The Lie Division

Jim McDermott

Abbreviations and acronyms used in the text

**DVdI** – Deutsche Verwaltung des Innern: German Administration of the Interior, the Soviet-zone puppet internal security administration prior to the establishment (1949) of the German Democratic Republic. The *VolksPolizei* fell within its remit

**FHO** – Fremde Heere Ost: the Wehrmacht's Military Intelligence Service, eastern section; responsible for data gathering and disinformation on the Eastern Front

**KDP** - Kommunistische Partei Deutschland: German Communist Party

**MGB** - Ministerstvo Gosudarstvennoy Bezopasnosti SSSR: Ministry for State Security, counter-intelligence successor organization (from 1946) to the former **NKGB**, and forerunner of **KGB**

**NKVD** – Narodyi Komissariat Vnutrennikh Del: The Soviet People's Commissariat for Internal Affairs, domestic (including military) security agency of the Soviet Union

**NSDAP** – Nationalsozialistische Deutsche Arbeiterpartei: German National Socialist Party

**PSh** – Podozreniye Shpionazha: 'suspicion of espionage', a catch-all offence often alleged (in lieu of evidence) against those arrested by **MGB**

**SBZ** - Sowjetische Besatzungszone: Soviet Occupation Zone of Germany

**SED** – Sozialistische Einheitspartei Deutschlands: German Socialist Unity Party, a Soviet-imposed merger (in April 1946) of the **KDP** and **SDP** in the Soviet Zone of Germany.

**SPD** – Sozialdemokratische Partei Deutschlands: German Social Democrat Party

**SSU** – Strategic Services Unit – short-lived American successor (1947) to the **OSS** (Office of Strategic Services) and forerunner of the **CIA**

**SVAG** - Sovyetskaya Voyennaya Administratsya v Germanii: Soviet Military Administration in Germany, based at Karlshorst, Berlin; known also (to the German population) as **SMAD** (Sowjetische Militäradministration in Deutschland)

**USFET** – United States Forces European Theater; US Military administration in Germany. **USFET (G2)** was the Army counter-intelligence department to which the Gehlen Organization reported directly until, in late 1947, it was transferred to the purview of the newly-created **CIA**.

**Volkssolidarität** – The People's Solidarity: charity, founded in Dresden in 1945, which spread rapidly throughout Soviet-occupied Germany.

**WASt** - Wehrmachtsauskunftstelle – The organization responsible for the registration and notification of German military losses, which also administered records regarding captured personnel in German POW camps. At the end of the war the Allied Control Commission determined that it should continue to function, and, from June 1946, the French section of the Commission took responsibility for its administration

# Prologue

He lived with evil, and the stench of its poison in his pores tormented him. He had done one evil and it had bred another, nurtured and fed it, wrapped itself through the new growth until all had become a dense, choking strata of foulness. When he peered into it he could no longer distinguish intention from act, act from consequence, consequence from motive.

He prayed, every day, as a man who lay upon his death-bed might. But he asked neither for mercy nor redemption, and he denied nothing. He wanted only to understand why and how to make it stop. His only comfort was that he had been a good man once, or at least good enough.

Looking back at that person he wondered at the journey from there to here. Once, he had rejected war, had believed that to shine the boots of a soldier was no less wrong than to carry a rifle and aim it. His original sin had been to deny his beliefs, to collaborate willingly by accepting what he could not change. But then compliance had become acceptance and then collusion; the soldier's boots had not been so much cleaned by him as caressed, kissed, worked carefully to such suppleness that the marks of their march across shattered continents had been quite wiped away. And then he had embarked upon his own war, a war entirely waged upon innocents. He had not intended it, but a sin commissioned helplessly is no less a sin.

His faith told him that a soul might be redeemed by good works, but all of his works were tainted – hadn't he seen the proof of that? How could a man make good with further offences against God, offences that ranked as the vilest of human acts? He had nothing to say on his behalf - were he his own judge he would have insisted that there could be no mitigation.

He no longer had the will to eat or sleep, had abandoned all but the most basic ablutions and wandered the streets like a lost soul (which is what he was, of course). He yearned to have it over with yet feared what would follow death; penniless men couldn't bribe priests to forgive what shouldn't be forgiven, couldn't build monasteries to ease their passage, couldn't endow chantries to have prayers said for their lost souls. In any case, he had never believed that wealth, however applied, could ease sin. It was why he was what he was, and why he knew that damnation awaited him.

So he prayed to no purpose, using the words like a knotted lash upon his back. He prayed for the dead, the many dead, for some sign that their suffering had been brief, and small. He prayed for a better world than this, one in which deranged theories remained the property of their conceivers, not raised up by entire nations as truths to be enacted. As his senses abandoned him he even prayed (because God was God) that the physical world might be reversed and returned to a time before the horror commenced. But even in his fevered state he knew that this was a pointless fantasy because human will, allowed the choice, always seeks the further, darker boundary to cross. It had been done once, it would be done again. People committed enormities because they had not the capacity to deny themselves. Wasn't he – a good, virtuous man, once – proof of that?

He thought of the countless thousands who had fallen, the fields of Europe sown with a new crop, stripped of identity and dignity - fields over which memory drifted, dissipating. He thought of the chosen, beautiful few, sat in their new homes, knowing and seeing nothing, and he wept for all of what he'd done.

1

He felt her breath warming his head and expected a kiss, but she stepped to one side instead, to watch his hands as they moved in tiny, controlled sweeps.

'Otto, this isn't *real* work.'

She said it quietly, carefully, wearing her *this is difficult but it needs to be said* face that he was coming to love like a damp morning. She had worn it for the first time when he suggested that he might look for employment as a document translator with the British; then when he tried to persuade her that Berlin held out the most promise of future prospects; then after he painted their one-bedroom apartment *Heer* green (the only commonly available colour, now much-avoided) and asked her what she thought of it. She didn't like to argue but she couldn't just let things pass. Given the choice he would have preferred either to the face, but being in love still with the idea of being in love, he applied himself to removing it gently.

'There are always going to be plenty that need mending. You know how the Russians are – they play them until they break and then steal fresh ones. The east is littered with them. Earl's friend says he can send as many as we can take.'

The gramophone's bowels were strewn across the room's only table. His skills, non-existent a month ago, had advanced to the point at which he was fairly confident that everything he stripped out would go back in, and probably in the correct place. It was his fifteenth such piece of *work* (whether she thought of it that way or not), and for each he had been paid enough to keep them in turnips and kohlrabi (even potatoes, sometimes) for almost a week. They were living at a profit of sorts, and not many of their countrymen could say the same.

'I can't see who'd want such things, these days.'

'The GIs do. They can't bring their own players over here and Earl sells them so cheaply they can afford to just abandon them when they go home. Or sell them back to him, of course. It's a good side-line.'

'And I don't like Bremen, Otto.'

He sighed and sat back to give his aching back some respite. 'It won't be forever. You've made friends here, at least.'

'Two girls with *besatzungskinder*. We're just untouchables sticking together.'

'Earl likes you.'

She managed to pout and shrug simultaneously, and as always it fascinated and goaded him equally. 'Earl likes everyone. He's sweet.'

'And what's so wrong with Bremen? As German towns go it hasn't been too pounded, not away from the docks and the factories. It's pretty and historic - almost *gemütlich*.'

'It doesn't feel like home.'

'Where does?'

'It's full of Americans.'

'They provide our income at the moment.'

'They despise us.'

'We're despicable - we lost, remember? And if we get too tired of being despised by them we only have to walk a couple of kilometres in any direction to be despised by the British instead.'

She laughed and put her arms around his neck. 'Otto Fischer - the only German who sees the sunny side of night.'

He took care not to move, letting her half-strangle him, enjoying the smell, the closeness. She had meant it as a joke, but its kernel of truth surprised him greatly. In Stettin it had been she who dragged his spirits out of the mud, but now? When and how had he misplaced his bone-deep pessimism about everything and everything's extended family? Was this what a woman did to a man? If it was, why hadn't he been warned?

'Can we invite Earl for our anniversary feast?'

'Anniversary?'

She freed one hand to thump his shoulder. 'Six months, next Tuesday.'

'Yes, of course. I'll order a rack of venison and champers for three.'

'Don't be glib. You know what Earl's like – he'll want to surprise us with something you can't find in Germany anymore.'

Fischer smiled. It was true, and shameless of her to think of it. If there was one thing Earl Kuhn enjoyed it was to feel needed.

'Seriously, Otto, this isn't a real job, to be tinkering with junk. If you won't let me work anymore you'll have to find something steady, with prospects.'

'I wanted to translate for the British but you said no.'

'They pay nothing. Why not ask the Amis?'

'Because every third one of them has German grandparents. They don't need us.'

'They need women.'

'I've told you, any more of that and I'll divorce you in a minute.'

'I know. It was another joke. I'm humorous today.'

'Jokes are funny. Getting on to your back for other men isn't.'

'It doesn't have to be like that. Some of them like to fuck against a wall, or take me kneeling down …'

These days he could be teased about it without getting angry, or impotent. They had agreed that their wedding day was Year Zero, every slate wiped, and he was certain that she'd never break her vow - or vows, for that matter. He was a reasonable man (he told himself), one who could hardly object to what she'd done to survive the even-worse-than-these years.

She stroked his head, the ruined side. 'Don't worry, I'm an old hag. There's plenty of younger fanny in this town - it's a port, after all. They're probably unionized.'

He picked up his painter's fine brush and applied oil to one of the smaller gears he'd laid out neatly in line. 'You're mad, woman. When I walk down the street they point and say 'Look, there goes that monster Otto Fischer. He makes a slapped arse look pretty yet he managed to seduce Cleopatra. How is that fair?'

She applied a death-grip this time, and he gave up the gramophone's secrets as a temporarily lost cause. They hugged for a while, rocking slightly, saying nothing, and then went to bed behind the hanging blanket, their barrier between the new world and the only pleasure still allowed to Germans that didn't require written permission.

2

On his seventeenth day at Bautzen he decided to die. By his estimation the regulation diet was giving him less than a thousand calories daily, and twice already he had witnessed the kind of casual brutality that killed a man slowly - or, if he was lucky enough to fall badly, in an instant. He had known too much of that to want more. A part of him said that he shouldn't be done with life before his fortieth birthday, but he comforted himself with the iron truth that the world no longer cared for what was or wasn't natural justice.

Like every other inmate he had been strip-searched when he arrived, but NKVD had employed their usual methods - too violent, too perfunctory, by-the-flawed-book. He'd held the needle in his hand while they gave his mouth, colon and foreskin all their attention, and he'd managed not to loosen his grip when the sergeant punched him playfully in the face. When they'd doused him in DDT powder and allowed him to dress he slipped it back into his jacket pocket. A seamstress would have called it blunt, but it was fit enough for what he had in mind.

As hopeful creatures do he had wandered the camp during the first days, hoping to find some of his own kind. Reason told him that it was a stupid thing to do, but stupid patted his shoulder and urged him on. Eventually he found a few of them, Party members who'd had the shitty luck to be carrying paper to that effect when they were picked up. But they weren't the sort of men he'd fought with, honourable men used badly by fools. He shouldn't have bothered looking.

He tried to get a feel for what this place was. The more optimistic among his fellow prisoners were convinced that it was a detention camp, a terminus, but after making a complete circuit he wasn't minded to agree. During the war it had been part of the Gross-Rosen complex, a transit facility for poor bastards on their way to Sachsenhausen or Buchenwald, and its new owners didn't seem to be expanding or modifying it. There were too many men for too few beds here, so it was a waystation to somewhere else, and *somewhere else* was more likely than not to be a copper mine or a quarry, and in either case Siberia. He'd had his full ration of snow (what man in his old regiment hadn't?), and, lacking other options, settled upon dying instead.

Each evening, after what might barely be described as a meal, they were made to line up at the latrines (perhaps the Soviets crapped to order, and expected everyone else to do the same). Usually he managed to squeeze out something, but on this particular evening his mind was on a different sort of business. He'd be noticed, of course, but who would try to stop a man from checking out of this place?

When his turn came he stepped inside and shuffled to the back wall, letting those immediately behind him pass by. The needle had worked its way around the seam to the back of his jacket, so his body was twisted and his head down as he tried to tease it back again when the cosh came down, and his right ear took most of the impact. It was agonizing, but he was on his feet still, only slightly stunned by what, better-aimed, should have finished him off. Before the next one arrived his knees bent slightly and he punched short and straight, into the throat. When the head bounced up off the floor he kicked it hard, and a second time for luck's sake. Then he thought about what had been interrupted and added a couple more.

He slid down the hut wall and tried to catch his breath while the hut cleared as fast as a dozen pairs of dropped trousers allowed. The corpse lay face up, watching a selection of balls flashing past, apparently unconcerned by the view. The face was messed up but recognizable still; it belonged to the leader of a gang of thugs, vicious sorts who had tried to ply their habitual street trade under the new regime and failed. The camp was full of his sort, as many as there were honourable servicemen, or NSDAP *zellenobleuten*, or social democrats - it was a clearing house for all the shit that war and its aftermath had collected, a sluice to rid the new world of its old detritus. But now they were just two comrades in an otherwise empty latrine, both of them frustrated in their intentions. It almost made him laugh; if the stupid swine had waited a minute more he could have tossed the cooling body for whatever he imagined was in its pockets and they'd both have been satisfied with the arrangement.

Then he *did* laugh, and found it difficult to stop. On the occasion of his attempted suicide he'd made a clutch of new enemies who would be doing their best to kill him *and* committed an offence for which the certain punishment – following a brief hearing before the camp's ranking officer – was death. Best and most perversely, his urge to be out of the world had been quite excised by its near-fulfilment.

When they came for him he had plenty of warning. Boots made no real sound across their dirt yard but NKVD guards liked to shout a lot (even if they had no audience to appreciate it), and they hardly ever opened a door when kicking it in did the job just as well. He stayed where he was, and when they saw what he'd done they kicked him too; but it was desultory stuff to the body, for form's sake. It was part of the code of guards everywhere, he supposed, to lay off a little when the recipient had an urgent appointment with a firing party.

They dragged him to the commandant's office, even though he could walk perfectly well. It took longer that way but he didn't mind; it gave him time to think, to get it right in his mind. By the time the corporal rapped very respectfully on a door he'd found and polished the stone that would kill both birds.

*Werwolves*, he told the NKVD Colonel, passing themselves off as small time hooligans because it got them where they needed to be, inside the enemy's fence, working to recruit men who had nothing to lose. He was asked why he cared enough to kill one of them - didn't he think of them as patriots? No, he replied (not entirely untruthfully); he'd always despised Hitlerites, even though he'd fought in one of the Regime's elite units.

The Colonel thought about that, and then asked if he'd consider doing further valuable work for the anti-fascist front. He forced himself to be silent for a few moments, pretended to weigh up the offer as would a man who had principles, a measure of self-respect, a sense of belonging. And then he said yes, he'd be very happy to consider it.

3

The sign, in English, announced *West Side Records*. On the day it
went up Fischer had pointed out that, technically, the establishment stood
somewhat to the north of central Bremen, but Earl Kuhn was adamant. The
name - conceived, breeched and nurtured during his Stettin *longueur* - was
open to no further debate.

It was a large hut, a nissen, erected by the British before they
graciously withdrew to allow their American cousins squatting rights in the
city. The latter had no use for the place but Kuhn did, it being only half a
kilometre from the old Flak Kaserne, now US 1st Division, 18th Infantry
Regiment's Camp Grohn. There was no official lease, only the goodwill of
a quartermaster sergeant who had charge of organizing local storage
facilities and had been willing (for a reasonable fee) to draw up and sign
something plausible.

Along one side of the hut Kuhn and Fischer had constructed a rack
that was passably a second-cousin of the type to be found in real record
shops. It was sparsely populated still, but the establishment was gradually
acquiring a jazz catalogue unrivalled in central Europe (not a notable
achievement). Two months earlier, Kuhn had dipped into his war booty of
stolen Swiss francs and paid for a hundred posters, printed in German and
English, offering hard currency for gramophone records in good condition.
For a further outlay (principally cigarettes and hard liquor to 21st Army
Group transportation personnel), he'd arranged for them to be distributed
across the British Zone as far as Hamburg. For almost two weeks thereafter
not a single customer had visited their premises, and Fischer had endured a
series of anxious monologues on the *market* and its whimsies. But then an

old gentleman who had pushed a pram-full of shellac all the way from Ganderkasee heralded a near-crusade of dusty folk pushing similar, all of them hoping to be relieved of their music collections at rather more advantageous terms than they had their gramophones. True to his word, Kuhn bought everything that could be played still, no matter what the repertoire. Much of it was poison to a jazz fan, but as he pointed out to Fischer, a world that could accommodate the depraved philosophies of National Socialism must have a place for light opera and *schicksalkmusik* also.

Ironically, most of what Kuhn acquired and filed under Ear Rape proved to be the means of expanding his core repertory. An American lieutenant came into the hut one day and introduced himself as the son of the proprietor of Klossmayer's Music, Conestoga, Pennsylvania. He examined the B stock briefly and offered dollars for it, German music of all genres being understandably scarce in his home state yet much sought after by its large, sentimental Teutonic community. Kuhn, restraining his eagerness, had refused the cash and made a counter offer. On trust, the lieutenant brought a jeep to West Side Records and took away everything that wasn't jazz. Three weeks later, a first consignment of American Decca, RCA, Columbia, Dial and Swan pressings arrived, all new, pristine copies of music that Bremen's occupiers – presently enduring a heavily-censored diet of AFN pap - were missing like momma's pie.

For years, Kuhn's world had been filled with expectations of America and Americans, and his first live one – shallow, venal and hip – was almost too perfect. He wanted desperately to be *buddies* with Lieutenant Klossmayer, but the man had serious character flaws. He quickly developed an affection for Beulah May Annan, the premises' four-legged security system, and made several inappropriate offers for her (like any father, Kuhn took this badly). Worse, he wasn't of African descent. Kuhn – a bone-deep racist – held Negroes to be the only truly admirable Americans, and felt their sufferings at the hands of Whitey much as he would his own. So Klossmayer remained only a trusted business associate, though Kuhn was soon amply compensated for this emotional disappointment. When the first Black GIs began to patronize the establishment he fell into a state made popular by St Theresa of Avila, to the point at which Fischer had to remind him that the time he devoted to following them around the hut, pestering for details of their lives and jives, was time in which they weren't browsing or buying records.

The repaired gramophones (advertised as *phonographs*) were displayed on a table opposite the records, and at least three of them acquired new American owners each week. Kuhn's money bought the wrecks, and the profit on what could be mended was split equally. Fischer knew he was being treated over-generously but he couldn't afford to stand upon the luxury of principle. He had a new wife, an extremely modest but expensive apartment (as in any occupied city, Bremen's landlords were as grasping as mantis brides) and a vague but growing awareness of what put the stoop in family men's shoulders.

He was finding it difficult to come to terms with the several hells of domestic life. The threats of death and systemic abuse that he and other Germans had faced in Stettin had given way to sleep lost upon matters of housekeeping, and on some days he couldn't say that he didn't miss the existential things. He wasn't in control of his own life anymore, because now he was obliged to care whether it ended sooner rather than later - and if it was to be *later*, the matter of occupying the time between now and then demanded attention. He couldn't recall the last time he had felt the need to plan his affairs, to draw a line with a goal at its far terminus, to own what amounted to expectations. He was becoming a worrier, and that worried him.

More than his own situation he worried about what he was going to *do* about Earl Kuhn. They had fled to the west together with little more than a thick money-belt and hopes for the goodwill of others, and each had found his most ardent goal. But their happily-ever-afters had different signposts, and the fork in the road was looming. Maria-Therese was fond of Kuhn because he was Fischer's friend, not because she saw him as family, a surrogate son. And she was right about Bremen, much as her husband defended it. A place could be pretty, and safe, and still not feel anything like a home. Fischer needed to have a difficult conversation, and soon.

But he couldn't see how it would go. West Side Records was threatening to boom, and the putative hordes of shysters and thugs he was supposed to deter with his face – at least, that was the rationale Kuhn had deployed to employ him - had proved imaginary. He hadn't been truly of use since their brief stay in Berlin, where his one, sterling contact in the city's *VolksPolizei* had vanished them more effectively than a stage pigeon (and in an official vehicle, no less). Their most harrowing experience since - the frantic search of Lübeck's refugee camps for word or sign of Maria-Therese - had been Fischer's problem, not Kuhn's. That ordeal had lasted barely a day, and ended by an almost-human British DP officer who not only kept precise records, but - and this was what most astounded his appellants - required no bribe to open them to Germans. Fischer found her in the care of the nuns of St John's Convent, wonderful women who cared nothing for her Magdalene past. She'd been safe there and angry, having waited too long for a man whose own deliverance had been no less due to the charity of others.

They had married quickly, without plans, and the force of Kuhn's insatiable longing to plunge into the recorded music business had been enough to drag them to Bremen. Fischer owed him at least a little of his time, though what faculty the boy had discerned in a veteran of one too many battles was a mystery. It was probably just his company, the comfort that a fellow Stettiner offered in a strange land.

So he had been deputy-führer of West Side Records for more than four months now, it was time to move on, and despite having earned the Reich's highest honours in battle he would willingly have run whimpering from the moment at which he had to broach the subject. His friend deserved more than excuses, but excuses were all he had. The future was a fog still, thick and unhelpful, and at the moment he was making a reasonably lucrative, half-secure living from distressed gramophones' secret places. What variation of *goodbye* wouldn't make him sound like an ingrate?

It was cowardice that made him ponder substitution. He had been introduced to Maria-Therese's friends, the two girls who'd opened their legs for GIs but missed the wedding ring; they were both young, both pretty, and he wanted desperately to find an innocent excuse to introduce one of them to Kuhn. Like most men of his generation he had neither the soul nor talent for match-making (masculine conversation on the subject rarely moving beyond the quality of the terrain and getting into it), and after several days' fruitless pondering he was sufficiently desperate to ask Maria-Therese how he should go about broaching the matter. She looked at him as though he were block-headed and told him to just *say* something.

What the hell was *something*? He hesitated for a few days more and then - it being a tender business - stumbled into what seemed to be a propitious moment and launched himself like a cavalry assault. He and Kuhn were working, naturally (Kuhn ate, slept, defecated and prayed to the Gods of phonographic reproduction in West Side Records, and could only be persuaded out of doors when holding the other end of Beulah May's neck-tie); the proprietor was standing at his desk, humming quietly as he deposited US dollars in his money box. Their sole customer and his new copy of *Jazz at the Philharmonic* had just walked out of the door, there was no music playing on the establishment's official gramophone, no urgent matter to attend while awaiting further custom and no reason to put it off any longer. Fischer even resisted the temptation to clear his throat to give himself time to think of a better way to put it.

'Earl, do you like girls?'

Kuhn looked up from his money box and contemplated the hut's opposite wall.

'That question usually means 'do I like boys?' No, I'm quite conventional, Otto. Why, is heterosexuality tiring you already?'

'It's just that I've never known you to mention the ladies, even to express an opinion.'

Kuhn blew out his cheeks. 'I don't have one, most days. And when I do, Madame Hand relieves the pressure. What is it? Are you trying to set me up with someone so you can fuck off?'

With an effort Fischer kept his lips together.

'Yeah, I thought so.'

'Why? I mean, how?'

'Did you know that you wince - I mean visibly, *wince* – every time I drop the needle on a record? And that whenever a customer talks loudly – which is most of the time, because they're mostly Americans – you keep a blank but very fixed expression on your face, or find an excuse to go outdoors quickly? Do you think I employ Beulah May as a seeing-eye dog?'

Fischer sat down heavily. 'I'm sorry, Earl. I don't dislike working here. It just doesn't feel like …'

'A calling? That's alright, it's my dream, not yours. You got me out of Stettin alive and unholed, and I wanted to repay you, not condemn you to a thrilling career in retail. Where will you go?'

'I don't know, really I don't. My gut says Berlin, but Maria-Therese says no.'

'Clever girl. The Russian warned you never to return, even to the western sectors.'

'He did, but I can't see him bothering to search Europe's largest ruin for me. I suppose it isn't *where* we go so much as what I'll do when we get there, and I can't yet see that either. I just didn't want to surprise you one day soon by not being here.'

Kuhn lifted a copy of *Black, Brown and Beige* from the nearest rack, frowned and carefully wiped dust from its outer sleeve with his own. 'Would you be police again?'

Fischer shook his head. 'I didn't want the job back then, and I couldn't do it now. In any case, being required to press lips to British or American rears wouldn't be a step up from selling records.'

'Education, then? The British are trying to restore the schools. They need reliable non-Party men.'

'I *was* in the Party, remember? Anyway, what would I teach? How to land without breaking your legs or strangling yourself with parachute cord? Silent killing, theory and practical?'

'What about English? You speak it well enough, don't you?'

'Not idiomatically.'

'Well I don't know what that means, but if you can teach the little buggers to say 'please', 'thank you', 'I surrender' and 'mummy will suck your cock for cigarettes' you've covered the necessary stuff.'

'German children have been through enough traumas, Earl. What would my face do to them?'

'God, I'd forgotten your face - hard to believe, when I'm looking right at it. Lessons from you might be an ordeal.'

'An object lesson is all I could offer. No, it's going to need more thought, or a shove.'

Kuhn laughed. 'Most Germans could say the same. Have there ever been losers like us?'

'At least we know we're beaten this time. Another Führer wouldn't make any difference, whatever shit he spouted.'

'Yeah, there's that. No-one's making speeches any more, thank Christ ...'

The door's inferior British hinges announced the arrival of more visitors, a small reconnaissance party of black GIs. Kuhn advanced to engage them, arms wide enough to welcome or restrain them.

'Hey guys! Vat's the vord?'

Recalling recent criticism, Fischer made an effort and smiled. Horrified, the American soldiers stared at the apparition then moved hurriedly to the stock. Kuhn followed them, sparing a brief, angry glance for his partner, and gingerly patted two of the smaller backs in front of him.

'How about zem Dodgers, eh?'

4

His tutor was a former university lecturer named Naryshkin who now held the rank of Major. He thought of him this way because there was nothing obviously military about the man. The mild manner and easy humour were something of a front, obviously, but the fellow was by several kilometres the most human member of the Soviet Armed Services he'd encountered. He'd even offered his hand, and it hadn't been making a fist.

His journey - his odyssey - from Bautzen had been the purest experience of travel, unspoiled by distractions like food, much water or other than the most occasional toilet halt. He knew that he had been brought to somewhere west of Moscow because their truck had passed through a mass of rusting missile batteries, relics from the winter of 1941/2. He'd faced them back then, though not closely enough ever to see what was trying to erase him. There was nowhere else in Russia that its rulers cared for enough to have defended that thoroughly, not unless it bore the Boss's name.

When they dragged him from the truck he was too weak to stand, but after that the treatment improved considerably. Their destination was a large but forgettable public building, the sort that had housed minor nobility (with equally minor taste) before the Revolution. Its grounds were laid out formally but long neglected, and so extensive that anything that happened here would be a rumour at most to the world beyond the gates. Inside, he was given a large mug of sweet Mongolian tea and made to shower. When he smelled a little less like a farmyard's darker corners they dressed him in a Soviet uniform stripped of its insignia and took him to a staff cafeteria where he was given a bowl of decent chicken broth. Three minders – large, ugly, silent types - sat at the table while he ate, blocking the view in most directions. It was one of the finer meals of his life (lacking only a certain ambience), but before the last mouthful went down he was beckoned upright and shoved along more corridors than he cared to count, to the office of a major who signed a piece of paper presented to him by one of the types and nodded them away.

Naryshkin introduced himself formally, as if his guest had arrived for a job interview. He offered a seat and a cigarette, asked about the camp, the journey, the offer that had been an attractive alternative to summary execution and took the trouble to seem interested at the answers. He went so far as to allow questions.

'Do NKVD want …?'

'NKVD want nothing. This is an MGB facility.'

'I don't know what that is.'

'Formerly NKGB, Counter-Intelligence, now reorganized and renamed as our masters are pleased to do occasionally.'

'What is it that you do here?'

'Among other things, the examination of Soviet soldiers returned from imprisonment in Germany.'

'Examination?'

Naryshkin laughed. 'It isn't always the case that they're marched straight to the nearest wall.'

'I'm surprised that many of them survived the experience.'

'So were we - and not pleasantly, to be honest. The Vlasov business has shredded nerves, as you might imagine. Shaken loyalties are so much more attractive when they're the enemy's.'

'What is it I'll learn here?'

The Russian didn't answer immediately. He took a pipe from his tunic pocket, filled it slowly from a pouch and struck a match on the table. He sucked at least a dozen times before shaking the match and letting it drop. The message was taken – a thoughtful, methodical man.

'How to hide, deceive, obfuscate. The first thing, of course, is that you need the life of someone else and the memories that go with it. Above all, we want to nurture an ability to invite belief.'

'No military training?'

'What could we give you that your own people didn't? What we require is rather more in the nature of a long term commitment.'

'You want me to be a traitor.'

The Russian waved that one away. 'What constitutes loyalty anymore? You can't be apart from the struggle; it's a matter only of choosing your side. In any case, the German psyche is predisposed to being directed. It's what makes you such effective soldiers.'

Was that true? He couldn't recall when he'd last exercised the degree of initiative that counted as free-will. Childhood had offered an illusion of it, but nothing since had come close - school, the *Wandervogel*, cadet training and then the war – a breeding bull could have laid greater claim to choosing the direction of its life. It wasn't something that had ever concerned him. He didn't intend to let it get under his skin now.

Naryshkin sat up and placed his pipe on the table. 'Germany's been occupied for more than a year now but the situation is fluid still, and *fluid* means opportunity. As you'll be aware, freedom of movement across and within the Occupation Zones isn't consistent. Soviet personnel can enter American controlled territories openly - a concession, we think, authorized by Eisenhower in the rather unworldly belief that we will reciprocate at some point. We can't expect this happy situation to endure indefinitely, and it's vital that we have in place a robust intelligence network before the Americans realise that they've been dolts. Fortunately, their own intelligence facilities are extremely rudimentary as yet, but they're doing something about that. Firstly, and shrewdly, they've begun the recruitment of a native German agency – you Germans, after all, know a great deal more about us than they do. No doubt they will attempt to resurrect the assets you had in place during the war, but this will be futile.'

'Why?'

'Because most of your spies in the Soviet Union were double agents, and those that weren't have either handed themselves in for debriefing or taken up residence beneath large rocks from which they will never willingly be extracted. So the new agency or agencies have only one other source of useful material. Or rather, they will have, soon.'

'Am I allowed to know?'

The major shrugged. 'It isn't a secret. There are about three million of your countrymen resident in our detention camps. Clearly, we have neither great use for them in the long term nor the inclination to put bullets in their heads – they are, after all, the compatriots of people we wish to make allies of, eventually. So, at some nearing point a phased return of Germans from the east will commence, and this will be a very, very rich source of human intelligence. It's to our advantage that there are so many such men, because the task of examining them will be onerous. We intend to make it ineffectual also.'

'Your men will be in place already?'

'It's what we intend. Particularly, we need to ensure that enough of them are involved in the screening process to compromise its value to the Americans and their German subordinates.'

'You want those you've turned not to be discovered?'

'Exactly that. Those returning to the Soviet Zone of Germany are of course safe already, but the truly valuable ones will be going home to Stuttgart, or Köln, or Hamburg, or the western zones of Berlin.'

'Am I to be one of those doing the screening?'

'No. To give you a credible intelligence background would require far more time than we have. Your role will be more … flexible.'

'Flexible?'

'Let's talk more about it when you've become someone else.'

5

'Farming? You're joking, yes?'

'Not farming. Market gardening.'

'What's the difference?'

The face was back, and Fischer knew that if he couldn't shift it in the next minute or so it would defeat his best arguments.

'Scale, intensity, profits. We rent *schrebergärten*, preferably two adjacent ones, buy seed and grow what Germans are desperately in need of. It'll feed us and the surplus will buy everything else. We sell locally of course, so there'll be no transportation issues. And I'll be doing something *useful*.'

Maria-Therese raised her hands and spread them. 'But you don't know anything about agriculture!'

'Not a lot, no. But near Flensburg there's a man who does, and he'll teach me everything necessary.'

'Who's that?'

'An old comrade – or rather, his father. We have enough money to pay our way through what's left of this foul winter while I learn from him. When the ground warms we'll start.'

'But won't everyone else be doing the same? There are hundreds of thousands of allotments …'

'It doesn't matter. The east was Germany's bread-basket, and we've lost it to the Poles and Russians. This zone alone has more than two million extra mouths to feed, *ostflüchtlinge* like us. Until German agriculture gets back to its feet, how much of a food surplus do you think there'll be?'

His wife stared doubtfully at him. 'What would we do for fertilizer? Where would we buy seed? Who would have money to buy from us, even if we grew enough to sell?'

Fischer rubbed his chin and tried to pretend that he'd thought these things through already. 'I know, basic supplies are a problem right now. But the British and Americans are trying to do something about it, and we have a couple of months yet. As for money, we can barter for stuff we need, at least in the short term.'

'And what will we do while the crops are growing? Eat their leaves?'

He closed his eyes. He'd prepared himself for stubbornness, not a string of bloody good questions he had few answers for. He must have looked as deflated as he felt because she abandoned the interrogation suddenly, put her hand on his shoulder and squeezed.

'Otto, it's a good idea, for us. Everyone needs to eat, and a community garden's perfect. But I'm a farmer's daughter, and I know there are too many things that could go wrong for it to be a safe living. Why don't you go and see your friend at Flensburg and talk about it? He'll give you a better idea of how easy or difficult it could be.'

He knew that the punch was being pulled (she probably thought he'd abandoned his senses somewhere on the road between West Side Records and their apartment), but it wasn't bad advice. To date, his personal experience of horticulture amounted to following his father around the family allotment with his toy wheelbarrow, tearfully begging to be allowed to help.

'I could be back in two weeks, less if I don't hear good news. You wouldn't mind?'

'I'll have one of the girls stay with me. She'll be grateful for the extra hands to help with her little American.'

To have delayed the business would have added to his humiliation, so he told Kuhn the same afternoon. His proprietor seemed even less concerned for his absence than his wife, and took obvious pleasure in warning that the journey would be hardly less onerous than the Israelites' through Sinai, war damage in Hamburg and elsewhere making the *through* in through-traffic a flight of mad optimism.

Fischer boarded his train the following morning, took a window seat and was promptly pinned there by a woman whose girth gave the lie to every statistic on food shortages in post-war Germany. For more than an hour he endured her efforts to place him immediately outside the chassis, wriggling occasionally only to give his lungs a chance to do their job. Then, at Elsdorf, what he fervently hoped were her preparations to disembark became only a struggle to remove a bag from beneath the seat. She opened it, removed two battered carrots and without a word offered one to him. Shame wouldn't allow him to take it. A lingering childhood allergy, he told her.

His ordeal ended at Hamburg. The connecting train wasn't scheduled to leave for an hour, so he departed the almost-intact station to wander around the city that, for its size, had taken the greatest and most protracted aerial pounding of any German centre. There was much a wise man wouldn't want to see, and he particularly didn't want to see the ruins of St Nicholas' church, so of course his feet made straight for it. Only the tower remained, giving the finger to its departed tormentors, and the sight of it sank his spirits considerably (as he'd expected). His only previous experience of the place had been upon his sister's wedding day, a joyous occasion marred by his introduction to the woman who became his first wife and with whose collusion he had done his best to make hell of two lives. Of Germany's thousands of ruined churches, it was the only one whose fate he might have wished for.

British troops filled the city, though the only ones he saw carrying arms were guarding the train station. They had erected a large board in the main hall that declared proudly (in German) that almost all rail routes in the BiZone were now functioning normally. He glanced around and begged to differ. Packing the concourse were refugees from the east, wretchedly thin or just wretched, squatting on piles of battered luggage, waiting to be assigned, redirected or otherwise given a faint hint by the authorities of what their futures might hold. He'd avoided their fate by chance and so couldn't speak to the experience; but none of what he saw constituted any form of *normal*.

At least the train for Flensburg train was punctual. It was an old locomotive pulling four equally old carriages; but it was clean, and, when fully loaded, still comfortable. Fischer took another window position and had the rest of the seat to himself this time. They pulled into Schleswig at 4pm. The prospect from his window couldn't have been more different than what he'd seen in Hamburg. The city's pretty, seemingly untouched rooftops marched towards and around the Cathedral, pretending that such things as wars and foreign occupation had never rippled its bourgeois calm. He tried to admire the view, but felt as far from it as if he were sat in a bar in Patagonia, leafing through a faded pre-war brochure on Things to See in Northern Germany.

The train reached Flensburg after dark, and the absence of street lamps prevented his audit of the town's condition. The Dönitz Government had set up shop here in the dying days, so he couldn't imagine that war damage was too severe (though the proximity of the Danish border might have been an equally strong attraction). From the old Naval Academy the British supervised the displacement camps that ringed the town, but here the refugees were mainly Slavs and Balts, poor bastards dragged to the Reich to serve as slave labour and now condemned by their homelands' new masters as collaborators or worse. They were waiting for a turn of fortune that would never happen, a future that had already scraped them off its porch. As a Stettiner he knew exactly how they felt about it

He found a small, pleasantly shabby hotel run by a one-armed *Kriegsmarine* veteran, dined sparsely and slept well. In the morning he was outside the town's municipal office before it opened, first in a queue of three. The clerk to whom he spoke couldn't have been more helpful; he pulled the address within minutes and gave detailed directions to the farm, which stood conveniently close to a stop on the Flensburg – Gelting bus route. When the applicant departed he wrote down the details of the enquiry as he was required to do, placed the docket with others completed during that shift and put it from mind (though he recalled the man's terrible face a number of times over the following hours – how could he not do?).

Two days later the docket was examined at Hamburg, in a small office staffed by men who worked for no as-yet recognized organization. When the names on it entered the mechanism they nudged a cog, one that had been balanced precisely to sense and capture something that roamed a disordered wilderness.

6

'Isn't she beautiful?'

Princess Karoline Mathilde glanced up briefly, barely acknowledged the compliment with a sniff and closed her eyes once more. He stroked her body and she groaned slightly, shifting to allow him to reach her swollen belly. His hand was as rough and calloused as the rest of him, the whole prematurely aged by hard usage, but it somehow managed a devout gentleness as it caressed her young, perfect skin.

With the greatest will, the young man who watched this display of affection could find nothing endearing in three-hundred-and-fifty kilogrammes of womanhood. It was a matter of taste, he supposed. Some saw beauty in horses, others in moonlight; a few (the princess's suitor among them, presumably) found it in unashamed corpulence, as if *more* of something could only improve the principal. Certainly, she was impressive, even to his untutored eye - how could anything so large not be? But he had often thought the same of bombs and bombers without becoming ardent about them.

'Yes, father. She's a real stunner.'

'She's the last in all our district, thanks to hungry idiots not thinking of their tomorrows. Bless her.'

'Shall I feed her now?'

'Is the water at body temperature?'

The younger man wanted to ask *which body - mine, yours or hers?*
'Just about.'

'Well, set it down, then. She'll want a drink before she eats.'

*I'll get her a fucking napkin, shall I?*

'What?'

'Nothing, father.' The young man placed one pail at the edge of the straw pile, removed the other from the crook of his right arm and positioned it a metre from the first. Princess Karoline Mathilde regarded him momentarily with a baleful eye and clambered clumsily to her feet. Her snout briefly checked the combination of turnip peelings, acorns, brambles and earthworms (the last foraged by the younger man earlier that morning against the strong objections of his stomach), and then plunged into the lukewarm water that stood almost to the brim of the other pail. The older man watched fondly, ignoring the quantity of liquid that splashed on his boots and trousers, holding his hand just above her back as if unsure whether a stroke might upset the rhythm of her gulping. When half of the water had been drunk or redistributed she transferred her attention to the food. To the young man's ear the noises became even more revolting (if that were possible), and he had to make an effort to push the residual image of writhing *oligochaeta* from his mind.

The farmer shook his head. 'I'm worried about the worms.'

'She seems to like them.'

'I mean, if the ground freezes hard again. She's two weeks yet from serving, and the barometer's falling quickly. They'll burrow deeper.'

'What *would* you have given her?'

The old man looked at his son as he might any imbecile. 'Well if the world hadn't turned for the worse, *meal!*'

The young man sighed. He had never taken to farming life, one of the reasons he had gone off to seek glory and lose the best part of a limb in the war. Farmers breed boys to be the same as them, so he knew that his father regarded himself as a failure in this respect. But at least his son had returned (as so many German sons had not), and if a fatted calf had survived anywhere in Schleswig he was certain that it would have been murdered to mark the occasion. Knowing this, and wanting to be a better son than he presently was, put him under something of an obligation to do his very poor best.

'I meant, if the world wasn't quite as it is.'

That was a better question. His father pursed his lips and frowned at the princess's vast arse.

'God lets her process just about anything, but her womb needs good nourishment, better than for her own needs. When the last of the acorns go, well ... Do you know where we can get some corn?'

'No, father.'

'Fishbone, then?'

The young man sighed once more and shook his head.

'If the British ground their flour here in Germany we could try to beg the midds. But they don't. Most legumes would be fine, and she could just about *make do* with forest truffles ...'

It wasn't like the old man to joke, and certainly not about pigs. His son, surprised, looked for a hint of smile and found none.

'… but of course, if she was a city pig it would be easier. There's always something to be found in cities that even hungry folk won't eat.'

Yes, a city would be good. The young man thought of Berlin, his second home until recently. There, he knew all sorts of people who could get their hands on things for a price. But that was the trouble both there and here - nothing was for free, and all that his father had to trade was the very item he wished to preserve. She was porcine gold, a treasure of marbled fat - the means, perhaps, by which a family would survive what Germany had become.

Her Highness scoured the pail's bottom for the last morsel and then extracted her head, squealing slightly as an ear caught on the handle. She gazed at each man in turn, a slightly disbelieving look that they should expect her to be satisfied with such scraps. The farmer scratched her head, whispered 'I know, darling, I know' very softly and tried to interest her in what remained of the water.

The younger man thought hard, if only to acknowledge the compliment of his being invited to a discussion on husbandry. 'We used to have dice snakes around here, didn't we? And grass snakes?'

'We did, but too much cultivation's done for them. It's a good idea though, Detmar; she'd do very well on snake meat.'

The farmer reached for his son's only hand and squeezed it. He had never been the sort of man to let his feelings show, so the gesture meant something. For a moment Detmar Reincke wondered if he'd accidently let slip some spark of competence, or even promise. It didn't seem likely. If one arm had been any use around a farm the British wouldn't have released him - he'd be across the Channel with almost every other German soldier they'd captured, working their soil instead of Germany's, assisting them to piss very politely upon the Geneva Convention. Here, he was just another useless mouth to feed.

No, that wasn't quite true - he had returned with something more than his wounds and a talent for inhabiting dreams that sometimes woke the entire house. He had acquired a single piece of war booty that had not been re-requisitioned by the victors, that had required no threat or violence to take, that had come gladly, even lovingly, with him. He had brought home the miracle of a Danish wife, a girl whose own father (his farm a mere twenty kilometres across their border) owned a breeding boar - a young, beautiful woman in whom the past had not laid its poisonous eggs.

As always when Kalle trespassed upon his thoughts she lingered, teasing a better mood from him. It became better still when she appeared, several moments later, at the door of the sty. He was surprised; it wasn't nearly time to eat, and she had set herself to helping his mother that day with the laundry, by a fair distance the worst job on the farm. She smiled at him - a secret thing, not her usual, open-to-the-world sunniness.

'Detmar, there's a man to see you. Come to the house.'

The old farmer looked up from Princess Karoline Mathilde, a frown gathering his face's many other creases. Like most Germans he had cultivated a deep anxiety about unexpected callers - a faculty that, since the defeat, had sharpened considerably. Detmar, feeling no more at ease than his father, patted his shoulder.

'Did he …?'

In the doorway behind Kalle a man appeared, a vision from a time too recently passed. The entire right side of his face was a work of art commissioned by Vulcan – torn, twisted, melted and then re-assembled into a protean sculpture of a being struggling to be formed or unformed. Seeing it, looming behind his daughter-in-law, the farmer gasped a word that his son had never heard from those lips, not even at the worst of times. It was a shocking slip of the tongue, but Detmar Reincke laughed gaily and slapped the shoulder he had just tried to comfort.

'Otto! What a fellow you are, pretending to be dead!'

7

The building was pretty, far too much so, given what had happened within its walls. Captured Allied airmen had been brought here on their way from crash-site to POW camp, offered bed, breakfast and a thorough debriefing by Luftwaffe Intelligence. Though the interrogators had spurned *Stapo* tactics (their prisoners tended to be able to walk still, afterwards), their sense of chivalry, the brotherhood of the air, had died after Hamburg and what followed. Later, the Americans returned the favour, interrogating captured senior Wehrmacht staff here. Even today, barbed wire surrounded the compound – a reminder, to keep the new tenants' minds on who they were and who they worked for.

But the thick-set, hard-faced old fellow wasn't complaining. He had a job, a good, unexpected job and hopes for advancement that a German in his early sixties had no right to entertain. His sense of optimism had been disinterred, brushed down and told to report for duties, though the whole thing felt strange still, something that needed more time to settle in his mind and conscience. He had never imagined he might become a collaborator.

The trick, he found, was to repeat to himself often that a man had to shape himself to realities. He'd never been too squeamish about how he got results in his work; why should he care now about the means by which his family would find security in the least secure of times? It was a good argument, at least for as long as it sat in his head. It put balm on the rawest edges of his conscience, kept the important matters to the fore.

He looked down at the brief report once more. It was dated the previous day, so someone had been doing their job - someone in much the same situation as himself, perhaps, hoping to demonstrate his competence the way a puppy did with a new trick, to earn the knuckle on the head, the *good lad!*, the biscuit. He liked the way it was worded – clear, concise, nothing pompous or off the point – and decided to take the trouble to thank his correspondent. A new man didn't have a network, and a network was most necessary in this kind of job. It was wise to keep the good ones friendly.

And he had been sent the best news he could have hoped for. His new bosses were nervous men, as eager to please as their subordinates, but in their case the price of failure wasn't just a dismissal notice. He'd made perhaps too much of this business, promised something that wasn't in his power to determine with any certainty; but to deliver the package would be a good first step in a dance in which trodden toes were expected.

He had to do the thing himself, obviously. Sitting back and letting someone else take it on wasn't feasible - he wanted the rabbit in the trap, not skipping under a hedge at the first hint of a pot. He was happy to organize things, make the journey and take responsibility for it all going smoothly. The only unpleasant matter would be applying for the means; the rumour was that expenses had to be prised from their paymaster's dying hand.

And the man was as tight about detail as the cash. He'd want to know everything – why, how and where, all of it wrapped in a detailed diagram of the rabbit's very soul. A full life-history would be demanded from the point at which the fellow's mouth had departed his mother's teat for the last time, and any gaps, omissions or opaque passages would close the door upon the business quicker than a Heligoland breeze. But then the ordering of facts had never been a problem for him. Even when they didn't fit it was only a matter of widening the hole to accommodate them. That's what his old job had been all about, largely.

He had a small bottle of Schnapps in his desk, the last – the only – thing he'd brought out of Berlin during the final days. He'd had it since before the war began, a means of celebrating something that hadn't ever quite happened (the fall of France had made everyone more, not less, nervous, and from the start Barbarossa had been just too big a potential fuck-up to celebrate even when things were going well). He was tempted now to crack the seal and have a small swig, but he recognized the urge as a symptom and quashed it. To anticipate a successful operation at this point would be as good as urinating in the Fates' favourite pot.

Yet his hopeful mood persisted. He was effectively a prisoner here, confined behind wire except for occasional home leave or 'road service', a tiny resource in a bigger, anxious pool of similar, all trying to please their new masters, step on their competitors' throats and lay a first course of bricks upon which something might be built. But today, the sum of all that hardly pressed upon his broad shoulders. In a world done with Germans he was alive still, holding a degree of initiative, working options. It made him feel less than optimistic yet more than craven, and that counted towards a fine day.

To soften the news of his abject defeat, Fischer went to West Side Records before returning home, to beg a bottle of cheap spirits from Kuhn.

The proprietor shrugged, opened a cupboard and removed one of several bottles of Delamain Réserve. 'I was going to bring it along to your apartment next week anyway.'

Reverently, Fischer stroked its label and wondered why it hadn't been repatriated with other stolen fine art. 'Why?'

'Your anniversary. You hadn't forgotten?'

'Yes, I had.'

'She'd have murdered you, twice.'

'Probably.'

'You'd better take the champagne truffles as well, then.'

'How …?'

'Don't ask, it spoils the fun.'

'It would be too much. I want her to think I'm a failure, not a bigamist.'

'You had no luck?'

'To be put off so emphatically counts as luck of a sort, I suppose. I led my brilliant idea into the woods afterwards and shot it.'

'What was wrong with it?'

'Everything - timing, the absence of necessary agricultural supplies, the British habit of requisitioning at random. I think Detmar's father regards me as half-deranged for considering it. He was very kind, though, which made it worse.'

'Well ...' Kuhn waved at one of the hut's rear corners; '... more gramophones came in yesterday, so you can be busy if you want to.'

Morosely, Fischer stared at the small pile of beaten machines. He'd staved off the worst of winter at least, and not many of his compatriots could say that. But then, he might have told himself exactly the same several days ago and saved himself a pointless, costly journey. As usual, Maria-Therese had seen everything far more clearly.

Kuhn did his unnervingly clairvoyant turn again. 'Otto, don't try too hard, she isn't measuring you. Not when you're dressed, anyway. Now, go on, take your brandy and get off the premises. Charlie Parker's calling to me, and I don't need the Wince.'

The apartment was empty when he returned. Drying baby clothes were hung in a rope across the kitchen range, steaming gently, and the place was as untidy and as welcoming as he'd ever known it, even if the colour on the walls hinted at a forward command post. It was only several seconds after he entered that he noticed the noise, or absence of it. She'd fixed the broken window pane. He examined it closely - a good, neat job, better than he could have managed. It brought him down even further, made him wonder why she thought she needed him at all.

Carefully, he removed from his bag the four eggs he'd brought from the Reincke farm, his journey's only success (they'd had to threaten torture to make him take them), and placed the brandy on the mantelpiece where she couldn't fail to see it when she entered. He was about to make a start on tidying the place when he glanced at the baby clothes again. He was vaguely aware that infants' rear ends evacuated more often than an Italian Front, but the quantity of *windeln* seemed excessive. He began to count them, and had reached thirty-three when the door opened.

'Otto! Be a darling and help me with this.'

Maria-Therese leaned to kiss him as he grabbed the pram handle and dragged it into their apartment. It was full of clothes, more baby clothes. A pungent fragrance cleared his sinuses like an ammonia douche.

'It came to me three days ago, while I was burping little Freda. We have the range and all the wood we need to keep it hot, and a lot of families around here don't, of course. So I put out word that I could take in laundry for mothers. They'll pay with food, which is just what we need. I asked Earl if he could find some detergent ...' she nodded towards the kitchenette, '... and he brought about ten kilos of *Mersol*, don't ask me where he got it from, and ...'

She kept talking, giving him the full business plan, but Fischer hardly heard it. With a fraction of the effort he'd expended upon his fantasy she had organized a horribly demeaning yet profitable means of keeping the wolves from gnawing their door *and* expertly amputated his remaining manhood. He sighed.

'It's a very good idea, my love. But won't it ruin your hands?'

She lifted one of them, spread her fingers and examined it critically. 'They were never good. Perhaps Earl knows someone who can find hand-cream.'

'I'm sure Earl knows someone who can find the Ark of the Covenant and a cure for death, but he's done enough for us already.'

The frustration in his voice gave her the news more efficiently than a telegram. She stood on her toes and kissed his forehead. 'Don't worry. Your gramophones and my washing can keep us until something good enough comes along.'

'When, and how?'

'I don't know. But a smashed country's a good place for new opportunities, isn't it? Everything that's been lost has to be replaced.'

He shrugged, though he wanted to believe. 'How can we know, until the Allies decide what to do with us? It's hard to have a plan when you don't know the rules.'

'Exactly, so stop feeling guilty. If you can't change things you're not to blame for them. Is that brandy for drinking?'

'It's Delamain. It's not for rubbing on wounds.'

They opened it after a lunch of cabbage soup, marvelled at its old world taste, the way it did its business without removing throat tissue. He wanted to talk more but had the sense to drink too much instead. Later, she applied another balm, and by the time the light faded across the steep-pitched roofscape he felt better than he could recall. His head had cleared of the many ways he was failing his wife, the future had receded into grey mist, every extremity was warm and he knew, really knew, that sleep was about to fall upon him like a wall. But that was the moment before the door almost departed its hinges. As a former *kripo*, Fischer had often used that knock himself, and he was fairly certain that it wasn't trying to beg a cup of *Mersol*.

9

The Russians released him before dawn at a bus stop on the outskirts
of Wandlitz and gave him a ticket. He reached Berlin two hours later to
find a sleet-swept, grey day in prospect. He'd expected to feel something, a
tug, but from Mitte to Schöneberg not a single sight or odour worked upon
him. The city had been erased almost, beyond the power of memory to
recover. He hadn't been here for years, not since the RAF's first,
ineffectual raids had slightly ruffled Berliners' composure and given them
cause to pat their own backs, feel they were sharing something of the
ordeal their sons were enduring at the Front. At the end, all fronts had
come to them, and with a little help from their allies the Russians had
recreated Stalingrad on the Spree.

Would anyone here recall him? Nothing was beyond possibility, but
he'd always been a stranger, a passer-through. His face might stir
someone's dusty corners but the name, the context, would be as lost to
them as their *heimats*. As for the other fellow, the one whose history he'd
been briefed into, *he* had never visited Berlin, never wandered further than
the capital of his *kreis* before war put a gun in his hand and despatched him
to exotic, supremely luckless climes. For both of them, this atomized
cityscape was an excellent place to start again.

He had been forbidden to attempt to make contact, but that was fine
- he had no idea who to make contact with, who to avoid, who to follow.
All was to be revealed to him gradually, carefully, in a manner that
attracted no attention. His only orders were to find something with a roof,

pay rent in advance and then park his arse in one of three designated cafes for as long as required. Any form of preliminary reconnaissance, ground-laying (though for what, he couldn't say as yet) and potentially useful acquaintance-making were all equally *verboten*. He was told he must not use women other than prostitutes, engage in no opinionated conversations (in extremis, he might say enough to avoid giving an impression of reticence that might linger in a mind), commit nothing to paper, pay only small amounts in US dollars and absolutely shun those who wished to know more about him. He had no problem with any of this. In effect, they were demanding that he be himself.

He found a fine residence in Steglitz, near Fueurbachstrasse s-bahn station, a spit's distance from Rosa Luxembourg's old family home (he doubted the gesture would earn him points from his new employers). It was a cellar, reasonably dry to the elements, with basic ablutions and a small woodstove. He paid two months' rent, an amount that didn't come close to contravening his instructions. His landlady seemed perfectly suitable – very old, damnably talkative but incurious of matters other than her own, half-blind and without close family. She lived in a garden hut above and slightly to one side of the cellar, her former home being now a quantity of rubble and almost fresh air. He gave her his new name and allowed her – very briefly - to take his card to register his details as required by the American authorities. She offered to cook for him for a further, nominal sum (so nominal, in fact, that he suspected he would be tasked with finding the food that she would prepare for both of them), but he told her that he preferred to make his own arrangements.

He had no doubt that she would scour his cellar for calories whenever he was out. He didn't mind that; he carried with him all that he needed and might attract attention. She would find his spare boots, underwear, a tattered copy of *Moby Dick* and a pristine non-smoker's matchbook. If she could gain nourishment from any of it, good luck to her.

His first night was spent largely in the hunt for a broken spring in his thin mattress, a playful thing that stabbed him whenever he drifted towards half-sleep. In the morning he went out early and found the first of his cafés, a former rail-workers' den in Dürer-Platz. He had to wait almost an hour before it opened and used the time to familiarize himself with the lie of streets, the overlooking windows and frequency of American foot patrols. Whether this counted as the sort of reconnaissance that had been forbidden to him he couldn't say, but he was careful to make it all seem like a bored, hungry man's indifference to anything but breakfast. No one seemed to notice him.

At 7.30am a shabby fat fellow unlocked the café door, nodded and shuffled back inside. The smell of ersatz coffee pervaded the place already, rousing his stomach, and rather than wait to see what was on offer he placed a dollar bill on the counter. The proprietor's eyes opened very slightly and a hand promptly disappeared the note. Halfway through the first cup of *muckefuck* a plate arrived at his table bearing a thick piece of rye bread decorated with fried pork belly. He ate quickly, before other customers arrived. The next three cups were free; he drank them slowly over the course of the morning, read the Occupation newssheets to familiarize himself with what was required of (or forbidden to) him as a good German and took care not to let his careful examination of every face that entered the establishment attract the merest attention. He dealt with the boredom as did all former soldiers, by reminding himself there were far worse things than nothing happening.

He left before noon, wandered for a while to stretch his legs and then set a course for the second café. This was a larger, busier place, used by off-duty GIs as well as civilians, though custom or regulation kept the two strictly segregated. He joined the German queue (the Americans were being served what smelled like real coffee at their tables), used his coupons at a long counter and accepted a bowl of wretchedly thin broth. He ate in a corner, sitting with just one other person (an old man interested in nothing but what was in front of him), and began to wonder how this was going to be done.

How would they know which of the three appointed cafés he would visit on a particular day or time? Would he be followed to one or more of them, or was there some point between two of them at which he would be accosted and given instructions? He didn't know with any certainty whether a physical meeting would take place. *Contact* could mean anything – a letter drop, a sleight-of-hand transfer, a detailed departmental briefing. He was where he was supposed to be, and that was about all he could judge of his work so far.

It was possible of course that someone who knew him – knew of him, his new role – might be in the café at that moment, watching, appraising. He didn't bother to commit the faces here to memory; there were too many of them, and any display of *interest* on his part might earn him a reprimand or even retirement. The thought almost raised a smile. Was it possible to pretend or imply *disinterest* in a manner that didn't attract attention to the performance? He might yawn a lot, he supposed, or pick his nose obliviously; but either would attract the distaste of neighbouring diners, which was another sort attention.

This business was more difficult, or more ridiculous, than he'd imagined. The only subterfuge with which he had much experience was the kind that put a man too close to an enemy to miss, and in such a way that didn't advertise itself beforehand. He'd been quite adept at that – skilled, even. It was what he had been trained for, had practised, and then performed too many times to recall. Sometimes the surprises had gone the other way; one or two of them had been bloody disasters, debacles from which the survivors had needed to be extracted like infected teeth, swiftly, leaving dead and dying comrades on the ground (unlike the Americans, his people hadn't been too sentimental about their wounded - *don't get caught without your final bullet* had been the sum of their crisis training). After the last mess he'd become just another soldier, meat for the machine, an anonymous element of far vaster fuck-ups. He couldn't say that he'd found it more reassuring to be one of a hundred thousand potential corpses, rather than several dozen.

He looked up and glanced around the café before he could catch himself. How long had he been dreaming? One of the GIs – actually, a lieutenant – had turned in his seat and was looking directly across at him. He forced himself to nod slightly and not season it with a smile, but the soldier's eyes kept moving, past and through him, carelessly taking in the sights to be had in foreign, conquered parts. He relaxed slightly, and then nearly departed his skin as something nudged his elbow.

'Aren't you going to eat that?' The old fellow was gesturing covetously at a centimetre's depth of cold broth.

'No. Please …'

The bowl was swept up before anyone else could put in a claim and its contents devoured in one gulp, unassisted by a spoon. Watching this, whatever appetite he still possessed excused itself and departed. He waited ten minutes and then followed it out into the street. This was his first day and he was tired already - tired of people, of ersatz coffee, of being an object awaiting a purpose. It took a great effort of will to point himself towards Schöneberg and his final designated rendezvous, and only the cold rain that doused him on the way restored something of his energy.

The third café was closed, long closed, with a fading notice on the door that apologized for the death of the proprietor and re-directed disappointed patrons to Café Else, an establishment only some two hundred metres' distant, apparently. Puzzled, he re-read the notice and tried to get a sense of the game's rules. All he could think was that this was a deliberate misdirection, but for whom, and to what? Did it mean that Café Else was his third appointed location, or – and this worried him immensely – was he being worked by some incompetent who had selected the three cafes at random, and from an outdated guide-book?

'It's a great shame.'

He turned quickly. An elderly lady, resplendent in a tattered fox fur stole that looked older than her, had emerged from a door in the adjacent property. She gestured at the notice.

'Hansi used to serve the best coffee cake south of Mitte, but he had a heart attack last winter. I think it was because of the defeat, the shortages. He felt he had no place in the world anymore if he couldn't make his old customers happy. He'd been here more than forty years, you know.'

'Yes, that's very sad.'

The lugubrious expression on her face disappeared, and she smiled. 'The Ambassador Café in Friedenau is further to walk, but it's every bit as good. I mean it isn't, obviously, but the owner manages somehow to get things that no one else has, so it *seems* as good, if you see?'

'Thank you. I'll try there.'

She nodded and shuffled away. The tension in his head dissipated as he realised that he worked for some very clever people after all. He was glad it was the Ambassador and not the other place; it seemed not to attract Americans, it was much closer to his new home, and if he thought about it he could still taste the fried pork belly.

10

Maria-Therese found it hard to drag her eyes from their visitor. He was huge but squat, a frightening sight, like something that used to wear the black uniform but did its work in cellars, not at the Front. A bear, only slightly smaller; a carefully shaved, over-muscled bear, walking upright, affecting human mannerisms, fooling no one.

Her husband couldn't stop laughing, cavorting, almost dancing with the bear. She hadn't seen him this happy since he dragged her away from the nuns, and that had been a much quieter, more dignified sort of happiness. If she hadn't known for a fact that he was only half-drunk …

'You old rogue! How the hell did you get out of Berlin? And look at you! Dressed like a tea-dance pimp!'

The bear seemed to take this in very good part, though Maria-Therese thought the comparison offensive. He was grinning, showing gold teeth, and one of his hands pressed into Fischer's shoulder so hard the thumb had almost disappeared.

'Aren't I exquisite? Have a feel - finest *entartete* tailoring, courtesy of the Amis.'

'You're …' Fischer paused, turned the volume down on his own grin and recalled his manners. 'Sweetheart, I'm sorry; this is Gerd, Gerd Branssler. He's a very old friend, an ex-*kripo* like me but from the very biggest-time - the fourth floor of the Police Praesidium, Alexanderplatz, no less. Gerd, you may kiss the hand of my wife, Maria-Therese.'

'Wife?' The bear's eyebrows (the only collection of hair on his entire head) moved up to his frown lines. 'Are you deranged, madam? Or was it perhaps a debt that you couldn't discharge decently ...?'

They both fell to laughing again, and Maria-Therese's outstretched hand remained unshaken. She tried not to feel irritated but she stood well outside the joke, watching it play out, and still felt the shiver that *Alexanderplatz* had roused. One needn't have ever visited Berlin to know what had happened there.

'You're working with the Americans?'

'*For*, Otto. A German doesn't do anything *with* the Amis. Yes, for two months now.'

'How's that possible? Of course you deserve it, but ...'

Branssler glanced down at one of the apartment's two chairs. Maria-Therese hurriedly swept up a clean pile of nappies and he sat down heavily, forcing its arms apart.

'It was thanks to one of our old friends, a very unlikely one. When things settled down after the surrender I brought Greta back to Berlin and tried to ease my arse into police work, but no one wanted to know – the Alex thing is death on a *curriculum vitae*, as you'd guess. The house was gone of course, along with the rest of the street, so we had a bad time of it last winter. But I kept in touch with some of the fellows from the old days who'd been luckier, and they put me in the way of just about enough work to keep us alive. Anyway, something started this spring.'

'Something?'

'Not much - questions being asked, someone looking for someone else.'

'Who?'

I didn't know who was doing the looking, but the word was that former Abwehr personnel were being hunted down. I don't mean literally. The poor bastards were almost wiped out after the July Plot, so no one was holding a grudge still. But the survivors were being sought out and, well, recruited.'

'By ...?'

'It's hardly anything, yet. But the Amis are resurrecting German Intelligence – at least, one arm of it. Not the old system, of course. *That* thing had more tentacles than a fucking squid ... I'm sorry ...'

Red-faced, Branssler looked at Maria-Therese. She gave him her best shrug-and-pout.

'The problem for the Americans is that they know nothing about Russians. In fact, they have no real intelligence about anything other than the Japanese. We did have, and they want it.'

'Intelligence? But you were never involved.'

'No, but desperate men can be too honest. The fellow I was introduced to had some shit from me about working with the industry - I worked with *you*, didn't I, so it was only a small, dry piece of shit. But he wasn't just going to take my word. He asked for a reference, someone who'd know, so I gave him the only name I had. You won't believe it, but the name came right back and did me a big favour.'

'Who?'

'Schapper.'

'*Gottfried* Schapper?'

'The poor sod's a widower now, dragging his little boy around Berlin, trying to find work for himself - but he was electronic surveillance, and the Allies have their own assets, don't they? Anyway, when they asked him about me he told them I'd been *instrumental* in the success of a major anti-SS operation. They loved that bit, offered me a job on the spot. I'm the lowest rung, but so what?'

'Where?'

'Near Frankfurt. A place called Oberursel.'

'Didn't that used to be …?'

'Yeah. Ironic, isn't it? The Americans watch us like we're ticking, and I have to put up a hand if I want to dump one. But I report directly to other Germans, even if *they* report to a Yank general. It could be a lot worse.'

'Who are *they*?'

The one who recruited me, he was Abwehr once, their top expert on the Russians - one of Canaris' top men, apparently. How he survived the hangings I don't know. He's called Baun. The others, including *his* boss, were foreign intelligence, Eastern Front.'

'FHO?'

'Yeah. It was a hidden archive of their material that did it, persuaded the Americans they needed Germans if they were going to understand Russians. The guy who hid them had precisely that end in mind.'

'What's *his* name?'

'Reinhard Gehlen. He was a general.'

'He headed FHO during the war.'

'Until Adolph got sick of his stupidly accurate reports, yeah. He should have composed fairy tales like everyone else.'

The Reich had been burdened by more intelligence agencies than all the Allies put together, most of them treating each other as the real enemy. Fischer had skirted them, glanced off a few, been dragged into one or two of their more byzantine arrangements and experienced not the slightest urge to apply for an interview. His own organization, nominally another such agency, had merely created lies to blur the enemy's understanding of Germany's true weakness. He counted that as the work of heroes.

He was delighted to see Branssler, and didn't for a moment think that this was a case of an old friend getting back in touch. He'd offered too much detail for this not to be ...

'Gerd, forgive me, but why are you here?'

'Otto!'

Maria-Therese (who had a former whore's hatred of bad manners) stared furiously at her husband. He ignored it, concentrated on Branssler. The big man didn't seem quite as offended by the question.

'And after you tell me that, *how* are you here?'

'No, let me start with how. You'd think, wouldn't you, that in poor, smashed Germany it would be difficult to track someone? In fact, it can be wonderfully easy. About three percent of Germans are trying desperately to be forgotten, while half of the rest are desperately trying to find the other half of the rest. I hardly had to do anything. I just put markers against certain names and wait.'

'I went to see Detmar Reincke.'

'Yes, you did. I recalled the names of about half a dozen of your comrades from Berlin and flagged them to every one of our ID processing centres.'

'So if I needed to ask directions I'd light up.'

'I'm very pleased with myself, Otto. I had you within three days, because you were honest enough to give your correct address.'

'Why wouldn't I?'

'You'd be amazed how many people don't. They have long memories of what happens when officials know where they live.'

'That's *how*, then. *Why* are you here?'

Branssler turned to Maria-Therese, opened his palms and winked. 'He's sharper than a gangster's pipe-cleaner and he asks *why*.'

'You said that this is all about Americans having no Soviet desk. I couldn't be any use with that.'

'Why not? You fought the Ivans, lied to them, interpreted data on their dispositions … '

'I *made up* data and fed it to our own people. Afterwards I made up German data and fed it to the Russians. I still don't see how that helps you.'

Branssler laughed. 'You're over-qualified! I bluffed my way into this, but you, you're exactly what they need. Alright, you didn't gather intelligence and you didn't analyse it; but hell, you can spot crap before it clears the horizon! The boys I work for are academics, almost. They sit in rooms, poring over reports, seeing about as much of life as tank fish do. Their foot soldiers, the gatherers, the fellows who used to risk their arses behind enemy ones - they're all gone, dead or turned. I think they've worked it out by now that I'm only an ex-*kripo* with a tiny bit of spook experience, but they don't care. They need men who can look into other men's eyes and see the truth.'

'Spook?'

'It's what the Amis call intelligencers. You can't work for them without picking up the slang. In fact, if you don't pick it up you'll wonder what the fuck they're talking about most of the time.'

'I should introduce you to another friend of mine, you'd get along splendidly. So you're offering me a job? As a *spook*?'

'I can't offer anything, but the reference I had from Schapper covered you too. And when they asked me about you I laid it on, told them that you'd gone up against SS, SD, Abwehr, that bastard who ran Peenemunde, granny killers - everyone I could think of. My boss wants to meet you, if only for your autograph.'

'It pays well?'

Branssler snorted. 'Not nearly. But it's as secure as any job a German can find, we get free access to PX and the whole business is new, virgin ground. You could be a general in ten years.'

Fischer looked at his wife, who she didn't need to say a word (*'this is real work'* might have been hung in fluorescent lighting over her head). It was all too much to weigh up rationally, but at first glance he couldn't spot the flaw. Frankfurt was a good place to be, possibly better than Berlin; it was the centre of American government in Germany and the place – if any – from which they'd begin their re-building. If it made Maria-Therese happy that was another good thing, and at least he could be reasonably certain she'd be safe there from most of the countless pits that had opened beneath German feet. The only itch beneath his skin was a half-dead sense of loyalty, though whether to his country, his military oath or his 'honour' he couldn't say. He reminded himself that a lot of important men were scrambling to become American lap-dogs at that moment, and for a newly-married man with no valuable skills to resist on a point of principle was wilful. The itch persisted, all the same.

'If I say yes, what comes next?'

Branssler jumped to his feet with far more energy than his older man's bulk hinted at. 'You'll go to Oberursel probably, get introduced, let them decide if they're happy about you and get your basic training over with. I can't say where they'll want you eventually, but in the meantime we can find accommodation for you both in Frankfurt. If they decide that you're to work at Oberursel they'll demand that you live in-compound, but at least Maria-Therese will be close by, and you'll be allowed domestic leave each month. That's it. You get paid monthly, in arrears, but you can draw on their PX immediately. How does it sound?'

Branssler, a friend, one of the few men that Fischer trusted instinctively, had come bearing a gift he could hardly refuse. He held out his hand and it was enveloped, half-crushed in the bigger man's fist. The other one thumped his shoulder, almost toppling him. Delighted, Maria-Therese clapped her hands and reached for what remained of the Delamain. For once, a small celebration didn't seem wildly inappropriate.

11

The pause between his knock on the door and the response was entirely expected. *Oberrat der VolksPolizei* Kurt Beckendorp wondered if it was just a certain kind of German or dolts everywhere who didn't regard it as a cliché, a pointless, empty gesture that neither impressed nor intimidated. He was tempted to wait, to make the arse speak a second time before he entered. But that would have made him an arse, too.

His second assumption was also on the mark. The chair for guests had been moved into the corner, so he'd be required to stand before the desk like a schoolboy awaiting the cane. Without looking at the man sitting behind it he limped across to the banished item, brought it back to its usual position and sat without being invited. The weasel eyes narrowed.

'Chairman Pieck was extremely disappointed.'

'I'm not surprised. We were shit.'

If the fellow had owned a pair of balls he might have leapt over the table at that. But he was a typical Party man, possessing an intimate knowledge of the anatomy of the human back and how to place things in them.

'Is insolence appropriate, do you think? Are your pitiful efforts not a cause for shame?'

'I could have been canvassing with Jesus, Mary and bags of gold, and still we'd have tanked. As long as folk think we're taking Red Army cock we haven't a chance. We made it as hard for the SPD as we could without actually breaking legs, yet they snatched half the vote. They're seen as Germans. We're not.'

'How can you say that?'

'How can you not? Anyone who bothered to speak to me on their doorstep said the same thing – that we're no more than a shotgun marriage, blessed by the Ivans but at each other's throats still. Christ, I fought Weissensee, it's as Red as a *florenzer*'s foreskin and what did I poll? Thirty-two fucking percent!' He tried to resist but hadn't the self-control. 'Remind me, comrade – what was your share?'

The man's face was quite puce now, a marbled hint of heart strain, but to his credit he didn't ignore the question. 'Rather less than thirty-two percent.'

'And it's not *your* fault, either. The election came too soon after the war and much too soon after the new party was formed. We needed two more years, minimum, but we were pushed into this. Now, Ostrowski's stitched together a coalition we couldn't break with iron bars.'

'Not legally, no. Obviously, it's a disaster.'

'Yeah, but if we'd won the Americans and British wouldn't have given us a clear run. Berlin is Berlin; it's the occupiers who set the rules, not the council. The Mayor no more owns the city than I do.'

'You're a good fellow, Beckendorp, but you don't see beyond your nose. None of us believed we'd seize the administration outright, but to gain so few seats is going to reduce our ability to wield any patronage. Clearly, we need to find a new strategy.'

'I assume you'll be wanting my resignation, then?' He made to rise but was waved down.

'Actually, no. You've become valuable by default. We expect the new Mayor to try to purge the police very soon, particularly in Western Sector stations. Obviously, SVAG will resist this, but it will be more difficult now. You have good relationships with many non-Party members of the force, yes?'

'Police work first, politics second.'

'Good. We need robust, continuous intelligence on what City Hall is thinking. By all means express frustration and disappointment with the Party. Imply, if you wish, that your beliefs are shaken by the scale of our defeat and that a permanently western-leaning city is now inevitable. Try to make friends.'

'You sound like you need a spy.'

'As you say, Berlin is Berlin. On a front-line, who isn't trying to know things?'

'And if I bugger it up, you'll wash your hands?'

'Thoroughly. But let's try to make it so that you don't. You hold the rank of *Oberrat*, don't you?'

'Provisionally, yes.'

'We'll get Markgraf to confirm it and then immediately appoint you to the rank of *Commandeur*. At that level you'll have far more access to the Council.'

'A promotion? For what?'

'You must have done *something* of note.'

'I put together the squad that brought down the Pankow currency gang. They had automatic weapons, we had shovel-staves.'

'That was last month, wasn't it?'

'Yeah. We lost three men.'

'Were you physically involved?

'I had to get one of the lads to kick down the door, obviously. But I led them in.'

'Then you're a hero. We need hardly argue your case to the *Kommandatura*.'

'Will my pay packet get any fatter?'

'I would imagine so. It's disappointing that your motivation is greed.'

'I'm acting in future character. A would-be capitalist who doesn't want more money isn't going to convince anyone.'

That raised a near-smile, and he relaxed. He enjoyed teasing politicians, but it was a dangerous pleasure when they were also the favourite glove puppets of *Sovetskaia Voennaia Administratsia v Germanii*. He owed his job to the Ivans at Karlshorst, but he had no illusions as to how valuable he was to them. The moment he became more of a pest than an asset they'd reach for the rat poison, bake a cake and shoot him as he ate it. It was the reason he'd worked harder and better at this job than any of his previous paid employments, and why he wasn't going to make the slightest fuss about being invited to make all the wrong friends.

Weasel-eyes removed a cigarette case from his inside pocket and offered it. They were probably Russian but he took one anyway, allowed it to be lit and pretended to enjoy the result. It was the strange thing with true German *kozis* - they'd spent so long in the Soviet Union while Adolph was spoiling things that they were natives now, more comfortable with Russian ways than their own. In fact it was best to think of them *as* Russians but with excellent German diction. He suspected that the bleak, shortage-ridden situation of which they now found themselves masters-at-one-remove made them homesick for wartime Moscow and its iron certainties. For them, the real shock of the recent elections was they had happened at all.

But he smiled cockily and flicked ash on to the carpet, playing to his reputation as a man of the people, a hard-case, a hopeful scoundrel they needed badly. It was a role he wore easily, because he needed them even more. They had plans, stratagems, long-range projections for the triumph of the socialist model and the nerveless determination to see it happen. He, in contrast, had no plans whatsoever. If his family were kept warm, well-fed and safe from all possible futures (and all three relied absolutely upon Soviet goodwill, whatever the results of the council elections), he didn't mind how it all fell out. He had no complaints. A man who wasn't what he claimed to be, who wasn't even the name he wore, had no right to be ambitious.

The other man fumbled in a desk drawer and brought out a bottle and two glasses. 'Vodka, comrade *VolksPolizei-Commandeur*?'

What else could it have been? He sat back in his chair, thought about putting his feet on the desk and then thought again.

'My very favourite. Yes, please, Herr Secretary.'

12

'I don't know why the Americans are here still, really I don't. They act like Lords of the Earth but I think they just want to keep their place in Berlin. They don't mix with us except to rape our girls, and they plan nothing beyond making their lives as comfortable as possible and enjoying our suffering. Perhaps they think we'll have a revolution and kick out the Russians, then they can just take over. They sit in the old *Leibstandarte SS* kaserne at Lichterfelde like princes in their high towers, and we're less than serfs to them. I don't suppose you have any food, Herr Baer?'

Despairingly, he took from his pocket the half sausage and bread he'd wrapped at the café and had brought home for his supper. She had the grace not to snatch at it, though her eyes lit up like a fox's would if it woke up on a meat counter. She nodded and shuffled out of his cellar, taking her treasure to where she wouldn't have to share it.

He had been disastrously wrong about his landlady. For two days, what he'd imagined to be indifference to his business had been a Berliner's natural reticence when confronted by a strange face. As soon as it became more familiar she had laid into him like a hardened *blockhilfer*, demanding his history and present hopes, the means by which he earned his hard currency, his political loyalties, his shoe and collar sizes. Rebuffed on all these points, she changed tactics and began to offer her opinions upon the entire tapestry of human affairs, probably in the hope that a reaction would tell her something of his own. The door to his cellar had no lock (an irrelevance to a man with no possessions), but short of punching her in the face he couldn't think of any other device that would protect his privacy. He wondered if he could requisition one, or a gun.

This was his fifth day in Berlin, and he had yet to meet his contact. Frustration hadn't set in yet but he'd expected swiftness, resolution, opportunities spotted and seized. Perhaps he'd assumed too much of espionage, if that's what it counted as. He had to remind himself that every job had its mundane passages, its clock-watching hours that made the day creep. Even war was more about manoeuvring than fighting, waiting than killing.

Yet café life had lost its last shard of novelty. A succession of dollar bills had enticed some fine morsels from the *Ambassador*'s obviously connected proprietor, but the man had no conversation and didn't seem interested in refreshing his stock of reading material beyond what the Amis circulated. The liquid assault upon his bowels by over-roasted acorn or chicory was another problem; it collaborated with his bed's fugitive spring to keep him far from sleep most nights, to the curious point at which days of enforced indolence were wearing him out. An even more curious consequence of his routine was that a man who had never had any great engagement with (or empathy for) other human beings was becoming an accomplished people-watcher, a student of behaviours.

At the *Ambassador*'s only corner table, for example, was Mrs Margot, always called that despite the obvious fact that Margot was her given name. She was an old acquaintance of their host, often recalling some shared memory of better times involving now-lost members of his family. Yet there was also a subtle hint of … he thought about it occasionally over the space of two full days, until it occurred that her manner towards him stood somewhere between affection and deference, that once she had been a family servant, perhaps a nanny, and that the careful sadness with which she drew her recollections hinted at unexpected tragedy, long accepted. His mind wandered over a crib death, a motor accident, invited headaches to resolve the mystery.

The old man who propped up the counter each day from noon onwards was a former railway worker. This needed no great feat of perception because he wore his work clothes still, either because he had no others or was trying to keep his morale a step from the half-death that retirement often was. He was a cantankerous fellow also but a walking archive of Berlin's rail history. With or without encouragement he would rehearse the growth of the city's network, it's quirks and oddities, the secret lines that seemed to run nowhere but led to places not to be mentioned, the war damage (how, when and the attendant deaths) and the statistics, above all statistics, pouring from his old head like the torrent released by a storm valve. His name was Peter, but everyone called him Steam.

He reserved his most careful, discreet attention for the attractive woman whom no one called by name, who claimed a seat near the stove and remained for hours each day, eating and drinking nothing. The café owner didn't seem to mind this abuse of his hospitality and always said *good morning, my dear* when she arrived. Others offered similarly intimate addresses but took care not to intrude upon her oblivious, twitching reveries or muttered conversations to absent friends. He didn't need to tempt a headache for this one. *Bereavement, battle shock, rape - most likely all.*

He had too much time to waste and these observations were diverting, but the obvious problem was that he was becoming one of them, the *Ambassador*'s regulars, and this wasn't the best way to remain anonymous. Even the proprietor, who appreciated his hard currency, had taken to casting long, thoughtful glances at this man who didn't need to work, who spent all day every day doing nothing much and paying for his leisure in Hamiltons. Worried about this he rehearsed a few almost-plausible explanations about a convalescence, an inheritance, a successful salvage operation, and almost wished someone would end the tension by asking outright.

He was being noticed at the café and interrogated at 'home', a fine start to his career as a shadow-man. If it *had* started. He began to wonder if this task was a jest, a sophisticate prank to keep his handlers amused in a tiresome posting, or whether his contact had been intercepted by the Americans and was presently coughing up blood somewhere, ready to give names as quickly as they could write them down. In his uninformed judgement either might be equally likely.

So it was upon this particular evening, having been robbed of a meagre supper by his wolfish landlady and lacking any wood to light the stove, that he began to consider his early resignation from the espionage business. This would require no formal notice, obviously - a hitched ride westward to the French Zone, where Germans were treated worse than anywhere else but where true administrative chaos reigned, would serve as emphatically as any signed document. What could they do then, send someone after him? He knew nothing, could reveal nothing, was capable of betraying no one - in any case, they probably expected a certain percentage of recruits to run or fail. How much effort would they consider worthwhile to recover an asset that had yet to prove itself as such?

For several minutes, the prospect of becoming his own man warmed him more than a lit stove might have done, but common sense reined himself in. He had no resources other than the dollars in his secret pocket, no friends other than the men who directed him like a locomotive upon a switching plate, no prospects other than those they half hinted at (unless he were to offer himself to the Americans or British, and that would bring him right back to this but with the bonus of a double-double-dealer's momentary life-expectancy). He realised that had to wait, to let things happen the way his paymasters intended. He could make decisions when his new world was seen more clearly, when a blurred prospect sharpened and ghosts became men with readable faces.

He had just persuaded himself of this when behind him the door that lacked a most necessary lock creaked and opened. He sighed.

'Really, Frau Best, I have no more food. Tomorrow, perhaps …'

He turned. An old man stood in the doorway, dressed in manual worker's clothes so worn that they might have been heirlooms, passed down through generations of dogged grafters. A rope served for a belt but had missed at least half its loops, so that it seemed more to be holding in his generous stomach than preserving modesty. Incongruously, the trousers were tucked into battered *knobelbechers* that had been split at their sides and folded down ankle-boot fashion (though 'fashion' was an accusation hardly to be cast at any item of his ensemble), their top-straps protruding rakishly as if to clear a path or collect pollen.

The gentleman hitched his departing trousers with one hand, removed the pipe from his mouth with the other and scratched his head, oblivious to the ash that fell upon it.

'But *I* have bread, Rolf. And instructions.'

'My name isn't Rolf.'

'It is now.' The old man removed a pack of papers from his jacket pocket. 'Take these and burn the ones you have. The name they gave you is for your landlady, in case someone comes asking who the new fellow is. To everyone else you're going to be Rolf, Rolf Hoelscher. I'll tell you all about yourself, right? And you can call me Wolfgang. Just Wolfgang.'

13

'Why here?'

Fischer peered around the room. It was small but public, and half-filled with American uniforms. He couldn't imagine a setting less suitable to clandestine business.

Branssler shrugged. 'I do what I'm told.'

The heavily-timbered bar of the *Hotel Die Hirschgasse* was a throwback to a time before Germany, before the Confessional Wars even. The view from the window was equally amenable – a grand sweeping vista of the Neckar, its right-hand aspect only slightly spoiled by the untidy mass of medieval red roofs tumbling towards the water. This was Fischer's first visit to Heidelberg. Earl Kuhn had imagined it the ideal post-war location for his record business but settled for dirtier, busier Bremen instead. War had almost passed it by, the sole damage (three arches of its pretty old bridge) inflicted by withdrawing Wehrmacht demolition units rather than USAF. It was too beautiful, too perfect, too unspoiled.

'At least General Patton died here. The town can say it's done its bit.'

Fischer snorted. 'The town was so far up Adolph's rear that its university had a book-bonfire before being told to.'

'Yeah? That doesn't surprise me. The picture-box places were always the worst. It was the prol shit-holes like Berlin that saw through him. Over there.'

Branssler gestured to a table in the far corner of the room. At it, a dapper man with a thick moustache was examining a menu. He had his back to the rustic, bare-stone wall, his flank covered by a large briefcase sitting upon what had probably been a carefully-laid place setting.

The man looked up, beckoned to Branssler and stood as they approached. Fully erect he was almost as tall as the ex-Bull but cadaverously thin. It looked to be his natural build, not the result of the enforced health regime everyone else was currently grateful for.

'Herr Oberstleutnant, may I …'

'Just names, Branssler. No redundant ranks, please.'

'Right. Otto Fischer, this is Herr Baun, one of my bosses.'

Fischer took the hand. 'Not Hermann Baun?'

'Yes. Have we met?'

'No, sir. I recall that some briefing papers circulated to my department had your name on, or in, them.'

'Of course. You were with the War Reporters' Unit, in Berlin.'

'For a while, yes. Then Luftwaffe Counter-Intelligence East.'

'And you were police before the war, like Branssler. Very good.'

'Really? I would have thought you'd have preferred Abwehr or FHO men to someone with my …'

'Ideally, we would. But it isn't possible to recruit entirely from within the profession. FHO's eastern network was smashed towards the end of the war, and many Abwehr men were too closely associated with the Admiral to escape the noose. So we can't entirely pick and choose. You're not offended?'

'No, sir.'

'The fact is, any background in investigations and data analysis is useful to us. Branssler will have told you about the conditions, I think?'

'Yes, sir. I hadn't realised things were moving so soon after ...'

Baun was tapping the table with a knuckle, not really listening. Fischer took the hint and became an audience.

'It's a slow process, God knows. But the Americans are finally coming to accept that the Soviet Union is the threat, not Germany. One of them must have found a map of Europe and coloured in the parts occupied by Stalin. Fuel, raw materials, vast new reserves of manpower - he's not going to give up all of that, whatever Truman thinks. We've put it to General Clay that the borders of the Soviet Union have moved westwards by several hundred kilometres, making every previous attempt at political ascendancy in Europe seem half-hearted by comparison. He's seen the light, finally, and we're needed once more.'

Fischer was unconvinced but said nothing. Russia and Russians had always warmed Abwehr's collective arse. They would have called it a necessary *preoccupation*, others a near-obsession; it's why Canaris had risked and lost everything in an attempt to ditch Hitler, secure a peace in the west and realise his vision – hallucination - of western civilization standing shoulder to shoulder, ready to repel the Eastern Beast. A more impartial head might have acknowledged that the Americans and Russians were going to wrestle come what may, and if Germany was *needed* it was only as the battleground upon which the new struggle would take place. It was hard to be enthusiastic about the prospect but this was a job interview, so he gave his serious, thoughtful face to Baun, who seemed eager to have him convinced.

'The Soviets won't stop at the present demarcation lines – history tells us that. There'll be another war, eventually – it's inevitable. Bur first, they'll infiltrate German civic institutions, to subvert hearts and loyalties. The Americans don't understand how strong our domestic socialist tradition is, despite the most strenuous efforts of National Socialism to extinguish it. They seem to assume that their brand of democratic capitalism will insinuate itself into the German psyche and re-shape us in their image. This is wishful thinking – perverse, even. The Russians understand far more clearly the German yearning for security, order, a world emptied of surprises, even if the price is a degree of political authoritarianism.'

'You know the Russians well?'

'I *am* Russian, in a way. I was born in Odessa, the Volga German community.'

Fischer realised now why Baun was so energetically anti-Soviet. Following the invasion in '41, the entire Volga German community had been offed in cattle trucks to Kazahkstan or Siberia, despite the fact that most of them were Mennonites who wouldn't have touched the war – *any* war - with a shit-covered stick.

'So, can we expect you to join our little band, Herr Fischer?'

'Have I any time to think about it?'

'Not really, because *we* have no time. We're attempting to build an organization from scratch, impress the Americans with our indispensability *and* resurrect a network in the East that may already be corpse-cold. I'm looking at three other prospective candidates today, and will have added more than two hundred kilometres to my odometer before I see my bed again. You'll appreciate that this opportunity – if you feel that's what it is, of course – isn't the sort we can place in the trade papers and hope for a decent response.'

'No, sir.' Fischer glanced at Branssler, and could almost smell the force of the man's eagerness to bring him in. He still wasn't certain why he should be regarded by anyone as suitable material for this kind of work, but he had no doubts on one point at least - to even consider saying no would require that he had other ideas, or prospects, or at least the prospect of having an idea. Had he been given even slight encouragement by Detmar Reincke's father he'd now be scouring north-western Germany for seed and fertiliser, probably getting nowhere yet thinking himself a man with a path before him. Why should he baulk at an opportunity that had pulled on its boots and marched towards him bearing a salary?

Baun's hand was half extended, as if the question were a moot one. Fischer took it, and a thought came to him some minutes behind schedule.

'Do you – we – have a name?'

'Not yet. It's been difficult enough to get the Americans to accept the idea of employing *Nazis* without throwing something on the lines of *GeheimeNachrichtenDienst* at them.'

Nazi? I was obliged to be a Party member, but ...'

Baun waved it away. '*Anyone* who served in German uniform during the late war was - *is* - a hardened National Socialist to most Americans minds, even the intelligent ones. Their world is quite straightforward, inhabited only by good and evil, right and wrong. Hopefully their opinion of us will moderate in time, but so far we've gained their slight trust only by emphasising that they have a new, larger adversary. If you can conceive an amenable, non-Germanic name for us you'll certainly earn our gratitude. And an early bonus, perhaps.'

14

Fischer was puzzled by Branssler's reaction to his successful recruitment. After Baun's departure the big man reminded him of a puppy being introduced to its first stick, insisting that the two of them remain for lunch at the hotel, paying in Allied marks for a two-course affair finer than any Fischer could recall then demanding that the waiter bring them two rounds of cheap brandy to bed it down. All the while he burbled on happily about the people they would work with, their elusive American masters, the politics that scarred the day-to-day efficiency of their organization already ….

'Politics?'

Branssler threw back the last of his brandy and shrugged. 'History, then. Baun's a one-man-act, never happy unless he's on the road, running his field agents, paying them with fistfuls of cash. But the real boss, Gehlen, he's more … measured, and hard to read. He's the one who really convinced the Amis, went across to the US, argued the case for a German Intelligence asset and then set up Oberursel. Obviously, he ran FHO during the war, so he's got the record. He employed Baun back then, dragged him over from Abwehr and calmed him down a bit, made him shoot lower. It's what I heard, anyway.'

'Shoot lower?'

'Baun's prone to enthusiasm, I've seen that. The rumour is that while Gehlen was in the US he went at it on his own, promised too much to the Americans and couldn't cover the ticket. But no one knows the Ivans like he does, and he's been damn busy building a network in the Soviet

Zone. Between here and the Oder we have dozens of agents now, and it's eighty percent Baun's doing at the least.'

'So where's the problem?'

'Baun runs the fieldwork and wants to keep it that way, a separate structure to the evaluation and analysis side. Gehlen says no, that's what made such a mess of our Intelligence during the war, when everyone had his own kingdom, building walls around it. From now on there'll be one organization that does everything, like the British SOE. The Americans agree, so the boss is going to win this one and Baun's not happy. They don't argue about it openly but it's there, in the air, like you've walked in ten minutes after a lovers' tiff.'

'It sounds like you're Gehlen's man.'

Branssler shrugged again. 'I'm for the fellow who pays my salary, and I work purely on evaluation.'

'So why am I being interviewed by Baun?'

'He does a lot of recruitment, for both divisions. Gehlen trusts him on that at least.'

'When am I going to Oberursel?'

'Soon. Eventually.'

'In the meantime …?'

'Don't worry about that now. We can talk about it more when …' Branssler pulled out his wallet and rummaged in it. 'I think we can go to another round of drinks. That's a nice suit, by the way. Where did you get it?'

'Stettin, my personal tailor. What is it that you aren't telling me, Gerd?'

'How do you mean?'

'For an ex-*kripo* you have a very readable face. I say readable; I mean betraying. Since you came to see us in Bremen I've had the feeling that something's not being said. It's not that I'm ungrateful, but unless you've become someone else it's like watching a poor actor rehearsing his lines.'

Branssler glanced around, accounting for the fellow diners remotely in hearing. Fischer's eyes followed his, and he noticed for the first time that they were the only civilians – the only Germans, other than staff – in the restaurant.

'Shit. Sorry, Otto, but I had you get you to say yes. The job's everything I said it was, I promise – poor money, good prospects and the Americans treat us almost as human beings. You couldn't do better, really.'

'But why me, particularly? There are men who are far better at everything I've attempted – police work, soldiering, lying professionally for the Reich. Why not one or more of them? You probably have any number of contacts from Alexanderplatz still who'd bite off your hand to do this. Is this just a favour you're doing me?'

Branssler was fascinated still by the view around their table. 'No, but I can't say more here.'

'Where, then?'

'Come on.'

They left the hotel and walked west, towards Heidelberg's old town. Fischer said nothing, letting the silence do its work while some inner battle working itself out. It was curious how a career in police work had failed to teach either man how to think one thing while flagging something else, or nothing at all. A pack of cigarettes came out of Branssler's pocket three times, and only at the last did he fumble inside and half extract one. Even then it remained there, forgotten. It was at moments like this during a suspect interview that a shrewd *kripo* would send out a subordinate for a blank statement sheet.

They came to the river, and that was where Branssler ran out of runway. He turned to Fischer, his habitual frown softened by what, in a less brutal face, might have been taken for a hint of desperation.

'It *had* to be you, Otto. I know something they don't, and if they found out I'd be gone in a minute.'

'Why? Surely, the more they know …?'

'Not this. It's about something that's already started, that Gehlen particularly wants and Baun – for once – particularly wants to help him with. It'll put them both well in with the Amis and give the organization some credibility.'

'So, let it happen.'

'I can't, and neither can you.'

'Tell me then.'

Branssler took a deep breath and held it. He was looking across the river, probably at nothing.

'Gerd?'

'You know how espionage works?'

'Bribery, betrayal, deception – sometimes, a selfless sense of duty.'

'Yeah, sometimes. Not this time. The Ivans are doing their best to turn Germans who work for the Americans, or plant their own pet Germans in useful positions. Obviously, we're trying to return the favour.'

'It's sensible.'

'It is. Baun and Gehlen have been looking at our old *kozis*, the ones who fled to Moscow before the war and stayed there until it was safe to come home, or those that hid in deep places until Adolph was gone.'

'But they're hard cases, aren't they? Redder than the Soviets?'

'Most of them. Me, I think the organization's wasting their time, but I don't get to say so. They've found a few likely ones, who might be vulnerable.'

'It turns out that they're former NSDAP, you mean?'

'That's right. The threat of exposure may or may not work. Neither the Americans nor Russians mind employing former Nazis *if* they're useful enough, do they? We don't even know if they've admitted it already to their bosses, so it could be a pointless exercise.'

'So why do you – we – care?'

'One of them is living a slightly larger lie than a former Party membership. A weakness we can definitely exploit, no question about it.'

'Girls, boys, Jews?'

'Worse. He's pretending to be someone he's not. That's the thing I know, and I almost wish that I didn't. Because Baun and Gehlen know it too.'

For a moment Fischer wondered why Branssler should care. He opened his mouth but it hit him before the question was out. 'Not … *Freddie?*'

Branssler nodded. 'Hamburg council's been busy sorting out the stale pools of fat in their ruined cellars. Under one of many piles of rubble they found the remains of a family, poor bastards who decided to face out the firestorm together. There were papers in a tin which put a name to them.'

'Beckendorp.' Three years earlier, Fischer had been careful to lift the *volkscartei* of people who had been listed missing, presumed dead. Once the paperwork had been disappeared they were truly missing, so the family's resurrection hadn't stirred any *OrPo*'s curiosity. It had worked, so well that the Beckendorps – née Hollemans – had survived a Regime that tried to know everything about everyone. But if Branssler was right, the Peace was going to be less forgiving.

'The real Kurt Beckendorp was a die-hard communist, wasn't he?'

Fischer nodded. 'The Hamburg Rising, 1927. Freddie told me.'

'Obviously he managed to avoid being put against a wall, then or later. The Party never found out who he was, and he was careful to do all the right things after that, even volunteering for the Luftwaffe. But somehow Abwehr dug up the full story, and like everything else they kept it to themselves. I think they were planning to use him at some point, until his death made them lose interest. It's possible they would have noticed

Freddie's Lazarus act eventually, but then came the July Plot, and after that they were too busy burning files and trying not to earn a piano-wire noose to care about past plans.'

'So this was just evil luck.'

'Well, Freddie's may have held still, except that Baun of all people got the news from Hamburg, remembered the name and went straight to Gehlen. The guy's a fucking Hollerith machine - he put the data with that of an up-and-comer in Berlin's *VolksPolizei*, also name of Beckendorp, and burrowed until he got the names of the latter's entire family, which …'

'… matched precisely those in the tin in the Hamburg cellar.'

'There was a daughter too, but they're assuming she died in the meantime. They've got Freddie by the balls.'

'And they'll squeeze, hard.'

'They're going to make him their man in Berlin's *kozi* network. And when he's caught and takes one in the back of the head, what are the chances that Kristin and the twins get a state pension?'

'How did you find out?'

'Accidentally. I saw the Hamburg report before it rang anyone else's bell. I knew what it meant immediately of course, but I was a new boy and unsure of how easy it was to bury stuff. By the time I decided to light a small fire it was on its way to Gehlen. After that I made sure I was involved. Luckily they have absolutely no organization in Berlin yet, so I could play up my police experience in the city, all your connections there – I made up that bit - and how useful we'd be to the operation.'

'We? *We're* the ones who are going to snare Freddie?'

'Who else? It's going to happen for certain - who better than you and me to do it?'

'They don't know that we know him.'

'No, that's part of the only luck we have. They don't know because they don't know who Freddie is. All they know is that he isn't Kurt Beckendorp, because no one is anymore. So, we have a small opportunity, though fuck me if I can think what it might be at the moment. It *has* to be us.'

Fischer thought it through and could find no obvious way to say no. Freddie Holleman had always enjoyed the services of one organ more than most of his species. His heart took care of the blood, his liver the cholesterol, his pancreas the infections and the surplus item the pure, undeserved good fortune that had swept the path before him for most of his life. Had he been born a firing post a bullet wouldn't yet have found him, but *yet* was about to expire. An offer was going to be made, a choice of falling into the staked pit either soon or very soon, and he would be allowed about a minute to decide which. The best they could do for him was to carry the offer personally. After that, they had only the Americans, Russians and most of Germany's surviving Intelligence to distract.

15

'Give me a brief idea of what this is, before I wipe my prettiest feature with it.'

*Unterkommissar* Beyer grinned, reached across the desk and recaptured the sheet of paper he had placed in front of his boss. At no point since entering the office had he attempted to stand to attention, and now he placed a foot on the guest stand chair and leaned on his knee while he glanced down the page. His superior, Commander Kurt Beckendorp, ignored this egregious display of disrespect.

'It's marked *Secret*, so naturally it sat in the pool in-tray for several hours before I noticed it.'

'Cocks.'

'It says we have to get ready to put the knife into a few backs.'

'A few?'

'To begin with.'

'Social Democrats, I assume?'

'Despicable Judas-bastards.'

The eyebrows at the other side of the desk rose slightly. 'You're referring to our fraternal brethren.'

'That's a tautology, isn't it?'

'A fantasy is what it is. Anyway, didn't we just get the word to treat them like our favourite aunts?'

Beyer grinned again. 'That was last week. But yes, all decisions made at committee level must be fully discussed with former SPD members before being signed off. Consensus must be seen to consense.'

'That isn't a word.'

'It should be. But *this* says that while we're embracing them we should squeeze hard enough to cut off the oxygen – specifically, to make sure that any meeting at which ex-SPD votes are cast comprises of a majority of KPD colleagues.'

'To make them count as much as a skat seven.'

'Exactly. It's a marriage, so appearances have to be just that.'

'Fine.' Beckendorp sighed and stood, shifting his weight instinctively to ease the pressure on his amputated leg. 'Do I have to respond with anything?'

'No.'

'Good. Now, Beyer, you're a policeman again. What's happening with that throat-slasher in Hellersdorf?'

Beyer came smartly to attention. 'Nothing, Commander.'

'Nothing at all?'

No, sir. He was identified yesterday morning by an old woman who almost tripped over him as he worked. Luckily for her he panicked and ran. But it doesn't matter.'

'He's Russian?'

'Probably Mongolian, from the description.'

'Shit. Well, send what we have to Karlshorst. With luck someone there will locate their conscience and shoot the bastard.'

'They'll bundle him out of the city, at least.'

'Still, I'll miss the warm glow of a job well done.'

Beyer pulled a face. 'It's what we have. At least we can wash our hands of the case.'

'Any more hand-washing and we'll need new fingerprints. Anything else going on?'

'Two raids, both on suspected cigarette fences. A couple more missing children to add to the list. The rest is the usual – breaking up fights on points of who owns what cellar or rations, or wives earning a bit on the side.'

The other man shook his head. 'They could train up cats to do this job. I remember …'

'What, sir?'

'Never mind. Bring in anything that needs my signature; I'm off home early today for my boys' birthday.'

When Beyer had gone he limped to the window. Down on Keibelstrasse the rubble was almost gone, a collateral effect of the vast Alexanderplatz clearance just a hundred metres to the south. He wasn't sure if the prospect of the resulting wide, empty spaces wasn't worse than the original devastation - at least the tumbled buildings had held an echo of what had been here. A swept-clean urban desert had nothing to which to attach memory, to hold down a sense of belonging.

The thought of what memory could do roused him. He had to be more careful - if he'd let spill just a few more unconsidered words young Beyer would have been on to it like a *wachtelhund* on a pheasant. It was all very well playing the bluff, don't-give-a-shit popular hero to the cheap seats, but falling asleep and letting the character take over was asking for trouble.

'Beyer!'

A head appeared around the door. 'Commander?'

'A couple more, you said. The list – how long is it now?'

The head moved slightly, and though the body couldn't be seen it offered strong evidence of a shrug. 'It's hard to say. A proportion of them will be dead somewhere from malnutrition, or run away, or found and removed by out-of-town family, but ...'

'Your best estimate?'

'More than six, fewer than twelve.'

'Jesus Christ. What are we doing?'

'What we can - speaking to people, putting up notices, fending off distraught mothers. Not much, in fact. You know what the manning situation is.'

'Who's your least incompetent *oberwachtmeister*?'

'That'll be Müller.'

'Was he police before the war?'

'An advocate.'

'Well, if he knows the law he must be as intelligent as most cats. Put him and an *anwärter* on to the missing kids, full time for now.'

'But we're at least sixty percent below complement. How ...?'

'You'll be losing two men from a murder case you can't chase and assorted domestic affrays that you don't care about anyway. It isn't going to make any real difference to our results, and at least we can say that we're trying.'

'Is that an efficient use of them?'

'I couldn't say. But my bowels tell me it's better to fail diligently on the important stuff than wipe up trivia. Don't worry, I'll clear it with the Inspector.'

16

Wolfgang walked the rail lines in Steglitz, ensuring that no war damage, rubble or suicides impeded the passage of Germany's resurrected rolling stock. It was healthy employment but boring, and he eased the hours along by whittling any interesting pieces of wood he encountered into rudimentary naval vessels (he being a former mariner who recalled his First War experiences with more fondness than they deserved). His other hobby was nudging the means and benefits of production into the hands of the proletariat, a pastime first taken up in the days following the Kaiser's abdication, when he had been one of only a few dozen members of the *Volksmarinedivision* to join the Spartacists' revolt against the traitor Ebert and his Freikorps friends. Coming second in that struggle hadn't diminished his belief in the inevitability of Capitalism's imminent demise - in fact, his obvious satisfaction at Germany's defeat, her partial subjection to Soviet rule and enthusiasm for the continuing struggle might have wearied an impatient temperament.

But Wolfgang's new colleague – *Rolf*, as he now was - didn't tell him to shut up, or take a breath, or even try to change the subject when the martyrdom of poor Karl and Rosa came up for the thirtieth time. The man's need for camaraderie – doubtless nurtured during the long years he spent being very necessarily mute on political matters – made him garrulous (an ill-advised quality in his trade) and, therefore, informative. He was a wellspring of detail on the present state of Berlin politics, the loyalties of various departments within the city's curious, divided-yet-whole government and who among the clench of timer-servers, yes-men, Janus-shamers and professional rodents was most likely to be peering down upon the rest from the top of the manure pile when things settled down.

That was a curious thing about Wolfgang – he had no partialities when it came to his fellow Germans. Hard left, centrist, fascist or uncommitted, he despised them all; only the Russians could claim some part of his affections, and probably because to date it was they alone who had successfully thrown off the shackles of class despotism. But he had responded well to the first handshake, and took pains to infer that he didn't necessarily hold a man's nationality against him.

'The thing is, Rolf, Germans are always happier being nudged in a direction. We took the Roman coin, we gave ourselves French lessons, we kissed Swedish arse and then we touched our toes for an Austrian half-wit. And now that almost everyone's come to live with us, offering one thing or the other, we've a choice to make.'

'And you think it's the Soviets, Wolfgang?'

'You and me both, Rolf, obviously. Who'd want to be an American, tied to a workbench with eighty million others, toiling to keep the Vanderbilts living like Renaissance princes?'

'What about the British?'

Wolfgang sniffed. 'They had their chance in 1649 and buggered it. Now they're just burned-out lap-dogs of the Amis. No, it's the Soviets who'll give us what we need – bread, potatoes and class-struggle. I swear, if we all do our job, in ten years' time there'll be a united, fraternal, socialist Europe.'

Rolf didn't argue. He had always been entertained by the naiveté of true believers, whatever their faith. Besides, he was supposed to be an enthusiast himself, the reason he was taking instructions from Wolfgang - instructions, and packages. He was surprised by the latter, particularly the quantity of US dollars that one of them contained. He wondered how ethical it was from a socialist perspective, to be suborning the Federal Reserve to bribe minor German officials away from their bourgeois principles. In any case, wasn't a bribe just a means of confirming those principles?

At their second meeting (in a half-ruined signal shed at the Ebers-Strasse junction), Wolfgang dismissed these qualms. 'Marx never said we shouldn't use Capitalism to defeat it. In fact, he said it was inevitable. Well, something like that.'

'So I'm to make friends with the gentlemen on this list and ... what? Offer money to have them vote our way?'

'No, just offer them the money, tell them it's an appreciation of the good work they're doing and leave it at that.'

'Are they? Doing good work?'

'Are they fuck. What we're giving them is the means by which we can hold their balls over a fire when the time comes to demand the ... um ...'

'Quid pro quo?'

'Yeah, that. Some of them will be sharp enough to see it right away, guess who you're representing and tell you to shove your money. Them you don't press, just back off with a smile and an apology for having been insolent. Some will be too stupid to get it until the day they hear from us. Most will have a fair idea what it's about but be too greedy to say no.'

'These men are local politicians?'

'About half of them, yes. Others are in various jobs in management or administration - fuel distribution, transportation, food supplies, even police. The sort of people a city needs to keep it running.'

'And they're all loyal to the western Allies?'

Wolfgang tapped out his pipe on the shed wall and shrugged. 'Who's to say? We need to make sure we know where their loyalties will lie at a certain point in the future, not where they are now.'

But they're all are in the Allied Zones of Berlin?'

'They live or work here. We try not to cross west-east too often in this business, it gets us noticed. There are others doing the same elsewhere in the city. But Rolf, you look disappointed.'

'Well, it seems a little …'

'Ordinary?'

'Sordid.'

'Welcome to the struggle, mate. Like any other, it's nine parts paperwork and one part shitting away your colon.'

'This other bundle?'

'Leaflets. Leave them in public places, but don't get caught.'

'Anti-American propaganda?'

'No, forged American instructions to their GIs, about how filthy German women are, how we're all Nazis, the usual.'

'Will anyone believe that they're genuine?'

Wolfgang laughed. 'They're almost exact copies of what the Amis gave their men last year, before they changed their strategy and pretended to be sweet. We're just reminding folk of what they really think of us.'

'Is this all a test?'

'Of course it is. No one's going to ask you to assassinate Truman on your first day, are they? Be reliable and you'll get noticed; bugger up and they'll put you in the Teltow Canal.'

'I get it.'

'Now, you'll have worked out that you're going to need to watch these fellows, get familiar with their routines, so you can approach them without being seen. The list's in order of who you're to speak to, but it's likely that things will go wrong and you'll have to adapt it as you go. Just keep me clear about what's going on, right?'

'Where will I find you?

'The Ambassador Café, Tuesdays and Thursdays, from ten o'clock. I'll be dodging work, so I can only be there for half an hour each time. Don't ever speak to me, or look as if you want to. I'll leave when you walk in, you follow after ten minutes and keep walking. I'll decide where we talk.'

'What if …?'

'What if what?'

'Something happens to you and you don't come?'

'You mean the Americans spot me and put me in the ground? Keep going back to the café each day until someone new contacts you. We're none of us indispensable.'

'You might talk, implicate me.'

Wolfgang smiled. 'I might. I never did enjoy pain. But don't worry, it's alright if I do, you're no bigger loss to the cause than I am. If *you* get into trouble and can't find me, get back into the Soviet Zone, quickly.'

'To where?'

To Mitte, Linienstrasse 112. It's mainly a ruin, but there are two intact rooms. One of them has an unbroken window with a pair of curtains. Get in there, lock the door with the key that's under the mat and close the curtains. Someone will notice them.'

What sort of trouble do you mean?'

'They sort you can't put right. You'll know what it is when it happens, believe me.'

17

Lehter Bahnhof was functioning, which was all that was to be said for it. Once Berlin's most elegant station building, a palace upon the Spree, it was now a proud monument to the Allied Air Forces' adept bombing skills, which had destroyed almost all the beauty without crippling its purpose. Fischer hadn't passed through here more than half a dozen times in his adult life; he wished that he'd paid more attention then to what was missing now.

It was a bright, late winter afternoon, and he was in a foul mood. Six hours earlier he had said goodbye to Maria-Therese. As he packed his meagre wardrobe, bundling his three heavily darned socks into each other and folding his only two ties, she had started to cry. He hadn't seen her cry before. A few moments later Earl Kuhn joined in. Had the small suitcase been his coffin their grief might have been more touching than irritating (though he would have known nothing about it, of course), but to mark the departure of a man hoping to be away for a month at most they had both crossed the line well into maudlin.

Kuhn had sniffled rather than sobbed, and saved both their blushes by pretending he had a head cold. But Maria-Therese had been inconsolable, a dam wall bursting at its base. It had touched and exasperated him, made him too uncomfortable either to take her emotion for what it was or soothe its edges with anything more useful than a clumsy hug. And ever since then he'd kicked himself for not being better at what husbands do.

At least she would be watched over. Kuhn had promised to visit each day (an onerous undertaking, to be dragged from his emporium), and if necessary would excuse Beulah May guard duty to keep company with the war widow. He couldn't have hoped for more, and once the Berlin thing was done he planned to find her a place to live in Frankfurt, close to his new workplace - or better still, Bad Homburg, where princes used to take the waters, at most a couple of kilometres from where he'd be serving the victors behind barbed wire. It was comforting to think of it, something he could tie hopes to. It almost amounted to a plan.

But the Berlin *thing* added its weight to that of parting, making him doubly miserable. He'd brooded over it a great deal over the past days, and each time his nose had met a wall when he tried to imagine how it could be done. He feared Branssler's faith in a man whose only palpable success to date had been to remain upright in a collapsed world; he feared this city, its territories claimed by new and unfamiliar piss marks; most of all he feared himself, what might be required of him in an age in which loyalty – even identity - was bartered, surrendered or subsumed into the service of filling one's belly and drawing breath for another day.

He was waiting at the appointed place, beneath the station clock that had been stood down by the raid of 25 February 1945 and never restarted. A stream of humanity passed by and around the broken man and his one battered suitcase, a near-motionless monument to the larger damage around him. No one appeared to notice him, no one told him to move on; the bustle was as all bustle was, oblivious and preoccupied, but to his eyes its components had a weary, broken character. An optimist might have called it convalescent, a bustle that was recovering tenderly after a long, serious illness, but signs of better, healthier prospects were hard to find. In almost half an hour he didn't see a single civilian in clothes that hadn't been mended or re-worked to fit the new standard, ultra-trim national figure. To someone with kinder eyes they might all have been of that breed of self-effacing rural Englishman who patched the elbows of his perfectly sound tweed jackets to affect an air of shabby gentility.

Gerd Branssler couldn't have hidden in that crowd. As he crossed from the main entrance Fischer watched commuters shuffle quickly to void a potential collision that would have been much to their disadvantage. How a man of sixty and several more years could have maintained his muscle mass would have been a small mystery in any age; in the midst of the present, general want it bordered upon an affront to an entire nation. His belly was less generous than formerly but little else had followed it, and if he'd chosen to resurrect his career as a *kripo* he could have replaced half a squad of the present, whipped intake in weight alone.

Branssler's bullet-head swivelled, and he caught sight of his friend. This time there were no hugs, no broad smiles. The big Berliner looked as glum as Fischer felt, and the handshake was brief enough to leave no bruise.

'A shitty business.'

'As you say. What's the procedure?'

Branssler glanced around and reassured himself that none of the passing herd was paying attention.

'It has to be done in less than twelve hours - the initial encounter, the abduction, the offer, the safe return and our detailed report to Oberursel.'

'That's not possible.'

'The timing of it's at our discretion, obviously, but once it begins they want Freddie caught, coerced and back at his desk in Keibelstrasse before anyone notices.'

'Why not get to him at his home?'

'Because that would bring Kristin and the twins into the business, and families aren't reliable. They might panic, push Freddie to run or worse.'

'Kristin wouldn't do that.'

'No, but we aren't supposed to know that she wouldn't, are we? We have to do it their way. They're already nervous about this.'

'Why?'

'This is their first attempt at turning a *kozi* who's someone. It's probably why they let me talk my way into it - if it goes arse-up they won't have lost too much. Anyway, I've no intention of visiting Freddie *en famille*. The Hollemans – sorry, the Beckendorps - live in deepest Marzahn these days, and that's much too far into the Soviet Zone for us to do it safely.'

'It's the countryside, nearly. I hope Freddie's lungs can take it.'

Branssler almost smiled. 'We've arranged a safe house in what's left of Ziegelstrasse, so Freddie's return journey won't eat too much into the schedule we've been given. If things go wrong we can run and be back in the British sector in less than ten minutes. It won't stop any pursuit but at least they'll have to make an effort not to shoot us. I think.'

'Where will we stay?'

'In the shittiest, cheapest hotel in Moabit – *the Bad Gastein*, if you can believe their nerve. We'll have a mattress and a roof, and that's it. Gehlen doesn't do perks.'

Fischer considered how many things could go wrong, and forced himself to think of something else. 'We have to find a way of making twelve hours something more like twenty-four.'

'You mean to give ourselves time to come up with something?'

'I mean we need time to convince Freddie that he has a better choice than being a spy for the Americans or running.'

'And has he?'

'I don't know yet. But if we snatch him, give him the ultimatum and send him straight back to the *VolksPolizei* Praesidium I doubt that he'll make any sort of sensible decision. Would you?'

'I tried to argue the same at Oberursel, but Gehlen's too desperate to give the Amis a success story to play any subtle long game.'

Fischer studied the ground's shrapnel-chipped masonry. 'We need to think about this. It doesn't have to happen today, or tomorrow.'

'No. But if we spend a couple of weeks seeing the sights and spending American cash they'll ask questions.' As he spoke Branssler patted his coat pocket nervously.

'How much do we have?'

'I signed for eighty dollars, and for that I had to pledge a kidney. Gehlen's operation isn't what you'd call flush with greenery. It was made clear to me that the bulk of should be regarded as emergency money, to be squandered only in an extremity. Or two, preferably.'

Perversely, Fischer was reassured that their perceived worth was apparently so modest. It offered a small hope that no one would consider their failure – deliberate or otherwise – something for which a spectacular example needed to be made. Probably, there were dozens of schemes being put into motion all over Germany, pawns being moved around a board whose boundaries were as yet only half-drawn, the rules not yet fully set down. Like scouting parties in a strange landscape, men were being sent out more in hope than expectation of their goal. If that were the case, perhaps the sanctions were similarly fluid, the price not …

'That's it.'

'What is?'

'*Two* extremities, you said.'

'It was meant as a joke, even if I'm not laughing.'

'We'll do what we're told to do, and take Freddie.'

'That's it?'

'No. We take him twice.'

Branssler thought about it, and this time the smile managed to fight its way to the surface. 'But only the second time is official.'

'This way we can give him some warning, at least. It's probably the only advantage we'll have.'

'There's something else. You remember what it was like, back in the good old days?'

'Which part?'

'The world of so-called Intelligence.'

'It was a bloody mess, everyone stabbing everyone else, clambering over the corpses to kiss the Führer's hand and pass on information that was shit, usually.'

'Well, you're about to get nostalgic about Berlin. Think of the same, only with howitzers instead of knives. The Russians, Americans, British and French are playing the Great Game, and each of them have several intelligence departments in the city, all fighting each other like rats in a bag, trying to be the ones that bring home the prizes. This really *is* a mess, playing in four languages, and we have a small edge.'

'Which is?'

'We're jumping into waters that other boots have muddied beautifully. And it's *our* mud.'

18

Five men stood in the interview room. Though no one had insisted upon it they were in a rough line, facing the only exit. Two were peering at the floor, attempting to glean something of the next few minutes' events from the random pattern formed long ago by setting concrete. The other three couldn't take their eyes from the closed door. One of them wore the uniform of Berlin's *VolksPolizei*; the others were in civilian clothes, dignified only by green *VoPo* bands on their right arms.

There was no shouting or other merciful warning, so when the door burst open five pairs of feet almost lost contact with the floor. The sight that replaced the badly-peeled grey paint and solitary coat hook did nothing to tempt them back down.

'You useless bastards!'

The big man limped in and immediately tacked to pass across the line in front of him. It was a risky naval manoeuvre but no one tried to take advantage of it.

'I could squeeze out turds, put them in uniform and hope for better than this! What, you needed tanks? *Panzerfausts*? It's fucking pitiful!'

The *hauptwachtmeister* who had followed the big man into the room cleared his throat.

'What?'

'It wasn't their best moment, Comrade Commander. But …'

'Jesus! You think not? What will be, having a collection and sending the cash after the guns they surrendered?'

The *hauptwachtmeister* winced. 'Obviously, it was planned carefully. The gang knew exactly where to …' his voice died off, and he gazed at the five men as a disappointed father would at an idiot son.

'And what threat did these desperate criminals bring to bear? Cruel insults? Observations of a wounding nature? You were armed, for God's sake!'

All five men were by now intensely interested in the floor beneath them. One of them mumbled something before his animal sense of self-preservation could assert itself.

'Eh?'

The man looked up, swallowed hard. 'We didn't have bullets, Herr Commander.'

The big man raised his hands, clasped his head at the temples and spoke carefully. 'You were in Neukölln, at midnight, with empty magazines?'

The *hauptwachtmeister* coughed once more. 'Orders, sir. After recent … incidents, the General Inspector told us that each armed patrol was to have only one loaded weapon. The last time, in Lichtenberg, we lost four carbines and a pistol, all of them loaded.'

'But these sorry sods had *no* bullets!'

The other man blushed. 'The rota was re-drafted and there was a misunderstanding. Georg here … 'he gestured at one of the men, 'thought that Gregor had the loaded pistol, and Gregor thought that Georg …'

The Commander groaned. 'So a defenceless patrol was set upon, kidnapped, held for two days and then dumped at the gasworks, and Berlin *VolksPolizei*'s reputation as law enforcement's purest *muschis* climbs another notch. Who was it, by the way?'

'Gregor says the Lichtenberg gang, definitely.'

'Well, at least if they'd broken skin your men wouldn't have been infected. They're east Berlin's penicillin kaisers, aren't they?'

'And pecithin, obviously.'

'Well, fuck.' The big man sighed and stared at the five reprobates. He had read their personnel files during the fraught days when he'd expected to be breaking the bad news to their families. Not one of them had been professional police prior to their present employment; the streets of a city plagued by increasingly bold gangs of violent black marketeers, rapists, murderers and heroically ambitious thieves was protected by a shabby, greying cohort of former railwaymen, miners, civil servants and … he looked with disgust at the lean, forlorn fellow with obvious kyphosis who formed the left extremity of the line … at least one lecturer in Classics, currently missing a sinecure.

'Feed them and send them home. Have them report back the day after tomorrow.'

'Right. Is this to be taken as official leave, or …'

'What do you think? We sent them out unarmed into a war zone and then wait, fingers up our arses, hoping that someone has the heart to send them back unopened? If this wasn't Mad Land they could sue us for gross neglect. So no, we don't steal their leave.'

The *hauptwachtmeister* seemed pleased. He nodded at the men, and they shuffled out of the interview room. 'Thank you for coming, Comrade Commander. They appreciate it.'

His boss shook his head. 'This is shit. It took us months to get the Ivans to allow our men to carry ordnance, and now we're voluntarily disarming ourselves. It's as if we're hoping to conquer with pathos.'

He stayed in the building for a further half-hour, showing his face, shaking hands, spouting the prescribed fantasy statistics, pretending not only that there was a strategy but that it was proceeding robustly. He recognized no faces from *back then* during his perambulation, but he'd expected – hoped for – that. Lamenting the lack of real policemen in the police (as he did often) was purest hypocrisy, given that their absence was utterly necessary to his survival. It would take only a single sharp memory, one that could put him back in an *OrPo* uniform and forget the limp, and he'd be on his way east faster than a homesick stork.

Still, the police in him couldn't be happy about things as they were. Each month he and his fellow commanders were dragged before the *Magistrat* to explain why it was that a city occupied by four victorious Powers and a twenty-five-thousand strong *VolksPolizei* force was increasingly resembling Deadwood on Free Drinks Day. The obvious, shouldn't-need-to-be-explained-to-an-imbecile reasons – the breakdown of social structures, atomization of families, the loss of the entire public health infrastructure, black market opportunities in a city where two thousand calories a day was more of a dream than policy, the burden of building a criminal investigations department from scratch, a manpower crisis unprecedented in German history – were at once irrefutable and summarily ignored. *Try harder, do more* they were told. *But don't ask for more resources.*

For the first time in his life he was afraid of failing. They had made him one of the guardians of a wretched, flattened city of phantoms, of indifferent conquerors, of grudges repaid nightly, of shadows passing from unspeakable past crimes to future exile, of a deep, insatiable hunger for something *else* and he was no more than a cypher, a false identity pretending to be a good communist and anything but an ex-policeman. It was no wonder that he was getting nervous headaches. A dozen times he had almost told his wife how it was, how any half-competent new head of the *VolksPolizei* would dismiss every other man on the payroll and start again, and he couldn't say that he didn't deserve to be one of them. He knew exactly what to do, how to turn around a pitiful standard of policing, make at least some of the streets safe for the herd. And he knew that he'd never step into the firing line by suggesting any of it. Every German in a position of power in Berlin was looking over his own shoulder, gauging the reaction to a cough, a sideways glance, a lateral thought, the slightest initiative. It would require a man without fear of making mistakes to do something memorable, and he suspected that such a man no longer existed - at least, not one who had been born between the Rhine and Oder. Defeat had made Germans fear the wrong step because they knew the worst of what might follow it.

He wished heartily that the Allied Powers were running Berlin still as a conquered city, not as the playground in which they fought for each other's marbles. By withdrawing most of their troops to barracks they had handed Berliners the worst of worlds – one in which decisions couldn't be made and order couldn't be achieved. With Eisenhower's blessing the

Soviets had control of the Allied Marks plates, and they were printing money like crazed Guttenbergs. Their men could spend this only in Germany, so they congregated in Tiergarten and Alexanderplatz (where the black market was hardly less conspicuous than a traditional frost-fair) and promptly bought every watch and pack of Lucky Strikes they could prise from the wrists and pockets of GIs. Their wallets bulging with this new wealth, the American soldiers took themselves promptly to any street corner in Berlin, where one or more of the city's half-a-million prostitutes (the majority of them women of formerly impeccable moral character) offered their private places for next to nothing, wiped themselves half-clean afterwards, bought bread (and milk, on those oddest of days when it was available) and went home to put some nourishment into their children, a great many of whom were the unasked-for blessing of Russian semen, forcibly offered the previous year. This was as close to a functioning economy as the city possessed, and the *Magistrat* wanted to know what could be done about it, soon.

The thing was, he didn't want to *do* anything about activities that put calories into German stomachs. It was the other stuff, the offences he couldn't touch, that tormented him. Half the real crimes committed in Berlin (and three-quarters of the thefts) were those of the Occupiers, the untouchables. The Russians pillaged and called it reparations, the British 'requisitioned' and called it regrettable but necessary, the Americans commandeered and shrugged about it, and the French …

He smiled. He was coming to like the French, almost. They stole blatantly because they wanted you to know how it felt to have some jack-booted bastard stroll into your parlour, lift your grandmother's clock, tip his hat politely and stroll out again. It was exactly what Germans had done to them (other than the polite hat-tipping, obviously), so they made a point of never disguising, excusing, justifying or otherwise avoiding the question of guilt. In fact, they preferred not to take stuff from empty houses, because no point was being made if they did.

The *VolksPolizei* could prosecute none of these crimes. At best they could make a tentative identification and inform the *Kommandatura*, trusting that the Russians would push the Americans to punish one of their own and vice versa. Sometimes a soldier would dispense retail justice at the *locus quo*, as in the previous year when a British sergeant had beaten an Azeri rapist half to death and then dumped him in the Soviet Zone (the Ivans had thought it fair punishment and made no fuss); but most of the time the perpetrators got away with it, or were transferred to other units, or found themselves sent home under a half-cloud with a severely slapped wrist - except for the French, of course. None of them were punished, ever. They even regarded rape as their gift to grateful German womanhood.

Crimes committed by Germans could of course be chased and punished, but usually they weren't, due to one or more of the many waved-away reasons regurgitated at the *Magistrat* each month. Things weren't going to change until they had a plan and the budget to pursue it; in the meantime, he visited the stations most under siege, offering his hand or boot (the latter, usually), talking up a dire situation and generally doing nothing that real police would call useful. The only comfort he could take from any of this was that he was being paid almost regularly, his family were fed and housed and when the Soviets finally outmanoeuvred their so-called allies in the next local elections he would be sitting in one of the Senate's rear seats, spouting crap about proletarian internationalism or whatever it was that gripped *kozis'* foreskins the most and anticipating a retirement that for much of the past decade he hadn't seen any way of reaching. In a vast, communal latrine he had at least access to a half-decent coat sleeve.

A passing truck's horn roused him. He was standing on Dresdenerstrasse, outside the station house to which he had done much the same. His driver was out of the car, waiting with one hand on the rear door handle. He shook his head.

'Take it back to Keibelstrasse, Reinhardt. I'll walk.'

The driver's eyes widened almost imperceptibly but he knew better than to say anything. No doubt the one good leg and its tin partner would make the best of the first kilometre, but he knew that as soon as he got the car into the station garage there would be a message turning him right around, and when he picked up his boss a chaffed stump was going to make the rest of the day similarly painful for anyone in its path.

Still, it was an hour in which he wouldn't be getting talked at about this, that and stuff he'd never heard of until it was abused heartily in his ear. He drove slowly back to Pretzlauer-Berg, stopping on the way to buy horse-meat for his mother's supper, and parked the battered Opel in the first of only three bays, ready to take it out again. He was mildly surprised not to find an irascibly-worded summons waiting for him already, but he waited a further two hours before putting his name back on the available-for-duty roster. In the afternoon the General Inspector himself visited Keibelstrasse without prior warning, and everyone forgot everything that wasn't to do with spit, polish and implausibly massaged statistics.

19

Rolf held the man by the back of his jacket, pressing him to the wall until his legs gave way. The body took most of the splashback of blood; only a few spots stained his cuff, and in almost exactly the same way as he recalled it had in Belgium and Greece. A testament to his training, he supposed.

He gagged dryly, almost staggering into the wall and its mess. Being adept hadn't ever made killing easy for him. Others had managed with greater apparent ease, though he had never advertised his aversion - it wouldn't have gone down well, not in the Regiment. He'd done his job well enough not to be noticed, and there had been a Mess board somewhere with his name on it, commemorating their greatest, bloodiest debacle - Maleme. No one could say he hadn't served the myth.

It had happened too suddenly for him to have thought it through, and now that it was over he couldn't gather his thoughts. How the hell had it come to this? The man's name was on his list, third down, and he'd followed his instructions precisely, accosting him in an alley, a pass-through between streets where they couldn't be overheard, politely confirming his identity and offering the money – *from friends who appreciate your work.* The target – one Peter Beckmann – had been surprised (who wouldn't be, to have US dollars shoved at you for no apparent reason?); but his reaction had been more curious than discouraging. He hadn't dismissed the transaction with a *fuck off*, like the second man on the list.

Rolf had explained that nothing was required, no service necessary in return for the money. At that Herr Beckmann had laughed, shook his head and begged to suggest that there was always *something* required when hard currency was in point. He hadn't known what to say to this. Was he supposed to persist, to continue to press the envelope upon the man, or should he shrug and walk away? He recalled that he mumbled something about no one witnessing the offer so there couldn't be any harm in it, but even to his own ears it sounded strange, almost a plea. Beckmann wasn't convinced but he didn't walk away, didn't continue his morning commute to work at Tempelhof. They stood in the alley, two men paused around an unusual encounter, one not knowing how to end it, the other thinking it through, taking his time. And then the fellow had done the crazy thing, turned and shouted for help – help that he hadn't remotely needed.

Rolf looked down at the body, realising now that it had been blind, naïve panic on both their parts, nothing more. Beckmann had called out, but so what? There'd been no danger in that, no risk of exposure, yet he'd lost his nerve and slashed the man's throat. He should have retreated gracefully, begged pardon, made himself only briefly memorable.

*What do I do?* The briefings he'd had in Moscow, and Wolfgang's more cursory instructions, hadn't addressed the possibility that he'd be crassly, fatally stupid. Perhaps they'd assumed that someone trained to fight in desperate situations could be trusted not to lose his head over the matter of a cash transaction. But poise was easily achieved in battle - it was the calm of a near-certain moment, the stool rocking beneath one's feet, the noose tightening. He hadn't lived in peace long enough to know how to deal with it.

If he went to the café and told Wolfgang, what would *they* do? Did a most expendable man deserve another chance when the first had been squandered so madly? He saw a quiet stretch of the Teltow canal, its only-recently cleared navigation spoiled once more by a half-floating corpse, his own. He didn't for a second believe that the decision would be an onerous one, reluctantly made - these were serious people, set about a big business. He was not only a fool but had made himself weak, open to exactly the same manipulations as those he'd attempted to bribe. Really, what other sensible decision was there?

Was there an excuse, a sleight of circumstance that would keep him alive? No one would believe he'd acted in self-defence, not against a man ten years older and a hundred flabby pounds heavier. He considered getting rid of the money and then feigning surprise when they told him about the deadly assault and robbery upon one of his contacts. Everyone knew the crime statistics - it wasn't as if any German was truly safe in this city, not unless he was protected by the Occupiers. It would be plausible.

But this was Friday, and Wolfgang wouldn't be at the café until Tuesday, so he might be dead before he could even attempt to explain himself. It went against his most basic sense of self-preservation but he realised that pretend innocence wouldn't do – he had to be a victim also and have a reason, a good reason, for fleeing to the Mitte safe-house. There, they would have to speak to him, to listen to what he had to say before making a decision. In any case, he couldn't be certain of getting out of the alley without being seen. It had to be done the right way, so that anyone recalling him wouldn't contradict his version. Before he could think too much about it he picked up his knife, braced himself and grasped the blade firmly in both hands. For a moment the pain was agonizing but he kept his mouth closed and fell to his knees, letting the momentum prise his fingers free. He concentrated on breathing, shallowly and often, until he could trust himself to look at what he'd done. It was a mess, though it looked more spectacularly bad than it was. He grasped his jacket to stem the flow but made sure he bloodied the alley wall a good half-dozen times before he reached Württemberger Ring. A smartly dressed woman was walking toward him, her head down; he stumbled, fell, held out his torn hands.

'Help me, please! He attacked us!'

She stopped, mouth wide with shock, and then turned and ran across the road – a sensible Berliner's reaction. But others had seen him. Two men, manual workers, dropped a section of wood they were carrying and ran towards him.

'My friend, down there. Please help him.'

One of the samaritans paused to give him a brief inspection, thought better of it and then followed his friend down the alley. When their attention was fully on the corpse and the envelope that lay prominently beside it he stood quickly and walked northwards, his burning hands in his pockets, his eyes on his feet. No one followed or shouted after him. Other than the fact that the incident had occurred in broad daylight there had been nothing about it to stir anyone's curiosity for more than a few minutes. Their society expected disorder and casual brutality, adjusted its expectations and went about its business.

He couldn't risk taking public transport and being closely observed, so he walked into central Berlin. He was in Mitte within an hour and could have gone straight to the refuge in Linienstrasse, but he decided to be prudent, taking a roundabout route that allowed him to recce the neighbourhood. As he'd expected, *VolksPolizei* patrols were conspicuously absent, but he saw and avoided several groups of Soviet infantrymen whose loitering seemed too strategically well-placed to be unintentional. At one point he entered a shop and joined a queue, turning his head to the darkness when three Russian officers strolled past. There was no glass in the front window and he feared that every hair on the back of his neck was stood to parade attention, betraying him. He found that he couldn't move, until a woman waving a kohlrabi under his nose startled him back into sensibility. As hungry as he was he declined the offer, keeping both pieces of evidence firmly in his pockets.

He was running, hiding, from men who were supposed to be his allies, and it unnerved him. From the shop he turned north again up Monbijoustrasse, determined now to get into the safe-house as quickly as possible. It occurred, much later, to wonder why he hadn't kept his head firmly pointed at the pavement, to hide his face and save himself a deal of trouble.

He was crossing Ziegelstrasse when he saw them, arguing in front of a burned out corn merchant's premises. It wasn't the argument itself that caught his attention (he was too distant to make out the detail, and squabbling was Berliners' preferred mode of conversation, after all), but the protagonists – or at least one of them, the one doing the least shouting – brought him to a dead halt in the middle of the road. Probably, he wouldn't have recalled the face when it *was* a face, because he'd seen it that way the one time only. But they had met again, later, when God or something very, very hot had rearranged it. Back then, he had recognized the man despite the alterations because he'd been stood right in front of him, examining his papers, trying to keep his own face from showing the shock at how much had changed since their last meeting (if *meeting* was what one did in the middle of a disaster). Perhaps it had been the dislocation of those wounds, framed by the plush calm of the Air Ministry, but all he'd managed to offer was a brief nod of recognition, poor fare for someone he had nearly died with. He couldn't even recall the name, only that he'd been someone that General Bodenschatz himself had expressed an interest in, and summoned.

And here he was once more, alive still, arguing with a big civilian and someone in the uniform of a senior *VolksPolizei* officer, and whatever itch they had it wasn't any business of a man who wanted desperately not to be seen. He stepped on to the pavement and was almost around the corner when the civilian grabbed the policeman's arm and pulled him into the alley that ran down the side of the ruined building. The other one, his old wounded comrade, stood for a moment, glancing around as an abettor would to account for unwanted witnesses, which is how their eyes met.

He forced his legs to move, to take him quickly away from Ziegelstrasse. He told himself that it had been a moment only, that there was little chance his own, unmemorable face could have been dragged from the memory of a man with so much more *past* to occupy him. But even before he reached the refuge in Linienstrasse he knew that he couldn't leave it at that. If he survived his looming interview (a prominent *if*) there was now another s-mine ahead, waiting to jump up and cut him off at the knees if he didn't do something about it.

20

'You mad bastards!'

Former *Rottmeister der Ordnungspolizei*, fighter-pilot and serial deserter Freddie Holleman had temporarily suspended his impersonation of police-killer, hard-line communist, ghost of Hamburg and *VolksPolizei* Commander Kurt Beckendorp and was attempting an aneurism in an armchair.

Twice he had tried to rise from it, but Gerd Branssler's hand shoved him back, using gravity and the victim's one good leg against him.

'Freddie ...'

'Fuck off with *Freddie*! My best, closest comrades turn up without as much as a carrier pigeon's warning, drag me off the streets – *my* streets – and tell me they're going to bend me full over. Shit!'

Fischer glanced at Branssler. The expression on his face was somewhere between pleading and murderous, though he couldn't have expected anything but this.

Squirming beneath the hand, Holleman turned to stare at Fischer.

'What do you think I'm going to do? Stuff myself into every sensitive meeting I hear about, then pop around to give General Gehlen the news, pick up my ten dollars and limp back to Keibelstrasse? And don't look at me like that, of course we know about Gehlen. Do you think the Amis keep anything secret in this city?'

'How did you ...?'

'The usual way. One lot doesn't like what the other lot's doing so they let slip enough to … what's the word?'

'Compromise?'

'Yeah, *compromise* their work. In Berlin it's the military that pulls the strings, and they haven't taken kindly to SSU opening shop here.'

Silently, Fischer appealed to Branssler, who shrugged.

Holleman snorted. 'It takes top fucking spies not to know what their own people are up to.'

'I'm surprised you do, Freddie. I thought you were just police with political connections.'

'All the sewers meet in this city, it's necessary to know. Anyway, the Americans are at each other's throats. Someone in SSU got tired of taking it up the arse from General Clay, so somehow *we* got the nod about what USFET are letting Gehlen set up at Oberursel …' Holleman paused and looked up at Branssler. 'Seeing as how they pay your badly-earned wages, I assume you know who USFET are, and that you can explain it to the virgin here?'

'Fuck yourself. And who do you mean, we?'

'We the *kozis*. K-5, to be precise.'

This time it was Branssler who offered the dumb look.

'You can have that for free, to take back to Gehlen. You know we have politicos in every station, the Ivans' pet Germans? Well, they have a name now, the Fifth Kommissariat, and an organization, and they're doing for the Soviets what Gehlen's doing for the Amis. Officially, they're still

police, but crime doesn't interest them. They spy on their own and yours –
anyone, as long as they're Germans. They know that Oberursel intends to
vet all POWs returning from the East, so K-5 are going to be doing their
best to get men into the process to bugger it. They report directly to
Karlshorst, so it's all wonderfully circular. The Soviets turn Germans in
the East and send them home, you interrogate them, we get word on who
breaks and then pass the word straight back to the Soviets, who promptly
turn more. Somewhere, someone has a job for life.'

'Let this come from you directly, Freddie. The more you can tell
them that won't hurt you, the better.'

Holleman rubbed his face. 'It isn't what I tell that's going to hurt
me. It's talking at all. If MGB get a whiff of it – and they will, the bastards
- I'll be PSh'd.'

Fischer looked helplessly at Branssler once more. 'You'll be …?'

'It's an offence they use to bury you when they can't be bothered to
look for an offence. It covers espionage, anti-social activity, bad breath,
anything.'

'Then we have to think of something. At the moment Oberursel
know they want to use you, but it isn't clear yet if they're willing to be
subtle enough about it to be able to use you long-term.'

'If they're like ours they'll work me as long as it's worth it and then
drop me like a warm turd. How the hell did they find out about
Beckendorp, by the way?'

Branssler gave him the story. 'It was an accident, just bad luck. But
you've been due some.'

'Yet somehow I don't feel deserving.'

'You're a *VoPo* Commander?'

'Since last month, yes.'

'That won't help. Oberursel briefed us that you were just an *Oberrat*, though they knew that you stood in the City elections last year for the SED. The new rank may give them second thoughts on how valuable you could be.'

Holleman groaned. 'I don't want another fucking career! I've got a nice requisitioned apartment near the countryside, Kristin and the kids get to eat most days, any year now I'll be able to afford a weekend break on the Baltic *and* the Ivans let me carry a gun. Who'd want to risk that?'

'What choice is there? It's why we made sure we were the ones to give you the good news. '

'Yeah, I'd guessed that. Thanks, I think.'

Fischer pulled a flask from his coat and offered it to Holleman.

'Freddie …. is there anyone you could approach on your side, trust them to take the news of this the right way?'

'How? Even if they were happy to work me as a triple-Judas they'd have to be told *why* it had happened. So I'd be admitting that I wasn't Kurt Beckendorp, wouldn't I?'

'Hell, of course you would. Sorry, Freddie.'

Branssler pulled a face. 'I've had more time than you to think of bad ideas, Otto. I considered that one and flushed it.'

'Well, then. He can't run or hide, because both sides would be looking for him. He can't confess to being Freddie Holleman to his own people. If he gives Oberursel nothing worthwhile they'll almost certainly be spiteful and let Karlshorst know the worst, probably by way of an ad in the papers. If he gives them too much it would be the same as shoving a detonator up his family's collective arse. If ...'

'Christ's Wounds, stop!'

' ... we can think of some way for Freddie to tread a very narrow, middle path, something that keeps one side satisfied and the other suspecting nothing, it should give us what we don't have at present.'

'What's that?'

'Time. To find something better.'

'Let me up, Gerd.'

Branssler released his grip. Holleman struggled out of the deep armchair (it had been made deeper by the large rip in its seat) and took a moment to regain his balance. He didn't look happy.

'That's as much of a plan as engaging the fellow who puts the guillotine pin in polite conversation.'

'I know. It's all we have. The K-5 information's something they would have had in a month anyway, but it's good that you can give it to them. A further few dozen revelations of that quality and we can relax.'

'You've become an optimist, Otto. Or a complete arse.'

'A German who's one must be the other, these days. We have to send a report to Oberursel, to tell them you've agreed – there's no alternative. But Gerd and I wanted to give you more than a moment's warning of it. We all have to think, hard.'

Holleman opened his hands. 'I'm empty. You've just told me my resurrected life's been given notice to quit. What could we possibly *think* that would change that?'

'I don't know, yet. But this is a business of deception, isn't it? If lies and misdirection are its guts, we have to become surgeons, quickly.'

21

*[Most Secret]*

'Should we write that?'

'What do you mean?'

'I've always wondered why the fact is stated. I mean, doesn't it just flag the point to the wrong people, the ones who aren't supposed to read it?'

Fischer paused. Branssler had a point. If they were part of a large organization with secure walls and a rule book it would only be prudent to warn that circulation of a thing was restricted. But they weren't, and this piece of paper was going to leave the building in every sense before it found itself in the hands it was intended for. He tore it up and started again.

*To Herr Schmidt*

'He couldn't have thought of a more convincing alias?'

Branssler shrugged. 'There are any number of Schmidts. If you don't want to be seen you hop into the forest.'

*Subject: Vacancy for Floor Walker*

'Is there a usual form of words for this sort of report?'

'No one's been doing this long enough for anything to be *usual*. Just make it bland and to the point.'

*An interview was held on the 21st inst., by invitation. The candidate expressed disinterest initially as he feels that his current employment is satisfactory in most respects. However, when the terms and conditions on offer were fully explained he indicated his willingness to give the position his careful consideration. It was stressed that we wished to fill the vacancy as a matter of urgency.*

*We explained that his prior work experience was extremely relevant to the new position, and that he would be expected to fully draw upon it. He indicated that he fully understood this.*

'He told us to fuck a meat-grinder, didn't he?'

*A timetable was agreed upon. The candidate will consider the offer and give a decision within seventy-two hours. If his response is satisfactory he will meet with his supervisors who will fully explain what is expected. He indicated his satisfaction in principle with the terms offered.*

*Respectfully,*

'A work of art, Otto.'

'Of fantastical fiction.'

'Seventy-two hours. Shit! What can we do in three days? It's no time.'

'It's time to think. At least Freddie took it fairly well.'

'He went berserk.'

'Half-berserk at most. We've seen him worse. *You* would have been worse.'

'Probably, yeah. So, we gift him to Gehlen, and he becomes his *rat*.'

'Another Americanism?'

'It is, and for once an apt one. Rats have short, miserable lives, mostly up to their necks in it. It's only a matter of time before someone with a brain works out that little secrets are finding their way west. They'll search, interrogate, plant traps, wait and then arrange a quiet retirement party, but with no gold watch. We don't want Freddie retired.'

'No.'

'Once it starts I can't think of any way that you or I can control what happens, or when. They'll take us off it and put Freddie in someone else's hands, someone who knows how likely it is that SVAG will discover the business sooner rather than later. It'll incline Gehlen to take risks with him, to get as much as quickly as possible.'

For the first time in his life, Fischer wished he had been given the blessing of ignorance, of having unconsciously avoided Branssler and his organization, of not knowing of Freddie's quandary, of having only the small, convenient pain of providing for himself and Maria-Therese, of worrying only what their private tomorrows would bring. At that moment he might have been sat in his Bremen apartment, brooding at the prospect of his wife cheerfully half-buried beneath shitten diapers, conducting a discreet audit upon his talents and coming up very short of the mark. But he had wished for more than that, and paid the price in new guilt for a thing that was not in his power to stop or alter. What sharpened the guilt considerably was the certain knowledge that he had given birth to it. Three years earlier, when Freddie Holleman had needed a new identity urgently, his good friend Otto Fischer had extracted one from a vast pile of surrendered lives. Unerringly, he had chosen one that came with strings – or rather, fuse wire – attached. All that remained to do, what he and Gerd Branssler had volunteered for, was to prime the detonation box.

'We need ...'

'What?'

Fischer looked down at the brief report. It was as bland as Branssler could have wished for – a German masterpiece of words wrapped in soft cotton, anodising a looming human tragedy. No doubt their K-5 counterparts were equally versed in the proper forms, equally careful to say nothing that might offend when setting loose their dogs. He almost smiled. Their reports would make the Ivans scratch their heads, wonder exactly what it was they were reading ...

A bell sounded dimly, rousing him. They couldn't protect Freddie; they couldn't persuade Oberursel that he was worthless; they couldn't stop other men using him until the plum had been squeezed dry. What remained was to do what armour specialists did to render an impact less than fatal. But that would require the certain, prior removal of the *other*, and there was only one way to ensure that.

'We need to make Freddie valuable.'

'He is, too much so. If he wasn't, who would care?'

'No, I mean to his own, to the people who are going to disappear him when they find out he's a traitor. We have to make them love him.'

'How? Paint him red? Help him kidnap Lucius Clay?'

'He's going to do what *we're* doing. He's going to turn someone in the west. Actually, he's going to turn *me*. We'll make this so confoundedly, unknowably incestuous that no-one's going to take the wrong decision for fear it will return to shit in their lap.'

'But we don't know anything.'

'We know everything, Gerd. We just haven't made it up yet.'

22

His given name was Engelbrecht (he preferred *Engi*), and he was a rat, a shadow, a thief, and that was almost all that he knew about himself. Once, he'd had a father – his mother had spoken wistfully of a wise, decent man who had died in the war, somewhere cold and very far away – but he recalled nothing other than a vague presence, lost like every other fragment of his early childhood. His last recollection of *her* was too painful to permit, so he was always careful to think of something else, quickly, when he was reminded of her hair, her warmth, the smell of her neck.

He was about ten years old, and lived where he chose to live - but that wasn't quite true. If his life had offered choices he would have lived in a house, one that had windows still and a stove to warm it, and someone there who could protect and cook for him when he was hungry. He was always hungry.

He knew very little of the city, but a great deal of the small part between Unter den Linden and the Charité, where his hiding places were. He didn't know how or even why he'd come to be in Berlin; his earliest, best memories were of a large garden, and fields, and smells entirely unlike those now familiar to him. He recalled the journey from *there* to *here* imperfectly- its confused, interrupted stages, the press of people all moving the same way, the roadside overhung with trees, where …

There had been another, older boy, Paul, who'd found him sobbing beside her body, given him half the piece of stale bread he'd stole from someone's bag and took him on as a sort of apprentice, teaching him how to wrap himself into himself against the cold, to find the small, filthy places that you shared with rodents but not the wind, to know which broken conduits leaked water that wasn't too tainted to drink (not if you didn't mind getting the squirts occasionally). He had also learned the necessary art (or craft) of making his face shine with innocence as he stole, of putting his hand in a pocket without bothering its owner unduly and of disappearing swiftly once the transaction was completed. He was aware that Paul had probably saved his life, and regretted that he hadn't been able to return the favour when the weather had turned deadly, made them take risks, tempted them to steal food from the wrong people. They had fled but in different directions, and though he'd tried to find Paul afterwards the river had been too close when it happened for him to hope still.

Since then he had been alone. There was a mission on Parochialstrasse, open three days each week, where he could find just enough nourishment to keep him alive. Occasionally, he loitered near a Soviet patrol, risking a kick for the more uncertain chance of a whim, the momentary kindness of bread or half an unwanted sausage. Once, he had been tossed a boiled egg by a man whose eyes had come from some faraway world, who'd shouted something that might have meant well but had terrified him as a bear's growl would. Engi had run from him too, though not so quickly as to put the egg at risk.

His luckiest encounter by far had been an old man, the caretaker at the only-half-ruined Hartzmachinen offices on Schumannstrasse, whose pocket he'd tried to pick and had received a hearty smack in return. Before his ear had stopped throbbing he'd been dragged into a hut, given a marvellously hot mug of something sweet and horrible and allowed to sit by the stove as he drank it. Not wanting to test his luck he'd returned thereafter only on the coldest mornings in the hope of chasing the worst of the numbness from his bones. If the old man was in a companionable mood he might extend the welcome by talking about the war before last, his heroic exploits against the British and the fond memories he'd given a host of pretty French women (the last stressed with a wink to another man of the world who didn't need the detail spelling out). On days when sciatica tormented his joints he remained civil enough to offer the hot drink, and if his conversation extended no further than a nod the silence never pressed rudely. If any shard of Engi's territory came close to his hoped-for ideal it was this, a small, overheated room that smelled of kerosene, damp wood, rough tobacco and old man.

But as spring came the caretaker died too, or went away. The half-ruined offices he had guarded were demolished, and his wonderful hut disappeared the day the gangs started their work. Engi stood at the fence that morning, watching them busily removing his idyll, letting the tears well up until they almost choked him. When some humorous fellow noticed him and threw a small rock in his direction he ran away, and never returned.

For a few days after that (it may have been weeks - like many children without a routine he hadn't learned to distinguish time), he drifted aimlessly between his several hideouts and places where he might find enough food to survive, not wanting more than to ease the cold and the pain in his belly. Mostly he avoided other people (especially the gangs of feral children that infested the city centre's countless ruins), fearing the prospect of company as much as he needed it. Only at the Parochialstrasse mission did he feel safe enough to watch others around him, hoping for some sign of that quality the old man had carefully concealed beneath a dirty face and vast whiskers. But he couldn't recognise what he didn't know to look for.

One day he ran from boys hardly older than himself, whose faces, harder by far than their years, spoke to him more loudly than any threat. He was so frightened that he hid for hours afterwards in a dry sewer, breathing as shallowly as his pounding heart permitted. When he crawled back to the surface it was dark, and in the unlit street he couldn't get his bearings. The buildings around him were shells, ghosts of the past city, and though he knew he shouldn't be scared (all buildings loomed, they couldn't help it) he began to run, stupidly, with no direction or purpose in mind. He was aware that a person running in this city was regarded as fleeing and treated accordingly; that if he was seen by the bad boys they would chase and hurt him, or the *VoPos* would arrest him, and he was almost certain that the Russians would shoot at him for sport. But the panic that had gripped him couldn't be calmed by this large helping of more anxiety, and if he hadn't run straight into the wall he might have kept going until his heart burst.

Fortunately, he'd slowed slightly to avoid rubble only a moment before, and his nose was only moderately punished by the brick. He sat down, hard, and for a moment the pain in his arse took away even his fear of being lost. It slowed his head, helped him to think, of finding a sanctuary. Paul's first advice to him (offered very solemnly) had been Always Hide – hide from people, hide from the cold, hide for the sake of it whenever there was nothing more useful to be done. They had explored enough entirely ruined buildings together to know that they were a poor prospect, that their uppers storeys tended to have beaten a path to the cellars and filled them. Partially destroyed properties were more promising, forlornly occupying a limbo between fled tenants and the repairs necessary to make them worth occupying. He didn't need much - a boy-sized space known only to himself that didn't let in rain or wind, with just one way in or out - to call a shelter.

The wall, his assailant, turned at right-angles, making what had seemed to be an alley a cul-de-sac. He turned and tried to make out shapes in the darkness. After a moment his lateral vision could distinguish the black of empty windows to both sides of the entry; they were low enough for him to have climbed into any of them, but he didn't know what he'd find inside, and his heart was still far too strained for him to be brave. He walked, slowly, back out into the street.

There were no working streetlamps along its length, and only a few buildings showed lights at their windows. He saw a solitary figure moving away from him about two hundred metres distant, but nothing else stirred. He felt the lump in his throat lessen, began to breathe more regularly. He still didn't recognize the street, but he was fairly sure that he hadn't run too far or kept to a straight line. Familiar territory was close still, the night wasn't too cold, and as soon as it was light he could find the mission and get something to eat. He'd been in much worse situations than this.

He began to move again, keeping his body close to the wall, crouching slightly to make himself insignificant. For once he was glad that his boots' soles were almost worn through, the nail heads long since shorn off or blunted into the leather. The only sound he made as he moved was the slight rub of his hand on brick, keeping him from grazing himself on its pitted, irregular surface. At a corner he paused and stared down the street to his left, trying to make out enough to spot a landmark. A small bonfire burned at its far end, and he could see at least two figures gathered around it. He'd often done the same himself, trusting to the company of others in similar straits to himself, but the day's events had made him timid. He hurried across the street he was presently on, darting to the safety of the intersection's far, darkest corner.

When his hand found the wall he moved on as before, but after a few metres he paused. The brickwork had become smooth and undamaged, yet the first window he encountered was emptied, and he realised that unless a freak explosion had managed to destroy everything but the outer wall there would probably be a roof still, or at least floors. He pushed his head cautiously into it, and sniffed. There was no hint of tobacco or unwashed bodies, of unspeakable decay or more than the usual staleness of a damp, emptied property. He put his hands on the window frame and began carefully to heave himself up.

Living on the streets had given him bats' ears, and the shuffle behind him, soft as it was, almost stopped his heart. Frantically, he threw himself forward through the window and landed badly on a pile of smashed wood. For a moment he couldn't move and he held his breath, waiting as in dreams for something that could neither be seen nor stopped; but a small, insistent urge told him not to close his eyes or wish the world away, to rouse his body and crawl deeper into the room, away from the window.

From the floor he kept his eyes on the rectangle of almost-blackness. Nothing had followed him through it. He told himself that could have been an entirely innocent encounter, perhaps a local resident curious about a stranger. It might be someone as lost as himself, looking for company (he knew how strongly the need not to be alone pressed sometimes), or a passer-by innocently going about his business, entirely unaware of the boy he had almost collided with. But there were too many other, worse possibilities. The gangs were more brazen at night, safe from patrols that tended to withdraw to their stations. So too were the usually decent civilians made desperate by want, warped by a jungle instinct to find food against the competition of too many others. Worst of all, night brought out the lone wolves, the degenerates set free by society's disintegration, wandering their chosen ranges looking for young meat to spoil. He feared all of them, but mostly those who needed what the city had become.

He kept telling himself that he couldn't just lie there in the dark, waiting. If someone wanted to harm him they were waiting for him to emerge, and testing their patience wouldn't make him safer. He began to move again, dragging himself across the floor, trying to find a wall where he could at least protect his back. His outstretched hand found a doorframe instead, and in the same moment he saw another dim rectangle directly ahead of him. He pulled himself into the second room and squatted against the wall. It wasn't much, but the cold brick removed him a degree or so from the sense of helplessness that had chased him all that day.

He held his breath, trying to hear the outside, to work out whether he had a problem still. Perhaps someone was doing the same out there, but all he heard was the slight breeze and a distant engine backfiring upon the unrefined piss that poisoned it. It was difficult to know how many folk lived in a neighbourhood these days; electricity was rationed like everything else so radios were used mainly by the military, and the abiding lack of oil and wood sent even the hardiest families to bed early. Everything here was still, quiet, and if it wasn't for the odours he might have imagined himself somewhere in the country, waiting for first light and birdsong.

He waited for a few minutes more, breathing as shallowly as possible, and had almost convinced himself that the threat was gone, or hadn't existed, when something in the room creaked, too high for a floorboard, and he felt the terrible press of proximity. Before the urge could trip-start his muscles a hand was on his shoulder, feeling its way to his neck. He kicked out, found a leg, and then something far larger and more powerful than an under-nourished boy pressed down on him, pinning him to the wall he'd thought might protect him.

The hand reached his neck but kept going, upward, passing over his face. A sigh, so close to his ear that he felt its warmth, accelerated his already frantic heart and he felt dizzy, almost insensible. The grip upon him slackened, but he had no strength, no will even, to run. He slid down the wall to the floor and waited.

He heard the creak again. It had more shape to it this time – a chair protesting the weight of something. Whatever was in it sighed again, something that sounded more like frustration than regret.

'You can't be the one.'

23

The man introduced himself as Gerhard Wessel. Branssler had warned Fischer that the morose face was an act, that it belonged to an acutely intelligent man, a sifter who could find a small lie in a mountainous heap of plausibility. It didn't make either of them feel any less nervous about what they were doing.

Wessel looked at each of his subordinates in turn, taking his time. 'I don't see why you want to do this.'

Branssler pursed his lips, and looked serious. It was something he'd practised in front of Fischer, a slight polishing of his habitual scowl.

'We want to show that we *can* do it, sir. It's no secret that General Gehlen prefers his old comrades to new faces. If we don't have a chance to prove ourselves we'll spend the rest of our careers shuffling other men's work across the desk. We know Berlin better than anyone who isn't ex-police. We can work this fellow without leaving a trail.'

'But you have no fieldwork training. Eventually, perhaps ...'

'With respect, we have the very best field-training. Both Fischer and I are used to running *spitzels*, men who mixed with – and betrayed - the worst, most dangerous criminal elements. I've never lost or had to remove a source, not in thirty years' police work.' He turned to Fischer. 'You, Otto?'

Fischer shook his head. This was the solid part, because it was true. In Stettin (not Berlin, of course, but he needn't bother Herr Wessel with that detail) he'd routinely run a dozen *lockspitzels* - 'stoolies', Earl Kuhn would have called them. A *kripo* department couldn't have functioned on legwork alone, not in areas where brotherhoods of the knife and cudgel had made their own rules. His unluckiest informer, suspected of telling tales, had been beaten so badly that he lost an eye, but he had managed to talk his way out of a midnight swim and even been found a permanent night-watchman's job thereafter – an apology, of sorts.

Wessel was giving attention to a file on the table in front of him. Fischer assumed it was what information Gehlen's organization had on one Otto Henry Fischer. For once he hoped that it was accurate, and reasonably comprehensive on the matter of plots, stratagems, subterfuges and their messy human consequences, and on his part – reluctant or otherwise – in them. He could imagine far less relevant *curriculum vitae* than his.

'Our man has political ambitions, doesn't he?'

Yes, sir. Beckendorp stood for the SED in Weissensee last April and lost, badly. But he remains a Party favourite, for his role – his assumed role – in the 1927 uprising. He's admitted to us that he's being encouraged to put it around that his recent failure's brought a change of political heart. With his rank it won't be difficult for him to become friendly with leading social democrats on the City Council and feed information back to the *kozis*.'

'Ironic, then, that we have him.'

'He's scared, certainly. If his people ever discover that Kurt Beckendorp died in Hamburg ...'

'Which they will of course, eventually.'

'They will?'

Wessel looked indifferently at Fischer. 'Typically, a turned man lasts a year - less, if we press hard for what he can give us. It's impossible to control the risks, given that the only eyes we have into his situation are his.'

'I had assumed ... ' Branssler glanced at Fischer once more, '... that we were looking to run him over the long term.'

'If we had a mature network in the Soviet Zone, it might be feasible. We don't. Right now, a small group of individual operatives are attempting to establish a presence that can withstand the discovery of one or more of its elements. Until that happens, well ...'

So Freddie Holleman was already a casualty on Herr Wessel's balance sheet of assets; he just wasn't aware of it for the moment. Fischer's urge to throw something into the Gehlen organization's spokes tightened a notch.

'Then ...'

'Yes?'

Fischer cleared his throat. 'If Beckendorp is to be used efficiently you'll need someone with experience of interrogation. Do you have many such men at present?'

Again, the long stare. It was a tried, even clichéd technique, and Fischer (who had used it himself more times than he cared to recall) de-focussed his eyes slightly to avoid wilting beneath it. Eventually, Wessel bored of the game.

'We do not. Most of our former FHO and Abwehr operatives are from evaluation backgrounds, not fieldwork or ... the necessary things.

Baun's men on the ground are almost all recently trained. We lost most of the old cadre in the war's final months'

Branssler nodded. 'I've taken your training - a month's worth, yes? Six weeks, perhaps?'

'It isn't much. One day we'll have proper facilities and funding for a more effective programme.'

'Even then, you'll need men with experience to *give* them the training, particularly in how to keep their contacts alive and talking - which is what Herr Fischer and I have. We can make Beckendorp productive more quickly than anyone who's been through Oberursel, I guarantee it.'

They had come to the dangerous moment, the one in which a suspicious mind – and Wessel's mind was little else – might take self-promotion as pleading. The last thing they wanted was to give the impression they had money on the cockroach. Fischer waited until the latest silence became painful and then shrugged.

'It's your decision, sir. But speaking for myself I've done more than enough desk work.'

For the first time since the two men had entered Wessel's office - a panelled room in a prettily-shuttered, *faux* Alpine lodge (surreally re-named Alaska House by the Americans), sitting incongruously behind barbed wire a mere stone's throw from the impossibly pretty river that gave the place its name - the General's stern face allowed itself a slight smile.

'I appreciate ambition, but you'll forgive me for asking - is your face the right one to pass unseen?'

Fischer held back his own the smile, which would have confirmed Wessel's point precisely. 'Sir, in Berlin it's the unspoiled face that gets the second look.'

24

'Why you, Comrade Commander?'

Freddie Holleman wondered how a man did an *earnest* expression. It wasn't something he had ever been required to perform. Before the war one had to rise higher than he in the *OrdnungsPolizei* to need to pretend any ambition, and his interview for the Luftwaffe had consisted of an eye-test and some fellow in a white coat squeezing his scrotum with less tenderness than it deserved. Neither job had required the sea-lion-earning-a-fish routine; he feared that he might overdo it now and seem merely demented.

'Because I know the man, sir. He's ex-Luftwaffe, like me, only I got away with a misplaced leg. He was badly burned, unlucky enough to survive it and had a lot of head problems after that. I saw him in Berlin two days ago. He was following me, too obviously, so I bought him a drink and we did the *old days* business. He was twitchy, like I would have expected, but there was something else, something he wasn't saying. And then the poor bastard blurted it and made a clumsy attempt to recruit me.'

'On what terms?'

'Money, of course, though he wouldn't give me a precise figure. He hinted that the Amis are generous with non-cash benefits, as if I have a use for nylons. The thing was oversold, but being new to the job he probably needs to impress his bosses, the Gehlen gang.'

'And he wants …?'

'He knows that I'm in the SED – it's hardly a secret. He'd like to know any Party business, particularly the anti-SPD stuff, and anything we're up to that contravenes the *Magistrat*'s rules. He's also sufficiently deluded to believe that I have, or can get, access to data on German POWs, turned during their captivity in the USSR, who SVAG intend to use in Berlin and the west. He'd very much like to know about them, apparently.'

The other man's eyebrows rose slightly. 'Men like me, you mean?'

Holleman risked a shrug. 'You aren't going west, comrade. But yes, men like you. He told me it's the Americans' worst nightmare, to have the Allied Zones infected by secret communists who know the place far better than they do. It would be like occupying the territory of an invisible enemy.'

Direktor Jamin leaned back in his chair and studied the ceiling. He was a tidy man with a fuller head of hair than a former Siberian tourist might have expected to retain. Holleman knew that he'd been the worst sort of SS, one of Oskar Dirlewanger's creatures (though he exhibited no obvious derangements), who'd experienced a quite remarkable – or self-serving - damascene moment during his captivity and emerged as a certified *kozi*, so trusted by the Ivans that he'd immediately been appointed the top job in the newly-fledged Fifth Kommissariat. Holleman didn't need to speculate whether the man could be peevish if he suspected he was being played.

But Jamin he could gauge, at least. It was the other one, the silent fellow at his side, who made him really nervous. It wasn't the face, obviously - had it softened slightly and sat upon a woman's body he'd have found it as amenable as a view of the Harz Mountains. No, it was the nondescript Red Army uniform and its supremely relaxed slouch that was putting his bowels through basic training. Every time Jamin opened his mouth his head tilted slightly towards Pretty Boy as a dog's would to a shepherd, waiting for the command that would drop him to his belly. Which meant the fellow was MGB, or some sub-set of the species, and that a file on this business had already been opened at Soviet HQ, Karlshorst. The bowels lurched once more, and Holleman almost had to ask for toilet-leave.

Jamin was pursing his lips too tightly for it to be good news. This time he glanced directly at his handler before speaking.

'This is a counter-intelligence matter. K-5, as you know, are concerned only with domestic security for the moment. And while we appreciate your diligence in the matter, Beckendorp, your further involvement wouldn't be productive. Therefore ...'

Pretty Boy coughed politely, and Jamin almost left his seat. 'May I ...?'

'Yes, of course.'

'Thank you.' The Russian smiled graciously and turned to Holleman. 'Herr Beckendorp, how well do you know this man?'

*Shit*. How much was precisely enough? *Hardly at all* or *I married his sister* wouldn't do. Only one version would stand up to scrutiny if they were so unlucky that the records survived still, and that was something as close to a half-truth as he dared.

'We served together in the Belgium campaign, in '40, Comrade. Well, not together; he was Fallschirmjäger and I was air-station support, but everything was moving so fast in those days that we were tangled. My unit helped pull the regiment out of Fort Eben-Emael, and the survivors used our Mess all that week, so we got to know each other a little. Three years later I was at Reinickendorf Lazarett having my stump checked when I ran into what was left of the poor bastard. His head was messed up inside and out, and I think he was grateful for familiar company. After that, I didn't see him again until this week.'

'I see.'

Holleman hated that phrase - it meant to say precisely nothing, and in a way to make the steadiest conscience wonder what it had done. But the Russian smiled and nodded as if he'd been given the right answer. Jamin's face was set to zero, registering nothing that could commit him one way or the other.

Pretty Boy turned to him. 'Herr Direktor, would you mind if we allowed the Commander to take on this thing? It's not usual procedure, obviously, but the personal connection is something we should use. If this … what was his name?'

Here it was, the unavoidable rock in the road. Holleman hated the idea of what had to come next, but there was no way that a false identity would stand the most cursory glance if the Reds already had a man – a willing employee or worked stooge - in Gehlen's organization. Despite himself, he cleared his throat.

'Fischer, Comrade. Otto Fischer.'

The Russian thought about that for a moment. 'Well, if this Fischer is vulnerable, I'd prefer that he be run by someone he considers to be a friend. MGB shall of course assume direction of the business. As you say, K-5 isn't interested in counter-intelligence.'

Jamin was still reeling from the novelty of *would you mind*, but he managed a nod. The Russian opened a slim file and shoved a single piece of paper to Holleman.

'You may use this as a first taste of what you can give to Gehlen's men. It's a short list of Germans who are presently employed by the Americans in various roles at Camp Andrews, Lichterfelde. Assure your friend Fischer that they are, to some extent, in our pay also.'

Holleman counted eight names – all, presumably, expendable sods who imagined they had some sort of future still. He looked up into the Russian's guileless face.

'You don't mind losing them?'

'Why should we? I imagine they're all perfectly loyal to the Americans, though of course they can't prove that. We're merely spreading a little disharmony and creating vacancies that, with luck, we may at least partly fill with our own people. Camp Andrews is *very* important to us.'

Why is that, Comrade …?'

The other man smiled amiably, but didn't take the hint and offer a name.

'Because, Herr Beckendorp, it's the only major sovereign territory of the United States of America that lies a convenient bicycle ride from my office.'

25

At dawn, when pale light coming through the window ended his last chance of anonymity, he realised that he had a choice – to kill or to feed his unwelcome visitor. He removed one of his last three *eiserne* rations from his pocket, put it on the floor and kicked it across the small room. The boy recognized it instantly and snatched at it, opened the seal expertly and devoured the contents in less than three minutes. He didn't seem to find horsemeat unpalatable.

When his fingers had scraped the tin almost to a state of sterility he sat back against the wall, licking his lips like a satisfied cat, his eyes fixed once more upon the threat. He was a runt, a *kümmerling* of the nondescript species that infested this and every other German city of the new age. The clothes that hung from him were a parody of a grown man's, everything two sizes too big and holed more comprehensively than the building in which he presently trespassed. His face was dirty of course, but that was something of a blessing in that it helped to conceal much of what malnutrition and the mid-century's hardest winter had done to his complexion. He was pitiful and pitiable, a theatrical costumier's overwrought interpretation of a side-plot from Hugo, or Dickens.

'What's your name, lad?'

The boy's mouth twitched; he licked his lips once more, swallowed hard and said something unintelligible.

'What?'

'Engi.'

'What sort of name is that?'

'It's short for Engelbrecht.'

'You poor bugger. Engi it is, then.'

The boy watched his host carefully, a slim but wiry man, tall, with cropped hair of a style now avoided (except, curiously, among some Russian officers who strutted around Berlin much like their exemplars once did). The face was hard, one to run from; if he'd been free to do so he would have fled that moment, but he knew that he'd be caught before he reached a window. He noticed now that the man's hands were bandaged, and wondered whether that should make him more or less frightened. Only his stomach argued that a man who fed you and asked your name wasn't in the murdering business, and having just been pampered its judgement couldn't be trusted.

But he gathered his small store of courage and tried to look tougher than he was.

'What's *your* name?'

The man laughed. 'That's a very good question. It *was* Rüdiger, and for a very short time it was Hans, but now it's Rolf ... I think. Which is best?'

Engi shrugged. One name was much the same as another.

'Well, let it be Rolf, then.'

'What are you going to do with me?'

'Do? Nothing. I'm dead, and dead men don't do things, good or bad.'

'You're not dead.' If there was a subject upon which Engi regarded himself as an expert it was the nature and appearance of death. His education had commenced with *her* and continued almost on a daily basis since.

'Well, dying then. And it's you who's killed me.'

'How did I do that?'

'You came here.'

'That's not killing.'

'Someone was supposed to come, but not you.'

'There was someone outside last night. I was frightened, so I jumped in the window.'

'I know. You scared him away.'

'I don't scare anyone.'

'You made him cautious, then. I don't suppose he saw you properly in the dark, that you were only a kid. But if he doesn't come back I'm dead.'

'I'm sorry.'

Rolf shrugged. 'You weren't to know. It's hard, being frightened.'

'Have *you* been frightened?'

'Almost all the time, during the war. It's called being a soldier.'

'Did you kill anyone?'

'Probably. I pointed my gun at a lot of people. Some of them fell down.'

'Were they Americans?'

Rolf smiled. 'I don't think so. There were Belgians and Greeks, a few New Zealanders and some Russians. Actually, a *lot* of Russians, which is ironic.'

'What does that mean?'

'It's hard to explain. A lot more things are ironic these days than used to be. Don't worry about it. Would you like some more food?'

Engi nodded vigorously and remembered to say *thank you* when another *eiserne* ration was tossed at him. He ate this one more slowly, sitting at the table to which Rolf beckoned him. It was the first at which he'd eaten since the times he preferred not to recall (but which, of course, he recalled now), and he had a vague memory that when you ate at a table you weren't allowed to wolf down your food. It was a tradition, he supposed, or a custom.

While he was eating Rolf went to the curtains, put a bandaged finger between them and peered through the gap. There were noises outside now – the hard percussion of hooves on the broken asphalt, the squeal of badly-maintained axles (horse-power having replaced the internal combustion engine for all but military and official personnel), an occasional voice half-raised in some complaint or other as it passed by – all of them the standard distractions of life in a city on its knees. Rolf watched but didn't seem to be interested in any of it.

'Where do you live, boy? Do you have family in Berlin?'

Engi shrugged.

'Yeah, I thought so. We've both got problems.'

'You can hide, like I do.'

Rolf sighed. 'It's tempting. But if you stay in the same place for long enough someone always finds you.'

'Do you mean *your* someone?'

'That's another very good question. I don't know. Is *someone* the person to make a decision about me or just the messenger? Do I wait here or go? Do I find Wolfgang and stick with the story, hoping that it sounds more believable in his head than it does in mine? Will they think I'm worth keeping, or that they'd be inviting more mistakes if they did? What do you think?'

As Engi had no idea what any of these words meant he said nothing. After a few moments Rolf put a hand in his jacket pocket. 'Well, we've got just the one ration now, so we'll need more food. Can I trust you with money?'

These last were words that Engi very much understood. He nodded, trying not to seem too eager. Rolf laughed again and removed his wallet. 'I doubt I'll see this again. Go to the market on Ackerstrasse, get bread and whatever tinned meat you can find. Coffee would be good too, any kind. If there's money left after that you can keep it, alright?'

Engi nodded again. He didn't like to be seen outside during the day but this was too miraculous an opportunity. He folded the marks reverently and put them in his trouser pocket, the one that had a button on it still. 'Can I go?'

'Do you know what a moral obligation is?'

Very truthfully, Engi shook his head.

'I fed you. Return the favour, please.'

26

Fischer saw it immediately - you didn't work with men for so long, get into their minds and habits, without spotting the hints, the subtle signs. Gerd Branssler and Freddie Holleman were drunk.

He and Branssler had parted two hours ago at the entrance of their extremely modest hotel in Moabit, Fischer to check for telegrams at the telegraph office and Branssler to meet Holleman and convey him discreetly to the safe house in Ziegelstrasse. Clearly, they had arrived earlier than anticipated and used his absence energetically. His theory was given bones when he saw an empty bottle protruding from beneath the sofa. He might have spotted immediately, only Holleman was almost sitting on it.

'Otto! Pull up a piece of floor, we're solving our problems.'

Fischer helped himself to one of two unopened bottles of Purveyance Board vodka (Holleman's contribution, he assumed) sitting precariously upon the small, pitted table. Branssler was supporting the wall opposite, rubbing his head with a half-full glass, humming quietly. Suddenly his eyes popped open.

'A tank!'

'What?'

'A Sherman tank! It shouldn't be difficult - the Americans have so many they can't possibly account for every one of them. I'll bet there are some in Frankfurt. We can drive one here to Berlin and let Freddie give it to the Ivans.'

Holleman burped. 'They've got lots already. The Amis sent them thousands during the war. The Red Army think they're crap - they call them *five-man cremation wagons*, apparently. What about rocket technology? Come on, Otto, this is your subject - pull your weight, man!'

'What are you idiots talking about?'

'About what we can give Freddie to give to his people, to keep him …' Branssler belched loudly, '…alive.'

'Jesus.' Fischer swallowed his first mouthful of vodka and replaced the cap. 'Forget *things*! What both Karlshorst and Oberursel want is information, mainly about what the other is doing. We're *spooks* now (Branssler nodded blearily), or at least we're doing what spooks do, and spooks deal in data. But it can't be *real* data, or we're all dead and buried. We have to make up something, and we can't make up a tank, or a rocket, or even a pistol, can we?'

Holleman pursed his lips and thought about it. 'I don't know. What about the Mark IV *Teufelsturm*? We can give that to the Ivans.'

'What is it?'

'I have no fucking idea. Um, it's an integrated anti-aircraft system. The Americans found the prototype in a cave in Thuringia and whipped it back to the US before Zhukov could get his damp hands on it. They're building one of their own right now, somewhere in Arizona.'

Fischer almost laughed. 'That's not entirely mad - unprovable, irresistible, and even if it *was* exposed as a hoax you'd only be doing your job by passing it on. But perhaps something less complicated? We have to be able to write it convincingly.'

Well, like I said, rockets.'

'*Vastly* complicated. If the technology confounded Dornberger and von Braun I don't see us making a better job of it.'

'A new gas weapon?'

'I didn't study chemistry. Did you?'

Branssler (who had slid down his wall to spend some time with his knees) groaned. 'Why don't we stop buggering around and give the Ivans the Atom Bomb?'

'A masterstroke, Gerd. Simple, plausible *and* risk-free.'

'Jesus, I don't know, then. Three ex-police, we aren't experts at *anything*, are we?'

Holleman shook his head lugubriously. 'Otto can jump out of aircraft without shitting himself ('not quite true' murmured Fischer). I can – *could* – pilot a variety of now-extinct fighter 'planes, though their insides were always a mystery to me. You, Gerd, you're even less useful, not having served and failed gloriously in uniform. So what we can possibly construct? Killing or catching folk is all we ever learned. Pass me that last bottle, there's a fellow.'

Fischer handed over his own, almost untouched ration as it came to him - a wonderful, perfectly simple *thing*, requiring only imagination and credibility, of interest to both parties for as long as might be required to allow the three of them to find a way out of this.

'What are spies most exercised about?'

'I don't know, Otto. What?'

'Other spies. So that's what we give them.'

'How? We don't know any. And if we did, would we betray them?'

'Not real ones. We give them dead people.'

Holleman's face was a study in vacated space. 'Eh?'

'What does Germany have more of than almost any other nation?'

'Fuck-awful luck.'

'And confusion. We have millions of dead, missing or displaced persons. How would anyone begin to trace them?

'*Kennkarten*?'

'And who issues these?'

'Right now? Hardly anyone, and then only to the Jews. Most of us are making do with our Reich IDs still.'

'That's right. So the *volkscartei* files are still the only comprehensive means of checking identities.'

'Yes, but they were stored in *OrPo* stations, and how many of those have survived?'

'My point precisely. We give dead people to Oberursel and Karlshorst. All we need to do is find names from jurisdictions where we know the *OrPo* stations were destroyed, resurrect them and put them to work for us as alleged spies.'

Branssler had started to smile, but it became a frown instead. 'Otto, I doubt that either Gehlen or … what's your fellow's name, Freddie?'

'Jamin.'

'… would be so dumb as not to try to check the names. They'll be lucky with some of them at least, and then they'll realise that these people don't exist anymore.'

'I truly hope so. Because then they'll think what?'

Holleman stared at the floor for a while before getting it. 'That the other side's setting up ghost identities.'

'Why would they do that?'

'To use them to insert their own people, obviously.'

'Yes. And the advantage for us is …?'

'I have no fucking idea.'

'None of it has happened - *yet*. Gehlen fears the tide of German POWs returning from Siberia, but they're a trickle so far and he knows it. No doubt Jamin and his MGB masters are bracing themselves to deal with Gehlen's network of spies in the Soviet Zone, but it doesn't exist at the moment. All we'll be doing is feeding each side the details of a story they think is being written already. It makes a little time for us.'

'Christ!' Holleman looked up respectfully. 'We'll be betraying everyone – two sorts of Germans, the Amis, the Ivans, even the dead!'

Fischer smiled modestly. 'And we don't need degrees in physics or chemistry to write it plausibly.'

Branssler took a long swig of his vodka and belched once more. 'Dead males, presumably of a certain age?'

'Hardly. Virtually everyone between conception and senility got a uniform towards the end. It shouldn't be difficult. The real beauty of it is, the fact that our information's bad more or less guarantees its authenticity in the minds of those we'll feed it to.'

The drunks on the floor laughed. With infinite care, Holleman wiped the rim of his second bottle of vodka and offered it back to Fischer.

'Who'd be spy? You can't trust night to follow day! But you know what this is, don't you, Otto?'

'What *what* is?'

'This thing we're doing.'

'Tell me, Freddie.'

'We're resurrecting the War Reporters' Unit. Up shall be Down, Black shall be White, and the truth whatever we say it is.'

The weight of what they were about to attempt pressed upon Fischer's mood like a falling gantry, but the laugh came straight from his belly and kept going. At the Air Ministry they had taken mere truths and fashioned gloriously implausible unrealities, turning military reverses into brilliant re-alignments, defeats into crushing defensive actions, retreats into consolidations and all with such brazen clarity that a rational person reading their stuff might have doubted his own judgement and sanity. Technically it had been what the Ivans called disinformation – propaganda, perhaps, put to the service of a very bad hand being played disastrously. But the men of the unit had a different way of seeing it and a secret name for themselves, a name they had carried with intense pride.

'We've Lazarus'd the Lie Division.'

27

'What did you do in the war, comrade?'

*Oberwachtmeister der VolksPolizei* Albrecht Müller winced and looked up from the report he was trying to assemble into something credible.

'I'm surprised you ask me that, Kalbfleisch. We are Germans, you'll recall, which is to say that we try not to be curious about certain things.'

*Anwärter* Sepp Kalbfleisch, a man much too old to have acquired the wrong sort of record during the recent business, shrugged. 'I know, but it's strange, working with folk and not chatting about life. Let me start, then. I was a watchman at the Seimens-Schukert-Werkes until the Reich decided to ignore my club foot and give me a rifle. When the Russians came I threw it on the floor and they treated me very decently - I got a slap and a couple of kicks up the arse, but then after a while sitting behind a wire fence they told me to go home. Which I did. In all, I was a soldier for a little more than six days.'

Müller sighed. There wasn't a chance he was going to get away with a mysterious past. In any case, he'd be giving nothing away. His bosses were unusually particular about not taking on men who might be dragged off to the Allied Tribunals at a moment's notice.

'I was an advocate, in the People's Court.'

Kalbfleisch grinned. 'Not a difficult job, allegedly. Did you defend anyone?'

'I had many clients.

'That's not what I asked.'

'Until the Reichstag fire I defended *all* of them. After that, I was expected mainly to hold their hands, or explain that they'd been naïve to repeat bad things about the Führer, or about the way the war was going, or the price of ersatz cheese. This was on the rare occasions the judges invited me to speak, naturally.'

'Well, they're stringing up *those* bastards now, at least. A pity the Americans dropped one on Freisler before the people could have their revenge.'

'I appeared before him, twice.'

'Really? Was he as odious as they say?'

'It was a long time ago. I was young and he was merely bombastic. But we all saw what such men became, given free rein. All I know is that when he died no one shed a tear, not even those who handed him the piano-wire nooses. It was as if a cancer had been cut away.'

'You'd almost want to believe in a hell. What do you think His Honour would have made of these?'

Kalbfleisch nudged the thin paper files sitting on the table they shared. Each of them contained a single sheet of paper recording the approximate age, apparent wounds, identifying features and location of discovery of a dead child. There were seven such files; an eighth was slightly thicker, containing the statements of frantic mothers reporting the disappearance of their sons and daughters. Occasionally, a new tragic discovery allowed Müller and Kalbfleisch to remove one of these statements and open a new, thin file (a bureaucratic progression that gave them no satisfaction whatsoever). It was onerous, important work, and though neither had yet admitted it to the other, they shared less than a sense of delight at the trust that Commander Beckendorp had placed in them.

'Very little, probably. He had a conscience that could send obviously innocent folk to the guillotine. Mere depravity would hardly disturb it.'

Kalbfleisch sighed. 'You'd think that this city had hosted quite enough guests of a certain disposition not to be advertising vacancies for more of the same.'

It was the most elegantly stated opinion that Müller had heard escape those particular lips (being more usually employed by a cigarette butt), and he looked up from his report, surprised. But his subordinate had put down his pen to excavate a nostril with his finger, and the moment passed.

'There are peculiar things here.' Müller swept the files with a hand.

'So you keep saying. But all it boils down to is that the same person or gang's doing it.'

'The children died within an extremely brief period, perhaps two or three days, the last of them a fortnight past. So, either the thing's finished or the killer's gone to ground, unnerved by his success. Visible damage to the bodies is limited, the sort of wounds that might have been inflicted during a struggle, or even in the normal course of living on the street – none of it so severe as to cause death. So how did they die?'

'Suffocation, most likely. That's what the surgeon says.'

'This would be Herr Doctor Jensen, who couldn't locate a haemorrhoid in a cherry-red colon?'

Kalbfleisch grinned, said nothing.

'Yet no post-mortem was carried out on any of the bodies.'

'You're a comedian, comrade.'

'The victims were discovered within an area two kilometres' square, in mostly ruined houses that are occupied either by their owners, or tenants, or squatters, all of whom happened to be elsewhere during the act. Again, the bodies were so placed within a three day period. So, he ...'

'Who?'

'The monster - he knows when people are going to be away from their homes. Who would have that information?'

'A doctor?'

'There hardly *are* doctors anymore - which is why, against all reason, Herr Jensen is drawing a police salary still. Who else would know when someone was going to be away for one of half a dozen reasons?'

'A blockhilfer?'

'Once, perhaps. But how many blockhilfers are left in the city? Most of those who didn't die defending their territories during the Russian advance got it from behind, payment for their careers as informers. Or they ran before their tenants thought to do it. In any case, no one admits to having been one, these days'

'Well, I don't know. A clairvoyant?'

'Don't be amusing.'

Kalbfleisch's finger paused in its valuable work. 'Someone who knows certain properties will be empty on particular nights because he has the authority to empty them?'

Slowly, Müller nodded. 'Very good, Kalbfleisch. A city official of some sort, or perhaps …'

'One of Berlin's foreign guests.'

'Shit. Still, it won't be difficult to interview the occupiers of the properties and find out who got them out of doors. I wonder why they weren't asked when they gave these statements.'

'Perhaps they *were* asked, but whoever got the answers had the sense to forget that he'd asked.'

It wasn't unlikely. An overworked, underpaid *anwärter*, dredging for details of yet another casual enormity that would probably never be chased (much less resolved), had little incentive to place himself in Allied cross-hairs. In any case, he would have known that if he reported it his superior would do what he himself longed to do anyway, which was to carefully bury the offending information.

'Still, we're going to have to ask again.'

Kalbfleisch nodded. 'I don't want to upset anyone who's got an army behind him, but there are worse things than a bullet.'

'Beckendorp.'

'God, yes. All I can think is that he had a worse war than the rest of us. Or he married Medusa's uglier, nagging sister.'

28

Watching the boy eat, Rolf was reminded of a pre-war newsreel on the lives and habits of moray eels, and what they do to passers-by. It was efficient, he supposed (in that a maximum number of calories were captured in the shortest time), but an unpleasant spectacle, a habit that needed a mother to curb.

*Poor little bastard.*

He was surprised by this slight tug of compassion. During the Greek campaign, he and his comrades had made children of a similar age stand with their mothers while their fathers were put against a wall and reminded that civilians shouldn't be armed. He hadn't felt too wretched about it at the time.

It was the only 'recipe' he knew, filling and reasonably nutritious, one that could be cooked quickly on a field stove (or in this case, the small pan he'd brought to the refuge). You ripped up stale bread, added whatever raisins or other dried fruit you'd managed to pillage and wet it with just enough milk to make a glutinous mess as it heated up. Germans didn't have an official name for it, though some of their British prisoners had called it *pobs* (for God knew what reason). He thought of it as grouting for the stomach, and the boy seemed to enjoy it. When his spoon had extracted all that it could he discarded it and used a forefinger to clean the bowl forensically, smacking his lips to preserve the taste as long as possible. It was impressive. The quantity (served up in two portions) must have represented at least eight hundred calories – a feast to a modern Berliner.

The glutton sighed and pushed away his bowl. 'Thank you, Rolf.'

'You're welcome. But you ate too quickly. In an hour you'll be hanging over a ditch praying for it to drop out in a single load.'

Engi shook his head firmly, and Rolf suspected he'd not had much use for latrines recently, not on a regime that would leave a rodent sharp-set. He pulled out a cigarette pack and offered it. Carefully, the boy took two and put them in a pocket - currency, not another unfortunate habit. He seemed nervous still, glancing around every few seconds to reassure himself that an exit was available if necessary. But he'd surprised Rolf by returning with the food he'd been instructed to buy. He could have run with the money, a fortune to a street waif.

'So, what do we do?'

'Do, Rolf?'

'About my problem. If I stay here someone will come, and I don't know if that's good or bad, do I?'

'No, Rolf.'

'I could get on the road, go somewhere else, stay out of Berlin. Where, though? Would I be safer there or here? And what would I do for work? The only job I ever had was Army, and Germany doesn't have a use for one of those anymore.'

Engi stared at the floor, considering this. 'Go to America?'

'I don't speak English, and who believes all that shit about fresh starts and liberty? Wherever you go it's the same, good or bad, better or worse, a future or nothing. Besides, I don't suppose the rest of the world's welcoming German migrants these days.' He stopped and winked at the boy. 'Except for a certain sort of discrete gentleman who can pay his way on a South American line, no questions asked or answered, the sort who started all of this and then fucked off smartly with his Jewish inheritance.'

As was usually the case when Rolf spoke, Engi wasn't quite sure what all the words meant. He didn't know what *Jewish* was, or *inheritance* for that matter; but he recognized the weariness behind the words, the way Rolf seemed not to really care about the things he spoke of, as if it he had no hand, no say in them. Engi often felt like that about days and where they went.

Rolf's face didn't show much emotion. He pulled it occasionally, or smiled, but there wasn't any real hint of what he was really feeling, or meaning. It made it hard for Engi to know whether he was safe in his company (though he'd been given more and better food here than he could remember). It was what kept him on the tip of his toes, even when he was sitting on the floor. If things went bad you only ever had the one chance to get away.

At the other side of the table, Rolf played with his own ration of *pobs*, watching his guest trying to decide if it had been a good idea, coming back. He was a good kid in a very bad situation, thinking himself streetwise but really a casualty-in-waiting. Feeding him was prolonging the torment, staving off the moment when he looked the wrong way at a bigger kid who'd entirely forgotten – or never known – how kids should be. He knew that he shouldn't care - it was no one's business, least of all his. The same tragedy was working itself out all over the city, all across Germany, a new generation nailed to the cross its parents had joyously raised.

But there was the thing. He *kept* thinking that it was none of his business, and he wondered why. He had no better life to offer, no lessons to impart, no force to invoke that would change anything. All he could do was to feed the boy until his dollars and Allied marks disappeared, and that would be to apply the very worst poison of all – hope.

He glanced around the refuge. Obviously, his contact wasn't returning soon. He didn't know whether this was procedure, prudence or cowardice, but the little runt sitting across the table had done for him, killed his last chance of putting a case to his employers before they formed their own opinion about what had happened in that alley. He had only two options – to run or to face Wolfgang and hope that his story acquired a smear of credibility as it passed through the air. He laughed, and Engi, surprised or scared by it, stared at him, waiting.

*A good kid, my killer.* 'What do you think, boy?'

'About what, Rolf?'

'I can't stay here, so where do I go?'

'I don't know.'

'Well, do you want to come too, to this place neither of us know yet?'

The animal in Engi told him not even to think about refusing a food supply, protection, the chance to get out of a city that killed children by rolling over them. An even baser instinct warned him to run away, find another hiding place, hold his breath, trust no one he didn't know. But the boy had the casting vote, and for all that the man in front of him might equally be a cannibal, a deviant or a best friend, his need for something more than the company of ghosts spoke loudest of all.

'Yes, Rolf.'

29

'Unfortunately, we'll need to bribe someone. Fortunately, that *someone* will almost certainly be French.'

Freddie Holleman smiled. 'The French are wonderful. Who else can do corruption as an art-form? But why?'

'Gerd's going to ask one or more of his old *kripo* mates to pull the data on smashed police stations, so we'll know exactly which *volkscartei* records are lost. Then we need to find dead soldiers to match those jurisdictions. Which mean *Wehrmachtsauskunftstelle*.'

'*Is* there a WASt still?'

'Surprisingly, there is. But only because they administered all records for Allied POWs and casualties as well as our own war dead. The Amis captured the archives, but since last June the organization's been assigned to French control, apparently.'

'Where is it now?'

'Right here, in Berlin.'

'Lovely. But won't it be difficult, matching boys correctly to their home addresses?'

'It'll take a little time. And we need a plausible story why one of us is poring through the records, because someone's going to be curious. The files are either going to be in alphabetical order of surname or by unit, so it'll be a case of ploughing on until we hit the towns or districts on Gerd's list.'

'You do it, Otto.'

'Why me?'

'Your wounds. The French like to be awkward, but who's going to make it difficult for a man who wears his war like you do? Listen, tell them you're the former commander of a unit whose boys were lost heroically defending one or other retreat. You've sworn by Odin's white beard to find their parents and tell them how poor Hansi or Ruprecht entrusted their last words to you to take home for them. WASt is the only hope you have.'

Gerd Branssler swallowed hard. 'Jesus, Freddie. That's beautiful.'

Modestly, Holleman shrugged. 'It's my poet's soul.'

'Alright, I'll do it. Awkward or not, the French are the best we could have hoped for. They dislike the other Allies as much as they do Germans, so I doubt that they share more information than they need to.'

'Do you speak French, Otto?'

'Enough to make myself understood.'

'Then lay it on thickly about France being the cradle of culture and all that shit. They'll love it, that and the bribe.'

'What do we give them?'

Branssler pursed his lips. 'Not money - that would make them wonder what it is you're really doing. It's got to be something that *means* something, just like your story.'

A recent, pleasant occasion stirred Fischer's thoughts. 'What about vintage brandy? The real stuff, I mean, pre-war French brandy?'

'Perfect. You'll tickle their egos *and* palates.'

'I'll need to speak to Earl Kuhn. A couple of bottles shouldn't be too hard to find.'

'Don't drag your feet. We're going to have to tell our respective bosses that this thing's moving.'

'I know.' Almost in formation the three men glanced around a room whose walls pressed suddenly. Whatever qualities defined a safe-house this place didn't have them. It was paid for by the Gehlen Organization but sat in Soviet-controlled territory, on a street patrolled by Freddie Holleman's men – men who believed him to be someone he wasn't. Looking at it that way it was more of a dog-pit, and the three of them were topping the bill, given no choice other than to win but plotting to throw the fight, call it a misstep, bad luck, a victory of sorts and hope that they didn't get put down by their disappointed owners.

'Oh God.' Branssler sighed and picked up his hat from the holed sofa. 'I should be sat at my desk at Oberursel, wondering what Greta's doing, hoping that one of the girls has written from Dusseldorf.'

Holleman looked wretched. 'Sorry, Gerd. You two are in this because of me – again.'

Fischer shook his head. 'It's my fault. I dragged Kurt Beckendorp back from Purgatory and stuffed you into his skin. If only ...'

'... we could shit gold bars we'd all be in Montevideo. Shut up, Otto. You kept Freddie alive for two years with those papers. It's just bad luck the originals sat in the only cellar in Hamburg that didn't become pure glass *and* that Baun recognized the name when he saw it. You'd think the mightiest military arse-fucking in history might have blurred some of the detail in his head, wouldn't you? No one's to blame. It's what it is.'

Holleman sighed. 'I daren't tell Kristin any of this.'

'She doesn't know?'

'What could I say? That the old gang have got their heads together and somehow it's going to work out? I can't see that bit myself, so how convincing could I be? Every way I can think it through, at least one party to this fisting's going to feel something and object violently. We seem to be relying upon our bosses being blind enough for us to organize this and then stupid enough to take the results indefinitely. How could I explain that? No, the first she hears about any of it is when they pull us out of the Spree.'

Fischer and optimism weren't in a close relationship (as a man who'd taken the glass in the face he found it difficult to have an opinion on where its level stood), but he was fairly certain that a plan relying upon the best efforts of three dejected masterminds wasn't being given the best start in life. He applied himself to the hopeful case, the one he hardly believed in himself.

'If we were doing this anywhere else, or at any other time, I'd be the first to argue it down. But as we keep saying, this is Berlin, it's nineteen forty-seven and everything – *everything* – is fogged in. The Allies are cracking their spines trying to get ahead in a game they've started without really knowing the rules. They're making assumptions about what the others are doing, but apart from the brotherly thing the Amis and Brits have got going, actual intelligence isn't crossing any lines yet. That's why they're using Germans, and why – right now, though perhaps not even in a year's time – there's a gap between what they *want* to know and what they can effectively know. You're right, Freddie - if it closes we're dead, but between the two hard places there's room still to do something. Gehlen needs to impress the Americans, and he wants to believe in something that may stuff the Ivans' plans for the west. The Soviets *know* that capitalism is a vast plot, so evidence that the SBZ is being infiltrated is hardly going to hit a wall of scepticism, is it?'

'Yeah, food for hungry mouths, I understand all that. What's chewing at me is us. No offence, Otto, but we're not spies. I know I'm speaking for you and Gerd both, but we haven't a clue about any of this. What if we blunder into trip wires we don't even know exist? I mean, *real* spies must have all sorts of clever techniques for spotting shit, the way we do when some poor bastard's making it up in the interrogation room. We're beginners, like kids picking our first pockets.'

Branssler nodded. 'He's right. I know more about the spy business than either of you, and that's down to some very basic, basic training at Oberursel. All I learned was how to avoid the more stupid moves, like talking in my sleep or subscribing to *Stars and Stripes*.'

Fischer rubbed his head. 'I *know* that we're beginners. But *they* – K-5, Gehlen – know that we're beginners too. That's part of what makes this feasible. Look, we give them names, men who we think are going to be planted in the East and West to work for the other side. Fairly quickly, both parties realise that the names are crap, those of dead men, and they think, 'ah, but this is exactly what *we're* doing, so the enemy must be doing it also - isn't it so predictable that they fooled the well-meaning dolts we set loose with a prayer and fifty dollars?''

'We're using stupidity as a strategy?'

'A tactic, Freddie. They aren't going to suspect naïve journeymen of being master spies. And there's a further advantage to it, I hope.'

'That they'll think I'm useless and leave me alone?'

'Hardly. But Gehlen has a big job and a small cash-box, so he has to establish priorities. Without a major coup perhaps he'll revise his hopes, see you as occasionally useful.'

'I don't want to be occasional, Otto. I want to be forgotten.'

'I know, but you're too innocent for that. If only you were wanted for war crimes - we could arrange for sympathizers to disappear you to Spain, or South America.'

Holleman brightened slightly. 'I strafed folk back in '40, during the advance.'

'Did you hit any Jews?'

'Probably not. It was an armoured column.'

'So we add Belgium to your list of enemies.'

'Shit.'

Branssler laughed mirthlessly. 'He'd have no problem with Gehlen's people if he *was* a Nazi. We've been told explicitly *not* to chase anything that looks like a certain kind of past.'

Fischer was surprised. 'Really? But the Americans ...'

'I know. I suspect it's one reason why Gehlen insisted that his organization works autonomously. He may not have been a blood-loyal

Party man himself but he doesn't want to be handing over Germans to the Tribunals. Like I keep telling you, it's the Reds he's got an erection for.'

'Well, we can only make a start on this and see if it's enough to keep them happy for a while.'

'What if they ask for something specific? Like Soviet troop deployments, or Beria's hat size?'

'That's a pit we'll wade when we come to it. In the meantime, get a list of burned-out *OrPo* stations and I'll find something that'll tweak a French official's heart.'

30

Rolf departed the Ambassador Café at 12.05pm, less than a minute after Wolfgang. He kept his eyes on the old man's back, following him down Cranachstrasse. Behind him, on the Begas-Strasse side of Dürer-Platz, a young boy watched both men. He wanted to follow, but pretended instead that his feet were cemented to the ground beneath him, as he'd been instructed. He couldn't understand why Rolf had been nervous about this meeting. The man he followed was much shorter and flabbier than him, moving with the slouching gait of someone who carried a lifetime's bad habits with him. But then this was a strange part of the city, and who was to say what danger looked like here?

When Wolfgang reached Heckerstrasse he stopped, pulled out his pipe and fed it from a pouch. Rolf paused beside him, forcing himself not to glance around like a burglar about to prise a lock. When the pipe was lit, Wolfgang threw the match in the gutter and stared into the road for a while, drawing on his smoke. If this was intended to unnerve Rolf it almost succeeded. He kept his bandaged hands out of his pockets, letting them speak for themselves, trying not to start the conversation he desperately needed to have.

'Rolf, mate, you've become a topic of conversation.'

'I know. I mean, I assumed so.'

'What happened?'

Rolf gave him the story, the innocent-victim-of-unlucky-circumstance version he'd rehearsed. Wolfgang listened, his lips pursed.

The frown deepened when he heard that the money had been lost. He seemed much less upset by the description of the gentleman's death at the hands of their mysterious assailant.

'So you went to the Linienstrasse refuge.'

'I didn't want to wait this long to explain what happened.'

'No, you did the right thing. But someone else was there.'

'It was just a child, a coincidence. He ran away. Your man didn't return.'

'If he came upon someone else he wouldn't, it's standing instructions. Typically, they'd send someone else a little later to clean up things.'

Rolf didn't need to ask what Wolfgang meant by *clean*. On his third day in his new career he'd given them great cause to think they'd made a mistake, and wise heads put mistakes right quickly. But his story was plausible and he hadn't fled Berlin, which is what a guilty party, someone who'd held on to the money, would have done.

The older man sighed. 'For the moment you're to do nothing. Hold on to whatever dollars you have left, but don't try to contact any more of the people on your list. Wait for new instructions.'

'When?' A stupid question, but he couldn't hold it back.

'When it's decided what you're to do next, obviously.'

'Will it be you who finds me?'

'Possibly. I don't know for certain.'

It was hardly good news, but unless he was employed by sadistically playful people it meant that he was being given some sort of second chance. With that load off his shoulders he relaxed a little, and for the first time noticed Wolfgang's mood. He seemed preoccupied, almost uneasy.

'Is something wrong?'

'Wrong? No, Rolf. Things are … moving.'

'What things?'

The older man failed to resist the glance-around. 'Karlshorst's told us to stand down.'

'Us?'

'Just about the entire native network in Berlin. It's happened before, in the days leading up to the local elections.'

'Do you know what it is?'

'It may not be anything. The Soviets want the other Allies out of the city, but it's a delicate business. If they try too hard it might look too much like a line in the sand; if they do nothing then nothing's what they'll get. The trouble is, everyone's got an idea on what should be done, and Christ knows if Stalin's any better than Adolph was at taking advice. Perhaps he listens to one thing one week and something else the next. Perhaps it's just the turn of *something else* now.'

It sounded plausible to Rolf. The Soviets had tried to manipulate the elections and it had gone badly wrong for them. The city council was now a western-leaning coalition, the communists firmly side-lined, and it wasn't likely that SVAG were taking their failure philosophically. Back in

Moscow someone would have paid for the miscalculation, probably, and a new fellow stepped into his place.

But how long would the new strategy – if that's what the idea of the moment counted as – be tested? Stalin hated losing face, and the city elections had almost amounted to slapping it. Soon, probably, there would be slight escalations, provocations, to let the Allies know that what looked like their little victory was something else. And if he could see this he was damn sure that Wolfgang could too, which was probably why the man's nerve-endings were visible. The city was Germany's trip-wire, the place where any *next* would begin. Not even a die-hard Spartacist would want to be sitting on that front line when it lit up.

'Do you think another war's coming?'

'Christ, I hope not. I doubt it. Moscow prefers to counter-punch rather than start things – I mean, look at '41. The Americans have made it more tempting, sending home most of their good troops and replacing them with dross, but who would want another one yet? The Soviets will try some sort of foot up the arse, probably - a hint that things would be a lot more comfortable if the Allies pulled out of Berlin and went home to Frankfurt and Bad Oeynhausen.'

'They'd never do that.'

'Not today, they wouldn't. But those elections have bitten SVAG on the arse. They can see a status quo coming and they don't like it. If they can't control Berlin through the ballot box it's a case of making the place more trouble than it's worth …'

'So we just wait.'

'We do. We stay low and quiet, smile a lot, do nothing bad and genuflect when GIs grope our wives.'

Give the cue a line of US Army Ford trucks passed by, moving northwards on Cranachstrasse. The sparse domestic traffic, most of it horse-drawn, moved hastily out of their path. Half the trucks carried troops – sloppy, slouching, miserable boys who seemed to regard this particular foreign clime with disgust. Rolf watched them, thinking how homesick someone with roots must feel, so far away from what was familiar and without even a war to distract them anymore. Or *yet*.

'They don't look like much.'

Wolfgang sniffed. 'It doesn't matter. They've got Pittsburgh and two oceans on their side. They can out-produce anyone else *and* take their time getting ready for whatever shit's thrown at them. They aren't surrounded by perfect tank country, they're not a short, convenient flight from the enemy's forward airfields and they're not pushing any of the rubble that History's dumped in most other nations' prams. If Stalin's going to take them on it's got to be with a good chance of finishing it quickly.'

'That's what the Japanese said.'

'Yeah, stupid bastards. They had no more sense than Adolph, and at least he had an excuse.'

'What?'

'He was madder than a shit-house rat.'

The trucks stopped in Dürer-Platz, parking along the flanks framing Friedenau station, and the troops deployed in patrol groups of four or six. It was just a presence, a gesture to remind this part of Berlin that its occupiers weren't asleep.

'Wolfgang?'

'Yes, Rolf?'

'Does this mean I'm alright? About the incident?'

'Why shouldn't you be? It was just bad luck, your dollars being seen by the wrong person. I'll explain it, tell them you're fine. But don't be unlucky again. Russians are superstitious about things like that.'

31

*Oberwachtmeister* Müller pushed away the paperwork in front of him, sighed and shook his head. 'A waste of time.'

This was undoubtedly true, but *Anwärter* Kalbfleisch couldn't let the injustice stand. 'Yes, comrade. *My* time.'

The seven statements were neatly typed, with copies placed in each case-file. Müller was impressed by his subordinate's industry (the station didn't employ secretarial staff below the third floor), but he resisted the temptation to admit it. The idea had been Kalbfleisch's in the first place, and it had gone nowhere.

'Well, at least we can forget about coercion.'

'But the killer had some way of knowing they wouldn't be at home when he dumped the bodies, didn't he?'

'They were absent for various reasons. Look, this fellow was out hunting for firewood, these two were visiting her mother in Dahlem, this lady was helping out at her local Inner Mission and *this* one ...' Muller peered at the typescript, trying to make sense of the garbled narrative, '...appears to have been at Divine Service.'

Kalbfleisch coughed. 'Actually, he was wandering the streets in a blanket and sandals. He's a prophet, sent to announce Christ's return.'

'When?'

'Any day now - Tuesday, his best guess.'

'And Our Lord has chosen Berlin for His return?'

'Why not? We've had our End of Days already.'

'Well, until Jesus takes this one off our hands, let's think about who would have the addresses of these people.'

'*We* do, obviously. Also, ration-card and housing committees. Functioning schools have parents' addresses and the Allies have their political, war-crimes and criminal conviction data.'

'But none of our witnesses are any of the latter.'

'No, just unlucky citizens with an unwanted gift.'

'Alright. They left their homes on errands, or visits, or to go to their employments. This was in daylight. In each case they returned in darkness, didn't they?'

Kalbfleisch checked the files. 'After dusk, yes. At this time of year that's not unusual.'

'No. But we can assume that our fellow knows he has time enough, and that he won't be seen. No intact street lamps near these properties, I assume?'

'I didn't notice any. It isn't likely. The Prenzlauer-Berg - Friedrichshain border was badly smashed up.'

'So, did he bring the bodies to the houses, or kill them at the scene?'

'Without blood being spilled it's hard to say. If there were screams, would anyone notice?'

'The properties are at the southern end of the borough, near allotments and the Friedrichshain rubble dump. Did he do the business there and then carry the bodies to them.'

Kalbfleisch considered this. 'Even in the dark, and without streetlights, would he risk it? There's always the slight chance of a Soviet patrol, or one of ours.'

'Unless he has a vehicle, even a hand cart. A man pushing a cart wouldn't excite interest. It's the modern mode of transport for just about anything.'

'If he's a foreigner he probably has a truck.'

'And almost certainly he'd be required to show no more than papers to a patrol. Either way, he isn't likely to be caught by chance, not unless someone stumbles upon the act.'

The two men stared at the statements. They had seven dead children, no definite cause of death, not even a hint of a suspect and the most peevish commander in Berlin on their arses on an almost daily basis, making it obvious that he wasn't going to unlock his jaws even a little. Müller knew that his appointment to this investigation was a compliment, but it was one he'd willingly have seen tossed in someone else's direction. He had fallen gratefully into a relatively secure employment in a supremely insecure age and wanted no opportunity to be measured. He was forty-two years old with a wife and three children (none of them raped or murdered as yet), an un-requisitioned house that had lost no more than its windows and chimneys and somehow he had survived the stain of his long employment as a bit actor in a deranged entertainment – the National Socialist justice system. He had been *too* fortunate, and this task felt like the first instalment of a reckoning.

The big problem was that the city desperately needed, yet lacked, a proper criminal investigation department. The smaller problem was himself. He had a fairly sharp mind and wasn't unwilling to deploy it, but as in any other job there was a knack, a faculty, that separated competence from excellence, and he was sure he didn't possess it. He had experience of crime but it was the wrong type, accumulated over too many years defending men and the occasional woman already marked for the guillotine. He didn't know how to sniff out an evil that wasn't sitting directly in front of him on the Bench, shuffling its papers, wondering how many more dockets sat in the way of a fine lunch.

Across the table Kalbfleisch pursed his lips, sending cigarette ash on to the statements. Like many *VoPos* of his rank, his qualification for the job consisted principally of being able to process oxygen still, yet he had occasional flashes of something intuitive that didn't belong in a former watchman's head. Müller suspected that any impartial analysis of policing qualities would place the man higher than himself on the results board, though he hadn't learned to extend his tongue sufficiently to please the right fundaments. That was probably fine with Kalbfleisch; he had a strong *us* and *them* instinct, with no urge to cross the divide.

Müller, even with a good man at his side, wasn't sure that he could do this. In past times a method-murder case could have drawn upon previous casework, information shared, a network of men with experience of similar. And then there had been the *blockhilfer* system - intended to stifle social dissent but also a marvellous aid to criminal investigations, a web of snitches burrowing tirelessly, betraying instinctively. It was all gone now, as dead as the Regime itself. The modern police force had ascended to its roots, become a collection of lone amateurs once more, stabbing into dark rooms, hoping to skewer something other than their feet.

He thought a lot these days about what a real *kripo* would do. The old bulls hadn't all been models of efficiency (as with every other profession their ranks had been diluted with the Regime's trash, brutes whose talents had extended to the interrogation room's four walls and no further), but they'd known how to be dogged, to chase until they caught their man or dropped trying. He thought of his boss, the man who'd given this job to him. He should have been able to ask his advice at least, but the word was that Beckendorp was one of the New Order's placeman, someone who had risen because of who he was not what he could do, a dyed-red thug in a green uniform. One rumour had it that the man had been a political assassin back in the days of the Republic, a revolutionary every bit as desperate as the Liebknecht gang. It seemed unlikely, but Beckendorp played to his reputation and Müller had no intention of testing it.

He picked up a clutch of the statements once more. A *real* bull would return, again and again if necessary, testing the evidence, finding the pieces that locked. He was only an *oberwachtmeister*, a junior chief of broken-pavement-pounders, and yet this case had been put into his hands without the option or possibility of him passing it on, down or up. He felt the wall at his back and sighed. Kalbfleisch looked up and pulled a face that managed both to acknowledge Müller's shitty luck and its owner's relief at being far too insignificant to get splashed by it.

'What do we do next, then?'

'Go back.'

'To where?'

'To the occupiers of these seven properties.'

Kalbfleisch seemed dumbfounded. 'And do *what*?'

'Ask different questions.'

32

It was when Maria-Therese asked whether he might be able to get hold of a supply of pecithin (and she used the word *supply*, not *some*) that Earl Kuhn began to fear that the nappy laundering business was not the endless round of pleasures it seemed.

She didn't utter a word of complaint of course, because her temperament inclined to the stoic (at least one branch of her far ancestors had borne their lot on the steppes until famine, wars or a stab of ambition had driven them westward); but Kuhn, having spent a great deal of time with her since Otto's departure, was beginning to catch the subtle stiffening in her manner that told the difference between good and bad days. He'd noticed more, rather than less, stiffening lately.

Her business had expanded too quickly. From being a godsend to her own building she was now extracting baby shit for half of Bremen-Mitte, a near-industrial scale enterprise employing two girls to assist with the unpleasant phase and a third to sort and fold the finished product, and all in her tiny apartment. Though two of the girls were hard and conscientious workers, Earl had a feeling that this responsibility for putting food on other folks' plates was getting in the way of easy nights' repose.

The third girl was another problem. A refugee from Danzig (and therefore hired almost as a family), she had proved to be not so much light-fingered as a dedicated redistributor of anything that wasn't nailed to a floor and capable of being lifted by someone who weighed about thirty-five kilograms. Maria-Therese was making excuses for her (a bad sign), blaming the near-feral existence that German refugees in 'New Poland' faced and the natural instincts of anyone who had already lost everything to people who didn't recognize, and weren't required to recognize, the difference between mine and yours. But even Earl, who had no employees and only a single voluntary associate, knew that something had to be done about the girl before the walls of Queerenstrasse 23 collapsed into the vacuum created by its lifted contents. He didn't say so, because it wasn't his business and he didn't want to make his only friend's wife discover the ends of her nerves more quickly than necessary; he merely listened when she felt like complaining and debated writing a letter to add to Otto's worries.

In the meantime he did his best to loosen the pressure valve. Beulah May was almost a stranger to him, now that Maria-Therese kept money in her apartment most nights and needed an adept throat-remover to deter burglars. When the laundry detergent he'd provided was exhausted he tried to find more, and failing in that he approached his good buddy Lieutenant Klossmayer, who (for a nominal consideration) arranged for some of his British associates to divert several crates of *Persil* as they departed Henkel's Düsseldorf works. He even found new accommodation for Maria-Therese's friend and her baby when the girl's landlord tired of her refusal to give him what she'd offered freely to an American GI. That was his noblest effort, because he had no absolutely no contacts in Bremen's overburdened real-estate market. After a squandered morning pursuing non-existent properties he vacated his own luxurious suite (a small, damp room with separate toilet and sink to the rear of West Side Records' retail area) and took up temporary residence on a cot under Big Bands, M-Z. The girl – Alisz – was wildly, incontinently grateful, to the point at which she promised that if ever little Frida had a brother he should be named Earl and half-heartedly offered, on two consecutive evenings, to put the business into motion. He let her down gently, telling her to wait until she found him entirely irresistible. It was meant as a joke, but despite himself he started to wash regularly, and even had his hair cut into something that didn't recollect a drowned, half-shaved cat.

So, with the travails of Maria-Therese's growing business and his new live-in non-girlfriend, Earl was beginning to find life in Bremen almost as complicated as that of his Stettin days. Admittedly, he was getting beaten up a lot less and eating considerably more now than then; but the rapture of owning and running West Side Records was beginning to fade to a mid-grey normality, his valued Negro customers still didn't seem to regard him as more than a particularly strange (if well-informed) Kraut, and, as in Stettin, he had a hole under the premises in which several thousand Swiss francs were invited the very worst sort of attention. It almost made him wonder what happiness was, and how some people achieved it.

He worried too that he was drifting with this tide rather than resisting it. He found that he didn't really mind having Alisz's company and was even experiencing vaguely avuncular feelings towards her daughter Frida. While the mother cleaned West Side Records to surgical standards (she did this every day, her means of supplementing the rent she wasn't paying), Earl perched the baby on his counter, and, as he carefully wrapped each sale for a customer, explained to her the place or relevance of the particular artist or album in the pantheon of jazz. Doubtless this made him seem an ever stranger (though undoubtedly well-informed) Kraut to the adults at the other side of the desk, but Frida liked the noises he made even if the finer detail of what she was hearing escaped her. When he had no customers he played selections from his favourite records for her, and though her mother's toiling back tensed considerably when this happened Frida herself appeared to appreciate the remarkable dissonances through which her sound-world moved. During daylight hours this all seemed a perfectly amenable distraction, but when he stared upward from his cot into the darkness he recognized it as the stirrings of a chronic infection, and fretted.

Then several things happened in the space of a few days which brought new, novel reasons to worry. With no prior warning his premises were inspected by the Provost-Marshal of Bremen Military District, who, after more than an hour's intense questioning through an interpreter, satisfied himself that West Side Records was not a brothel, drug-den or Nazi indoctrination centre (Kuhn himself regarded the encounter more as an interrogation, though this was the first in his experience that had not required him to kiss the floor several times and mop up his own blood thereafter). The following day a uniformed journalist came to the hut - having been sanctified by the Provost-Marshal's vanished reservations - and interviewed the proprietor. This seemed much less like an interrogation, though the hack was as interested in gleaning Kuhn's good opinion of America and Americans as he was in discussing their greatest cultural legacy to the world.

After that, business – which had been almost as good as Kuhn might have wished – took off like a slivovitz-fuelled missile. Previously, two, three or four customers would arrive in a jeep to peruse the stock; now, trucks with up to a dozen men rumbled up, sometimes two or three of them each day, announcing their arrival by shaking the corrugated walls and needles from their grooves (to the proprietor's great anguish). Stocks depleted rapidly, and Kuhn redoubled his efforts to secure sentimental

German shellac to send Stateside while Klossmayer upped his deliveries of US pressings from once to twice each month. Meanwhile, the hole under the floor filled much too quickly, and its curator was obliged to think the unthinkable – of opening a bank account.

He also began to see first-hand something of America – the *real* America, not its military-shaped image. When a group of white GIs entered, any of their black compatriots who happened to be browsing the stock quietly returned record sleeves to their racks and departed. He never saw a white GI buy a black musician's album unless he was unaccompanied; he never saw black and white GIs enter together, friends on a day's leave; and he never, ever saw a black GI buy a Frank Sinatra record (not that West Side Records stocked many, and those only because avarice had overcome taste). He mentioned these observations to Klossmayer, who shrugged and said nothing as one would when asked to explain mortality, or Opera.

And then, most curiously of all, West Side Records began to attract German customers. Obviously, these were men (always men) to whom the war had been kinder than to the multitude, men with cash for more than necessities - well-educated, much travelled fellows who, never intentionally, made Kuhn feel like the never-educated, parochial easterner he was. They chatted enthusiastically about real music, its unfortunate prohibition by National Socialism and their delight in discovering its Bremen renaissance, and, though none of them said as much, seemed to fully share Kuhn's sense of awed satisfaction whenever someone of African descent walked in while they were making purchases.

A double blow – his growing, unsafe wealth and casually-dropped invitations to drinks from two of his German customers – brought Kuhn to an uncomfortable revelation. He was now a businessman, potentially what used to be called a pillar of the community (when there had been communities) and no longer a lone, fearless outrider circling the conventional mores. He realised that recorded jazz, though his abiding passion, was merely the instrument of determining the direction and quality of his life, not life itself. Naturally, this made him think of investment opportunities.

But this was still Germany, still 1947; it wasn't just a matter of opening the financial papers to check the best-performing stocks because there weren't any of either. Nor was he acquainted with anyone who could point him discreetly toward the fledgling phoenix-industries, the future motors of German reconstruction (if that were ever to happen). In any case, he suspected that he could never be happy as a distant, passive investor, content to let other men play with his money. He rejected outright those obvious lines of enrichment he had pursued formerly (cigarettes, illicit alcohol, 'surplus' Soviet weaponry), because he didn't want this as-yet dim future to end over a small hole in a cell-floor. He also dismissed the notion of investing in commodities or manufactures of which he had no prior experience - knowing that, without trusted and expert advice, he would do as well to pin a target to his back before opening his wallet.

All of which brought him back to the recorded music business. Though he was as yet a trainee entrepreneur, Kuhn was fairly certain that the Bremen market couldn't accommodate a second branch of West Side Records, and without Otto Fischer's nimble almost-pair of hands the hardware strand of his current trade was flagging, much less capable of expansion. Common sense told him to tread water, to wait and see what obvious opportunities arose; but the hole beneath the floor was pushing greenback tendrils towards the surface, and he feared that the nose of every would-be gangster in that part of Germany was beginning to twitch.

It was young Alisz, pausing upon a patch of her super-cleaned floor during one of Kuhn's audible conversations with himself, who had the idea.

'Why not go into Maria-Therese's business?'

He laughed, and thought about it. He had no interest in babies (those that didn't like jazz, anyway), and as for their arses ... but it *was* a business, one that wasn't seasonal, subject to fashion or likely to be replaced by a new, more efficient model. Most attractively, it wasn't one in which you were likely to have heavily armed, scalp-tattoo'd competition. It was respectable, necessary, relatively straightforward, and – this was by far its greatest attraction – managed already by a woman he knew wouldn't expect him get his hands dirty, metaphorically or otherwise.

The same day, after closing West Side Records, he went to the Fischer apartment and put it to Maria-Therese. He found her drying her eyes, having just dismissed the girl who couldn't get on with the eighth Commandment, and almost decided not to mention it. When he did so she couldn't see it at first, because she had all the business she could handle and all the money from it that she and Otto needed to eat and pay the rent. But then he talked about larger premises, and proper laundry machines, and more staff, and security, and – eventually – a larger apartment, or even a house and the lifestyle that a comfortable estate brought, and the spark came back into her lovely eyes (he loved her eyes above all else, because as Otto's friend he never permitted his gaze to drop to the greatest assets of her former business). Graciously, she agreed to let him proceed with the matter.

The following morning Bremen's retail music business was suspended temporarily. Kuhn went to see his landlord, the quartermaster sergeant who pocketed the rents from West Side Records, and enquired as to other buildings previously requisitioned but now surplus to Camp Grohn's shrinking needs. From a selection he chose a former cobbler's workshop, a single-storey, plumbed and wired shed on Ostertorswallstrasse, and this time paid a one-off bribe of five hundred Swiss francs for a formal tenancy agreement, all subsequent rent monies to go where they should. The sergeant was nonplussed by the new arrangement but mollified when asked to find at least three washing machines and mangles, no questions asked. Kuhn's next port of call – literally - was the Hafen, where jobless men congregated in the hope of loading work. After two hours he found a competent former plumber and an electrician. Both were surprised but by no means unwilling to except small cash retainers, and agreed to give him a priority place in their potentially busy (but in fact entirely empty) work diaries.

In the afternoon he reported back to his new partner, to let her know what was happening and to chase away the inevitable second thoughts. She made him tea and he sat on her new-old sofa, trying to sip it while Beulah May whined pitiably in his face, begging to come home.

'Earl, I'm not a businesswoman.'

'Yes, you are. This is just bigger business. Anyway, all you have to be is good with people, and you definitely are.'

'But I'll need more girls.'

'Yeah, there is that. Who in Bremen would want a steady, paid job these days?'

'Look at the trouble I had with Beatrice.'

'And you got rid of her. It'll be easier the next time.'

'It's going to cost a fortune.'

'I'm meeting all the start-up costs – it'll stand as my investment. All you'll be finding are the running costs out of your income, as you do now. It'll be sweet.'

'What will Otto say?'

*Shit.* It was the question Kuhn had hoped not to be asked, because he had no answer. A normal man would thank his guiding angels and plan out his looming life of leisure, but Otto had come late to marriage and held wretchedly bourgeois ideas about his place in it. No, not ideas, *torments*. A wife's über-successful career might be just the thing to kill any chance of future stiffening. This, Kuhn decided not to say.

'Why don't we write to him about it, separately? If he's unhappy it's better that we hear it soon.'

They left it at that, and for the next two weeks Kuhn returned to the warm embrace of polyrhythms and syncopations. He was reminded of the matter once more when the quartermaster sergeant sent word that three serviceable Mieles and a Bendix machine awaited inspection. Before he accepted the invitation, Kuhn returned to Queerenstrasse 23 to test the water.

Maria-Therese's cheeks reddened slightly when he asked if Otto had replied to her letter. 'I was a coward. I just wrote telling him not to worry, that I'm fine. He hasn't written back yet. How did you explain it?'

Equally abashed, Kuhn admitted that, like her, he hadn't found an easy way to put it so hadn't tried, confining himself instead to general observations on the music business. He shrugged it off.

'Well, it's all done now, the laundry machines have arrived. It's a fait … what do they say?'

'I don't know, Earl. It's what Otto will say that keeps me awake.'

Otto Henry Fischer had no history of violence other than that which war demanded, but Kuhn wasn't sure he knew the man well enough to be completely easy on the matter. It was a good deal, he told himself - a sensible business to be in at such times and entirely legitimate, blessed – in a way – by the Occupiers, who surely welcomed any measures that went some way to placating their subjects and preventing further outbreaks of typhus. Really, however he looked at it, Kuhn couldn't see a reasonable objection. Which was why he couldn't stop worrying.

33

Fischer shook out a handkerchief, wiped the visible dust from the slab's upper face and sat down. Behind him Gross Bunkerberg loomed, its now-buried core the shattered remnants of the Friedrichshain Flak Tower. Like Gerd Branssler he was dressed in the up-to-the-minute mode affected by most people in the city whenever the weather turned cold unexpectedly, so little of his personal war damage could be seen. In a further flourish both men wore caps that were anchored to their heads by scarves, which more or less confirmed to passers-by that they were ausländer refugees, to be avoided.

In contrast, Freddie Holleman was rakish in a felt Trilby and a scant three layers of civilian clothes, but then he was on home territory, passing a Sunday morning in what once had been East Berlin's prettiest park. The *Märchenbrunnen* - a miraculous survivor both of the bombing and Soviet assault upon the Flak Tower - would have been a much more amenable rendezvous, but despite the pinch in the air dozens of Berliners were congregating there already, wishing themselves and their children into the fairy tales the statuary depicted. A conversation in the rubble was less likely to invite an audience.

Fischer removed a sheet of folded paper from his pocket and passed it to Holleman. 'I have ten names. Three were resident in what's now the Soviet Zone, four in the west. The other three were Berliners. Obviously, I chose westerners who died in the east, and vice versa. All were single still at the time of their deaths; all died in early 1945.'

'No married men because …?'

'Wives. They tend to have good memories for the faces they married.'

Holleman reddened slightly. 'Right. And 1945?'

'Karlshorst and Oberursel need to discover that the men we give them are dead, but not so easily they become suspicious. If we use casualties from earlier campaigns they could check them out just by talking to family or former neighbours. But you know how it was in the final months - everything was confused, WASt was too overloaded to inform relatives of the many deceased and half of civilian Germany was on the move anyway. It all makes it harder to the get to the truth – and they'll find it only in the WASt files.'

'Still, it won't take long.'

'It might. It struck me that someone who'd been there before them wouldn't want the ghost identities traced, so I waited until my Frenchman took a toilet break and then misplaced the relevant cards.'

Branssler laughed. 'You ate them?'

'That would defeat the object, Gerd. I literally misplaced them - in the correct boxes, so they'll be found but not immediately. There are at least five hundred cards in each.'

'How did you persuade the French to let you into the files?'

'I gave them Freddie's fallen comrades' story, for which I wore my best, only suit and leaned heavily on a walking stick. I think the contrast between the face and the serge threw them long enough for me to present the bottle of Remy Martin to the watch chief. After that I reminisced about my only visit to Paris before the war, the women, the opera – far better than German opera, obviously – and mentioned that I never shot a Frenchman. I think they liked me, almost.'

'Ten names. Will it be enough?'

'It's believable. If we gave them a spectacular coup, dozens of names, everyone would be on our arses, asking how the hell we did it. This way Freddie offers the four westerners and a Berliner to Karlshorst, we give the others to Oberursel, and then we wait while they check them out.'

Holleman frowned. 'What if they can't? I mean, they only have WASt, and if they don't find the cards you've shuffled they may assume these fellows are genuine. I mean, that they're living still.'

'In that case they'll think our information is good, that these names really are those of infiltrators. The longer it takes for them to realise that they're chasing dead men the more plausible our *mistake* will seem when it comes to light.'

'You mean if they were fooled by it, why shouldn't innocent cocks like us be?'

'Exactly.'

'Still, I don't like it, Otto. It's one thing to be someone I'm not – I've done it for so long I'm almost more comfortable being Beckendorp than Freddie Holleman. But selling *you* as a spy, that's hard. It means lying off the cuff, about things I won't always be able to nail down first. Christ, I've already given them your real name!'

'How much more will you need to say? You're supposed to be handling a traitor. A man like that would need to have his collar size beaten out of him.'

'It's the beatings I worry about. What if they decide they want more from you? Or less? What if they tell me to put you in the river before your own people can double-turn you?'

'Stop thinking, Freddie. We can't anticipate, we can't hide, we can't run away. All we can do is to lose sleep counting the possibilities.'

Branssler patted Holleman's arm. 'With luck we might all get shot tomorrow by a bored patrol.'

'Thanks, Gerd.'

'I mean it. It happens. This city's fucking lawless.'

Holleman bristled. 'We're doing the best we can. You never dealt with what pisses into my pot, and you had four times the manpower ...'

'Yeah. Sorry, Freddie.'

'... and they were all actual policeman, not pensioners with green armbands who draw lots for who gets to carries the only pistol with a bullet in it, and ...'

'You're right, of course ...'

'... patrol a city that's three-quarters smashed, occupied by tens of thousands of well-armed bastards who can do what they want to Germans, *and* a few thousand more ausländer refugees looking to give back a little of what we gave them, *and* a native population whose thirteen hundred calories daily ration's an incitement to help themselves to a little extra ...'

Fischer coughed. When Holleman heated up he could stay in the air longer than a fully-fuelled Storch. The noise made him pause, but only to draw breath. He half-turned and stabbed a finger at Gross Bunkerberg.

'I've got seven murdered kids on my books right now. We think here's where it may have happened, but that's a guess. We don't even know how they died. We've got no pathology, no forensics and a single police surgeon covering half of this side of Berlin who'd much prefer that we didn't interrupt his daily drunks with unpleasantness. If a German killed them we probably won't catch him. If he's an ausländer we haven't a hope. If he's a soldier we won't even try. So yes, Gerd, you're right, except for the *just about* bit.'

'Jesus.' Branssler looked shocked. He had grandchildren, and hopes of them growing up. 'Seven? Over what period?'

'Two or three days. That was nearly three weeks ago.'

'He's dead, then. Or transferred out of Berlin.'

Holleman sighed. 'That's what we're hoping. But he might just be out of town for a while, or keeping his head below the firing line.'

Fischer and Branssler looked at each other. 'Typically, a method-murderer can't break off as an act of will. Once he gives in to the urge it becomes a need, like food. If he's stopped, there's some involuntary reason, like Gerd says. Or he's doing it somewhere else now, and it isn't your business.'

'It makes us look like arses, either way.' Holleman took a notepad from his pocket. 'So, give me my dead men.'

Fischer dictated the five names. 'Don't embellish it. Just say that I lifted them from my superior's desk at Oberursel, and that you paid me. Why do I need the money, by the way?'

'A drink problem. It was that or whores, and … oh, shit. Sorry, Otto.'

'Never mind. Alcohol's more feasible. I'm trying to forget what the war did to me.'

'That's what I thought.' Holleman pocketed the notebook and stood up. 'There's one other thing. From now on should I meet only you, Otto. Gerd can't be seen with me, not in Soviet Berlin. I couldn't explain how western stooges are turning up in gangs.'

Branssler sighed. 'Yeah, we discussed that. I'll be our liaison with Oberursel and try to keep my eye on Otto's back. If anyone questions it we tell them we're too conspicuous together.'

'It's the truth. You're too well-fed and Otto's too ... Otto.'

Fischer smiled. 'I am, for sure. Freddie, have you met your handler yet?'

'Yeah. He won't give a name, but MGB leaked from his pores. A major, I think.'

'Did you get any impression of how keen he is to push this?'

'Not really. He seemed to admire himself overmuch, but then someone that pretty's got every right to preen.'

'Pretty?'

'Ravishing, really. A blond, shouldn't ever go near a prison.'

Fischer tried to keep his thoughts from his face and almost succeeded, but Holleman was watching too closely. 'What's the matter?'

'Nothing, I think. Or rather, everything – which is more or less what we have to watch out for while we're doing this.'

'Yeah, we know.'

34

Frau Best didn't like children. Her barren womb had spared her the ordeal, and her husband's early death had removed the last occasion for trying despite the odds. In her experience they were nasty, loud, dirty things, incomprehensibly silly and disrespectful to those who deserved better. It had been provoking that her brother's young wife had dropped offspring with hardly less frequency or fuss than a rabbit might, and the christenings had been trials which Frau Best, even thirty years after the last of them, recalled with great distaste and resentment (principally for the unavoidable outlay upon silver *schutz* angels). She had since taken care to avoid that side of her family assiduously, her nieces and nephews having turned out to be every bit as fertile as their parents and no doubt as much in expectation of the largesse of their relatively wealthy aunt. The wealth, of course, had disappeared with the war, and the surviving fragment of her estate (a small garden apartment, a much ruined garden and the rented-out cellar of what had once been her beautiful home) was even more to be guarded jealously against the depredations of unwanted *kinder*.

So when her only tenant asked if he might take in a young relative she refused with more force than was perhaps politic (he being a very satisfactory guest, respectful and a prompt payer). However, her immoveable position on this was swiftly moved and then removed by the gentleman's offer – in lieu of an increase in the rent – to provide for her table as much as his own. It was a fact that food was a far more valuable commodity than the money to buy food, its availability being subject to gale-force winds of chance and supply in modern Berlin (and even when the authorities managed to do their job her ration card allowed her just enough sustenance to keep a small rodent content). Her tenant had reinforced the attraction of the offer by presenting to her a small package containing a genuine *bregenwurst*, a delicacy she had imagined to be as plentiful now as unicorns' tears. It had made the finest supper she had eaten in years, and by the time her distended belly had accommodated the last of it the ugly prospect of a boy on her property had softened considerably. She intended to be rigorous, however, in holding her tenant to his full part in the bargain thus struck. The child had arrived, apparently, and she awaited her next meal impatiently.

'Don't call me Rolf in front of the old sow.'

'Why not, Rolf.'

'Never mind. Call me *uncle* instead.'

Engi didn't say so, but he was delighted at this hint of permanence to their relationship. He had known Rolf for four days now, and in that time eaten more and better than since he came to Berlin, better even than at the Parochialstrasse mission. Though not worldly, he had known enough of what a certain sort of man wanted to do with boys not to be slightly wary still, but Rolf hadn't tried to touch him after their first encounter in the darkened refuge - much less interest him in the strange, disturbing photographs that seemed to line the pockets of some older men who came to the mission occasionally, whose homes – they'd promised – were full of cakes and jolly games to play.

So Engi didn't really care why he was being offered a roof, safety and a food supply. He hoped only that Rolf and his cellar weren't going to go the way of the old nightwatchman and his hut, here one day and dead or gone the next.

The old woman wasn't to be trusted, though. She said to Rolf that he seemed to be a *dear child* but her scowl said much more, and he decided not to put himself in her line of sight. However, as soon as the decision was made Rolf told him that he would be on business the next day and that Engi should stay in the cellar until he returned. As long as the old woman stayed upstairs he didn't mind waiting (the cellar was dry enough, and warm enough, and the cot that Rolf had fashioned for him was a hundred times more comfortably than the floors he usually slept upon); but the door didn't have a lock, and his body's overworked nerve-endings were going to be on duty until his new uncle returned.

Rolf could see that the boy didn't want to be left behind, but there was no discreet way to do what he needed to do with a child hanging on to his coat. Wolfgang had told him to wait for new instructions, which gave him a little time to attend to his own business – that is, to determine whether it *was* his business. So he gave the boy some bread, told him to be patient and was out of the cellar, across Schöneberg and into the Soviet sector before it was fully light. The day was miserably wet, which added to everyone's anonymity, and he moved confidently. At Ziegelstrasse he found and stepped into the alley beside the old corn factor's warehouse into which he had watched three men disappear a few days earlier. It took only a moment to identify their likely goal. Along its short stretch only a single building remained that was remotely inhabitable, a small office or shop with – from the hint of curtains at the windows – domestic rooms above. He peered into one of the ground floor windows, saw no movement and gently gripped the front door handle. As he'd expected, it was locked. Quickly, he returned to the mouth of the alley and examined the buildings on the opposite side of Ziegelstrasse. Most were damaged but in use still, their doors and windows either replaced or shuttered; but one narrow premises, flanked by a boot repair shop and a seamstress's (most non-food businesses in the city were salvage operations of some sort) remained forlornly gutted. He entered the gaping doorway and at the back of the first room found an almost-dry perch beneath a half-collapsed ceiling. The smashed frontage allowed him a good view of the alley's entrance across the road; he squatted down, removed a flask from his coat pocket and waited.

Six hours later he discovered the far boundary of his patience. Twice, he had been obliged to relieve himself almost *in situ* (the volume of noise from the boot repairer's told him that the party wall was wafer thin, so he was obliged to move as little as possible), and the smell of stale piss was taking the edge off the day's other delights. He was cold, damp, hungry and not at all certain that he wasn't wasting his time when he could have been sitting in a warm café, faithfully following Wolfgang's instructions to be a man of leisure; but the thing pressed like a needle under a fingernail, and until he could gauge its meaning he wouldn't sleep well. He forced himself to wait, willing something to happen.

By mid-afternoon he was dozing, and almost missed it. The thick-set fellow, the only one of the three without obvious war-wounds, came into view walking eastwards along Ziegelstrasse. At the alley's entrance he paused for a moment to check the view and then disappeared into it. With several moments' further acquaintance than previously, Rolf decided that he wouldn't have much of a chance against this one unless he caught him from behind, or in front a speeding truck. What little hair the fellow retained was silver, but his shoulders were massive and he moved economically, the way prize-fighters do when the opposition offers little threat. He was, or had been, someone - police perhaps, or political, military, criminal - and wasn't used to making himself smaller than he was. Whether this was good or bad Rolf couldn't say, but his instinct to move lightly put on its ballet shoes.

He had to wait only a few minutes more before the man reappeared carrying a suitcase. The view was given the same attention as before and then he retraced his path towards Friedrichstrasse. Within moments Rolf was out on the street, following at an inconspicuous distance, trying to affect the average Berliner's crushed indifference to anything but his own business. The rain was heavier now and he willed his prey to find his destination quickly, but their sodden passage became a minor odyssey, taking in the Charité, Invalidenstrasse and Alt-Moabit. His enthusiasm for the chase had just about expired when the man stopped on Putlitzstrasse, shook a pond's-worth of water from his coat and entered a shabby building. After a minute Rolf followed and glanced nonchalantly at the faded sign as he passed by. Though he doubted the place's claimed association with Gastein Spa it was undoubtedly a hotel, the sort that in former times had catered for the straitened budgets of commercial travellers, or men looking to pass a half-hour with pleasant, cheap company.

Rolf walked on, but more quickly. Within five minutes he was crossing Tiergarten, heading south, back towards Friedenau. He scarcely noticed the rain now; his mind was upon men who had business in the east but accommodation in the west, who moved confidently but carefully and always took care to know what was around them. He was new to this job, this world of sleights and misdirections, but he didn't need an expert eye to recognize that they occupied one of its hinterlands. The difficult part was to know what to do with the knowledge.

35

Müller tapped the table. 'Well, what do we have?'

Though he could recall every detail of what he had looked through three times now, Kalbfleisch made a show of consulting his papers.

'A former costermonger, war-invalided, and his wife; a part-time notary, widowed; a labourer, wife and two young children; a former butcher, war-invalided, with a wife and one young child; a prophet, single; a housewife, widowed; a pensioner, male, widowed.'

'What do these people have in common?'

'They each own, rent or squat in a property, and came home to a dead child.'

'Yes, thank you, Kalbfleisch. Otherwise?'

'They live in the same district, a small area falling across the border of southern Prenzlauer-Berg and northern Friedrichshain.'

'They do. Anything more?'

'They're on hard times, like most other Berliners. Only two of the households have a regular income at the moment, and in each case it won't be much. They're surviving on their ration cards and the occasional pension remittance.'

'I agree.' Müller took a sip of his *muckefuck*, winced and placed the mug carefully out of reach so as not to absent-mindedly repeat the error. 'Did you notice anything else during our interviews?'

'To be honest, no.'

Müller thought about not saying more. He couldn't find a way of putting it that didn't sound faintly absurd, the sort of observation that a diligent police officer wouldn't think of making. His advocate's training made him respect his feelings, however - it had been a vital part of his work to gauge how a client might behave in front of the Bench, given the very real damage it would do to a defence lawyer's career were the absurd process to wander from its script.

'Did you not think, Kalbfleisch, that these were all very … decent people?'

'Well, no one got his cock out, not even John the Baptist. And his kind …'

'Not that sort of *decent*. I mean … worthy.'

'I don't get you, comrade.'

Müller paused, and almost reached for the mug again. It *was* absurd, but he'd formed the same, strong impression as he spoke to all seven householders. None of them had been conspicuously virtuous (except the Baptist, obviously); nor had anyone adopted the better-than-the-rest air that any policeman had to endure during the making and taking of witness statements. He'd just had a feeling of *rightness* from all of them, a sense that they were fundamentally good folk struggling with the generally awful luck to be a German in 1947 and the specifically brutal ordeal of finding a murdered child in their home. It occurred to him only now that he hadn't remotely considered any of them to be a potential perpetrator, which was a surprising – even disgraceful – admission from an investigating officer.

'I *liked* them, Kalbfleisch.'

'Which ones?'

'All of them.'

'Even the Prophet?'

'He didn't berate us for our sins, did he? In fact, he made a point of stressing God's infinite mercy.' Müller started meaningfully at his subordinate. 'Even to the godless.'

'He saw right through me.'

'You made it fairly obvious. What I mean is, I could imagine finding the company of all or any one of them quite amenable. That's strange, isn't it? In seven households you'd expect to come upon at least one or two unpleasant temperaments, and several more – if not all the rest – who didn't make any impression one way or the other. But they all seemed like *fine* folk - to me, at least.'

Kalbfleisch sat up. 'And if you feel that way …'

'So could, or does, our monster. Which means …'

'He chose them. So he knows them.'

Muller swallowed hard to quell his stomach's lurch. 'He … oh God!'

'What?'

'He wanted the children to have good homes.'

'Jesus.'

'How were they found? They sat in chairs, or lay in bed, or squatted on the floor in front of where a radio would once have been. And in each case they were posed as carefully as rigor mortis permitted. We thought he was mocking us.'

'He made tableaux, like wax models.'

'Or offerings. Or commemorations.'

'How the hell do we investigate *this*? We need a mind-doctor.'

'We don't have to understand him, just find him. He knows these people, so he can't be a stranger to them.'

'We can't interview them again!'

'We must. I'll speak to the Commander, tell him what we think. If he likes it at least we're covered.'

Kalbfleisch looked uncomfortable, as if something with a sting was wriggling in his pants. 'May I say something, sir? In confidence?'

To Müller's knowledge he'd never used 'sir' before, and this alone made it too curious to forego. 'Of course, Kalbfleisch.'

'I don't feel *easy* about Comrade Beckendorp.'

'Why not?'

'He's a bad sort, a killer, they say. I know *VolksPolizei* have to take what's available these days, and that fellows who were strong *kozis* when it wasn't healthy to be so get preference. But the man's risen a long way on the back of some bad stories.'

'That's probably what they are – stories. You though that *I* was a Nazi bastard, didn't you?'

Kalbfleisch reddened. 'Not really. Just weak and complicit.'

'Well, I was both of those for sure. I don't believe it about Beckendorp, though. In fact, I find it hard sometimes to believe he wasn't a policeman by trade. He knows how to use what he has to the best effect, he doesn't bluster or admire himself in the uniform and he tries to attend as few meetings of his self-important colleagues as possible. That puts him in a minority of one among Berlin's *VoPo* hierarchy, in my view. But there, Kalbfleisch - you're safe now. I've just been as indiscreet as you.'

The older man grinned. 'So you don't think he's a police-murderer?'

'He's too comfortable in a policeman's skin to be that. Again, that's only my opinion. Don't forget, though, if it wasn't for Beckendorp we wouldn't be chasing a child-killer.'

36

'This is good work, Beckendorp.'

Freddie Holleman took the compliment as he imagined an arse-licking, Ivan-loving *kozi* might – with a serious frown, as upright a posture as he could manage from a deep armchair and a palpable keenness to have his strings pulled.

'Thank you, comrade.'

His Russian liaison officer scanned the names once more and didn't care to keep ash from falling on to the paper he'd been offered. Holleman had noticed already that for all the immaculate presentation this was not a professional soldier in anything but name - the man was too easy, too *at* ease in a uniform that was designed to strip the last molecule of individualism from its wearer. He looked much more like the obligatory, centrally-casted blonde, blue-eyed, square-jawed specimen memorizing lines for his next scene in *The Great Patriotic War*.

'These men have already been trained and briefed by Gehlen?'

'So I understand.'

'Fascists, presumably?'

'That I couldn't say. They don't like Socialism, obviously.'

Pretty Boy laughed. 'You mean Russians? Who could blame them? These addresses are current?'

This was the ugly bit. From WASt files, Fischer had pulled names of men who had fallen in the war's final months. Holleman – Beckendorp, that is – was presenting them as alive still. So, some parents were going to get the joyful news that their sons had been miraculously misidentified, and would soon be home.

'We can't say that all of them are, but ...'

'No, of course not. May I expect more names?'

'My man says that Gehlen plans to have a network of at least two hundred agents active in the SBZ within a year. He'll do his best.'

'Really? Your man ...?'

'Fischer. Otto Fischer.'

'Yes. You think his information is good?'

Holleman managed a shrug. 'He doesn't have any ideological attachments. In fact, I get the sense he resents his lack of juice at Oberursel. Gehlen's known to favour his old comrades from FHO and Abwehr, so promotion may be a problem.'

'Good. And you say he drinks?'

'A lot, and if you'd seen his wounds you'd understand why. Pecithin doesn't begin to do it.'

'Very well. Play on your friendship, give him support when he needs it – on his black days, I mean. He needs to know you're the one man he can trust.'

'But I'm not, am I?'

The Russian shrugged. 'It's not your fault that war did to him what it did. And he attempted to recruit you first, keep that in mind. When will you see him next?'

'I'm not sure, Comrade Major. He's gone back to Oberursel for the moment. It depends on when he returns.'

'Do you have a pigeon?'

'A what?'

'It's a phrase of our trade. I mean, is there a discreet line of communication between you that can be activated if necessary?'

'Yes, comrade. He checks the telegraph office at Frankfurt every two days and I do the same here. When he's in Berlin we both look into the Artists' Café on Dircksenstrasse daily. It's convenient for my office.'

'When he's at Oberursel use the telegraph occasionally. Make up a plausible reason why. Keep his nerve endings exposed. I don't want him to become too sanguine and make mistakes that Gehlen's people will notice.'

'Right.'

'Well, thank you, Beckendorp. This is a very good beginning. See yourself out, will you?'

Holleman departed Karlshorst's main administration building through its plain portico and limped to his car. His driver was leaning on its hood, smoking, giving as insolent an eye to passing Soviet soldiers as wouldn't earn him a deposit of *kirza* in his fundament. When he saw his boss his dropped the cigarette, crushed it and came to attention.'

'Keibelstrasse, Comrade Commander?'

It was a hint, and not subtle. The man should have waited for his instructions, obviously, but he was probably sick of being sent home alone and then required to retrace the route when Holleman's stump began to throb.

'Don't worry, Reinhardt. I've no intention of trying to walk five kilometres. Give me one of those coffin nails, there's a good fellow.'

He smoked it in the car, and only half-noticed the view along Wallensteinstrasse and Hönower Weg as they sped north-westward. It had gone as well as he could have hoped, and still his intestines were trying to impersonate the Cloaca Maxima. Every word he'd offered had been a lie, to a man who had the power to place him and his two closest friends where only burrowing creatures would ever find them. Worse, he was going to go back, again and again, to tell more lies. One of them, eventually, would ring an alarm, and probably he wouldn't even know which (unless his executioner was kind enough to put him right just before he put him very, very wrong). He was dancing across glass, and it made him more nervous than at any time since September 1943, when first he'd taken up the poisoned identity of Kurt Beckendorp and fled Berlin with his family.

As the car passed the half-shattered Rummelsburg marshalling yards he almost had his driver stop the car and surrender another cigarette; but he wrestled with his bowels and anxieties and brought them to a brief, exhausted truce. Either or both might have demanded a return bout had some miracle device allowed him to turn his gaze around and spy into the office he had departed minutes earlier. The Soviet officer sat at his desk still, the list of names in front of him on the desk. But his pale, clear complexion had darkened dramatically, his shoulders were shaking and he held a fist across his mouth to stifle what was sending tears flowing freely down his cheeks.

37

Gerhard Wessel stared at the paper as if an act of will could extract the verity of what he was reading. Branssler waited, making fists beneath the table, trying to breathe regularly.

The former general scratched his temple with a finger and looked up. 'Just five names?'

'And the eight he gave us last week, the men working at the old Lichterfelde kaserne.'

'Camp Andrews, please, Branssler. This isn't much, even if it's reliable'

'No, sir. But he was fortunate to get even this so quickly. He doesn't have direct access to Karlshorst except when he's summoned. It was luck, really. The Soviets have provided the Fifth Kommissariat with names of men who aren't to be looked at too closely when they pass through Berlin on their way back from the camps. Beckendorp heard about it over drinks with a buddy from the Fifth, almost drowned the guy in cheap booze and lifted a partial copy. It was a close shave, apparently.'

*Buddy ... guy ...close shave* - Branssler dropped the Americanisms casually, as sour as they tasted in his German mouth. He'd noticed a certain type here among Oberursel's virgin intake, reconciled already to the New Order and keen to make a place within it; they dressed like their off-duty American bosses, affected the same extroverted manner and were bilingual almost (though their English would have been incomprehensible to an Englishman). He wanted his bosses to think he was one of them, a looking-forward-not-back sort of *guy*.

Wessel didn't seem happy, but then he rarely did. Most people pursed their lips for a reason, but in his case it seemed to be their natural set, a mirror image of the frown that kept his eyebrows in a permanent crash-dive towards his nose.

'Why is Fischer acting as the lead contact?'

'We decided that together we were too conspicuous meeting Beckendorp on Soviet ground. Someone would notice, eventually.'

'Yes, I see that. But you're the senior man; surely …?'

'It's Beckendorp, sir. He has an amputee's fondness for his missing leg. It makes him maudlin, self-pitying even. We thought that Fischer's obviously worse war would work on him, open him up to a fellow victim. I was a civilian back then and he sees me as one now, whereas he and Fischer were both Luftwaffe. I don't believe I could gain his trust in the same way.'

'No, that's … correct.' The admission emerged with as much willingness as a head rising from a forward trench. 'So, these are men turned by the Soviets during their imprisonment.'

'Yes, sir. Vlasovs to a man.'

'Hardly. General Vlasov was a patriot who joined the anti-communist struggle from the best of motives. These are traitors, men who'd betray any principle for a few more calories.'

The sentiment was exactly what Branssler would have expected. It made him wonder what it was about Germans that allowed them to divide so fundamentally against themselves, take up far distant positions from compatriots with whom they stood cheek-to-jowl. Perhaps it was why the Americans were making so much better a job of appealing to the natives than the Russians – they shared the same view of the world as a pallet of purest black and white.

Wessel was staring at the names still. 'Very well. Clearly, we do nothing regarding these men when they return.'

'Don't we, sir?'

'If the information is good we don't want to poison the source. The moment we picked up one of them the Soviets would tear up the present scheme and start again, or at least redirect their lines of communication drastically. We shall interrogate them as with all such returnees and then monitor closely as they slip back into their domestic lives. The important thing is to be able to identify those who follow.'

'We're working on that, sir.'

'In what way?'

'Beckendorp's a political, stood for the SED in the April elections.'

'Yes, we know.'

'He didn't win that, obviously. Still, they can use him because although he's deep-dyed Red he's not one of their own, the Moscow exiles. They see him as a credible populist, something they haven't a hope of being mistaken for. He's more or less admitted to us that he owes his promotion to *Commandeur der VolksPolizei* to his work for the Party.'

'Of course he does. The whole system's a wen of corruption.'

'So Fischer and me think that a man with those credentials would be better suited to a role in the Fifth Kommissariat.'

A slight twitch ruffled Wessel's baked-on expression, a reaction that in anyone else might have been mistaken for an involuntary orgasm. When he cleared his throat Branssler knew that he was caught.

'How would you – he – manage that?'

'The hardest thing will be to persuade his present line of command to lose him. He's probably the most effective ranking *VoPo* officer in Berlin, though the competition isn't strong. If we could provide some form of nudge to make him seem the ideal candidate …?'

'A nudge?'

'A small coup, sir. Something only-just-redundant that we could offer him?'

'All that concerns K-5 is the enemy within, Branssler. We don't betray Germans.'

*Not unless they're on the other side you don't.* 'Of course not. But perhaps we could hand over information regarding Oberursel's structure? There were several plans for the organization that didn't get taken up, I think. The advantage would be that we're shining Beckendorp's resumé in K-5's eyes *and* misinforming them.'

'That would be the Americans' business and paperwork. I couldn't authorize it.'

'Well, something else then. What about giving him photocopies of the franks and stamps used by us for restricted matters?'

'You're joking, I assume?'

'No, sir. We alter them, very subtly. Then we'll have the ability to judge whenever one of our documents isn't, so to speak.'

Forgetting himself, Wessel nodded approvingly. 'It might be possible. But it – and any other suggestion, for that matter - relies upon something.'

'What's that, sir?'

'Convincing Karlshorst and K-5 that Beckendorp has a contact in Oberursel who's willing to betray his own kind.'

Relieved of having to point out precisely this, Branssler sat up. 'That's fine. Fischer's your man. He's a broken, bitter invalid with no sense of loyalty to anyone or anything.'

Briefly, the plummeting eyebrows went the other way. 'He's confident he could do this?'

'Oh yes, sir. The advantage of not really having a face is that no one can read it. He lets it speak for itself, and it does.'

'He'll be exposing himself considerably.'

'Until six months ago he lived in Stettin. I think he's used to worrying about his tomorrows.'

Wessel stared at Branssler, then the paper in his hand, and then the opposite wall of his office. No doubt he was thinking that it was a risky business - as, indeed, it was, but only for a man they had taken on less than two months earlier, a man who didn't belong to their old cadre of spies, a man in whom they had no great investment. For that modest outlay, Oberursel was being offered its first stab at a real penetration of the Karlshorst - Keibelstrasse axis, something Gehlen could present to the Americans like a prize gun-dog with a fat goose in its mouth.

'I'll speak to the General. You'll have a decision later today.'

Perhaps it was the tone, or something almost imperceptible, a there-and-gone in his superior's face, but Branssler allowed himself to hope that he, Fischer and Holleman had managed to close the loop. Even if they were being watched closely, nothing they did from now on would appear to be anything other than what they had promised. They would be seen only as pieces on a board, pretend-betrayers of their own for gain or under coercion, tasked with being disloyal as proof of their loyalty, feeding a two-way stream of make-believe with a helping pat on the back from men who knew that they were cleverer than those they manipulated. Disinterred, brushed down and taking up its sharpened pencils, the Lie Division had been stood-to.

38

*Otto, Darling, you mustn't worry about me! The two girls are here most days (I pay them a little to help me with the laundry, so I'm an employer now!), and Earl is sweet enough to let Beulah May stay with me often. I have enough money and the weather's getting warmer. I miss you too much!*

*M-T.*

Fischer re-read the letter for the fourth time, Apart from its heroic brevity the same phrase leapt out at him each time. *Why should I be worrying? What's happened?*

The other letter offered no enlightenment. Earl Kuhn's aborted education, his early flight from orphanage life and the distractions of his subsequent career as a small-time villain had taken a club to his literary style - it read as a disjointed conversation, the sort he might have had with himself on a slow trade day, and gave only an up-to-the-moment survey on what continued to ail the recorded Jazz market in contemporary Bremen. At least it ended with hopes for Fischer's success and safe-keeping, something his wife seemed to have taken as read.

*Was she eating enough? Being chased by GIs? Christ, had some desperate situation forced her back on to the streets?* It took a great effort of will to calm himself. Earl would have let him know, put more in his letter than a protracted lament about how month-long military manoeuvres had stolen ninety percent of his customer base. At the least, he would have hinted that his friend should come home for a few days and then given him the bad news when he was in a position to deal with it.

Fischer was beginning to feel that marriage was an institution for kinder, gentler times. A man's daily preoccupations shouldn't include having to worry whether his spouse was alive, ravished or working the GI trade, not when the rest pressed like a falling wall. Had he and Maria-Therese been younger they would at least have had a rationale for it - to breed, to make good Germany's manpower losses in time for the next one. But he was certain that his loins, ever reluctant to pass on anything infectious, had now excused themselves anything other than recreational duties. They had married for love alone, in an age that penalized sentiment.

He pondered his estate on a low, uneven wall opposite the mobile post-office. The van had been there almost an hour, yet the queue's far end showed no sign of appearing from around the corner of Thomasius-Strasse. Many of those in it were as smartly dressed as Berliners could be, decked out in their best as if posting or collecting a letter was a form of human interaction and not just the means of it. He admired their spirit, the effort they made to pretend the ruins away.

Her letter begged a fifth reading but he folded it carefully, placed it in his pocket and thought about *time* once more. Time was the currency with which he'd bribed his two friends to undertake this, but he feared he'd overplayed it. He didn't believe that either Gehlen's people or the Fifth Kommissariat would remain content with a slow, steady stream of dead men's names. They would nod, say *well done* and then demand more, and more dangerously-acquired, material - because they were servants too, of masters who were determined to take an early lead in a new game in which the foot-soldiers, Germans all, were by far the most expendable pieces on the board. He'd had a good idea, and it wasn't going to be enough. He couldn't imagine what sort of data would keep them happy for longer than it took them to chase the dead men. And he certainly couldn't conceive how he and Branssler and Holleman might identify, much less acquire, it.

He had started something that had no viable ending. It was a pause only, offering a small chance to escape the trap they'd fashioned for themselves and then going to ground, or running. All over Europe, men who had committed acts beyond the power of God to forgive were finding safe haven and then safe passage; a few of the unluckiest had been caught, displayed and executed, but many more had been ignored or overlooked until it was too late, until they had found new homes at the other side of a world that pretended to want them extinct. Fischer and his friends had gone the other way, had emerged from the war as blameless as any three male Germans could be and then marched resolutely towards the guns. They needed urgently to learn from the sinners.

The thing was, bad people had friends, fellow travellers, an organization of willing colluders and the resources to turn better men's eyes from the holes into which they scurried. The Lie Division's predicament was a different sort of *hole*, one that was full already, its three occupants tightly wedged, and the only resources they could call upon were in the hands of the men they were trying to escape. He regretted now having teased Holleman about pushing him through the underground escape system. It existed, it seemed to be working, and it was far beyond the mortal power of Otto Fischer to access.

*You did it once - you erased a family*. For a moment he almost allowed the possibility. Neither the Americans nor Russians and their respective German proxies had nearly the same iron grip upon their subject population as had National Socialism; yet four years earlier he had manipulated the system to remove the Hollemans from its one fundamental plane of existence - the paperwork. Why should it be more difficult to do it once more, and for Kurt Beckendorp, a man who didn't actually exist?

The obvious answer came quickly, and hard. *Because paper proves nothing any more.* The very fact that documentation was so inadequate now was all that allowed him and his friends to create a plausible fiction from dead soldiers. From being the proof that a man existed at all it had become a debased, damaged, unreliable guide to who was who - if, indeed, someone was anyone at all. Almost by definition, good paper had to be forged paper, and if Holleman tried to disappear with yet another new identity, half of Germany's fledgling secret services would plunge after Kurt Beckendorp with only the man in mind, not his ID card. Even in a smashed nation, he doubted the ruins were plentiful enough to make a hiding place.

He sat on his broken little wall, watching people queuing to discover whether they had families still, and knew that he'd come to the limits of his cleverness. Holleman had been right - none of them understood nearly enough about the game to play it with any chance of escaping a beating. In a while - probably a very brief while - something they did would stir attention at Oberursel or Karlshorst, ring the wrong bell, and people who understood the rules very well would say to themselves that they had a small problem, one that needed to be excised smartly. Three bullets and a spade would do the job, and the trickiest part thereafter would be drafting the report. His *kripo* department at Stettin had shared a floor with Gestapo, and he'd known men who did that sort of work. Their skills rarely extended to touch-typing.

The worst of it was, the spikes at the bottom of the pit were his invention. He was almost certain that Holleman's 'pretty' MGB handler was former NKGB lieutenant Sergei Zarubin, the one person on this continent who could kick away the final leg of his composure, a man fond of taking a dense tangle and weaving something Gordian from it. He had been given Fischer's description and name yet done nothing more than to play the game as it had been put to him. He might easily have had Freddie Holleman followed and arranged a quiet, discreet pick up at what Fischer and Branssler fondly regarded as their safe-house; he might, even more easily, have arranged for several grams of standard issue Soviet small arms munitions to be transferred to their heads in an alleyway and congratulated himself upon a minor irritation, expertly quashed. But these were standard options, the expected moves in a short game, and Zarubin didn't play that way. He would examine the terrain more carefully than a diamond dealer looking for flaws in the product, calculate every permutation of stab and consequence and then do whatever amused him the most. In Stettin he had played his German hostage expertly, teasing, tormenting and herding him towards a goal that hadn't been remotely in sight until he'd fallen into it head first. By God's grace or whim Fischer had survived that, but now his brilliant plan for making Holleman valuable to his own people had placed all of them squarely back in Zarubin's sights

His mind churned on, trying to find something new in a dozen dead-ends. Since leaving the luxurious confines of the *Bad Gastein* an hour ago it had bounced between Berlin and Maria-Therese, so even had his skills as a ghost – a *spook* - been more refined he wouldn't have noticed the man who followed him from the hotel and now stood directly across Alt-Moabit at the south-eastern corner of Kleiner Tiergarten. On a working day he wore a grey suit but no tie and stood easily, leaning against a small portion of surviving railings, close enough to an omnibus-post not to draw attention to his lingering. A copy of the previous day's *Berliner*

*Morgenpost* concealed most of his face without impede his view. On a stretch of road that was never quiet during daylight, framed by the vast rubble pile of the Johanniskirsche, field camouflage couldn't have made him less conspicuous.

A shadow passed in front of Fischer, rousing him from his trance. A smart young woman was looking down at him, though not with the usual half-horrified expression spoiling her pretty face. She held out her hand and pressed something into his, squeezed his shoulder and walked away without a word. He didn't know her, but would have put ... he glanced at what was in his hand - an Allied five-mark note on there having been tears in her eyes. It almost raised his spirits, to wonder if the Age of Self was passing already.

But not quite. He pocketed his unwanted wealth, stood up and thought about the coming day, one that held nothing – literally, nothing – more than a block of hours in which he would await news. Holleman and Branssler were elsewhere, testing their superiors' gullibility with lists of dead men, and that was all there was to be done for the moment. The third member of their fraternity of misinformers – their in-house mastermind - was reduced to considering a perambulation, a day of sight-seeing, a diversion that, in modern Berlin, consisted of asking oneself, over and over, *didn't that used to be ...?* and *wasn't that where ...?*

He walked southward, into the Tiergarten. At least its few remaining trees bore leaves still, and if he couldn't walk upon the grass (grass having been declared obsolete by the British and thousands of allotments decreed in its place) the absence of rubble made a mere 200 hectares seem even more remote from their city than when both had been plentiful.

As he walked he examined the struggling crops with interest, as someone who'd recently considered the business professionally. Men and women, their coats discarded in the warming air, worked the plots, their backs tensing instinctively as he passed by. He could hardly take offence - their produce was soiled gold, worth killing for or to defend. Again, he noticed the relative neatness of their clothes, but wondered this time what possible convention required digging to be undertaken to a certain sartorial standard. And then the obvious, crushingly simple answer occurred to his dull mind. These people, the ones cueing for the post - even, perhaps, his pretty young Samaritan - weren't trying to be elegant in adversity; they were wearing all that remained of their wardrobes, their last and best, the items they'd expected to be buried in.

The thought brought him further down than anything he'd seen since returning to the city, and he quickened his pace until he was out of the gardens, across Tiergartenstrasse and into embassy land, the ghost-strip of fine buildings that now lacked a Germany with which to maintain diplomatic relations. It probably wasn't the best place to restore his morale, but at least the only human footprint here was that of foreign nationals guarding their redundant piece of home turf. It was quieter, emptier, less obviously Berlin.

Yet still the thoughts crowded, distracting him, making the work of the man who followed him – a man as unused to the business of subterfuge as was his target – much less difficult than it should have been. By the time that Fischer passed the ruins of the *Matthaikirche* and turned into Margaretenstrasse they were barely ten metres apart, but when the man in grey realised where this stroll was going he almost stopped. It took a great effort to follow further, into Potsdamer-Platz and the Soviet Zone.

He had already guessed their destination. Fischer paused at the end of Leipzigerstrasse, leaned against a half-demolished lamp-post and stared up at the vast, near-intact *Reichsluftfahrtministerium* – the old Air Ministry. As he did so his shadow slipped into the ruined courtyard of the Ministry's neighbour, the Prussian Upper House, and pressed himself against the wall. He couldn't be seen there but neither could he see his mark, his target. He closed his eyes, breathed more slowly and forced himself to think about what he was doing, why he was there. His hand touched his jacket, felt the shape of the knife beneath it, and he knew that a decision had to be made, quickly. He forced himself to move, back out on to Leipzigerstrasse.

Fischer was gazing still at the vast flank of his old workplace, recalling the statistics once self-consciously displayed in its Hall of Honour - seven storeys, almost three thousand rooms, seven kilometres of corridor (Christ, he recalled tramping most of them), a total floor-print of 112,000 square metres, the largest office space in all Europe. No doubt the Americans had plenty that were larger (and almost as ugly), but none with such a weight of wonderful, undeserved good fortune baked into their marble slabs.

He had taken up the job here when his wounds were fresh and cripplingly painful, yet his time as second-in-command of the War Reporters' Unit had been the happiest of his professional life. Here, he hadn't been required to investigate and chase the worst of what people did, hadn't been invited to kill or be killed under the authority of the State, hadn't been a shabby, starving pariah, something to scrape from a conqueror's boot. His sole duty had been to construct absurdly pleasing fantasies from depressing facts, and for that he had drawn a hauptmann's (later major's) salary, been allowed to billet in civilian quarters and enjoyed the company of men who cared as much for the triumph of National Socialism as himself. He doubted that the Führer's pastry chef had been more pleasantly burdened.

SVAG were inside these days, of course. They probably didn't have any real use for the building (Karlshorst was quite commodious enough), but an undamaged bureaucratic palace so close to the city's demarcation line made a fine point about putting down roots, getting feet firmly under the table. Besides, they needed the top storey to get a glimpse of the monument to their fallen dead that they'd inexplicably built in the British Zone before withdrawing. It made him smile, that other nations could make doltish decisions too.

He recalled the outright, brazen lies he and his colleagues had written here, the hilarious exchanges as they read aloud their efforts, the long afternoons in the *Silver Birch*, the drunken staggers back to the office to hide under a desk as the RAF dropped their loads upon everyone but them, and almost wished it all back again. Memory was treacherous, and a time in which the entire German world had begun to topple couldn't have been as rose-strewn as he recalled. But a sense of unreality could be an opiate, a balm, plate armour against what was coming. It had been that way for the Reich's leaders; why not its walking wounded?

The movement, at the extreme right periphery of his vision, was slight but enough to puncture his trance. He stepped back hastily, lifting his bad arm to ward off a blow. The assault fell upon his shoulder instead, far too lightly to be meant as one. He turned and stared at the man dressed in grey, his shadow, and old memories converged jarringly.

'My God!'

39

Despite his naturally lugubrious nature, Müller had spent the better part of the morning feeling as pleased with the world as any Berliner might. A note had been tacked to his desk when he arrived, requiring him to 'pop his head' into Commander Beckendorp's office before throwing himself into the day's work. He had almost lost his breakfast at that, but the man rumoured once to have been a merciless killer had opened his door personally rather than bark an order to enter, invited him in as pleasantly as any man in the uniform might and actually smiled when he offered the good news.

*Unterkommissar* – confirmed, not provisional - a three-step-at-once promotion and a strong vote of confidence, putting him on the first draft of Berlin *VolksPolizei*'s restored criminal investigations department. He was too cynical to be proud, too weary to be enthusiastic, but there it was – for the first time in his life merit, rather than a professional qualification and the right contacts, had raised him.

He was almost as pleased with his own, first reaction to the news. He had insisted that he *must* have Kalbfleisch with him still – demanded it, in fact, and of Beckendorp for God's sake! His Commander had stopped him with a hand, shown him the paper promoting his subordinate to *Wachtmeister der VolksPolizei*, effective from that day, and sent him off to give the old man the good word.

Kalbfleisch had taken it emotionally, which is to say that his eyebrows rose, the cigarette almost fell out of his mouth and he shook the messenger's hand with a grip that had lost twenty years in a moment. When he found his voice it was unsteady.

'Good fellow, the Commander.'

'Didn't you say that he was a monster?'

'Mere gossip, Comrade *Unterkommissar*. I only repeated it because it was interesting.'

'He told me that he made the recommendations personally.'

'So now we'll *have* to solve this thing, won't we?'

Müller's fine mood dampened slightly. 'I asked him about my – *our* - training. He told me that this was it.'

'The interviews, then. Who do we see next?'

The previous day they had visited the homes of three of the recipients of their killer's work. An hour with each, prying into the smallest detail of their movements, habits and associations had given them no coincidences, no patterns, no inspiration. They had four more to see, and though the former job description for an *unterkommissar* had been lost and the new one was yet to be written, Müller was certain that the ideal officer didn't shrink from the difficult ones but advanced towards them, fearlessly. He sighed. 'Let's get John the Baptist over with.'

They arrived at their witness's home (a storage shed in Lippehnerstrasse, formerly attached to a kindergarten that Soviet ordnance had relocated) as he was about to depart upon his day's work among the Fallen. With good grace he agreed to a third interrogation and offered them tea, which turned out to be an almost drinkable reduction of nettles and St John's Wort.

As he was preparing it, Müller gave the shed more of his attention than during his previous visit. Like most German domestic environments it was bare, though here the emptiness seemed intentional rather than the result of unofficial reparations. There was a bed pallet but no linen, a stand chair without a table to keep it company and a wardrobe that consisted of a short pole placed upon two rusting wall brackets. On it, a lonely clothes hanger moved slightly still, presumably having only recently relinquished the tenant's only outfit.

Which remained a disappointment. At their first meeting Müller had hoped for a loincloth or at least the promised blanket and sandals, but he realised that Kalbfleisch had been pulling his leg. The prophet's attire was conventional, if simple - a thick worker's shirt, heavy trousers and stout but quite spectacularly battered boots. Today the shirt's left sleeve was rolled up far enough to reveal the Baptist's (*Herr Bosch's*, Müller corrected himself) Waffen SS blood-group tattoo.

Kalbfleisch coughed. 'Better not show that off, comrade.'

Their host glanced down and smiled placidly. 'Shame should be looked upon, not hidden.'

'Yes, but *looking* might not stop at a kicking. What if some Ivan's favouritie brother got it from your lot and he decides to ease his pain?'

Bosch shrugged. 'I talk to them, tell them who I am. They don't hurt me.'

Müller glanced at his colleague. Perhaps, like native Americans, the simpler Soviet soldiers feared and respected insanity, or considered it adequate retribution.

'May we speak about your schedule, Herr Bosch?'

'Again?'

'I know, it's tiresome. But we don't believe that you and the others who reported these incidents are unconnected.'

'I speak to everyone and know no one, not in Berlin.'

'It may not be a case of acquaintance. Perhaps you share something else.'

'Whoever has two tunics is to share with him who had none, and whoever has food is to do likewise.'

'Yes, quite. Shall we walk through your day, so to speak? I mean your route, your usual or unusual encounters - perhaps any singular events?'

Bosch sighed. 'We live in the final times. All things are coming to their conclusion. I walk, I try to talk to people, to warn them of what they need to do.'

Müller was mildly curious. 'How do they take that?

'As people do, differently. Most ignore me and walk on quickly. A few stop and listen, and argue. Some ...'

'Yes?'

Bosch shook his head.

Kalbfleisch glanced at his boss, asking permission. 'Forgive me, Herr Bosch, but how do earn money?'

'I don't.'

'Surely you need to eat, and meet your rent, and ...'

'I rarely eat. And what remains of this building belongs to the Education Ministry, or whatever's followed it. No one's ever asked me for rent.'

Muller was beginning to lose hope for this particular interrogation. 'Come now, everyone eats. You don't look to be too undernourished.'

Bosch shrugged again. 'I rely upon kindness. It's wonderful that charity flowers in the general want.'

Kalbfleisch snorted. 'It's necessary, certainly. If it wasn't for the missions half the people in this city would have starved this last winter.'

Müller almost left the floor. *Food.* More than any other element of life, the matter of nourishment occupied the waking thoughts of Berliners – what, where, how much, how often. In a city lacking intact churches, nightlife, entertainment, organized sports or political rallies the only occasion upon which people came together regularly was to ease the pain in their bellies. Yet they almost never spoke of it. Pride made them ashamed of their need - they wanted to see themselves as they were, not as they had become. Eighteen months earlier, Müller himself, out of work and desperate, had been obliged to take his family to a local *volksküche* for their one daily meal, a wretched ordeal that had lasted several weeks. Even now his wife wouldn't speak of it, wouldn't allow house-room to the memory of their *shame*. He and Kalbfleisch had interrogated their witnesses about every aspect of their domestic arrangements but not put the question specifically, allowing the matter of sustenance to be answered by shrugs and variations upon *we manage*.

Of the seven witnesses, only one - the widowed notary – potentially had the means to support himself adequately. The others were unemployed or invalided, and several had families to share their good fortune. These were not people who could refuse help, whatever they thought of it.

'Where do you accept this kindness, Herr Bosch?'

'Wherever I happen to be when it's available. I walk the streets, as I said.'

'Do you have a regular circuit?'

'I try to go as far as possible, but the soldiers …'

The more you walked the more you were likely to be stopped by patrols who wanted to know your business. If Bosch was a source of entertainment – and to soldiers and the *VolksPolizei* he must have been – it would be a time-consuming business, an impediment to spreading the good word.

'Tell us your usual routes, and the places where you take food most often.'

Restraining his impatience, Müller waited while Kalbfleisch painstakingly wrote down the details of Bosch's meandering routes. The prophet named four places, all Inner Missions, where hot, basic food was available on several days or evenings each week; all of them were within a half-kilometre of his cellar, and of Friedrichshain Park. When he'd finished, Kalbfleisch passed the notes to his boss.

Muller glanced at the four locations. 'One of our other witnesses assists at a local mission sometimes. Do we know which one?'

'Frau Betelmann? The one on Pasteurstrasse, I think.'

Müller returned the notebook and picked up his cap. 'Alright. We're going back to the three we've just re-interviewed and then we'll question the remaining three. And we're going to insist that they not be shy about where they're taking the help of others.'

The sun was setting that evening when they returned to Keibelstrasse, to the second-floor cupboard designated as their office. Both men were trying not to feel too pleased with themselves.

Kalbfleisch sat in his chair and ran a sheet of paper into their new, very old typewriter. 'Do we go to the Commander with this, comrade?'

'As soon as you've typed it.'

'He'll be pleased, won't he?'

'He'll frown at it, sniff like a ripe turd's wandered beneath his nose and then say *this isn't fucking much, is it?* So yes, he'll be pleased.'

'And this is our first day doing *kripo* work proper. We've already earned our promotions.'

Müller stood down his smile. 'We received them from Beckendorp personally, which means we'll be earning them still when Herr Bosch's prophecies comes to pass.'

40

On Tuesday morning Rolf went to the Ambassador Café early and waited. He got a single, morose nod from the fat proprietor, who pocketed the dollar bill and brought a thick slice of almond-covered *butterkuchen* to the table. It looked disgusting, the sort of thing Frau Best would kill for. He slipped it into his pocket and tried to drink his *muckefuck*.

Three other patrons were in the café at 10.45am when the door opened and Wolfgang shuffled in, making smoke like *Prinz Eugen* had found his range. He ordered a drink at the counter, drank it there in a few gulps then departed without another word. Rolf forced himself to wait a further five and then followed.

'What are you doing here? Didn't I tell you to wait until we had orders?'

They stood on Cranachstrasse once more, facing eastwards towards the allotments and Nathanaelkirche. It was a bright, fresh day, something that the mixture in Wolfgang's pipe was doing its best to spoil. He seemed peevish, a man whose schedule had been trifled with and then stamped upon.

'You did. But this is important, something you've got to get back to the Russians. I've met someone who knows me from the old days.'

'Am I invited to the wedding?'

'Be serious. This man is an old comrade. We served in the same regiment.'

'You were friends?'

'No. We met only on two occasions that I recall, but the first was in the middle of a close-fight, and that sort of thing sticks in a memory.'

'Don't worry about it. It was always likely that you'd trip over someone from your past. I assume you gave him an adequate story?'

'I told him that I was working for the Americans, as a clerk and translator. It's what he said to me that's important.'

'What?'

'That he works for the Americans too.'

'So do many other Germans. It's how the world is these …'

'He works for the Americans, at Oberursel.'

An instinctive twitch of Wolfgang's left hand caught his falling pipe. 'He *told* you that?'

'He's worried. He thinks he's got himself too deeply into some shit and can't see the way out. Listen, Wolfgang, he told me that he's turned a fellow in the SED, a *VoPo* commander no less. The thing is, to do it he's had to pretend that *he's* the turncoat, the traitor - that he's supplying intelligence to be passed on to Karlshorst, but really it's all worthless. If it goes wrong – and he's sure it will - he won't know who's going to take the first shot, the Americans or the Russians.'

Wolfgang whistled between his teeth. 'Stupid sod. What's his name?'

'Fischer. Otto, I think. Like me, he was in *Fallschirmjäger* I Regiment.'

'I'll need a description.'

'Half his face is missing, his right shoulder sinks badly and the right hand's a bird's claw. Apart from that he's fairly anonymous.'

'This is good, mate.'

'It's something that SVAG would want, isn't it?'

'*Want*? They'll be on it like dogs on to a rat, except they won't chew him up all at once. I almost pity him and the *VoPo* bastard he's working.'

'I ...'

'You what, Rolf?'

'I don't know if this is right, but I arranged to see him again – to have a drink and talk about better times, you know?'

'That's exactly what you should have done. Whatever Karlshorst decides, keeping contact is vital. But be careful - don't ask more questions than a friend would. Keep it personal, keep him at ease, and if he wants to talk about things we'd like to hear just let him do it at his own pace.'

'What if he wants to know more about me?'

'Invent it. It isn't as though he's going to check the detail. What name did you give him?'

'My real one. *That's* something he could confirm from Luftwaffe records ...'

'Fine. If he hears differently from someone else, well, there are plenty of Germans with good enough reason to get a new name these days. Now, I have to be gone. Come back to the café on Thursday and we'll talk more.'

'Are you going to pass this along today?'

Wolfgang pocketed his pipe. His body was overweight and shabby as always, but it moved now as if a considerable electrical charge had been applied.

'This isn't a matter to *pass along*. We're told to report directly when something big happens, and I haven't seen anything bigger.'

'You'll go to Karlshorst?'

The old man grinned. 'Getting in's no problem, they say. In fact, I doubt there's anywhere east of Potsdammer-Platz that's more welcoming. The problem is getting out again.'

When Wolfgang had disappeared around the corner of Rubens-Strasse, Rolf turned and signalled with a hand. A block north, the boy emerged from a doorway and ran to him. He looked nervous.

'What did you do, Rolf?

'I just betrayed someone. A comrade.'

'That's wrong, isn't it?'

'Yes, it is. But it's a sort of wrong that's the new fashion. Good and bad, they don't work anymore.'

Engi considered this. His dim memories of *her* were filled with dos and don'ts, rights and wrongs, good and bad, heaven and hell and why a little boy should choose carefully. 'Why not?'

'Because no one can know which is which anymore. We can only try to do what's right for us.'

41

Room 34 of the Hotel *Bad Gastein* contained twin beds, a small table with a washbowl upon it and a console whose sole drawer contained a much-thumbed copy of the Dore Bible. The decor was equally modest. The wallpaper's Second Empire pattern was slightly misaligned from roll to roll, and a corner piece descended slightly as if inviting a guest to examine the only piece of artwork in the room, a journeyman daubing of a Black Forest glade. In his waiting hours, Fischer had memorized its every crude stroke.

He was looking at it once more as Branssler gave him the bad news.

'Wessel wants Freddie to give us K-5's structure.'

'How detailed?'

'Names, who reports to whom, departments, responsibilities, and, if possible, present operations.'

'Christ.'

'I almost said that when he told me.'

'And how does Freddie do this, exactly?'

Branssler shrugged. 'Wessel doesn't care how. He just told me – us – to push hard, and quickly.'

'I know we're pretending to put Freddie into K-5, but how the hell do they think he'll get this stuff before that happens?

'He's a senior *VoPo* officer. K-5 are nominally a *VoPo* department. That's close enough for Wessel.'

The Fifth Kommissariat was a new organization, perhaps 2 months old, an infant struggling to find its legs, but Fischer was certain that it had enough weight to land heavily upon any irritation that nipped its arse. And it worked closely with MGB – hell, it was MGB's domestic arm - which meant that Freddie Holleman was going to be squashed.

Fischer shook his head. 'It's my fault. I thought to dangle the idea in the first place.'

'Come on, Otto, we all agreed it. But Freddie's been right from the start – we don't know enough about this business to see when we're being clever or very stupid. Whatever we gave them, we *knew* that they'd push for more and at their pace, not ours. It's like we were at the top of a steep hill, sitting in a kid's cart, looking down at where we wanted to be. Once you release the handbrake there's no knowing where the fucking thing's going to end up.'

'Who would have this information? MGB, obviously, and *VoPo* themselves. Who else?'

'Who do *VoPo* fall under? That's the Soviet's pet Interior Administration – *DvdI* - isn't it?'

'I think so.'

'Freddie's well thought of by our native *kozis*, isn't he? He might be safer, have more reason, to try to access the information through *DVdI*.'

'I don't know, Gerd. It's getting too far from us. Freddie might be safer if he's just honest about this.'

'Honest?'

'He goes straight to his Soviet handler and repeats, word for word, what we're asking him to do.'

'*What?*'

'He tells them the truth - that his mate Otto Fischer has been ordered by Oberursel to get everything he can on K-5. What would they do?'

It was Branssler's turn to examine the Black Forest. 'They'd … give it to him.'

'They would, yes. It would be manipulated, spoiled, twisted, but again, he – and we – would be doing our jobs, acquiring information and passing it on. How could we know that the data was wrong?'

'They – I mean *our* people – will end Freddie when they find out.'

'It's going to take a while to be proved wrong, perhaps a great while. In the meantime I've thought of something that we need to chase, a possible way out.'

Fischer noticed Branssler's wince. 'I don't mean another too-clever idea. This is something more fundamental. We decided that Freddie couldn't run, didn't we?'

'He can't. Kurt Beckendorp would be exposed immediately as a ghost, and …'

'I know - he can't run as Kurt Beckendorp. But we've been so tied up in lies that we forgot to think straight. What if Beckendorp doesn't matter anymore? What if Freddie ran as Freddie?'

'If …?'

'As Friedrich Holleman and family, I mean?'

'How could that happen?'

'Four years ago, when Freddie became Beckendorp, I took the best care I could to erase Holleman – his *soldbuch*, *volkscarten*, everything. If I did it correctly, it's as though he never existed. If we resurrect him and he disappears west to the French Zone, how would they begin to follow? It would look as though a very frightened Kurt Beckendorp had fled – well, *somewhere*. In which case, a very pettish Oberursel would slip their damning information about him to the Russians, who would ... what? Beckendorp would be gone like a fart in a gale – which is what he is, really - never to reappear. Neither Gehlen nor the Americans have anyone in the Saar, much less the Russians. It could work. If Beckendorp disappears the nice house, the steady job and the pension go with him, but Freddie's going to be more interested in keeping his family above ground.'

'What about us? We've got family, too.'

'It's going to be painful. We'd have to admit to our bosses that we abjectly failed to anticipate Beckendorp's bolt. Then we do the decent thing, offer our resignations, and with a little luck they'll reassign us to eavesdropping on hotel rooms and station lavatories. If Karlshorst ever decided to return the favour and implicate me in the double-dealing I'd raise my hands and say *yes, it's what I pretended, to get more out of Beckendorp. But if I truly was in the Russians' pocket would they have betrayed me to you?*'

Branssler frowned, trying to see every side of it. 'You said *chase*. Chase what?'

'What dragged us all into this in the first place – the unforeseen. Before we try any of this, we – you – need to find out if Oberursel have anything on one Friedrich Holleman, something that I missed back in '43.'

'Like what?'

'How would I know, if I missed it?'

'Jesus, Otto, I can't just walk into the archives. I'd have to open my mouth, ask the question, and then they'd say *why? Why do you need to see this? What is it that you know?*'

Fischer rubbed his face. 'It's a risk, yes. But if they have nothing on Freddie you should be able to shrug it off, or make up something they won't care to follow. If they *do* have something then we're all against the wall anyway.'

'Aren't you worried about any of this?'

'Like a child in the dark.'

Branssler sighed. 'Me too. You know what it is, Otto? You shouldn't have married, or made friends. It's what I've been telling myself for years. When you're on your own there's no problem that can't be solved with a bullet. But when you're dragging baggage, an armoury's not enough.'

'I never thought of you as baggage, Gerd. Leathery, perhaps, and somewhat commodious.'

The big man laughed, the way that Fischer recalled his *Fallschirmjäger* comrades did at some pathetic quip a few moments before jumping from their glider – without conviction but grateful for the distraction. It lasted about as long, and then the frown returned.

'Do we tell Freddie?'

'Of course we do. If it comes to nothing it doesn't matter, but if it can be done he needs to be ready.'

'How would we get him out?' How many kilometres – how many *people* - are there between Marzahn and the French Zone?'

Fischer said nothing, because nothing came to his bruised mind. He was emptied, flushed clean of inspiration, twitching rather than scheming. Getting Freddie to the west was a lurch in lieu of a strategy, the moment at which, in a military campaign, one begged to be allowed the sort of withdrawal that counted as an evacuation. But this was a different sort of war, a clash of minds, and when his last wild shot went absurdly wide his friends would look to him still, trusting his cleverness, confident that he had something else, ready to be produced with a flourish. It was a too-apt metaphor – he was an illusionist with a slowing hand and a heart fearful of the trick being spotted.

'We'll think of something, even if it's to put him in *baggage* and drag him there.'

42

Müller stood to attention. Beside him, Kalbfleisch made the effort, but his body hadn't been designed for it. His shoulders went back and the belly protruded to compensate, as if awaiting inspection by the third man in the room.

Commander Beckendorp took his time to read the report. A cup of tea sat beside his right hand. Twice he reached for it without taking his eyes from the page but it remained there, untouched, cooling. When he'd finished he placed the paper carefully on the desk, stood up and went to the window, his back to the audience.

Müller wasn't going to be the one to break the silence he desperately wanted broken. He was confident that they'd done a good job, but the *VolksPolizei* was a young organization, with rules that hadn't yet solidified into something one could be sure of having conformed to or transgressed. Had he shown sufficient initiative or too much? Made progress or trod on toes? The longer Beckendorp gave them the Trappist treatment the less certain he was that a *good job* was necessarily a good thing.

Their Commander turned to face them. 'Excellent work, lads. You're sure about it?'

'Yes, Comrade Commander. With one exception, the witnesses attend the Pasteurstrasse mission at least once each week. The seventh is a volunteer worker there. She serves the food. Therefore, it seems probable that the killer also attends the mission, or works there.'

Beckendorp sniffed. 'Not a customer, I'd say.'

'May I ask …?'

'He not only knew when they'd be at the mission but where they live. As to the first, he would only need to see them turn up and then go off to do the business. But to know *where* to do it he would have had to have followed them all previously, or have the information to hand. Pasteurstrasse is a licenced mission, isn't it?'

'Yes, comrade.'

'Which means that people eating there have to produce their papers and hand over ration cards. That's a far more likely way of getting an address. It gives us another possibility.'

'The information is recorded and collated, so he might be *VolksPolizei*, or someone at the Food Commission.'

'Very good, Müller. Either way, we aren't there yet. You know that you're going to be spending considerable time at Pasteurstrasse?'

'We assumed so, Comrade Commander.'

'In plain clothes, obviously. Try to look hungry. In the meantime I'll get a list of who sees and processes the details of people visiting licenced missions and *volkskuchen*. That's it. Dismissed.'

When the door had closed Freddie Holleman almost smiled. It was a rare day when good work earned more than a sense of running on the spot. Even if the perpetrator turned out to be an untouchable, hunting him down would give everyone at Keibelstrasse a feeling that they were more than time-servers. The list of what they lacked was depressingly long, and right at the top of it was *morale*. A good method-murderer case, swiftly solved - they might just start to think of themselves as real police.

At ten am he told his secretary that he was making a surprise inspection of nearby stations, put on his plain overcoat and walked, via several side-tracks, to the Artists Café in Dircksenstrasse, a small, bohemian-shabby establishment almost opposite what had been the rear façade of Police Headquarters, Alexanderplatz. He sat at a table for almost half an hour, taking in what was left of that infamous building, his mind's-eye following Gerd Branssler in the old days, staggering back to his office after a lunchtime bender, using the same back alley where his partner had been gunned down early in 1945. The memory took him further back, to his own *OrPo* days before the war, when he'd worn down the surface of every road, street and alley around here and north into Wedding, stopping fights, banging heads, calming old dears, pretending to note down blockhilfers' little betrayals when all he'd wanted to do was shove his *schlagstock* up their …

Fischer was in the seat opposite before Holleman returned to Berlin, 1947.

'Hello, Otto.'

Being now by default a seasoned *kripo* commander, he noticed immediately that his friend was uneasy. This, he deduced, was either because he feared he had been followed to the café, or he was nervous about being in Soviet Berlin, or some part of their blindly hopeful scheme had cacked, or – and this was where Holleman's understanding of what went on in that destroyed face came fully into play – he was bearing news that no sensible person wouldn't want to hear.

'Get it over with.'

'You sound like Gerd.'

'He's a wise man. What is it, Otto?'

Fischer gave him the details of Oberursel's latest 'request'. To his surprise, Holleman stayed in his chair and used no foul language.

'We think that you should go straight to your Russian, tell him everything and get him to give you whatever version he decides upon.'

Holleman shrugged. 'Of course I will. The alternative is for me to wander the Fifth Kommissariat's corridors with a pencil and paper, saying 'excuse me, but would you mind giving me your name and a brief summary of what it is you do?' It's alright, Otto, you're the fellow who's supposed to have turned me, remember? This is the kind of information you'd want. They'll expect it.'

Fischer glanced around. 'It is, but it drags us deeper into what we're trying to escape. Freddie …?'

'Otto.'

'I've been thinking.'

'Oh shit.'

'Listen, I may have found a way to get you out of Berlin if things get bad – I mean, worse. It means you and Kristin having to start again, but there's a good chance you could do it without trailing any history. No one would be looking for you – at least, if they did they wouldn't find you.'

'Forget it, Otto. Really, drop it. You're a clever man; think of something else.'

'Why …?'

'Because Berlin's home. As shitty as life is here, and however it comes about, this is where the Holleman corpse is going to be fertilizing ground.'

'What about Kristin and the twins? If things go wrong …?'

'They *will* go wrong, like I've been saying since you and Gerd showed up with the good news. When it goes bad, get them out, west. I doubt that anyone's going to be spiteful enough to chase them.'

'They'd sooner have you with them, Freddie.'

Holleman sighed, closed his eyes. 'I know, but I can't go. The moment those fuckers at Oberursel got wind of what happened to Beckendorp and his poor bloody kin I was nailed to a cross. I can't run again. This job is the most important thing I've ever done, apart from the kids.'

'Nothing's more important than family.'

'I know. It's why I'm doing it, for them. Women and children need to be safe again, like they were once. They need to know that this city isn't a slaughterhouse, or a shabby little room with a sodden bed on which mama's going to make some fucking Ivan feel good because if she doesn't everyone goes hungry. The thing is …'

'What, Freddie?'

'I've never done anything like before, not anything. I fucked up at school, I didn't give a shit either as an *OrPo* or pilot, and then I ran away and hid from Adolph. That's it, the Holleman saga. These days – these bloody awful days – I can look into the shaving mirror and feel alright about myself because I'm doing my best, even if it's an airfield short of good enough. Those kids I told you about, the dead ones? We're going to get the bastard who did it. If he's a German we'll put him in a hole, and if he's an Ivan, or an Ami, or a Tommy, we're going to frog-march him to the *Magistrat*. After that they can do what they want with him, which is probably nothing, but everyone will know that the days when you could fuck with *VolksPolizei* are ending. We're up off our bellies and on to our knees, and I've done a little to help with that. So if they want to retire me the hard way, well ...'

Fischer sighed. As a motive, principle was impossible to argue. He turned and waved at the middle-aged woman who served behind the bar. She caught the gesture, ignored it. Holleman stood up.

'Never mind, the coffee here's cat-piss. Come on.'

They walked for a while, saying nothing. On Oranienburgerstrasse a goulash-cannon served a single dish, something grey and greasy that came in cardboard bowls. Fischer chewed half-cooked barley and tried not to guess at the other ingredients while Holleman slurped down his own portion with apparent relish. He seemed happier, or at the least more composed, than at any time since receiving the news about Beckendorp - as if he'd gauged the range of what bore down upon him and made his peace. He paused for a moment, belched, and licked his fingers.

'I haven't asked, but does this Oberursel thing have the making of a career?'

To his surprise, Fischer realised that he hadn't considered the matter since discovering why he'd been recruited so strenuously by Branssler.

'I don't know. I don't think so. Betraying Germans to other Germans doesn't seem ...'

'Wholesome? Fun?'

'Something that would allow sleep to come easily. Maria-Therese thinks that it's *real* work, but that's because so little else is, these days. When things get better, I don't know what I'll do.'

'I'd like to meet her, the woman who conquered you. Perhaps her seeing-dog will let me shake its paw.'

Fischer choked on his food. Solicitously, Holleman patted his back.

'Otto, why don't you come and be a good *kozi* like me? I mean, *really* betray Gehlen's crowd and come east? If we could find a way for me to survive not being Kurt Beckendorp the three of us could go places in the SED. All a man needs is to be able to spout doctrine convincingly, nibble arse and vote the right way – I mean, the way he's told to. The Ivans are kind to their pets, even if the quality of the bone isn't quite what the Americans toss.'

Fischer took the wet remnants of Holleman's bowl, jammed into his own and placed them on the goulash-cannon's counter. 'It's not a bad idea, Freddie. God knows, who could love the Americans? But I have history with the Russians that isn't likely to be waved away. Germans who came out of the war have to choose the side that's least likely to put them against a wall.'

'What about Gerd? Does he like his work? I worry about him.'

'He likes the idea of a pension. For a man with ten years' more work at most in him, it's an attractive word.'

'Tell him that Karlshorst's favourite German *kozis* get pensions, low-rent housing *and* subsidised holidays.'

Fischer looked closely at his friend. 'You haven't actually become one, have you? I mean, *believe* in it?'

'When have I ever believed? But ask yourself - what more could a one-legged fighter pilot who played for the losing side hope for, short of inheriting a girls' school? Do we want a drink?'

There were very few native Berliner venues that could lay their hands on anything other than home-distilled poison, so Fischer was about to decline. But there was something expectant, amused, in Holleman's eyes that made him pause.

'What?'

'Come and see.'

At a one-legged pace they walked north-westward, past the Charité, across Invalidenstrasse and into the British Zone. Fischer was intrigued. 'Are we going to find beer?'

'Of course not. Here it is.'

A tiny, windowless frontage on Dreysestrasse, less wide than Holleman was tall, advertised nothing. He grasped the rope that served as a handle and leaned on the door. Inside, a single line of tables against the right-side wall pointed the way to a makeshift bar that traversed the rear of the room. The feeble pallor from a single gas-lamp revealed half a dozen male customers, none of them wasting drunk-time on conversation. Beyond them a squat, homely woman stood behind a counter, drying clay tankards. She looked up and fixed Fischer with a glance that managed to convey both recognition and baleful indifference to it.

'No!'

'It's too strange, isn't it?' Holleman laughed and gripped Fischer's shoulder, shoving him on. 'As soon as someone volunteers she'll have the sign put up outside – *Tomi's Zwei*, or *How Flattened is My Tomi's*.'

Two years earlier the Soviet advance into Berlin, prefaced by every aerial bomb the Allies could spare, had been a biblical reckoning. At the spiritual centre of National Socialism the damage had been greatest, and within a square half-kilometre of the New Chancellery almost every building (the wilful Air Ministry aside) had been virtually atomized, including a subterranean establishment that had never aspired to anything so exalted as modesty. Its proprietor - a widow, Frau Margret Beitner – had been renowned among Mitte's drinking classes for her fidelity to the memory of her husband, Thomas Beitner, late of the XIV Reserve Corps (in the sense that he became *late* while serving therein), and for so lacking the traditionally understood qualities of a landlady – warmth, bonhomie, amenability – that her customers always had the sense they were colluding in a splendid joke, one that would become clearer once the second glass of her home-brew took hold.

It was the lady herself – moved only physically, apparently, by what 1st Guards Tank Army had lately done to Voss-Strasse - who now gave Fischer her most welcoming glare. Beneath it, his feelings were confused. Though he had warm memories of *Tomi*'s and the days when even a drunk German could imagine he had a say in his own future, they were tempered by the recollection of how much of his surviving throat tissue he had surrendered to Frau Beitner's special reserve.

'It's not the same recipe?'

'Apparently, yes.'

'She's serving it in *tankards*?'

'The British gave her a licence only on condition that she water it down.'

'What with, diesel? I'm surprised they allowed it on any terms.'

Holleman shrugged. 'The more Germans get dead-drunk the fewer complain about rations.'

Two pots sat on the counter, awaiting defusal. Fischer reached into his pocket but Frau Beitner scowled and shook her head slightly. He didn't waste breath enquiring of her health and estate.

They took the last empty table and sat down. Holleman glanced around, beaming at faces that looked up, made the uniform and hastily turned elsewhere.

'Lovely. I never really knew the old place, did I?'

'You didn't need to. The British bombed the *Silver Birch* after you'd fled Berlin. We had to make a terrible choice, and *Tomi*'s was the best of the rest.'

'Well, the lady has a proper sense of what a bar should be, bless her. But here's to the old *Birch*, and God bless it, too.'

For a few moments thereafter conversation became impossible, despite the polluting effects of water in the cause. Eventually, Fischer managed to gasp something intelligible.

'These children you're so keen to avenge. Tell me more about them.'

Holleman described the investigation, the curious placement of the bodies, the Pasteurstrasse Mission link, his assessment of potential perpetrators. Fischer listened, nodding occasionally. It was all good, sound police work, the more so for being handicapped by vast problems he had never faced as a *kripo*.

'Did you look at the parents?'

'We only have parents for four of the victims. The others, we assume, were street kids, orphans. They ...'

'What?'

Holleman, surprised, stared at his tankard. 'I never thought about it, but the ones who *did* report their missing children were all *Deutschevolk*, German refugees from the east or Sudetenland. What does that mean?'

Fischer shrugged. 'Probably nothing. Strangers recently arrived in the city are going to be more vulnerable, aren't they, particularly if they come with only the clothes on their backs? Unless ...'

'Unless they also ate at Pasteurstrasse, which means that the murderer chose his victims also, rather than at random.'

'It's another possibility. Tell me about the causes of death.'

'There were none.'

'None?'

'Not obvious ones, no. Bruising, one broken wrist, that's it. Our police surgeon – who's so fucking useless I wouldn't wish him on Churchill's anal fissures – says suffocation. Probably.'

'Was there cyanosis? Petechial haemorrhaging?'

'Hard to tell. Herr Useless Bastard said that a pillow would have lessened the latter, while a pallid hue's to be expected in children with crap diets. Clearly, we didn't have the equipment or resources for autopsies. And he wouldn't have been arsed to do them if we had.'

'These deaths occurred within three days of each other?'

'At most.'

Fischer started into his own drink. 'That's strange, really strange. Even someone who gives in entirely and enthusiastically to his urges would be sated for a while after each murder. Like after an orgasm.'

'Then we're honoured to have the exception on our patch. Anyway, my lads – good lads, by the way, even if they're not natural police – are going to be taking their meals at Pasteurstrasse for a while. If they do their job we should get something out of it, unless the sod's bolted.'

'Or dead.'

'Do these types ever kill themselves?'

'Rarely.'

'Good. I want to see his trousers fill when he's dragged to the post. Drink up, I have to get back to Keibelstrasse and make some paperwork.'

Their documents were inspected by a British patrol as they headed back into the Soviet Zone. Holleman nodded at the Tommies, perfectly at ease with all varieties of the city's conquerors. Fischer felt clumsy next to him and guilty too, but that was because he'd have to come west again later that day and hoped very much not to find the same group of men waiting for him. He considered saying good afternoon in English, but didn't want to pin himself in their memories.

He and Holleman parted beside the ruins of Schloss Monbijou. He watch the unlikely *Commandeur der VolksPolizei* limp past what had been an ornamental garden. His cap was in his pocket and his overcoat hid the uniform, and street kids, unaware that he was the enemy, emerged from the old Orange Terrace and surrounded him, begging for food or marks. Fischer heard the laugh, the banter and mock threats, watched him empty his wallet, smiled at the genial *now, fuck off!* (too loud not to offend ears in Hamburg) and was filled with a sense of how this city was stitched into the very fabric of Freddie Holleman. He'd been wrong to suggest running away, stupid to think his friend might agree to it. Starting again somewhere else would be just another way of ending it.

Curiously, understanding this didn't depress him. It was just mood, obviously; when he thought about it a little more, how the final tunnel out of their dark place had just bricked itself up, he would come down every bit as far as the situation demanded. But for now, Frau Beitner's poison and the lingering scent of the old days mixed finely with the Spring sunshine, anaesthetizing reality. He walked randomly, contentedly, observing nothing, and returned to the *Bad Gastein* only after dusk.

Gerd Branssler was waiting for him, with news that cured every last symptom of his good spirits.

43

Two large men with handguns, dressed as civilians, came for Rolf before dawn, shoving open the still-lockless cellar door with the force of a raid. He had time only to tell Engi not to run away, to go upstairs and put himself at Frau Best's mercy, and then he was outside on Fueuerbachstrasse, being bundled into a small Ford truck. They hadn't waited to let him put on his jacket, and that struck him as a bad sign.

One of them drove while the other sat in the back with him, saying nothing. The tailboard was up but the tarpaulin flapped loosely, giving him all the view he needed. They skirted Tempelhof, a slightly tortuous route that avoided American patrols, and crossed into the Soviet Zone via a minor road before it was fully light. He didn't need to wonder about their destination.

He hadn't ever visited Karlshorst during its Wehrmacht days, but when he was pulled from the truck he recognized the squat, plain façade immediately. His companions didn't think to offer the tour - the transfer from the vehicle park into the main building, up two flights of stairs and into a small office was only slightly less speedy than a delivery to the guillotine. No one waited for him there, but as his escort departed they closed the door softly, respectfully. It didn't ease the assault upon his nerves.

He waited, not daring to turn around, to sit, to glance out of the single small window, and tried to empty his mind of all the possibilities that had been quick-stepping through it. The desk in front of him held two small piles of paperwork (a reassuringly mundane presence), and the visitor's chair, though placed with its back to him, bore no obvious signs of blood or bullet damage. He told himself that an execution would have happened already, that a cautionary beating could have been delivered much more conveniently in the middle of Fueurbachstrasse.

The door opened and closed again as he stood still, almost to attention.

'Oh, please, Herr Hoelscher, have a seat.'

His interrogator – he assumed that this was going to be an interrogation – was a young, pleasant-faced Soviet officer of indeterminate rank, lacking an obviously military bearing. He was holding a file, which he glanced into.

'Formerly of … Bautzen camp, yes?'

'Yes, sir.'

'A rather harsh place, I understand?'

'It wasn't a rest-cure.'

'No. Well, NKVD don't like it, either.'

'They seemed to enjoy their work enormously.'

The officer dropped the file on the desk and smiled. 'Incredibly, NKVD have made several representations to Moscow, asking that the camps' regimes be improved. They're coming to think that we may be losing the battle for Germans' affections. As yet, Comrade Stalin demurs.'

Almost two minutes, and no threats. Rolf's diaphragm relaxed slightly.

'But we're not here to gossip. You reported contact with a member of the Gehlen organization, yes?'

'Otto Fischer, sir. A former Fallschirmjäger comrade.'

'Fischer, yes. What do you make of him?'

Rolf shrugged. 'I don't know him. We fought together on a single day, back in 1941. I saw him again two years later, but only for a few moments as I checked his papers. At some point he'd been injured very badly - mutilated, in fact. He seems to have recovered from it as well as anyone might.'

'What did he tell you of his work here in Berlin?'

'He's been ordered to gather information on the SED, he said. There's a senior policemen here who's well thought of it the Party; I don't know why or how, but Fischer believes that he can use this man. I think that I saw him – the policemen, I mean – about three weeks ago, with Fischer and another man.

'Where?'

'Ziegelstrasse, in Mitte. They were arguing, but not violently.'

The Soviet officer had become interested. He opened his desk, removed another file and extracted a photograph. 'Is this the policemen?'

Rolf studied the image. A large, ugly *VolksPolizei* officer was facing a group of hapless-looking cadets. The expression on his meaty face hung somewhere between bleak desperation and contempt. 'I ... think so. He was limped badly.'

'A war wound. This is very good. It confirms a good deal of what we know already. Herr Hoelscher, you can be very useful to us if you wish.'

Rolf didn't think his *wishes* were in point here. 'Of course, sir.'

'Please, no more *sir*. Comrade will be perfectly adequate - or *Major*, if you're nostalgic for your Luftwaffe days. I'd like you to nurture your acquaintance with this Fischer.'

'Yes, comrade.'

I won't ask you to gain his trust, or friendship, or anything else that makes it seem as if you're *trying*. Just have a drink together occasionally. Above all, don't lose contact. I need to know what he's doing and when he does it. Now, you were Fallschirmjäger.'

'As I said, comrade.'

'An elite unite. Presumably, you had sniper training?'

'Marksmanship was a required course. But we fought honourably, not as assassins.'

'I beg pardon, I meant no offence. Your skills may be required once more.'

'I doubt that I'd be much use after so …'

'Don't be modest, Herr Hoelscher. I believe that you demonstrated them quite recently, and very effectively.'

Rolf wanted very much to deny it, but *it* hadn't yet been stated. He held his breath.

'Your description of the assault in Schöneberg was convincing, but you were unlucky. The monies you alleged to have been stolen were, in fact, handed in to an American patrol by one of the good people who came to your assistance. I doubt very much that a self-respecting brigand would have done that. I believe that you killed the gentleman in the alley, though I have no idea why. No ...' he held up his hand, '... please don't, it doesn't matter. I'm sure you had good enough reason. Next time, however, it would be better if you did it only to order.'

'Next time?'

'You have a talent, and it would be a pity to let it lie fallow. Herr Fischer may be useful to us, or not. When the time comes we'll let you know. In the meantime take this.'

The Russian pushed a piece of paper across the desk. Rolf picked it up and stared at the Cyrillic script. It was a chit of some sort, pre-authorized by stamp, awaiting only the signature that had just been scrawled across it.

'What is it?'

'A requisition order. Ideally, I'd authorize a Karabiner 98k and a dozen stripper clips of ammunition, as it's probably the weapon with which you're most familiar.' The Russian laughed. 'We have a bloody great pile of them, it's very inconvenient. Wandering the western sectors with a rifle might invite a little attention, however. This is for a 9mm Steyr and a suppressor. We have plenty of those, too.'

44

Fischer couldn't recall seeing Branssler so nervous. It didn't look right on him, like lip-rouge never does on a circus seal.

'So, I showed my authority at Camp Andrews and they arranged an Army line to Oberursel, to the archives. I may have asked for the wrong man.'

'Who was it?'

'A fellow called Brunner - he started at Oberursel more or less at the same time as me and went straight into Records, so I couldn't see that he'd had time to get too deeply into the sensitive stuff. I put it as blandly as I could, just asked if he could have a look at whether we happened to have anything on one Holleman, initial F.'

'What did he say?'

'It's what he did, which was to almost drop the 'phone. I heard the gasp at my end, and I'll bet there was a shallow dent in the ceiling when he came down.'

'Oh, God.'

'For a moment I thought he was going to give me a straight *no*, but he had the sense to think about that. He asked – hell, he demanded – that I wait while he checked. He was gone for about twenty minutes, and when he came back I got 'no, nothing'. That was it, the lot.'

'So Freddie's in the files twice - once as Kurt Beckendorp and again as himself. Have they put the two together, do you think?'

'Shit, Otto, I don't know. His reaction suggests that they have, doesn't it?'

Fischer frowned. 'I can't see how. When I lifted Freddie's Luftwaffe records in '43 I may have missed something, but I can't believe it's enough to make a link between his old and new identities, not unless someone made him back in early '45 when we were chasing down the Lichterfelde killings. No, it can't be that. Whatever he's known for, it isn't for being Kurt Beckendorp's alter ego.'

'Why do you say that?'

'Because if they had enough on Freddie to link the two names, would we still be on this case? They have a file on him, so they must already have chased his pre-war records, the stuff I couldn't reach. At the very least, they know that *you* know him from his police days.'

'Yeah, that makes sense. But why the hell is *Holleman* in the files at all? The last time he did anything deadly was over Belgium, seven years ago. Why did his name give Brunner an infarction?'

'I don't know. But *we* need to, and quickly. What would it take, to get one of us into the repository?'

'A reason, authorization - and of course, we'd need to know what to look for, once we're in. There are different kinds of files.'

'The last shouldn't be a problem. You told me that Gehlen instituted a central card index.'

Branssler nodded. 'Everyone in Evaluation has access to it.'

'Well then, there'll be a card for Holleman, Friedrich, even if it only directs the enquirer elsewhere or tells him not even to think about it. Either way, we should know more once we've seen it.'

'You mean, when *I've* seen it?'

'Well, yes. I've taken the oath, but that's it. They don't know me at Oberursel, so everything I attempted would be watched. Make a reason to report back, and have a look at the index.'

Branssler sighed. 'I don't mind. When I pass through Frankfurt I sometimes get a chance to pop my head around the door and kiss Greta.'

'Can you go today?'

'What's my reason?'

'To report that I've spoken to Commander Beckendorp and he's agreed to get us everything he can on the Fifth Kommissariat. He asks for two weeks, tell them.'

'They get twitchy if it's anything over seven days, you know that.'

'Which is why you've returned to Oberursel, to get instructions. Stress that he's putting his arse into the sling for them. Say that he's got a meeting at Karlshorst in, um, ten days, and after that he'll give us the material.'

'Yeah, that's credible. If K-5 are anything like Gehlen's crew it would take him that long to work out who belongs where. I take it he's going to make up anything he gives us?'

'He's going to tell his Karlshorst handler that I've asked, so I can't imagine that what we get will be at all accurate. What about what's passing in the other direction? Have Oberursel decided what disinformation we're going to pass to Freddie?'

'I think they liked my idea about the altered franks, but I'll push it, tell them that Beckendorp needs something soon to offer to Karlshorst. Christ, this is getting too damned dangerous. We're like spotters in no-man's-land, signalling both sides where to train the artillery.'

'I know. Freddie won't run, by the way. He says if it comes to the worst we should get his family out. But he's staying.'

Branssler sat heavily on his bed and dragged out his case from beneath it. 'I'm not surprised. He's more native Berlin than pork and caraway. What would he do in the Rhineland? It might as well be Punta Arenas.'

'It means we'll have to find some other way out. And I've have no idea where or how.'

'That's alright, Otto, you can't always be the clever one. Who knows? Perhaps we're being too pessimistic. This could go on forever – us feeding shit to Karlshorst, Freddie feeding shit to Oberursel and both sides thinking their boys are top agents. We might retire with the thanks of several grateful governments.'

Fischer scratched his head. 'That would require a heroic degree of credulity.'

Branssler placed his last good shirt into his case and snorted. 'And what quality more defines our great once-nation?'

45

*Wachtmeister* Kalbfleisch stared into the bowl in front of him.

'What in the name of Christ's Wounds is this?'

Müller almost offered an opinion, but that might have made the grey mess even less appetizing. 'Eat up your *eintopf.* We're hungry men, remember? Your stomach can't afford to be fastidious.'

On a wet, cold evening they sat at one of the smaller side-tables in the Pasteurstrasse Mission. A sign by the door asked visitors to vacate their places once their meals were finished, but the two policemen had no intention of obeying this considerate reminder. They were dressed in office clothes that had seen service in some private ordeal (removed from corpses brought into the mortuary at Beelitz-Heilstätten four days earlier) and looked suitably destitute, men on the hardest ground.

They sat surrounded by every shade of something similar - people holding on, just, hoping to get through the hungry times to the moment when normality would resume, fearing that normal - the new, German normal - was here already. Müller had noticed that few of them seemed to have the average Berliner's native curiosity about their fellow citizens; they ate quickly, efficiently, heads down, steaming gently and malodorously as their sodden clothes warmed, forming close family circles against the outside.

A queue, orderly and quiet, snaked from the door to a serving counter at which four helpers dispensed portions from two large catering drums. A constant, barely muffled clatter from the rear of the building suggested that the building had proper kitchens and that food was prepared here rather than brought from elsewhere. But then, Pasteurstrasse Mission had been purpose-built as such over forty years earlier and not hastily requisitioned to meet the needs of the modern age. It wore its service to Need venerably, as cathedrals did their sanctity.

Müller and Kalbfleisch had eaten at the Mission three times prior to that evening. On their first visit their stomachs had been lulled – pampered, even - by a palpably identifiable *krautsuppe* that held a lingering aftertaste of bacon (though neither man could find a piece in his bowl); but since then the best that could be said for the dishes on offer was that they contained some of the basic ingredients required to sustain life, if not make it worth living. Only the chunk of dark bread handed out with each meal had a consistent quality, one that wouldn't recommend it to a delicate constitution or fragile teeth.

Their ordeal had not yet furthered the investigation, much less offered up an obvious suspect. The volunteer staff here knew each other by name and conversed easily, so Müller assumed that all had been doing this work for some time (and might, therefore, know something of those they fed, their regulars). On the other hand, the utter lack of interaction between the Mission's customers argued that Beckendorp's guess had been correct - that unless the victims' acquaintance had been made elsewhere and under different circumstances, their man wasn't likely to be a customer.

In fact, the mission was an oasis of resigned *apartness*, a marked contrast to the noisy, squabbling, co-mingled atmosphere of the wartime kitchens. Whenever two strangers came into chance proximity here – chasing the same seat at a table, or  grasping at the last spoon in the pot - they shied away politely, quietly, the centrifugal force of their common shame keeping the peace more effectively than an enthusiastically swung *schlagstock*. Muller watched as closely as he could without attracting attention and couldn't have picked upon a single word, glance or gesture that suggested any darker motive than survival.

This frustrated him considerably. Having achieved the breakthrough of identifying the probable common link between the unfortunate seven households he had expected a timely resolution of the case itself - a sudden, piquant deduction perhaps, or a meaningful meeting of eyes in which guilt could be read clearly. He realised that his expectations were perhaps warped by his prior experience of criminal investigations (derived entirely from cheap *krimi* novels), but this pause was deflating. It made him feel a little like a sprinter who, having exploded from the blocks, was then brought to a halt and made to wait while sheep crossed the track.

Kalbfleisch didn't seem to mind the sheep. He had a dogged temperament that took their lack of progress for what it was, and had settled comfortably into surveillance. Occasionally he would nudge Müller's elbow, drawing his attention to a new arrival who bore some near-invisible stigma of not quite rightness, or to someone whose mode of departure, or method of eating, hinted at asocial qualities. Otherwise, he contented himself with games of guess-the-dish and in-my-day, both of which added to his colleague's torment.

By now, they had memorized the faces of all the Mission staff other that the men and women who ruined the comestibles in the rear of the building. Müller estimated that an operation which fed several hundred Berliners nightly must employ at least six kitchen staff and probably more, but he could think of no plausible approach, short of waving his police ID, that would get him behind the serving counter. When he put the problem to Kalbfleisch the older man shrugged.

'The food is magnificent and you must pay your compliments to the chef personally.'

Involuntarily, Müller's stomach clenched. 'I need to investigate, not be restrained.'

'We're inspectors from the Food Ministry.'

'There isn't one.'

'Really?'

'A ministry would require a government.'

'Ah. One forgets the technicalities. The Allied Food Safety Inspectorate, then?'

'Is there one of those?'

'If *you* don't know, probably they don't.'

'True. But what is it that we'd be inspecting?'

'Kerosene burners. We're investigating a spate of explosions due to, er, faulty seals.'

'Good. Come on.'

As they approached the counter Müller removed his *Magistrat* ID, a card bearing Russian, English and French authorizations but not a single word of German and waved it in the face of the woman who dispensed the bread. The gesture was recognized immediately by the most of the front of the queue, which collectively shuffled back a pace. The woman scowled. 'What is it?'

'A safety concern. We're checking your ovens. It won't take long and we shan't disturb your staff.'

'You two came in yesterday. Why didn't you do it then?'

Müller drew himself to a bureaucratically-offended height. 'We have a list. It's your turn this evening.'

She shrugged and nodded at a small door behind her.

The kitchen was hotter and steamier than a Turkish baths. Two men stirred a large vat of what Muller assumed had poisoned him a few minutes' earlier, while two women and a middle-aged man sat by an open rear door, peeling discoloured potatoes. All five of them glanced up or turned at the distraction, stared briefly and then returned to their duties with every indication of finding the two men as interesting as the menu. Müller felt his latest stab of inadequacy keenly. Having penetrated Pasteurstrasse Mission's final mystery he had no idea what to ask that might elicit some useful information, being ignorant both of kerosene burners and an interrogator's skills (either of which might at least have started a conversation). But then he noticed that the man sat beside the pile of potatoes had paused and was giving the two disguised policemen a second look. He seemed faintly surprised, as if something unsuspected had occurred. The short knife in his hand paused in its business and surprise suddenly became a sort of awareness; he blinked twice and opened his mouth, trying to form words that the mind was attempting to decide upon. To Kalbfleisch this all looked as good as a confession and he advanced, deploying his notebook. His objective placed the knife carefully upon the floor, stood and stepped back, wiping his dirty hands upon his apron.

The policemen's shabby civilian clothes and profoundly unmartial bearing shouldn't have intimidated one of the kitchen's onions out of its skin, but the man was becoming disturbed. Müller put a hand on Kalbfleisch's arm, attempted a smile and considered whether this was the moment when an experienced *kripo* would state his business (though the notebook had done that already, probably). As an advocate he had always tried to comfort his clients, divert their minds from the probable consequences of falling into the path of National Socialist justice. Now, it was his duty to agitate rather than reassure, to disturb the equilibrium of suspects and witnesses in order to extract what was concealed or forgotten. The contrast between his former and present role wasn't a comfortable one and he had to steel himself to be unpleasant, particularly when the object of his rigour was a man like this one, a harmless, inoffensive fellow trying to do his best for others in an age when few enough cared to …

'I did it.'

Kalbfleisch licked his pencil with unprofessional relish. 'What is it that you did, sir?'

'I killed them. All those beautiful children.'

46

Most Secret

From: Wessel

Distribution: named recipient only: Gehlen

Subject: <u>Report of Alois Brunner</u>

Brunner: *'At 10am on 23 May 1947 I received a telephone call from evaluation officer Gerd Branssler, speaking from the American base at Lichterfelde. Branssler asked me if we held any information on (deleted; Red File ref. 'Andreas'). I undertook to check the archives and then reported to him that we had no data upon anyone of that name.*

*Branssler offered no indication as to why he required this information, and I thought it inappropriate to ask.'* Statement ends.

Branssler is a recent recruit, a former *kriminalkommissar* of Amt V, Alexanderplatz. No known political affiliations other than obligatory NSDAP membership, 1936 – 45. Satisfactory reference from Gottfried Schapper, former Ministerial Direktor, *Forschungsamt*. Demonstrated high degree of aptitude during training. Known associates: 1. Wife (resident, Frankfurt); 2. Two daughters, married, resident in or near Düsseldorf; 3. Otto Henry Fischer, also a recent recruit to the organization (solemn oath taken; not yet undergone training), who claims also to be a former kriminalkommissar, Amt V Alexanderplatz; however, preliminary research indicates that although Branssler and Fischer have prior acquaintance the latter served in Stettin, not Berlin, and came out of the SBZ only recently. I find this discrepancy disturbing, though Fischer was also employed by us at the personal recommendation of former Ministerial Direktor Gottfried Schapper.

The problem as I see it: Branssler and Fischer are currently acting in the field as the organization's lead contacts with Berlin *VolksPolizei* Commander Kurt Beckendorp (a rising member of the SED). As you know, this (so-called) Beckendorp represents by far our most important potential opportunity to penetrate the Soviet/German communist intelligence network to date, and has been given highest priority. Until now I have argued for minimal active supervision of the exercise in order not to put counter-productive pressure upon the subject; however, Branssler's attempt to access data upon 'Andreas' – though done openly – must raise strong questions regarding his wider motives, particularly –

1. Why did Branssler and Fischer argue so strongly to act as Beckendorp's contacts?

2. Branssler's suggestion - that Beckendorp's position with the Soviets may be strengthened by the pretence of 'turning' Otto Fischer - now looks suspect. Any tainted information that we consent to be passed to Beckendorp may be turned against us if these two are acting in bad faith.

I recommend, therefore:

1. That both Branssler and Fischer are monitored carefully until the Beckendorp exercise is concluded (or moves to a stage wherein more overt control may be exerted). If, prior to this, however, it appears that they are actively sabotaging or tainting the operation, consideration be given to removing them without recourse to formal process. To that end, it may be prudent to brief *Vidar* as soon as practicable.

2. That we give careful thought to information we allow Branssler and Fischer to pass on the Beckendorp, and that they be kept unaware of any manipulation thereof. Also, we should insist that they put pressure on Beckendorp to produce the information we have requested re: organization and structure of the Fifth Kommissariat within, say, seven days. This will, I believe, test all three men's commitment.

3. That, following the satisfactory conclusion or development of the Beckendorp exercise (and unless earlier action is required), both Branssler and Fischer are confined to the Oberursel compound and interrogated closely.

4. That if this exercise is compromised by the actions of Branssler and/or Fischer, damage to Oberursel's interests be minimized by immediately passing our data on Beckendorp, via a neutral agency, to Soviet Counter-Intelligence. Our loss of this source may well be fully compensated by the dislocation and reorganization such a revelation would encourage

Wessel


Most Secret

From: Gehlen

Distribution: recipient only: Wessel

Subject: Report of Joachim Brunner

1. Agreed, your recommendations in full

2. The file on 'Andreas' to be removed immediately from Red Section and placed in your sole care. Also the index card on only currently-known identity. <u>Please check and confirm that there are no other extant references</u>

<u>Gehlen</u>

47

Frau Best had not wasted the hours of Rolf's absence. The floors of her garden house had been washed, its curtains removed, beaten free of dust and replaced, and wood salvaged from some nearby ruin piled outside her door, awaiting conversion to stove-sized pieces. Engi, the instrument of her will, was sitting on the ground next to the latter trying to catch his breath when Rolf returned. An ax lay beside him, awaiting employment.

He glared at the boy, angry with himself for not making it clear that penal servitude wasn't one of the conditions of his *nephew*'s stay at Fueurbachstrasse.

'Come on. I've brought breakfast.'

They ate *blutwurst* and rye bread in the cellar. Rolf was tempted to give his landlady's share to her new slave, but before it became an intention she shuffled in, picked up her portion from the table and disappeared without a word of greeting, thanks or enquiry regarding his recent abduction by strangers. She had her world, and it was not allowed to be disturbed unnecessarily.

'Are you alright, Rolf?' Engi was nervous, having just sampled the blunt end of one possible future without his protector.

The weight and press of the Steyr beneath Rolf's coat reminded him of how far from *alright* he was, but he smiled and shrugged. 'They wanted to speak about some work, that's all.'

'Do we have to stay here?'

'For now, yes. But we can find somewhere else soon. Would you like to leave Berlin?'

Frowning, Engi stared down at the table. 'Yes, I would. Could we have a garden?'

*We.* It struck Rolf like a rock, what damage he was doing. A street-child wouldn't take food and shelter for what it was but as a pledge, a bright promise of better. All it had required was the correct measure of despair, diluted by a few deadly drops of kindness, and the boy had lashed himself to a sinking boat, a bad wager, a man without a functioning conscience.

'We could make one. There's plenty of torn up land that needs care.'

'I can plant things. I used to help my m ...'

'Food. That's the thing to grow. Then we can eat every day, twice.'

The unworldly prospect of multiple meals quelled the boy's tears. 'Potatoes?'

'Yes, and greens. And sometimes we could trade them for meat.'

Engi's eyes closed. 'I like chicken, I think.'

'Chicken is good. I haven't had chicken for a long ...'

Rolf bit his tongue. The trouble with painting magical lands was that it seduced the artist no less than his desperate audience. The only land he would ever work was that which accepted his body, a plot he'd have no hand in choosing, probably. But then he felt the Steyr against his chest once more, heard it whisper of a chance to make that choice.

'Engi, will you do something for me?'

'Yes, Rolf.'

'It's a thing you'll need to do every day. When we go out, I want you to walk behind me, a good way behind me, like you did when I met the old man near Dürer-Platz. You can do that without being noticed, can't you?'

He hardly needed to ask. A runt couldn't have survived for so long in this deadly city if he hadn't been able to make himself insignificant as the stick insect he was doing his best to resemble.

'I can, Rolf.'

'I want you to tell me if anyone takes an interest, or follows me, or does anything you don't like. It's a game, but a very important one.'

'I can come with you every day? And not stay here with the old lady?'

'Definitely not with her.'

'Are people looking for you?'

'I don't know. That's what we're going to find out. You're my rear gunner now.'

Engi thought about that. 'What will you be doing?'

'I'll be watching, too. One person in particular.'

'A bad person?'

'I don't know that either. It's my job to find out.'

'Is it the comrade you said you'd betrayed?'

Astonished, Rolf stared at his new assistant. An aborted education, loss of a mother and a deadly-bare existence as a sewer rat in one of the world's most butchered environments should have slowed a growing mind, but he'd known men with braid on their shoulders who hadn't half the boy's wit.

'Yes, it is. Am *I* a bad person, then?'

Engi licked a finger and wiped it around the tin plate to collect breadcrumbs while he considered this. 'It depends on what you do.'

Rolf smiled. 'I'm sharing quarters with a moral philosopher.'

'A what?'

'It doesn't matter. I'll think carefully about what I *do*, then.'

A slight scraping noise at the cellar door recalled recent visitors, and man and boy turned quickly. Frau Best re-entered, balefully regarded the now foodless table, turned and departed – again, without souring the atmosphere with conversation.

Engi shivered slightly. 'She isn't nice.'

Rolf shrugged. 'She's old. Age makes people care less about things that aren't themselves. You'll be the same, one day.'

'I don't think I'll ever be old.'

'You can't avoid it …' Rolf realised, too late, what the boy meant. He had no father's skill to make life seem less like a thing that crushed young hopes, and he absolutely couldn't do what a mother would to take away its pain in a moment. So he lied.

'Things will get better soon. You'll go to school, get a job that you'll need a suit for, meet a girl and have brats just like you. You'll become a fat man with a thick moustache, sitting behind a big desk covered in *kuchen* crumbs, treating all your workers like Frau Best treats you.'

Engi laughed, flattered that he could occupy someone's vision. 'No, I'm going to be a secret detective, because I'll be good at following bad people without them knowing.'

'So, this will be good practise.'

'When will we do it, Rolf?'

'Tomorrow, and every day after that. Where this fellow goes, so will we.'

48

The GI at the compound gate examined Branssler's ID card briefly and nodded him through. A few metres further in and he was stopped once more by one of Oberursel's German security staff. This time, the card wasn't returned.

'You're to go directly to General Wessel's office.'

Wessel's former rank was hardly ever mentioned, and Branssler considered the reminder a bad omen. Of what he couldn't say, but he nodded confidently as though he'd been expecting the summons.

There were only three permanent offices for senior staff in the compound (Gehlen was hardly ever at the site and didn't require one). Wessel's was the first of them, a modest box at the near end of a first-floor corridor in Alaska House. Branssler knocked and entered without waiting for a response.

The General was somewhere else. The third chair that Fischer had occupied during their interview two weeks earlier had been removed, and the remaining two faced each other across the plain campaign desk. Having the choice of making himself comfortable or standing outside in the corridor like a naughty child, Branssler parked his generous rear and unrolled the copy of the *Frankfurter Zeitung* he'd picked up at the station an hour earlier.

He was about halfway through the football reports when the old Gerd Branssler, formerly of the fourth floor, Alexanderplatz, enquired politely as to what the hell he thought he was doing. The file sections were located on the ground floor of the adjacent building, less than two minutes away, and had he done the job before coming to Wessel's office the delay would hardly have stirred the most suspicious mind. He thought quickly. A man coming from Berlin to Oberursel, a man summoned before he'd had time to have the shit that had been building all morning, could hardly be blamed for being absent for a short while. Quickly, he placed his newspaper where it could be seen clearly, opened the office door and strode out as casually as anyone of clear conscious might.

He saw no one between there and the front entrance, no one in the small road between the two buildings and only a single member of the organization - an old gardener, carefully tending a potted palm - in the reception area that fronted the file sections. Belatedly, Branssler paused there and thought of Brunner, of what explanation might persuade the man not to trigger every alarm immediately. *Beckendorp, of course.* His signature was on that file a dozen times already, a file he had more reason to request than almost everyone else here. He pushed open the fire door and walked in.

But it was Brunner's day off, apparently. A cadaverously thin, clerkish fellow sat at a desk, peering sternly into one of the card boxes. Branssler picked up a requisition slip, filed in the Beckendorp reference and coughed. The cadaver glanced up and gave him a broad, welcoming smile, the sort that the better innkeepers practise in a mirror.

'Good morning, Herr …'

'Branssler. Good Morning. I'd like this file please.'

The archivist took the slip, pushed back his chair and disappeared into one of the aisles that retreated from the front of the room. Quickly,

Branssler scanned the index drawers and found a gap between 'GS' and 'HU'; the *fuck* was halfway to his throat when he realised that the box he needed was in front of him on the desk, the one that the archivist had been examining when he entered. He flicked through the cards and found another gap where *Holleman* should have been. The profanity made it all the way out this time.

'I'm sorry?'

The happy cadaver was back already with the Beckendorp file. Branssler could think of nothing that would get him what he wanted unnoticed, not unless he clubbed this fellow to the floor, bound him tightly and hid him among the 'W's.

'I was looking for a card, name of Holleman.'

'Dear me, that's a popular gentleman today. Here ...'

A single card lay face up on the desk next to the box Branssler had been rifling. He felt his face redden considerably as the archivist lifted it and passed it to him.

'Thank you.' He tried to glance disinterestedly at its contents, then realised that he didn't need to pretend. They comprised just three words, flanked to the left by a red vertical band - *Hollman, Fritz. See: Andreas.* Below the main script were three small, pencilled letters – *G, W, F.*

He didn't know whether to be relieved or massively disappointed that he had risked so much for nothing. Why had Brunner gone into low orbit at hearing what he took to be this name? A better question, to himself – why should he even care, if Freddie Holleman wasn't in Oberursel's files? He could hand the card back, thank this unnervingly pleasant fellow and depart without having even slightly stirred the pot, having satisfied himself that a least one splinter in his and his friends' collective arse had turned out to be a gnat's caress.

But the old Branssler was there still (half-drunk after one of his long lunches, probably), prodding him rudely, asking what pots were for, if it wasn't to be stirred.

'May I ask – this red mark …?'

The archivist seemed puzzled at his ignorance, but not suspicious. 'Most restricted, to senior staff. Look, the initials – this means Gehlen, Wessel and Fuchs only.'

'Ah, yes, of course. This is the file the General requested I bring to him. Do I sign for it?'

The archivist almost snatched the card from his fingers. 'Oh, no, Herr Wessel must sign personally for it. We have very strict regulations.'

'Of course. But General Wessel is with General Gehlen at the moment, and this *is* most urgent. Perhaps if you call him? In fact, yes, that would be best.'

Branssler could read every tortured dither that passed across the fellow's face. A call to Wessel would relieve him of any responsibility, but it was a strong and confident temperament that risked irritating two former general officers in (no doubt) highly secret conference. The rabbit was caught between two cabbages, and in this case neither was appetizing.

'You'll sign for it, of course.'

'Naturally.' To his surprise, Branssler's hand managed it without shaking. He waited as the archivist disappeared once more, trying not to twitch like he was pissing himself, smiled as he took the file and was almost out of the door when the man coughed.

'Herr Branssler ...?'

*Shit.*

'You'll want this one too, won't you?'

He managed something like another smile and resisted snatching the Beckendorp file.

'Of course. What a dolt!'

He left the building, turned sharply to his left and went directly to the toilet block. In a cubicle he sat down and opened the file. The police report was short and he read it quickly, jotted down its bare bones and the two names in his best interrogator's hand and placed the single sheet of paper in an envelope. It was addressed already - *postlagernd*, to Alt-Moabit Mobile District Post Office, Berlin - and required only a name, which he scribbled hurriedly. When he left the toilet block the two files were on the floor still.

General, unclassified post from Oberursel was collected at the site's Post Room and included in the US Forces' bag. Neither of the two sorters there noticed Branssler enter and deposit an item just before the noon collection, nor heard the shouting, the running fight, the cursing and cries of pain as half the guard-room took casualties trying to put him on the ground outside the toilet block a few moments later.

49

Kurt Beckendorp had been summoned to Karlshorst too many times for it to test Freddie Holleman's nerves, but on that particular morning a septic testicle would have been as welcome.

His mood darkened when he discovered that his favourite driver, Dieter, was on sick leave. His substitute, a lugubrious fellow much avoided by the senior officers, was convinced that his prospects for advancement were best greased by a dogged and (literally) monotonous commentary upon the evils of National Socialism and capitalism, the sexual degeneracy of American GIs and any other aspect of Western depravity likely to be amenable to their Soviet masters. To date, no one had dared test the protocols of social egalitarianism (a relatively novel concept to Germans in the SBZ) by telling him to shut his mouth and watch the road.

Holleman broke the taboo as they passed Lichtenberg cemetery, during a diatribe about seamed stockings and the collapse of morality they portended. Not wishing to lay the ground for a lasting grudge he waited for an intake of breath, asked that he be allowed to read the briefing paper he had brought with him (for just this purpose, it relating a meeting held several days before) and then stuck his face into it so pointedly that the dolt couldn't help but take the hint. The car accelerated markedly once the monologue ceased, and at Karlshorst's main gates slowed only so much as to avoid leaving paintwork on the concrete.

Once more, mentioning MGB was enough to get Holleman into the main building without an escort attaching himself. His handler's office door was open and the man himself was on the telephone; a hand waved to a chair and the Russian conversation continued, a heated business. Though Holleman could understand nothing it seemed clear that this fellow was punching as hard as his adversary, and after slamming down the receiver he roundly invited someone to fuck their own mother. Holleman knew that much of the language, at least.

The Major's anger vanished like dye in a fast stream. 'Herr Beckendorp, good morning. Forgive me, that was a matter of authority and my abuse of it, apparently. Never mind. How are you this beautiful morning?'

'Well, sir. But very busy.'

'Of course – the child murders. A great coup, I understand.'

Holleman wondered how the hell news could had travelled from there to here in a little under eight hours. 'It seems so, yes. We have a confession.'

'You're done, then. To the Ministry for State Security a confession is as solid as honey cake, and almost as delicious. You may return to your triumph in a short while. I'd like a short conversation first, if you don't mind?'

'No, Comrade Major.'

'About Otto Fischer'.

'Really? I don't know what I can tell you.'

'The names he provided to you – of agents being trained to infiltrate institutions in the SBZ? They are all of men who died during operations in Belgium and the Rhineland in early 1945.'

*That was damn quick.* 'How did you …?'

The Russian waved a hand. 'I might have gone to WASt, of course; but the French like to ask questions, and I really don't like to answer them. The US Quartermaster General's Department and British War Office continue to hold comprehensive information on enemy casualties they inflicted, and both were admirably, or stupidly, pleased to share it with me. Unfortunately I did this upon my own authority, and I have to say that my Ministry feels quite the same way about initiative as did your Wehrmacht – hence the unpleasant conversation you interrupted.

'So, these men are corpses. The inference one might take is that their identities are to be assumed by Gehlen's agents in order to protect themselves and their network.'

'Yes, of course.'

'But I don't – take it, that is. I believe that Herr Fischer is misleading both of us. This data is useless. He is not as he presents himself.'

Holleman tried to keep his face straight, his voice calm. 'Why do you say that, comrade?'

'Two reasons. Firstly, because there *is* no network, and Oberursel doesn't yet have the resources to train men to be other men. To stand a chance of success they would require indoctrination facilities, teams of expert counterfeiters and support lines in enemy territory to maintain a fiction. At the moment Gehlen's operation is laughably sparse. His man Baun is obliged to tour eastern Germany in person, dispensing cash from an attaché case like a bootlegger's accountant, to men who live in constant fear of discovery. I know this because we've discovered quite a few. They're brave men to be sure, but not working any complex strategy.'

'The second?'

The Russian smiled, giving Holleman the benefit of his most un-Soviet mouthful of white, regular teeth. 'We already have reliable contacts at Oberursel, who assure me that Gehlen isn't using ghost identities – at least, not yet. No, the information is bad, and Fischer is not going to be of any use to us. At least, this is what he may believe.'

'What are you – we – going to do?'

The Russian sat back and regarded his ceiling. 'The correct thing would be to disappear him. But then Oberursel would try again, and we'd need to identify their new man or men. I have many more useful ways to earn my Major's pay. Let's continue to use him, then, at least to provide his people with shit.'

Holleman didn't allow himself a moment to decide whether this was the best time to pass on his latest news. 'He wants to know about K-5 – names and organization.'

'Does he? Well, give it to him.'

'*Really* give it to him?'

'Why not? The Fifth Kommissariat are the political arm of the *VolksPolizei*, so there isn't much that Oberursel won't know about them eventually. The request may be a test, in which case giving them accurate information will sooth suspicions in advance of material that we really need to taint.'

'So I've not been naïve, then?'

The Russian laughed. 'It's a foul business, isn't it? I quite envy you the company of mere method murderers. No, clench your stomach and continue to be Herr Fischer's good comrade, and if or when he becomes troublesome we'll take measures to make him less so.'

It took all the clenching Holleman could manage to make light of it. 'Nothing that I need concern himself with?'

'Not if you're sensible.'

'I was thinking of myself. I don't want to be in his company when it happens.'

'Herr Beckendorp, I assure you that we won't be using artillery. Our people will know that they're to deal only with the half-faced fellow. But we may need you to put him where they can do their job.'

*Not only do I get my friend killed but I'm to set him up for it. Fucking wonderful.*

'I have no problem with that.'

'Excellent. Now, you have your triumph to celebrate, and I've been summoned to explain my *initiative*, so one of us will have fine day. Shall we speak again on Friday?'

The now-taciturn motor-pool driver got the car back to Keibelstrasse in under forty minutes (despite having to negotiate a Red Army checkpoint *en route*), which raised him considerably in Holleman's eyes. The moment he reached his office he summoned *Unterkommissar* Müller and told his secretary to hold off any other visitors, including Marshal Sokolovsky if necessary. He was with Müller for almost an hour, and at the end of that time felt even less like celebrating their *triumph* than earlier, though he counted it a reasonable success that he managed to give his subordinate the impression he knew what should come next.

The day had been too full of unwelcome distractions, and Holleman was obliged to forego his daily visit to the Artists' Café. His non-appearance sent Otto Fischer back to the Hotel *Bad Gastein* that evening with two migraines, the one assisting the other nicely.

50

'Sorry, Otto. I had a bad day. That's what senior people say, isn't it?'

'I don't know, I've never been senior. But they're words I'd probably use about my own yesterday.'

'You too? And yet it didn't rain.'

'Freddie, I think Gerd's in trouble.'

Fischer took out the envelope and passed in across the table to Holleman, who ignored it.

'What trouble? What's he done?'

'He went to Oberursel to see if they have anything on you. I mean, on Freddie Holleman, not Kurt Beckendorp. He sent this to me, but he hasn't returned.'

'He's probably given himself a day or two in Frankfurt with Greta. Don't ...'

'No, look at the address. We agreed that he'd use Earl Kuhn's name if he had to walk into the mine-field. And he did, that's clear enough.'

'What do you mean?'

'Read what's inside.'

Holleman opened the envelope and removed the sheet of paper. It held the very brief summary of a police report dated 12 October 1946, containing a single name: *Fritz Hollman*. A second had been appended below it. He tapped the first with a finger.

'That's me, almost.'

'Almost. Spoken rather than read, and with only your initial offered, it's obvious how they mistook one for the other, and why they got upset.'

'You mean this 'Most Secret'?'

'It's a pity Gerd couldn't tell us *why* it's most secret. Do you recognize the other name?'

'No. Yes …. I mean, it rings half a bell.'

'For me, too. I've been thinking about it since yesterday and still it evades me. Does it mean that the two are connected?'

'Or the same man?'

'Or that. In any case, digging for this information and then getting it out of Oberursel's put Gerd in the shit. And they'll be looking for me too, probably.'

Holleman opened his mouth and paused.

'What?'

'You may as well have all the bad news at once. Karlshorst's made you, too. They know that we – you – gave them dead men's names.'

'That was quick. But it was inevitable.'

'Yeah. The thing is, my Russian's worked it out already. He doesn't believe that Gehlen's collecting ghost identities. He thinks that you're playing me. And, more to the point, him.'

'Jesus.'

'So, if Oberursel's on to Gerd and you, they probably think I'm rotten, too. Which means that our grand strategy's been bent over and slipped a large one.'

'Your Russian still thinks you're being straight with him?'

'It seems so. At least, he didn't tell me he didn't. But if Gehlen's mob make good their threat to drop Kurt Beckendorp in it, you, me and Gerd might be inspecting the same forest trench. And very soon, I expect.'

Fischer rubbed his face with both hands, as much to keep it hidden as to ease the pain. Holleman reached over the table and prodded his chest.

'Don't feel too bad, Otto. We all knew we were facing *panzerfausts* with bayonets. Why don't you get out of Berlin, back to Oberursel, and confess everything? If they're decent fellows they'll let you off with a kicking and dismissal. They'll only do to me what they were going to do anyway, and at least we won't have to spin a dozen plates on poles any more. I was getting very tired of that.'

'If Oberursel send Karlshorst the word about Beckendorp they won't let *you* off with a kicking, Freddie.'

'I know. But then sometimes I wonder - why not? I've been a good *kozi*, haven't I? *And* a straight policemen, better than they could have expected. So what if I'm not Kurt Beckendorp? What if I tell them the straight truth about why Freddie Holleman disappeared? Doesn't twisting Heinrich Himmler's tits count for anything?'

'They won't see it that way. The Soviets are just like our lot were with secrets – it means you're deeper than they'd prefer, and a bullet's the neatest way to solve the mystery. They don't enjoy being deceived.'

Holleman sighed. 'Yeah, well. Fuck.'

Fischer stood up. 'Come on. Let's ease the pain at Frau Beitner's.'

'No, I'm too busy to get bombed.'

'When were you ever too busy to miss a drink?'

'Whenever I solved a multiple murder and the itch didn't stop. Which would be about now.'

'You've got the killer?'

'So he tells me – insists on it, in fact. But that's almost all he's saying.'

'So perhaps he's not the one - just an attention-seeker, a lonely heart.'

Holleman sighed again. 'No, he isn't. He knows every dead child's Christian name and what they looked like, near enough. If he didn't do it himself he held some other bastard's coat while *he* did it.'

Not for the first time with this case, what Fischer was hearing puzzled him. 'He admits it but he won't say more? A method murderer can't stop talking once he's caught - it's the final act in his drama, the necessary step to the guillotine.'

'I know, I've been reading old files on similar stuff. But our fellow's different - he cries, tears at skin with his fingernails, begs us to put one in his head and gives us fuck all to take before the judge except *I did it*.'

'Did you ask him how he felt about his victims?'

'Yeah. He loved them all, he said. They were little angels. So why did you do it, we asked. And he just shrugged and cried a bit more.'

'That's guilt, certainly. Perhaps there's more than one person in his head.'

'I wondered about that. But he doesn't go away and come back, if you see what I mean - he's consistent, and penitent. Do you know what I wish, Otto?'

'That he was a sadistic swine you'd enjoy putting down?'

'That you could come to Keibelstrasse and help us to question him.'

Fischer laughed. 'This would be the Otto Fischer that Karlshorst has already made, walking into the building that happens also to be the headquarters of Berlin's Fifth Kommissariat? Why not smother me in honey and rent me out to a bear garden?'

'What if you're someone else?'

'This face would say that I wasn't.'

'No one would recognize you there. The only person in the Fifth who's got your description is Direktor Jamin, and he never descends from the top floor unless it's to catch the Moscow flight. Come on, Otto – you know how to interrogate people without breaking bones. If anyone dared ask I'd introduce you as an old comrade from Hamburg, a method-murderer specialist. You'd be in and out in two hours at most.'

'In Berlin's largest police station there's no one who could do this?'

'I told you, the only qualification for the police these days is not having been a Nazi. *Every* decent policeman in the old days had to be

NSDAP, and the Allies would sooner give the job to a wet leper. Probably the best *kripo* in the entire Soviet Zone right now is my man Müller, and he's as stumped about this fellow as I am.'

Fischer looked out of the café window, at the squat remnants of the Alex. Like the Praesidium at Stettin it had housed Gestapo also, and inexorably, the methods employed by one department had contaminated the rest. He didn't know how closely the new regime - one that had chosen to house its best police a mere two hundred metres from this monument to inhumanity - respected the traditions of the old. He was frightened to ask how far his old friend had been required to fall to rise so high, so quickly. And he had no intention of re-infecting himself willingly with what a decade's convalescence hadn't yet flushed from his conscience.

Holleman was watching him closely. He didn't seem hopeful.

'Freddie, I haven't faced a suspect across a table since 1937. How could I help?'

'By not charging right at him, like we do. You know the back ways in, the flanking stuff. Me, I just prod and prod until I want to punch. That's no good, not with this fellow. He'd probably feel better about himself if we made him kiss the floor.'

'Gerd has much more experience than me.'

'He's got his own worries, and we can't do anything about them today, can we? We'll need another one of your sharp ideas for that.'

'Do you have a name, even?'

'Egon Kofler.'

'Austrian?'

'Probably. He has a faint accent. I checked what records we can access. There's nothing, nothing at all.'

'That isn't unusual. Mass killers tend not to be criminal types, ironically.'

'Not unless they're in uniform.'

'Appearance?'

'Puny. About fifty years old, I'd say – he won't. Undernourished, inoffensive, not someone I'd need help restraining, even with this leg.'

'And no hint of satisfaction or pride at what he's done.'

'Anything but that.'

Fischer sighed. Nothing about this man defined his type. He should have been extroverted, self-possessed, strengthened by the consequences of his actions. Shame and self-loathing were symptoms of self-awareness, of a morality bound by conventions. In that straitjacket one might sin in extremity but not by choice, and definitely not repeatedly.

'Two hours?'

'Otto, I'll bring you back here myself, I promise.'

51

Most Secret

From: Wessel

Distribution: named recipient only: Gehlen

Subject: Family Business

You have my report on the incident and retrieval of data that occurred two days past. Branssler has been confined to site since then, but given our lack of purpose-built interrogation facilities – or indeed, expertise - this is an unsatisfactory arrangement. Preliminary questioning has produced nothing. The question is what to do next.

In other circumstances I would recommend that he be transferred to USFET HQ at Frankfurt and interrogated there, but the nature and sensitivity of the data renders this option unworkable. As it stands, therefore, we are at an impasse. The threat of sanctions against his family will be seen by him as less than credible as he is fully aware of policy in this respect. The only other obvious course – one which I'm sure you have recognized already – is to employ outside assistance. Several candidates are well known to us and can be relied upon to do what is required. My only reservation in this respect is whether we want any of them to be a party to extremely sensitive information.

As regards Otto Fischer, I suggest that *Vidar* be sent to Berlin immediately. We do not know if Branssler was able to communicate any of the stolen intelligence to his friend, but clearly we cannot allow the risk. Having examined memoranda and operational regulations established for this organization by USFET I do not believe we shall be contravening either the spirit or letter of our remit if the situation is regarded as a compromised field operation and actioned accordingly – that is, urgently.


Wessel


Most Secret

From: Gehlen

Distribution: named recipient only: Wessel

Subject: Family Business

Re: interrogation of Branssler. Agreed that one or more of our old acquaintances be engaged. I doubt that any revelations re: *Andreas* will be either surprising or interesting to them, but choose carefully. I would prefer someone who is of interest to the Tribunals, in case we need to exert pressure.

Re: Fischer. Agreed your proposal, with immediate effect. Ensure that all references to him are removed from Oberursel training and personnel files upon word of *Vidar*'s success.


Gehlen

52

Engi peered through the dirty, cracked pane. Directly across Putlitzstrasse a man emerged from the Hotel and paused on its three-step stoop to seal an envelope.

'Is that him?'

Rolf joined the boy at the window.

'Yes.'

'He looks like a monster.'

'Hush. A lot of lads who went to war came back ugly. This one was wounded very badly, in a fire. It would have been better if he hadn't survived.'

Engi considered this new information and studied the face as it turned to check the street in both directions. 'Poor man.'

'Are you ready?'

'Yes, Rolf.'

The man on Putlitzstrasse put the envelope in his coat pocket and pointed himself southward. Rolf waited a few moments and then eased open the unhinged door, squeezing himself through as small a space as would accommodate his wiry body. Behind him, Engi dutifully counted out twenty of his heartbeats and tried not to look at the empty racks that clad three of the room's walls, where in better times (Rolf had told him) a thousand lines of domestic goods had emptied hausfraus' purses. He had never seen a shop that sold more than half a dozen commodities and wondered if he was being teased; but since their first recce of the place two days earlier, the shelves' high, regular march had stirred uncomfortable half-recollections - of his lying face upwards, seeing something vague but similar to this. He had almost dared ask Rolf if they could find another place from which to observe their wounded man, but this was the only unoccupied half-ruin for almost fifty metres on either side, and he knew perfectly well what the answer would be.

At *twenty-one* he slipped easily through the gap, out into Putlitzstrasse and only just avoided a collision with a man in rough work clothes and a Breton mariner's cap who brushed past at a late commuter's pace. Beyond him, Engi could see that Rolf was close to the junction with Turmstrasse already, so he followed quickly, almost forgetting to be the eyes in the back of his friend's head.

At Turmstrasse, Rolf turned left. A few moments later Breton Cap did the same, and Engi's attention sharpened suddenly. He paused at the corner, crouched down to tie an imaginary shoelace and glanced eastwards. About a hundred metres away, Rolf was stood in front of the posters on Moabit Krankenhaus's southern fence, absorbed in the detail of the latest announcement, invitation or proscription inflicted upon Berliners, while the same distance beyond him the wounded man was haggling with the proprietor of a farm cart. Breton Cap passed by Rolf without any obvious sign of interest and carried on in the direction of the wounded man. Several moments he had passed by the farm cart and turned right at the end of the street, into Rathenowerstrasse. Engi realised suddenly that he had been holding his breath, and released it.

When the wounded man moved away from the cart he, also, turned right at the end of Turmstrasse. Rolf followed at a casual pace, even stopping for a moment at the cart to examine the produce. Engi couldn't manage casual but he forced himself not to run and tried to make it seem as though he was looking anywhere but at his friend - in the manner, he imagined, of an accomplished detective. When he reached Rathenowerstrasse he stopped for a moment and glanced around as if unsure of which direction to take, a small embellishment to his technique for which he was immediately grateful. When he turned to the south he saw that both the wounded man and Rolf were on the street's eastern side, passing the old Seydlitz Kaserne. At that moment, barely thirty metres in front of Engi, Breton Cap emerged from Dreysestrasse and crossed the street, putting himself in Rolf's wake once more.

This no longer felt like a game. His heart pounding frantically, Engi followed, down Alt Moabit and on to Friedrich-Karl-Ufer, where British and Soviet patrols monitored the east-west human traffic. Neither the wounded man nor Rolf slowed as they crossed Humboldt-Hafen and approached the Zone border, but Breton Cap stopped suddenly and glanced around, as if unsure of the terrain.

Engi almost stopped too, but the man was looking his way. With a great effort of will he continued, closing the gap, trying not to seem interested but desperate also to see the face beneath the cap. But as he passed it was turned away to the north, taking in the view over the Hafen's broad expanse, and only a single thought came to him.

'Good morning, sir.' Engi put on what he hoped resembled an unctuous, eager to please *Freie Deutsche Jugend* smile as the man turned. 'Are you lost? May I help?'

'No.' It was cold, abrupt, but the interruption galvanized the man. He turned away, and in a moment was moving again, eastwards towards the waiting patrols. For a moment Engi couldn't move. The face he'd schemed to see was in his head now, and he wished heartily that it wasn't. If only it had been obviously evil – something, perhaps, from the sort of dream one struggled to wake from, wearing an *aufhocker*'s slitted mouth, its beaked nose and eyes like a meadow viper's. But this one had been worse, because he had seen nothing in it at all - no human warmth, no geniality, not even a hint that it belonged in the company of men.

Anxiously, he peered in the direction of the patrols, and couldn't see Rolf. At the eastern bank of the Hafen the wounded man was presenting his papers to a Soviet soldier, but between him and the advancing Breton cap no one else was on Friedrich Karl Ufer. He turned around, knowing as he did so that it was stupid, that Rolf couldn't have doubled back unnoticed; but in his growing panic he looked everywhere, even into the water on each side of him.

A short, piercing whistle came from the direction of the Spree. Rolf was on the river – or rather above it, on the Alsenbrücke that led to Tiergarten, waving to him. Relieved, he sprinted across the road to the river bank and on to the bridge, his important job as a spy forgotten.

'Well?'

'Him.'

Engi pointed to the man in the Breton cap. He had stopped by the first, British patrol and was speaking with one of the soldiers. A few metres to the east, the wounded man had disappeared into the Soviet Zone.

'Are you certain?'

Engi explained about the double-back at Dreyse-Strasse. Rolf nodded, patted him on the head.

'He's following our man, not me.'

'Yes, Rolf. I thought we were following him, too?'

Rolf lit a cigarette and threw the match into the Spree. 'We were. But you don't have the papers to cross into the east, and I didn't want to lose my eyes. It doesn't matter. Look, he's lost both his interested parties.'

The man in the Breton cap was walking away from the patrols, westward back along Friedrich-Karl-Ufer. Rolf squinted, trying to make out features that kept themselves pointed firmly towards the ground. 'A popular fellow, my old comrade.'

'Do you think that one's an American?'

'I doubt it. Why?'

'He looks like a bad man.'

'Americans are like anyone else, good and bad. Except for their ears.'

'What about their ears?'

Rolf put a finger behind each of his own and pushed. 'They stick out.'

Engi wanted to laugh, but the face remained too clear in his mind's eye. In any one of his possible futures there would be dark nights, and he feared it would return to occupy them. He shivered, and Ralph saw it.

'Well, we're not going east today. Do you like chestnuts?'

'I don't know.'

'There used to be vendors sometimes in Konig-Platz. Let's see if any of them survived the Peace.'

53

Fischer was met at the entrance to the *VolksPolizei* Praesidium's garage on Wadzeckstrasse by a short, slim man in uniform who introduced himself as *Unterkommissar* Müller. Between the motor-pool and the third floor he kept a hand less than nonchalantly over the right side of his face, though to his knowledge no one noticed him. Shown into the office of Commander Kurt Beckendorp, he took a few moments to glance around and marvel at the relative comfort endured by senior *VolksPolizei* officers, but the room was too busy to dwell upon. Holleman sat behind his desk, looking every part the remorseless nemesis of evil. At his side stood an officer (junior only in rank), and in a chair facing both men a handcuffed prisoner sat slumped, his face pointing at the carpet.

'Come in, Herr Braun.' Holleman gestured to a chair next to his. Fischer nodded curtly, came around the desk and tugged his suit trouser seams with intimidating precision as he sat. Slowly, he removed a notebook and two pencils from his jacket pocked, placed them carefully in front of him and coughed.

'Some water, please.'

'Kalbfleisch?'

The elderly junior officer sprang to a side-table and poured water into a crystal tumbler, tsked and wiped the side of the glass with his sleeve. With an effort, Fischer kept his frown intact and gave the prisoner his best cold stare.

The fellow was no one's idea of an insatiable killer. Physically slight, with a stoop that made him seem older than he was, his abject, forlorn air almost invited pity. Fischer looked for signs of mistreatment, but unless the *VolksPolizei* were considerably more skilled interrogators than Amt IV or Gestapo had been it seemed that no one had yet attempted to beat out a more enlightening confession.

Fischer cleared his throat. 'You are Egon Kofler?'

Without looking up the prisoner nodded slightly.

'And you have admitted responsibility for the deaths of ...' Fischer paused, as if checking the facts; '... seven children, all refugees?'

Another nod, almost imperceptible.

'You stand by this admission?'

The prisoner mumbled something. Kalbfleisch walked across to him and nudged his shoulder.

'I did it.'

'Upon what dates?'

'I don't know, sir.'

'By what means?'

'I can't remember.'

'And you disposed of the bodies by placing them into the homes of decent people who had no connection with these crimes?'

'Yes.'

Fischer pretended to note down the replies, giving both himself and Kofler a few moments to think. No further evidence was needed to condemn this man to a swift, efficient execution; no one – not even the *Magistrat* - would expect more detail, a deeper view into a broken psyche, a reason; and no useful purpose could be served by continuing to divert terribly overstretched resources to this sordid case. But Fischer knew precisely why Freddie Holleman was so goaded by Herr Kofler. It was as if justice were merely an onlooker here, a guard of honour standing respectfully in the shadows, bearing witness to a self-indulgent *pietá*. A man shouldn't have done what this one did, and having done it should not then have expected to set the terms of his cleansing ordeal.

'Do you feel remorse for your actions?'

Herr Kofler looked up for the first time to meet the eye of his interrogator. He seemed mildly surprised by the question (though considerably less so than Kalbfleisch).

'I ... it doesn't matter.'

'If you had the opportunity to return, to make the decision once more, would you do the same?'

'I would have no power to do otherwise. I made no decision.'

Next to Fischer, Holleman sat upright in his chair but managed not to say anything.

'Then you were merely an instrument. But why you?'

Kofler's mouth made several attempts before he got it out.

'Because I'm possessed by evil.'

'Really? Evil, Herr Kofler? I ask because I've known some very …'

'Beyond redemption, then.'

'Ah.' Fischer glanced at the other faces in the room. Holleman's was carefully blank, Kalbfleisch's a model of puzzlement and Müller's …. the *unterkommissar* was regarding the prisoner either with surprise or recognition, as if a hood had been removed from one or the other's head.

'And this is why you did these monstrous things? Because you were predisposed?'

The cuffed hands went up and down again to the prisoner's lap. 'I had no say in it.'

'As you say. You work at the Pasteurstrasse Mission?'

'You know that I do.'

'Where do you sleep?'

Kofler seemed mildly irritated by the question's banality. 'At the Mission. I have a bed behind the kitchen. It's permitted.'

'And for how long have you worked and resided there?'

'Why is this necessary? I …'

Fischer raised a hand. 'The law requires that the necessary documentation be submitted. Without details we cannot complete the paperwork; therefore, we cannot proceed. Don't worry, Herr Kofler, we can be patient.'

'Please, I did this thing, I confess to it …'

'Well, that isn't quite good enough. But I need only a few details more, and then we can *proceed.*'

The prisoner thought about this for a few moments and sighed. 'Three months.'

'Thank you. And before that?'

'Nothing.'

'Nothing?'

'Like many others, I wandered.'

'You were a refugee, then?'

'For a time.'

'And before this?'

'I can't say.'

'It's a secret?'

'It's … painful.'

'Something of which to be ashamed, perhaps?'

'No, just …'

'Then please answer the question.'

'I was a friar, at the monastery at Graz.'

The real police in the room seemed nonplussed. Fischer cleared his throat and tried to find the correct question.

'What Order is that?

'Franciscan.'

'And when did you leave?'

'I don't know. A few months after the fighting stopped.'

'May I ask – you needn't answer this if you wish – *why* did you leave the Order?'

Kofler stared at his hands for almost two minutes, saying nothing. Holleman frowned away another nudge from Kalbfleisch, turned and beckoned Müller. The *unterkommissar* bent to listen, nodded and left the room. Before the prisoner spoke again he had returned with a file, which he placed in front of his boss.

'I ...'

'Yes, Herr Kofler?'

'May I have some water?'

Holleman nodded. Kalbfleisch went to the side-table, poured more water with as much reluctance as an only-recently ambitious *oberwachtmeister* dared and thrust it under the prisoner's nose. Kofler took two tiny sips and returned the glass.

'I had a crisis of faith.'

'You no longer believed?'

'In what I was doing, no.'

Holleman opened his file, removed a sheet of paper, pushed it in front of Fischer and tapped it. He took the time to read it carefully.

'Thank you, Commander. What does a friar *do*, Herr Kofler?'

'He helps the poor, the sick, the weak. For the glory of God.'

'An admirable calling. And yet you lost your belief in what you did. Or was it something else?'

'We are required only to help those in need.'

'And to pray, presumably?'

'The Offices aren't obligatory, unless one wishes to be ordained.'

'And you didn't wish to be?'

'Once, perhaps.'

'The poor, the sick, the weak. So many are such, these days. Has there ever been a time when you were needed more?'

'No. It's why I work at the Mission.'

'And yet, by your own admission, you are evil. Feeding those who are hungry strikes me as a curious way to demonstrate this quality.'

'I try ...'

'I know; you try to expiate your evil with good works. You're a Catholic, after all.'

'But it's pointless. Evil begets evil. Look at what I've done.'

'Tell us about the prior evil, Herr Kofler. The one doing the begetting.'

When he didn't get a reply Fischer tapped the piece of paper on the desk in front of him. 'Have you perhaps been *helping* in a manner that some might consider wrong? That *you* consider wrong?'

The silence from the other side of the desk showed no signs of abating. 'Let me put a case to you, then. As a friar you were obliged to assist those who sought help from you. You couldn't predetermine the nature of supplication that was made to you, naturally; nor were you permitted to apply your own judgement or discretion when discharging your duty. But it must be galling, I imagine, when one is obliged to assist those whose need arises from questionable actions or events?'

Open-mouthed, Kofler stared at Fischer. 'How did you know?'

'Never mind. Certain gentlemen presented themselves at your friary, requesting help?'

'Yes.'

'Your Bishop is Alois Hudal, isn't he?'

'He was.'

'And when gentlemen such as the ones we speak of turned up at your friary, you were obliged to inform him?'

'We were. It wasn't my responsibility.'

'What were you required to do, then?'

'We fed them. We gave them beds. We ...'

'Didn't mention them to anyone else?'

'No.'

'What happened then?

'We ... sent them to the Croats.'

'Who?'

'Our brethren at San Girolamo, the Croatian College in Rome.'

'And these brethren did what?'

'I don't know. It wasn't our business to know.'

'But you know why these men had asked your assistance. Were they all Germans?'

'Most of them. Some Austrians too, and a few Ukrainians.'

'Men named by the Allied Tribunals.'

'Some. Others were … expecting to be.'

'For terrible crimes - crimes against the weak, the defenceless?'

'Allegedly, yes.'

'That must have been difficult for you.'

Kofler took a breath, so deeply that a man underwater might have drowned himself with it. 'One of them came to us a dying men. He wanted me to hear his confession, not understanding that I wasn't a priest. So I listened, and afterwards I pretended to offer absolution. It was … monstrous.'

'And you consider yourself guilty by association with his crimes?'

'War shouldn't be waged like that. But if it is, those who do it should be punished, not aided.'

'So you were tainted. But surely, a sincere act of contrition would have removed the sin?'

'My faith isn't strong.'

'Yet your faith in the possibility of damnation is. That's very strange.'

Kolfer sighed and shook his head. 'You're very clever. But the proof of my evil is the children. I killed them.'

'I'm not a theologian, Herr Kofler, but it seems to me that your argument has two weaknesses. First, it would be a remarkably peevish God who punished evil with the deaths of innocents. Second, for such punishment to be effective you would necessarily need the capacity for remorse, a sense of moral obligation, a *soul*. It would be a poor embodiment of evil that displayed such flaws – as, indeed, you do.'

Kofler raised his hands helplessly. 'Then how could I have killed those beautiful children?'

'How *did* you kill them?'

'I don't know. But I did.'

'What did you do?'

'I don't know! I tried to help them …'

Tears welled in Kolfer's eyes. Fischer waited, forcing from his mind the question he most wanted to ask.

'These were all refugee children, from the East?'

'And the Sudetenland, yes.'

'The poor things must have been in a wretched condition.'

'They were starving, and very sickly. Some were orphans.'

'They found their way to the Mission. How?'

'The *Volkssolidarität* sent them to us.'

'All of them, together?

'And their families, those that had them. We fed them all.'

'How many times did you feed them?'

'I don't know. They came back to us for several weeks. They were being housed around Friedrichshain.'

'Did the children ever come on their own?'

Kofler stared at his hands once more, and said nothing.

'Was there enough food for the refugees and your regular people, the Berliners?'

'Not always.'

'It's hard, to see people go hungry - especially children, and most especially those whose need is so great already. Did you do something that wasn't permitted, Herr Kofler?'

'I ... fed them.'

'You fed them. With your own food?'

'No.'

'So it was food provided to the Mission. By whom?'

'The Danish Red Cross. It was ... good food.'

'Better than what's usually available, I expect. So you decided to help the very neediest, on your own authority.'

Kofler was crying again. 'It was *good* food, the best. I cooked it myself, carefully, and gave them only as much as their bellies could take.'

'The Mission was closed when you did this?'

'Yes. I went to them as they queued to eat the awful soup we served that evening. I whispered to them, told them to come back after we closed. God, they trusted me …'

'How long did they stay?'

'The kitchens are warm. We were to stay closed as usual, for two days, after Sunday. I told them they could sleep there. Later that night, before dawn, I had to go to Pankow to pick up more food from the station. I didn't return until the afternoon. They were all ….'

'You locked them in?'

'How else would they have been safe?'

His head in his hands, Kofler rocked in his chair, sobbing. Kalbfleisch went back to his side and patted his shoulder clumsily, a kindness for which Holleman gave him the same stare that had quelled the nudge.

Fischer coughed, and spoke gently. 'What was this *good* food, Herr Kofler?'

The prisoner said something into his hands. Kalbfleisch bent down, whispered to him and straightened. 'Pork liver, he says.'

Fischer closed his eyes.

'Jesus.' Holleman rubbed his face and waved Müller to him. 'We know where the kids are buried, yes?'

'St Georgen cemetery, Comrade Commander.'

'We need one of them brought up. No, two.'

'Yes, comrade. And …?'

'Tell that useless bastard Jensen to have a look in the intestines.'

'For what, comrade?'

'*Darmbrand.* Tell him to have a good look, a sober look, or I'll transfer him to a dysentery ward. Kalbfleisch, get those cuffs off.'

Fischer leaned forward, towards Kofler. 'How did the children get to the houses? Did you do this yourself?'

'I confessed myself, to a holy man. He told me that I must await God's swift justice, but that we should see the children taken to good homes. He brought a cart, twice, and we took them away.'

*Swift Justice.* Fischer turned to Holleman. 'Only one of the recipients of these children didn't have a broken window.'

Holleman cursed under his breath. 'The Prophet.'

'He put them where they'd be found - but not by us, or the other householders. He wanted them to be among the Holy, or at least the Decent.'

As he removed the handcuffs Kalbfleisch whispered to the prisoner. 'You weren't to know the meat was infected. You did what you thought was best for the children. Your offence was to be silent.'

But Kolfer redeemed seemed no less distressed than Kofler damned. He was weeping openly now. 'I tried to make amends to God, but …'

Helplessly, Kalbfleisch looked up. 'Comrade Commander, do we need …?'

Holleman shook his head. 'He stays at the Mission until we get the autopsy reports. You, if you try to run I'll nail your balls to our front door.'

Helped physically by Kalbfleisch, Kofler stood up and shuffled towards the door. Fischer turned once more to Holleman and whispered. 'That thing about the Roman escape route. Where did you get it?'

'From the Americans. It's lifted verbatim from a State Department report dated July, last year. They and the British know all about the route and how it works. Don't ask me why they don't do anything about it, I'm only a godless *kozi*. Apparently the Franciscans are as deeply into it as they could be and not wear the black uniform. They don't, do they? Wear black? Franciscans have brown habits, don't they?'

Several peals sounded thunderously in Fischer's memory, and he leapt up from his chair.

'Wait!'

At the door, Kofler turned. He looked ready for the worst, as if his reprieve had been a subtle joke. Fischer went over to him, took the folded note from an inside pocket and showed him the second name.

'Have you heard of this man?'

Kofler looked up, surprised.

'Haven't you?'

54

In a comfortable house in the Frankfurt suburb of Westend, an upper window afforded a view of the American Military Headquarters in the old I.G. Farben building, though to enjoy it one would need almost to touch the glass and peer to the extreme left. The manoeuvre was quite beyond the gentleman who sat in the room's only chair, as it was attached to the floor and he to it. Another man leaned on the window sill, watching the captive twitch occasionally. A third stood by the chair, catching his breath and shaking some feeling back into the arm that was doing the punching.

The man at the window lit a cigarette. 'Come on, Branssler. It's hardly a difficult question.'

'The fucker's too thick-set. It's like hitting a sandbag.'

'It's alright, Helmut. Take your time.'

'Can't I work on the face?'

'You know what we were told.'

'Fingers?'

'As visible as the face. Keep your attention on his gut. He'll feel it eventually.' The man in the chair farted loudly. 'See? He's feeling it already. So let me ask you again, Gerd - may I call you Gerd? Of course I can, we're friends here. Who got the information in the file you stole? Was it your friend Fischer?'

Gerd Branssler looked up at the comedian, whose pleasant, open face he strongly wished to spoil. The other one was a technician, a pair of hands

- he had no quarrel with that; but as a former *kripo* he had strong opinions on how to go about an interrogation. He detested the funny ones almost as much as those who enjoyed their work excessively, who carried on long after they'd got all they were going to get. There was something about a man who appreciated his own jokes that only a grave could cure.

'No one got it. I was curious, that's all.'

'Bugger me, it's a curious sort of curious that makes a man take risks like that. Eh, Helmut?'

'I wanted to know why the fellow in the archives shat himself when I gave him the name. It seemed strange.'

'Not as strange as *why* you gave him the name.'

'It wasn't the same man - a coincidence, was all. But I didn't know that until I'd seen the file.'

'So, who's this other guy?'

'Fuck off.'

Helmut's fist crashed into Branssler's stomach. He winced and farted again.

'Christ, let some air in!'

The man at the window put a hand behind him and pulled up the sash a few inches.

'Your friend Fischer doesn't know anything about this?'

'Didn't I just say not?'

'It's a shame he's got Vidar after him, then.'

Helmut whistled softly. 'So they're not worried about *his* face and fingers?'

The comedian smiled. 'From what I hear this fellow doesn't have a face to speak of. Not that he'll fret about it, once Vidar's done.'

'They must be shitting themselves, to bring that bastard in.'

The comedian shrugged. 'They're cautious people. They have to be, with the Americans sat on their shoulders. If there's any doubt, remove the doubt. Have you finished, Helmut, or are you just tired?'

'Sorry.' The fist crashed into Branssler's stomach once more, but the sarcasm had flagged the punch and he was ready for it.

'Fuck.' Helmut shook his wrist again and looked down at his customer with professional admiration. 'He's tougher than he looks. I felt a bit bad about this when I started.'

'Don't be too tender. He used to work at the Alex - one of the bulls left over from the Republic.'

'I thought Goering got rid of that scum when he moved in.'

'This one must have been good, then. Were you, Gerd? Did you keep our wives and streets safe?'

Branssler coughed. 'There's an arse under me that needs kissing.'

Helmut giggled. 'Don't do it, Rudy. He'll blow your head off.'

The comedian Rudy consulted his wristwatch. 'This is taking an age. Work on his jewels.'

Helmut pursed his lips and considered this. 'We'll have to get him up. The belly's in the way.'

'Alright.' Rudy removed a Sauer 38H from his pocket and waved it at the prisoner. 'Be good, Gerd.'

As the handcuffs were detached Branssler squinted into the gun's muzzle. 'You want me to stand up so you can kick me in the balls? No.'

Ignoring Newton's first law of motion, Helmut (out-weighed by at least thirty kilos) tugged vainly at a free arm.

'Can't you put one in his leg?' he pleaded.

'Not allowed.' Rudy sighed. 'It didn't used to be like this. Can you imagine Heydrich telling us to avoid doing any visible damage?'

Disgusted, both men regarded the job. His massive arms by his side, Branssler squatted in the chair between them like a half-deflated, sweat-drenched minotaur, inviting them to conceive a subtler form of coercion. After a few moments (during which he gripped the Sauer's handle with sufficient force to transfer its pattern to his flesh), Rudy rubbed the painful portion of his forehead with a knuckle.

'Alright, Gerd. Let's do it the strange way. If you give me an answer when I ask a question, we'll be that tiny bit closer to the moment when we can all leave this fucking room. Yes?'

Branssler coughed, spat blood, nodded slightly.

'Super. The file you took – did anyone else see it?'

'No.'

'Did you pass on information from said file to anyone?'

'How could I have done that? Five minutes after I left the archives half of Oberursel was sitting on me.'

'Not your friend Fischer?'

'He was in Berlin that day. You can check it easily enough.'

'So, taking the file - that was just you being idly curious?'

'I needed to know if it was anything I needed to know.'

'And it wasn't?'

'I don't know him.'

'Who?'

'The one in the file.'

'Whose name is …?'

'I forget.'

Rudy smiled. 'Good lad. Alright, Helmut, we've done what we were told. Clear up this mess.'

Branssler looked up and frowned. 'I can go?'

Rudy laughed. 'What do you think?'

55

Rolf was in his Putlitzstrasse observation post just before dawn. He had put the boy in the care of the manageress of a nearby workers' cooperative, whose reluctance to have her kitchens untidied was soothed remarkably by a handful of Allied marks. It had been enough to secure a piece of bread and some cheese also, both of a texture familiar to tank-armourers. He ate on his comfortable perch of bricks, without once taking his eyes from the frontage of the Hotel *Bad Gastein*.

It was fully light and commuters had begun their droop-eyed, oblivious odysseys when Fischer emerged. Today he descended the stoop, turned left and walked southward immediately, without bothering to check the street. Rolf pushed the last of the cheese into his mouth and waited. Less than thirty seconds later Breton Cap entered his left field of view and disappeared again, moving in the same direction. Rolf gave the Steyr another grope for luck, waited a further minute and followed.

Fischer had time on his hands, apparently. He kept his steady, unhurried course until he reached the river, crossed it and turned left on Holsteiner Ufer. At Tiergarten he meandered on footpaths, ignoring the geometrically-straight roads that would take a man with a destination swiftly out of the park once more. He paused at a bandstand to read the notices, examined allotments and generally gave the impression of a man pressed by no particular business.

Behind him, Breton Cap followed with professional disinterest. Had Fischer been as edgy as fox in a kennels he probably wouldn't have noticed his stalker, who at each pause managed to put himself where he could hardly be observed and yet cover any possible variation to his object's itinerary. During the same pauses, Rolf leapt in and out of the sparse shrubbery with such patent clumsiness that his own prey would have made him in a moment had he bothered to turn.

After almost half an hour in Tiergarten Fischer had gone no further than Grosse Weg, where he paused at the edge of the Neuen See, and, with what many Berliners would have regarded as unforgivable extravagance, began to throw pieces of bread to some of the surviving waterfowl. Breton cap paused about twenty metres from the water and started a conversation with an old gentleman repairing a bird net. He neither glanced towards the water nor reacted when Fischer had finished feeding the birds and began to retrace his steps towards Grosse Weg. The one passed the other less than two metres apart, and no one would have thought either man anything but oblivious to the encounter.

From a shattered copse of yews, Rolf waited, his nerves tearing. Unless he decided to reverse his course Fischer had three choices: to go south into the remains of the zoo and the Flak tower complex, southeast into the city once more or due east on the long, exposed stretch of Tiergartenstrasse. The first two options would require that he cross the Landwehr canal, where a body might be misplaced discreetly. The third would be unfortunate – a broad, relatively busy road, well overlooked and patrolled. If Fischer decided to go that way a looming problem would become a challenge.

As if reading the mind of his at least one of his followers, Fischer threw the last of the bread into the water, rubbed crumbs from his hands and turned eastward. Rolf cursed softly but stayed where he was, waiting for Breton Cap to finish his conversation. It took almost two minutes, by which time Fischer had almost reached Hofjäger Allee.

There, he paused once more, and for the first time Rolf wondered if he was being deliberate - a lure floating enticingly in a slow current. Breton Cap, who had resumed the pursuit, was in the open now with no plausible reason to pause; he kept walking, head down, closing the gap between them, drawing no attention to himself.

But then Fischer did something entirely unpredictable. A small bridge carried Hofjäger Allee over the outfall from the Neuen See. Instead of walking across it he descended the short, steep embankment to the bridge footing and the water's edge. For the first time that day, Breton Cap looked around to check on possible observers. Rolf had time – just – to change direction without being noticed. He forced himself not to glance back until he reached the closest tree and then leaned against it, removing a shoe as if to empty it of a stone. When he looked back at the bridge he could see neither man.

He hadn't run for years, not since creeping artillery barrages and flanking attacks had made it a very necessary form of exercise. But he sprinted now, his shoe abandoned by the tree. When he reached the embankment the water's surface was smooth and undisturbed. He scrambled down the incline on his arse and almost went into the stream, saved only by a leg, thrust out from the ledge beneath the bridge, which gave him a moment's purchase.

It was Fischer's. He was on his back, struggling to prise Breton Cap's hands from his throat. Rolf removed the Steyr from his jacket, and, taking care not to let the low arch hamper his swing, brought it crashing down on the assailant's neck. Assisted by a heave from one of the knees beneath him he toppled into the stream, barely conscious.

'I … thought you weren't coming.' Fischer sat up and rubbed his windpipe tenderly. There was blood on his head and a stain on the wall next to it, but the confined space had evened the disparity in strength between the two men and slowed the business.

'Your billy-goat-gruff strategy surprised me.' Rolf attached the suppressor to his pistol. Breton Cap – minus the cap - was trying to pull himself out of the water, but froze when the barrel touched the top of his head.

'Wait.' Shakily, Fischer clambered to his feet and leaned against the arch, catching his breath. 'It's not necessary.'

'What? You think he's just going to say fair enough and walk away?'

'He won't have a choice, if I'm right. But I need to see your Russian.'

Rolf eased the pressure on the trigger pin but kept the suppressor pressed against the assassin's head. 'That's a joke, yes?'

'As soon as possible. Today.'

'But he wants you dead.'

'Did he say so?'

'He gave me a gun, brother. It's a heavy hint.'

'Well, he can tell me about it himself. I won't be offended.'

56

Two former generals faced each other across a desk. One of them sipped tea from a bone-china cup; the other (who detested the pretence of composure in a crisis) tapped wood with a finger in the hope that its persistence was irritating.

Reinhard Gehlen licked his lips and placed the cup carefully in its saucer. 'So, what do we think?'

Wessel shrugged. 'Probably, he told the truth. But can we reassure ourselves with *probably*?'

'He was in the archives for a matter of minutes only. He had no camera, no access to a radio or telephone?'

'None, for certain.'

'The file?'

'*All* red files are now in my office safe. All cards in the index which refer to them have been lifted and destroyed. We need to have a conversation about future access, but definitely there must be no further opportunity for anyone to do what Branssler did.'

'No. It was remarkably lax.'

'The operation has been built quickly. Inevitably, some things weren't considered adequately. Perhaps the fence wire and our American guards allowed us to think that we were secure.'

Gehlen stared out of his window, at the wire in question. For all his apparent calm Wessel could see that he was pensive, upset. The Americans believed above all in his competence, his record for efficiency and accuracy - they wouldn't have put their faith and money in him otherwise. Not that they would be allowed to hear of this little disaster and its consequences. There were some things you couldn't tell even the best of friends, and they were by no means that.

'What do we do now?'

The question hinted at haplessness, usually, but in this case it addressed a wound. Wessel gave his finger a rest and thought about it.

'Clearly, we move cautiously. If Branssler was telling the truth there's no exposure. If he wasn't, then over-reacting will draw attention. I suppose the most immediate issue is: do we warn Andreas?'

Gehlen shook his head firmly. 'At the moment there's no connection between him and us. It would be damned foolish to create one. Let luck – good or bad – work itself out.'

'And Branssler?'

'It's too late to do anything about him – our associates saw to that. How are they?

Wessel shrugged once more. 'The one with the broken nose we paid off and sent far away. The other …'

'Yes?'

'He'll be discharged in a day or two. The pistol did a lot of damage. An arse makes a poor holster.'

Gehlen tried and failed to smother the smile. 'And the trail?'

'Cold as the steppe. Branssler got to his wife before we reached the apartment. His daughters live near Düsseldorf, but I don't for a moment think he'll risk that.'

'Well, we'll do what we can, for now. His friend Fischer is a concern still.'

'Vidar will have dealt with that.'

'I want to *hear* that he has. Herr Fischer may be as innocent as a March lamb, but the organization can't be put to the risk.'

'The Beckendorp operation?'

'Is horribly compromised. We don't know how much of what we've been given is good, if any. In a credible manner, let Karlshorst know they have an imposter in their ranks. I don't see why we can't share the pain of this damned comedy.'

57

Müller told himself that this was probably the best ending to a human tragedy, but still he felt slightly cheated. He and his assistant Kalbfleisch had pored over the evidence, made the correct deductions and – however aided by the man himself – brought the perpetrator to justice. Only they hadn't. They had chased down a monster and bagged an unfortunate bastard instead, a man whose back one would wish to comfort rather than push against a firing wall. It made it worse for Müller that he was obliged to see the fellow each day now, when he came to Keibelstrasse to report that he hadn't fled the city. It was like reading an unsatisfying novel without the power to put it down and walk away.

But finally, the final chapter loomed. On his desk he had the report (if a single page of resentful, scrawled opinion counted as such) on the autopsies of two children, wretched creatures thrown upon a kind charity that had killed them. The detail was sparse but conclusive: necrotic inflammation of the jejunum in both cases, which, given that these were apparently refugee children, and noting the timescale between infection and death (details that Doctor Jensen took care to stress were not known to him previously), almost certainly indicated severe food poisoning.

*If you'd bothered to open them up at the time you'd have smelled it, you dolt.*

So Egon Kofler could be released from discretionary arrest to continue the ascent to his personal Calvary. Kalbfleisch had been dispatched to Pasteurstrasse Mission bearing the glad tidings, leaving Müller to finish their report on the non-murders and wonder whether this constituted a triumph of police work or a waste of their horribly-overstretched resources. His own reputation and had been enhanced by the business, but the curiously vacant space where his sense of professional satisfaction should have resided irked him still. Perhaps it was the fault of his Christian schooling, the vague sense that evil ends should have evil causes.

He reminded himself that this had appeared to be a series of bestial crimes, and therefore had to be investigated. If there was fault here it belonged to God, or Fate, or whatever other agency had permitted humans to be too human, to allow the rape of a continent. The seven small corpses were only an eddy in the stream of consequence that flowed from it, and if all that he and Kalbfleisch had done was to confirm this (much assisted, admittedly, by the mysterious, mutilated 'Herr Braun'), it was no less necessary a task.

So he went back over the report, satisfied himself as to the number of times Kalbfleisch had managed to insert references to *vigilance, promptness* and *the people's safety*, and decided that if there was such a thing as The Book this investigation had been carried out precisely according to its precepts. He signed it, adding a little flourish to his habitually bloodless signature, and placed it into a buff folder he had labelled *The Friedrichshain Child Deaths* (to give it a chance among the anonymous pile of required sign-offs shoved daily before Commander Beckendorp).

That face came back to him again. When Beckendorp said not to ask any questions a wise man kept his lips pressed together, but what was a *Westie* doing in East Berlin's central police station, directing an interview in the biggest case they'd seen that year? Not that Müller doubted the man's qualifications – how could he, after witnessing a master-class in interrogation? No threats had been made, no fate insinuated, not even a voice raised (a pleasant voice at that, the light baritone nicely modulated), and at the end of it a man more tightly closed than an immature pistachio had more or less dictated his non-confession. Perhaps it been the face itself; perhaps a flayed countenance invoked some subliminal belief in its integrity. It had been unnervingly *open*, after all.

And the timing – that, too, bothered Müller. This fellow Braun was brought in less than forty-eight hours after Kofler had been marched into Keibelstrasse, which meant that his participation couldn't possibly have been authorized. Beckendorp was famously averse to toeing prescribed lines - you only had to pass his closed door most days to get his loud, oblivious opinion upon his superiors' competence (*they couldn't organize a Roman traffic-jam*) and the job (*a starving dog wouldn't do it for a fucking steak supper*), and he would think for less than a moment about putting a request through the correct chain of command. His friend had been brought into the building discreetly, had done the job smartly, had been conjured away again, and as far as Müller could see only himself, Kalbfleisch and the unfortunate Kofler had been parties to the business.

And there was Beckendorp's glibness, his lack of … gravity. When Müller had asked whether they should arrest John the Baptist, Kofler's abettor, he had laughed and said that there was no point. All the man had done was to break other folks' windows, and if he was taken he'd only be pardoned the following week - if he was right about Jesus, that is. Müller wasn't a pious man, but such things weren't to be joked about.

All of this put a weight on his shoulders. He was tremendously obliged to Beckendorp – for his trust, the promotion, the opportunity to be more than a *kapo* for the Russians. But if word got out that the man had done something that might wreck a career in the *VolksPolizei* he didn't want to be regarded as an accomplice to it. He had to think of his family, even if it made him a Judas.

He reassured himself that it wouldn't be necessary to mention that the man Braun was a westerner. To speak of the matter at all, even in the vaguest of terms, would indicate proper attitude, the correct level of concern about the Commander's impatience with regulations. If he put it as a duty reluctant discharged (that was hardly a lie), the matter might be quietly filed away and his arse covered without consequence. He told himself it was both the prudent and necessary course.

But contemptible also, without doubt. The old Müller – the craven collaborator, the false friend of pre-condemned souls, the coward who hated what he did but wouldn't for a moment think of doing differently – had returned, back from extended leave. In recent days he had been thinking of breaking the tradition of years and telling his wife something of his work, their collective success, to let her know that she was married to a man she could be proud of. Now, shame would keep it as buried as his glittering string of court cases, the multitude of defendants he had assisted into camps or directly out of the world with platitudes and a sympathetic pat on the shoulder.

He tormented himself for a further hour, conceiving penances for his betrayal and exonerations that would bear not a fleeting second-glance from a sound conscience, and then he went up to the fifth floor to make an appointment to see the Chief Inspector. He was almost relieved to be told that the earliest opportunity was three days away; it gave him time to agonize properly, to decide what to do if he was offered pieces of silver.

Kalbfleisch came in just before noon. He sat down heavily in a chair, threw his cap on to their shared table and lit a cigarette before nodding a greeting. He seemed to have emptied slightly, let some air into his uniform.

Müller returned the nod. 'How did our friend take the news of his innocence?'

'Indifferently.'

'He isn't pleased?'

'He isn't anything. After the Mission closed last evening he opened his wrists over the sinks. It was done very considerately. There's hardly a splash anywhere.'

'Why the hell would he do that? Why wouldn't he wait for the Doctor's verdict?'

Kalbfleisch shrugged. 'It didn't matter. What the *VolksPolizei* said he did or didn't do is beside the point. He was on a bigger wheel.'

'Christ.'

'Probably.'

'Was it was what happened here in Berlin, do you think? Or was it the Graz business?'

'I doubt he saw them as separate offences. When you work up that much guilt there isn't a place for logic or a ranking order.'

'Poor sod.'

'Well, he's made the best of it. Jesus can ease the pain better than we ever could.'

It was strange that Kalbfleisch would choose to be so dangerously facile, and Müller wondered if he was more upset about it than he seemed. Certainly, the news had brought his own day down a few more notches, made their triumph even less a cause for satisfaction. The children hadn't been murdered but they were dead in any case; their supposed killer was innocent and equally dead; the investigating officers were lauded but at least one of them was about to become an assassin, a cur, an outcast. Was it possible to be more depressingly, pointlessly successful?

Müller almost wished he were in the sort of occupation that allowed a man to finish his shift early, sick either in body or heart. The thought of an afternoon devoted to heavy drinking struck him as unusually amenable (the more unusual for that he was a staunch teetotaller), a few hours in a dark, comfortable place not caring where one's conscience and home address had been misplaced. The fantasy grew intensely more attractive just before his lunch break, when a near-geriatric *anwärter* stuck his head around the door and blurted that a squad of Soviet soldiers had arrested Commander Beckendorp and rushed him out of the building.

Müller didn't know whether to be terrified or relieved. He didn't know whether this was about the man Braun or some other matter on which the Commander's singular way of doing things had broken against the grey rocks of the new bureaucracy. He was only thankful – devoutly so - that his request for an appointment with the Chief Inspector was already a matter of record, and that he might not now have to keep it.

58

The Friedrich orphanage at Rummelsberg was like much of central Berlin, a good deal smashed up but with isolated pockets of near-normality, beauty spots spoiling a general disfigurement. The complex was well-spaced, so the bombs that had eradicated its church and almost all the girls' house had largely spared the two boys' houses. They were full now of war orphans, an abundant crop. Closer to the shoreline of the Rummelsberger See and adjacent to the district workhouse (infamous as the first stop for the Reich's repeat-offenders during their clearance to Dachau in 1937), the remains of their sister building stood forlornly among equally shattered trees, its one surviving, roofless room open to the water-side.

The view was quite attractive, despite the immediate desolation. On a fine day (as this was) the room might have served adventurous picnickers, its three remaining walls sheltering an almost *al fresco* lunch from the wind. But the uniforms and weaponry gave it a less pleasing ambience, the water's proximity a gloomier prospect.

A Soviet major sat incongruously at a badly-chipped child's desk, thereby reserving to himself the only two pieces of furniture in the room. He was flanked on either side by a heavily armed *soldat*, whose slightly hungry glares – directed at the room's two German guests – blanked with parade ground precision when he dismissed them.

The major removed a pen and placed it carefully next to the leather-bound notepad he had carried into the room (a purely psychological gesture, given that he had not the slightest intention of committing anything to paper). When the two objects were aligned to his satisfaction he looked up and smiled.

'I believe you gentlemen are acquainted?'

Despite themselves, Fischer and Holleman obeyed the silent whistle and glanced at each other.

'Yes, you are. Former Luftwaffe comrades, now mercenaries of ourselves and the Americans. A high-ranking officer of the *VolksPolizei* and … what? A spy?'

Fischer tried to smile, but it felt like a partial stroke. 'Hello, Zarubin.'

'It's *Major* to you, Major.' Sergei Aleksandrovich Zarubin smiled, pleased to have been the opening, but his face straightened in a moment. 'Didn't I tell you Berlin was to be avoided?'

'I think you mentioned it.'

'Yet you not only returned but attempted to corrupt one of our best men, Herr Beckendorp.'

'And he me.'

'His was a riposte, and therefore extenuating.'

'To a courtroom, perhaps.'

'You knew that he had been required to report the business to Karlshorst, to an MGB officer. Didn't you suspect me to be me?'

'The description fit.'

'And yet you persisted, passing on rubbish that you must have known would be discovered as such.'

'And receiving shit in return.'

'Which …' Zarubin's gaze passed pointedly from one German to the other and back again; '… you somehow also knew to be such.'

Fischer said nothing more. He had been feeding lines to an accomplished vaudevillian, a man who enjoyed picking apart other men's sense of how the ground beneath them lay. If a firing post was looming he had no intention of tying himself to it.

Zarubin was watching him carefully, and he returned the compliment. He had last seen the Russian only nine months earlier, but the man had grown into his new rank. He wore *this* uniform comfortably, not in the slightly sardonic, apologetic manner with which he'd occupied his senior lieutenancy. Then, he had been a one-man show, the only NKGB officer in Stettin, a permanently under-resourced onlooker to a disordered wen. This sleeker Zarubin wasn't apologizing for anything. Berlin was a far larger, more serious game for adult players, and he was helping to write the rule book.

But the man enjoyed a game still. He had known for a while that a certain German acquaintance was back in the city and done nothing about it – no warning, no interview, no quiet, discreet removal. Fischer wanted to know why, and couldn't ask. You didn't ask questions of Zarubin, for the same reason you didn't ask for answers during an examination. To do so would be cheating, or at least spoiling the *game*.

The Russian's careful observation was becoming a stare - a part of the entertainment rather than a pointless attempt to intimidate. Fischer decided to be surprised by it.

'Am I prettier these days?'

'Not really. But I have to say you disguise the ravages of your severe drink problem very well.' Zarubin turned to Holleman. 'So well, in fact, that I'm surprised you were able to diagnose it, Comrade Commander. I mean, his hands don't shake, his half-a-nose doesn't glow and his conversation seems a lucid as an abstainer's. Perhaps your imagination was at play? By that, of course, I refer to both your imaginations.'

Holleman frowned. 'I don't understand, comrade.'

'No? Well, I have a problem with Herr Fischer's little weakness. I didn't get a hint of it in Stettin – and Christ knows, *there's* a town that needs a stiff drink to survive. Perhaps the habit was in remission back then? But he's had so little time since to return to it since, given his recruitment and training by Gehlen's people and his energetic suborning of gullible police officers. Yet you attribute his dramatic ideological *volte face*, his willingness to be played by us, to an addiction to the bottle. I think you were mistaken, Beckendorp - that is, you weren't quite telling the truth. And why should you? What would be gained by admitting that you and Fischer are very good friends? In fact, conspirators?'

Before either man could respond Zarubin waved away something. 'Ach, do you mind if I call you Herr Holleman? This Beckendorp fiction is becoming stale.'

The punchline, delivered expertly. Freddie Holleman's mouth opened and stayed there. His gut turning, Fischer waited. He didn't bother trying to guess at the flaw in their plans that had allowed the Russian to drive sideways through the hole it made. He didn't need to. Zarubin would no more be coy about his cleverness than any other bad winner.

'You want to know how I know?'

'I know that you'll tell us.'

Zarubin laughed. 'Don't be petulant, Major. Obviously, from the moment *Holleman* gave me the name of this western spy he'd somehow ensnared I was similarly caught. I asked myself, why would Otto Fischer, a famously undogmatic gentleman, have tied himself to Gehlen's troupe of rabid anti-communists? They don't pay well, they have no retirement plan and tend to treat anyone who wasn't formerly Abwehr or FSO as scum. No, I couldn't see it. And yet there could be no doubt that he *was* a Gehlen employee. I looked for a motive. Excuse me, would you?'

Zarubin un-wedged himself from beneath the child's desk, went to the empty doorframe and shouted something in Russian. One of the *soldats* returned carrying a samovar and three cups, which he placed on the desk and retreated.

'Courtesy of our hosts, the orphans. Shall I pour?'

With a cup of steaming tea in his hand, Fischer felt even more disoriented, (which he assumed was the purpose of the small kindness). Beside him, dazed still, Holleman took and held his drink by its hot flanks, apparently feeling nothing. Zarubin didn't pour one for himself. He frowned for a moment, recalling himself.

'Let's speak first of the motives of the men at Oberursel. Clearly, they would like to control someone who had access to Karlshorst. This being the case they would identify a man either susceptible to pressure or under a degree of it already. So, why Beckendorp? The fact that he was their target intrigued me, and I had to investigate. This produced nothing initially, because his work for us and the good people of Berlin has been exemplary. Yes, his history was curious – a failed revolutionary who managed to avoid National Socialism's avenging hand by conforming and serving in the Luftwaffe – but credible. The life of the agitator is, after all, one that puts him outside the norms. Beckendorp had defied the Republic, hid his political convictions from the Reich and emerged in the cleansing light of 1945 to find us, his spiritual comrades, squatting in his *heimat*. We welcomed him as a brother, dusted him off, gave him a job and have since been tremendously pleased by the result. This man is not, I told myself, someone who can turned easily by the Gehlen gang.

'So my search for *why Beckendorp* revealed nothing. Which brought me back to you, Fischer – why *you*? Beckendorp had admitted that he knew you previously, so that was where I placed my artillery. I recalled his story of how you met originally - that his Luftwaffe support unit assisted in extracting units of *Fallschirmjäger* I Regiment during the Belgian campaign. This was easy enough to check, and proved not to be the case. So, magically, I had two results. The best policeman in eastern Berlin was lying to me - *and*, perhaps, I had the first sniff of a reason why Oberursel imagined they could turn him.'

Fischer took a sip of his tea to clear the jam in his throat. 'A reason?'

'Well, a hint of something. It was to do with you. You *know* him, clearly, though his version of it was a lie. But again I asked myself: why would you do Gehlen's work for him? You have no commitment to anything but your own, and every German's life is sufficiently interesting at present not to need a further portion of excitement. The answer, it seemed to me, was that you were doing it *because* of Beckendorp – that this was more than an acquaintance.'

Zarubin picked up the pen from the desk and placed it in his inner pocket. 'So, there it was. I merely checked the central medical archives for Luftwaffe leg amputations. Fortunately, Alexander Kaserne wasn't so badly bombed that this was a problem.'

Holleman finally found his voice. 'There must have been hundreds of leg amputations.'

'But you had mentioned Luftwaffe's Belgian campaign. I assumed you did so because you had been there in some capacity and could recall enough detail to be plausible, if asked. I found eight records for a six-week period, of which three related to left leg amputations and therefore couldn't be you. Of the remaining five, three died subsequently before the war's end. This gave me two possibilities, and one of them, poor fellow, had lost an eye also. So, I was left alone with Friedrich Melancthon Holleman. Presumably your parents were religious folk?'

'My mother ...'

Fischer interrupted. 'But this is still fairly tenuous. How could you know the man was your Kurt Beckendorp?'

'Because Friedrich Holleman turned out to be a most slippery fellow. When I went to Luftwaffe personnel records to confirm my theory I found nothing – as if he didn't exist. And yet the civilian Holleman was definitely on the 1938 voters' census, and had joined Johannisthal flying club the year before that. There was also a man with precisely this name who served in the lower ranks of Berlin's *Ordnungspolizei* until the outbreak of war. At some point thereafter, someone took great pains to extract him.'

'Even so ...'

'Please wait. I then went back to our friend Beckendorp. He was almost as troublesome, having a service record that trailed off abruptly in early 1943 without apparent cause. But he has a family and we know their given names, so it wasn't quite so difficult to narrow down the multitude who share this fairly common surname. And I found them.'

'Where?'

'Dutifully, Frau Beckendorp reported a change of address to the *OrPo* station in Lübben - on 14 September 1943, I believe, having moved from the rather distressed city of Hamburg to a pleasant lakeside property in the Spreewald. I now had the property address, so I checked the land registry.'

Holleman sighed. 'Shit.'

'The house had been owned by one Philip Holleman, since 1912. No transfer of title has occurred subsequently - not that it matters, the place was probably atomized during the fighting to erase the Halbe pocket. Philip was your father, presumably?'

Fischer managed to move his legs sufficiently to get his empty cup to the desk. 'What do you want, Zarubin?'

The Russian looked slightly disappointed. 'You really aren't going to address me as Major, are you? Want? I don't want anything.'

'Except my neck.' Holleman looked ready to make a rush, either for Zarubin or the door.

'Why would I want that? You're a very good policeman, I've said so. What would be the point of removing you from a job you're doing so well?'

'But I'm not Beckendorp.'

'Do you have to be? I mean, obviously you do, otherwise the paperwork becomes tiresome. But that apart, why do I need you to be *him*?'

'But ...'

Fischer took Holleman's arm. 'I don't think the Major cares about why you hid from the previous regime, Freddie.'

'... I'm not a *kozi*, either.'

Zarubin looked puzzled. 'Do you have a problem with our socio-economic model?'

'Not particularly. I draw a salary from it.'

'Well, then, don't feel that you're letting me down. I know men who can recite *Das Kapital* from memory yet can't find their arses with a finger. Most of them are politicians, obviously. Competence is rather more necessary in a policeman. If you keep doing what you're doing, I won't have any reason to gossip about you to my superiors.'

'Major ...'

Gratified, Zarubin turned to Fischer. 'Yes, Major?'

'You can be certain that he won't betray your trust.'

'Can I?'

'Oberursel has one thing on Beckendorp – they know that he isn't who he claims to be. Their only weapon is the threat of revealing this to you, to Karlshorst. Obviously, the threat means nothing now.'

'So this is why you involved yourself in their project. I'm touched.'

Fischer shrugged. 'It was me who disappeared him in '43. I feel a certain responsibility.'

'Presumably this wasn't because of any anti-Soviet activities? In which case I have no further business with Herr Holleman – who must once more and ever be Comrade Beckendorp, of course.'

The reprieved man still couldn't quite grasp what he was hearing. 'Really?'

'I think the Major has further business, Freddie. But with me, not you.'

'You, Otto? What can … oh, yeah.'

'Comrade Major Zarubin believes that he now has a convenient pair of eyes – and two sets of light fingers - at Oberursel. But I'm afraid he's wrong about that.'

The Russian's eyebrows lifted. 'I am? What a shame. Presumably, the attempt upon your life in the Tiergarten was General Gehlen's notice of dismissal?'

'You heard about it.'

'Naturally. Your guardian angel works for me, and though his interference wasn't authorized I'm glad he took the initiative. Yet I wonder why he did? Having been members of the same regiment hardly seems sufficient reason for him to risk his life and my disappointment.'

'We shared a shallow depression - at Maleme, in '41.'

'Ah, the heroic twilight of the parachutists. That would explain the blood-tie, and his willingness to feed me more of your shit. You and he have been working me. I should be very angry about that.'

'No, he thought you wanted me dead, and that he was to be the means of it. He warned me, that's all.'

'But he was mistaken. I only wanted him to be vigilant, and men called upon to kill are usually that. Really, I wouldn't consider harming a hair of your broken head.'

'I find that surprising, Major.'

'To be frank, so do I. I'm employed to see only enemies, yet I regard you as a blind spot, a blur. I suppose a head doctor might diagnose this as symptomatic of empathy, even fondness. But please don't expect a dinner invitation.'

It was Fischer's turn to be puzzled. 'So what did you intend?'

'Nothing. Don't worry, you won't be PSh'd. I knew already that you were useless to me. And the reason I knew is the same reason why I had little use for you anyway.'

'You have men in Oberursel already.'

'It's hardly an achievement. The organization's screening protocols are laughable – as long as a man can prove that he wasn't captured on the Eastern Front they don't care about anything else. As for you, you seem to have been there a very short time, and have access to more or less nothing - and, of course, they no longer trust you. In fact, they're doing their best – their very clumsy, left-handed best – to get you off the payroll. All of which makes you as useful as a perforated condom.'

Fischer glanced at Freddie Holleman, who was just beginning to get it. For the first time since 1943 he had a future that his blameless past couldn't pop up to ruin, a path that only would require him to keep to it, the faithful servant of whatever the Soviets were going to make of the SBZ. Fischer wished that his own prospects were nearly as unclouded - wondered how much further Zarubin was prepared to go than merely sparing him.

The Russian had reclaimed his notebook and was putting on his gloves. It looked like the day's business was concluded.

'Major?'

'Yes, Major?'

'Aren't you interested in why General Gehlen wants me dead?'

'Let me see … um, not particularly.'

'Why would they do something this drastic, even if it's only against one of their own? They aren't in the assassination business, and they know perfectly well that the Americans wouldn't condone it.'

Zarubin considered this. 'Probably not. How naughty have you been, Major?'

'Inadvertently, very.'

'As your business is entirely to do with knowledge, I assume that you've come into possession of too much of the commodity?'

'A quantity of the wrong sort, certainly.'

'Oh good, a tease.' The gloves were dropped back on to the desk. 'And you want, what? To bargain with this?'

'Trade, perhaps. A name for names.'

'What names?'

'How far have you penetrated the Gehlen organization?'

'To a modest degree. At the moment all senior staff at Oberursel are old comrades from FHO and Abwehr, feverishly committed to fighting the communist menace and therefore quite beyond our ability to tempt. In time our own Germans will rise through the ranks.'

'Did you know that the organization isn't chasing Nazis?'

'We did.'

'That they may at least be passively assisted wanted men – that is, by not turning them in to the Americans?'

'We know of criminals who could have escaped the Tribunals only by being aided - by the Church, or old comrades. And if we're aware of them, Gehlen must be. So, yes.'

'It's their names that I need. Some of them, at least.'

'And in return you'll give me just one? It hardly seems fair.'

'It's another fugitive. Oberursel are aware of him - in fact, they know where he lives.'

Zarubin pulled a face. 'This isn't so exciting.'

Fischer removed the piece of paper from his pocket and offered it. The Russian glanced at it, a frown spoiling his film star's face; but when he got the point he laughed disbelievingly.

'You went looking for this name?' He looked at Freddie Holleman. 'Of course you did. But you found *this* one instead! And Gehlen has it?'

'We took it this from Oberursel. From the restricted file section.'

'Fuck your Mother!' Zarubin shook his head in wonder. 'Why are you Germans so obsessed with documenting things you can be nailed to?'

'I suspect that the section has a lot of other names. They're referred to as the Red Files.'

'They would be - because if the Americans ever find out about it they're going to put a lot of arses over the fire.' Zarubin waved the paper, but carefully, as if he were trying to dry a precious document. 'Tell me about him.'

'There isn't much in the file. In October last year, two policemen in Rosenheim district visited a farm on which a released POW was working. They asked to see his release papers and recorded the name - Fritz Hollman. That was it, no further action taken. But their report ended up in at Oberursel with a red tag and that other name attached, so Gehlen's people must have other sources.'

'He's still on the farm?'

Fischer shook his head. 'I have no idea. He's very, very close to the Austrian border, and if he doesn't run he's a fool. Is this enough for me to have the other names?'

'The name itself? No. It interests me, but on its own it's hardly likely to be valuable. The Red Files are different, though – you've given me something to set my Oberursel Germans upon, eventually. With luck, it'll bring down Gehlen's entire operation, or at least make the Americans so angry he'll never again fart without needing it to be signed off. Very well. I'll send you a few names tomorrow, via my loyal subordinate Commander Beckendorp. In the meantime, Major Fischer …?'

'Major Zarubin?'

'Get the hell out of Soviet territory, would you?'

59

For two days, West Side Records saw not a single American customer, and Earl Kuhn began to fear that his premises had been placed off-limits. Allowing this possibility to become an ordained fact (by virtue of dwelling upon it for too long), he then began to wonder at the cause. Had the commandant received too many letters from servicemen's wives, complaining that their spouses had squandered their wages upon jazz rather than frivolities such as their children? Were the premises suspected to be supplying less noble product? Was Kuhn himself under suspicion of ... something?

The questions tortured him until he found the sense to lock his premises and visit his associate Lieutenant Klossmayer at Camp Grohn. At the front gate (which was closed), he was told to wait. A small rock found itself being kicked around for almost an hour before the American, armed and in battle-fatigues, appeared at the wire. However, he was then able to reassure Kuhn in a moment - in fact, in a word.

'Manoeuvres.'

Kuhn glanced around as he considered this. 'But the camp seems full.'

'Yeah. It's a close-down.'

'What's that?'

'An exercise that assumes the base is under assault from enemy forces.'

Bewildered, Kuhn scratched his head. 'This is Bremen. What enemy is there?'

'You. It's assumed that the local population's risen up against USFET.'

Once he'd started laughing, Kuhn found it difficult to stop. In fact, he didn't want to. Klossmayer seemed irritated. 'What?'

'Germans? We're too depressed to get out of bed, most days!'

'Yeah, well, you know what commanding officers are like.'

'No, I don't' said Kuhn, very truthfully. 'I hid from the war, remember?'

'If they've done nothing to piss the troops for more than a week they get a rash. So, we have an exercise. No boots out of camp until Saturday, and then only if the whole thing's declared a success.'

'You mean, if we haven't invaded?'

'Go on, laugh, you Kraut bastard.'

Kuhn did as he was told for at least the next hour. Freed from any urge to return directly to West Side Records he walked south from the Camp into Bremen-Mitte, confusing or irritating passers-by with an unsuspected giggle, a cheery *good morning*. When he reached Ostertorswallestrasse he was further heartened by the prospect of a small queue, mothers waiting patiently to leave or pick up their laundry. Above their heads, steam poured from the shed's ventilator pipe, and from inside the unmusical cries of girls hard at their work was nevertheless music to his ears. They were making money, and some of it was franked: *Earl Kuhn's special reserve.*

He excused himself and pushed past the head of the queue into the laundry. Though the enterprise had no name as yet it was a healthy infant employing six girls, all unmarried mothers. The evidence for this was clustered in a number of cots next to the Clean tables, most of them adding to the general cacophony. Curiously, this had been Kuhn's idea. When Maria-Therese had told him of her intention to hire girls who most needed the work it came to him immediately - that the answer to the problem facing all single, working mothers would also be a tremendous advertisement for the business: a wailing, noisome reminder of what a vital service they were providing. The girls would be happier having their little mistakes at hand, waiting customers could distract themselves with the inexplicable pleasure of goo'ing at other women's progeny, and, when the inevitable occurred, its hygienic removal could be addressed immediately – a small but appreciated staff perquisite. What other businessman, he asked himself, would have thought to turn babies into assets?

He glanced around the busy room and couldn't see Maria-Therese. This was strange, because she had a new proprietor's anxiety about every detail of her business and usually worked with the girls or hovered like a buzzard above a mouse. He waited for ten minutes and she didn't appear, though she was hardly missed - for all the efficiency with which her – *their* - workforce dealt with nappies and customers they might have been shareholders in the laundry. Eventually, he was noticed and a number of the girls began to falter nervously, expecting some comment upon their work. So he smiled, waved and made an open-handed gesture that managed to convey what he meant. One of them, Ursula (a small, dark teenager from Lilienthal who, a week earlier, had more or less dropped to her knees in front of Maria-Therese and begged a job), placed a folded pile of *windeln* on the counter and came over to him.

'She opened up at 7 o'clock but then went home again, Herr Kuhn. She says she has things to deal with.'

Without children of her own or an Otto to distract her at present, Kuhn wondered what *things* could have kept her from making money. He wasn't worried, because her apartment was at most five minutes from the laundry and worries needed more time than that to fester. So he told the girls to *keep it up* (not that they needed it, but he imagined tacit praise to be an indispensable tool of the good boss) and went off to ease his curiosity.

At Queerenstrasse 23 he ran up two flights of stair and rapped on the door of apartment 7. For two minutes he waited, wondering if it had been his imagination. He told himself not to be dirty-minded; that the fact she had been a prostitute back then gave him no right to even think such things. But the noise stayed with him, that particular kind of noise, hushed yet abruptly sat upon when interrupted unexpectedly, the noise one tried not to make when a money-belt came off anywhere but behind a locked door, or when …

No, it was impossible. He had never known a more *respectable* woman, someone who hadn't so much put the past behind her as amputated it cleanly. He knocked again, firmly, as someone would who suspected nothing, nothing at all.

He heard the soft noise again - or rather *noises*, coming from more than one location in the room he couldn't see. She wasn't alone, and she wasn't opening the door, and if it wasn't infidelity he could think only one other circumstance. He braced himself, wondering if his shoulder could deal with a locked door and his nerves with whatever waited behind it.

He had just about summoned the necessary recklessness when a key turned and the door opened. Blocking the view, Maria-Therese stood fully dressed (to Kuhn's immense relief) with a hand on her hip, glaring at him with something less than gratitude.

'What is it, Earl?'

This was so unlike her usual, affable self that Kuhn forgot to be hurt.

'You're not at the laundry.'

'Aren't I? I must have other things to do, then.'

*This* was so close to sarcasm that Kuhn almost forgot what he was going to say next.

'I ... can I help with anything? I mean, if there's something wrong?'

She held the stare for a few moments longer, but it was obviously an effort. The sigh deflated her a little.

'You'd better come in. But be quiet, please.'

Kuhn stepped inside the apartment, and something at the right-hand periphery of his vision moved, almost removing him from his skin. He turned as half the threat rose from the sofa. It was a man – ugly, thick-set, and very, very hard looking. He was about sixty, perhaps more, but Kuhn's thirty years' advantage seemed nothing like enough. He felt keenly the mistake of allowing Maria-Therese to close the door behind him, regretted now his decision not to return to West Side Records directly, even if he could expect no customers. But then he glanced at the other half of this threat and his diaphragm loosened slightly.

She was a woman of about the same age, but obviously of a much gentler disposition, and she was looking at Kuhn as though he were 'Stapo. *Now* he didn't know whether to smile politely or run, and only Maria-Therese's hand on his arm kept him still.

'It's alright. This is Earl. He won't say anything. Earl, these are two old friends who need to hide for a while.'

'You're Gerd Branssler.' As the words left his mouth, Kuhn knew he'd said precisely the wrong thing. 'Hello' would have been much better. Anything, more or less, would have been much better. If Branssler - and, presumably, his wife - were hoping to pass incognito, he'd not only put them right but given the ugly half of their partnership a good reason to limit the damage.

But the rage, or fear, had left Branssler. He sat down and took his wife's hand.

'How did you know?'

Having dropped tact, Kuhn left it on the floor. 'You're like Otto. You don't need much describing.'

Branssler laughed. 'He said you didn't dress things up.'

'It's all gone wrong, then.'

'Very wrong. We looked too deeply for something and they discovered it. I managed to run, but Otto's still in Berlin. He knows they're coming for him.'

Kuhn glanced at Maria-Therese. She was wearing her trying-not-to-cry face. 'Alright. What can we do?'

'That's up to Otto. If he needs to contact us he'll write to you, at your record shop. It's what we agreed.'

'They don't know about this apartment?'

'No. Sensibly, Otto forgot his address when they hired him. He gave them one that may or may not exist still. I wish I'd thought to do the same.'

Mrs Branssler leaned to her husband and kissed his cheek. 'You assumed it was a respectable job. You assumed they were good Germans, not scoundrels.'

Kuhn had liked her on first glance, but he wondered at a naivety that hoped for integrity from an intelligence organization. Though he knew no more than her about the spy business, he took it as a rule that the more secret a thing was the more brutal someone would be to keep it such or discover it. It was why he'd been nervous from the start about this job. Why had Otto thought it preferable to the obvious alternative? The worst that could happen with a faulty gramophone was you stabbed yourself while removing the needle. No one ever got thrown in a river because they repaired one badly.

Maria-Therese had stopped trying to hold back the tears. She turned on Branssler. 'Why? You said it was a good career, something with a future. What did you do wrong?'

This fearsome man looked at her, and then at Kuhn, and then his wife. His face had reddened, and he stammered.

'There's a reason I wanted - needed - Otto to join us. It's to do with the war, and a friend.'

For the next few minutes, Kuhn and Maria-Therese heard the saga of Freddie Holleman and the several fires over which three arses were now suspended. Mrs Branssler seemed merely bludgeoned by the tale, so it was obvious she had heard it in full already; but Maria-Therese's face began to descend the spectrum to match Gerd Branssler's, and Kuhn braced himself for the explosion.

When he had finished, the big man opened a hand and half raised it as if inviting the firing squad to proceed. Hastily, Kuhn got in the first word.

'I met him.'

'You met Freddie?'

'Yeah, last year. He called himself Beckendorp, but Otto told me his story. It was on a rail line, near Stettin. He helped us. I mean, he helped Otto, which is to say he helped me too.'

Kuhn had stressed *helped* each time, but it was as effective as a blanket tossed over a smelting pot. Maria-Therese was wildly, speechlessly angry, her hands twitching forlornly for want of a husband's neck between them. Her business partner wanted to sooth her, tell her that Otto hadn't said anything only because he didn't want her to worry; but he needed no deep insight into the female psyche to know that his own neck would be required for duties if he did. He glanced helplessly at Branssler, who had the air of a man desperately wanting to be somewhere east of the Urals.

It was Mrs Branssler who saved them both, probably. She got to her feet, took Maria-Therese's arm and led her into the kitchen, which, though small and underprovided, had the inestimable advantage of containing no men at that moment. When they were gone Kuhn turned to her husband, not wanting to ask the only question that pressed.

'Is it that bad?'

'It's worse. Greta's got a weak heart, so I told her I was questioned, not beaten and then almost executed.'

'Oh God. I thought that sort of shit was over.'

'Why? These people are in the war still, the one that didn't end. To them it was always about the Russians. If they ever think badly of Adolph it's because he stuck with the Japs in '41 and declared war on the Americans. If he hadn't, they say, Stalin would be holding cabinet meetings in Dushanbe right now and the Brits would be dreaming of lost empire. It's all crap, naturally, but Gehlen and his brothers breathe it in every day. To them we're in the same life-and-death struggle still, the right and wrong sides at each other's windpipes. And me, Otto and Freddie are definitely leaning east in their eyes.'

Kuhn considered this. 'Where's Dushanbe?'

'Never mind.'

'Would they try to kill Otto?'

'They tried to kill me. What do you think?'

Kuhn sat down, chewed his cheek, tried to think. This was worse than Stettin. Now, the bastards were bureaucrats, not rival entrepreneurs.

They couldn't be bribed, threatened, reasoned with, offered a partnership or escaped except to the mercy of other, slightly worse bastards - and, being bureaucrats, their opinions on right, wrong and what was required to put things right again was considerably less elastic than the typical Stettin gangster's. They'd be vindictive and persistent, two of Kuhn's least favourite qualities.

Branssler contradicted his unspoken fears. 'It could be worse, probably.'

'How?'

'The Americans won't allow Gehlen's men to be assassins, so they've brought in old friends. The two who worked on me were former SS, probably.'

'You're joking!'

'Why? They're loyal to the point of dumb, the more so these days because a wrong word would put them on the end of a rope.'

'How the f …' Kuhn glanced at the kitchen door and lowered his voice, '… could *that* be worse?'

'They're as twitchy as rabbits, Gehlen *and* his pet killers. If they find Otto they'll have to find a way to be discreet - it's not a matter of clearing the block and then Warsawing it, like in the good old days. Otto's expecting them, so he'll be twitchy too, and watchful. And the ones who interrogated me were the sort who use their heads mostly for keeping helmets company. It could be worse.'

'But they'll find this apartment eventually. They're … spies!'

Branssler scratched his big, hairless head. 'How? It took me days to find it when Otto wasn't expecting anyone, and even then he had to offer the address. Is he registered with the American administration here?'

'No. Only with the Brits at Lübeck. It was something he hadn't got 'round to doing.'

'Good. The British wouldn't help Gehlen even if they could – they detest his organization. No one's going to find Otto's wife, not unless she gets on a bus to Oberursel.'

'So what do we do?'

Branssler shrugged. 'Something. I don't know what. If I show my face it's likely to get shot off, which makes me fucking useless to Otto and Freddie. I have to get Greta somewhere safe, that's all I can think right now.' He glanced around the tiny apartment. 'We can't stay here, obviously.'

'Do you like pigs?'

Maria-Therese was standing in the kitchen doorway. Her colour had faded almost to normal.

'What?'

'There's a farm, about two kilometres from the Danish border. They'd welcome an extra pair of hands.'

'Who?'

'An old friend of Otto's. In the war they worked together.'

'Not the Lie Division?'

Kuhn gaped. 'You know about that?'

'Know? I more than … never mind. What's the name?'

Maria-Therese considered this for a few moments. 'Reincke, I think.'

'Detmar Reincke? A one-armed lad?'

'That's what Otto says. You see what I mean about the extra hands?'

Branssler pursed his lips. 'I look like one, I've been told. Why wouldn't I be good with them?'

'What?'

'Pigs. Nice and snug in the British Zone, on a border with somewhere else, and if anyone in Germany eats these days it's a farmer. What do you think, sweetheart?'

Greta Branssler sniffed. She was a grey, slightly-built woman, physically overshadowed by the mass of her husband; but it was he who seemed to shrink slightly as he put this one possible future to her. If she had a weak heart it was armoured by spirit.

'I don't mind pigs. I *do* mind being hunted like one. And we can't abandon Freddie and Otto. No, Gerd, it won't do. You have to go back, and rescue them.'

60

Engi had stopped asking questions. He wanted to know why they were leaving Frau Best's cellar (though he had no objection to that) and why it had to be done so quickly; he wondered why they had to go at night, when all the city's dangers were magnified, and whether they were leaving Berlin, to find their idyll in the countryside. But after Rolf had broken the news to his landlady, paid her a full month's rent (and a kilo of horsemeat) in lieu of notice and told Engi to keep quiet the boy had merely followed dumbly, trusting that an adult's understanding of the world would lead them to a better, safer place.

They each carried a single bag, and moved quickly. By dawn they were crossing the Tiergarten, keeping to minor paths to avoid patrols. North of Schloss Bellevue Rolf made Engi sit on a low wall and removed a bar of British 'Five Boys' chocolate from his pocket. They shared breakfast in silence, both glancing around to reassure themselves that they inhabited an empty world. When they were finished Rolf screwed the wrapper carefully and replaced it in his pocket as if, discarded, it might betray their passage.

'I don't have much money left. We'll need more, to get out of Berlin.'

It was the first thing he had said since Steglitz, and though 'we' reassured Engi the rest reminded him that he was at the mercy of a plan he hadn't heard. The next few, fugitive hours might bring the beginning of a kinder life or the end of one that, for all its ugliness, hadn't yet managed to finish him off. He wanted to be reassured, but Rolf's anxiety was contagious, and he kept quiet as they stood up and continued their journey northward.

It lasted only a further twenty minutes. At Alt-Moabit they turned left and came to the great ruins of the Heilandskirche. There, Rolf put a hand on Engi's arm and led him through the churchyard, across Turmstrasse and into Jonas-Strasse. The short street was heavily damaged, with hardly an intact structure north of the Arminius Markthalle, but Rolf counted the ruined plots to his right-hand carefully. At a particularly shattered property at the end of a short terrace, he stopped.

'Why are we ...?'

'Sshh.'

He held Engi's arm gently, and squeezed it as something parted from the shadows of the house. The boy wanted to run, an urge that magnified hugely when the *something* resolved itself into the hideously wounded man.

The two adults greeted each other like comrades, hands grasping wrists. Rolf glanced around.

'Why here?'

The wounded man turned to the rubble and gestured with a claw. 'My home, once. Before the world ended.'

'Family?'

'Almost. An old, infuriating woman, my landlady. I miss her.'

'She died in there?'

'No, resisting the Russian advance - or rather, a Russian's advances. Her sister wrote to me, said she managed to get in one good thrust with a potato peeler, bless her.'

'Bad luck.'

'Not really. I doubt she'd have wanted to see any of what followed. Are you leaving the city?'

Rolf shrugged. 'I think the Russian's patience must be exhausted.'

'It's hard to say. He seemed happy that you got in the way of my assassination, but he enjoys games. I wouldn't trust him.'

'Yet he let you leave the Soviet Zone. Shooting you would have been easier.'

'I know. Which makes me worry he's got more something in mind. Have you decided how you're going to do it?'

Rolf glanced down at Engi. 'I thought we could hitch to Rostock, then a boat to Lübeck.'

'Not bad. The Soviets are still pushing a lot of refugees west, so you should be able to lose yourself in a crowd. What do you need?'

'Cash, if you can spare any.'

The wounded man removed a wallet from his inside pocket. 'I'll give you an address. It won't make a home, but you can find your bearings there.'

'Why don't you come with us?'

'Going west doesn't help me. Even if Zarubin's being straight, I've still got Gehlen's people on my arse. And they have my friend. It's ironic, but the only person who seems to be safe now is the one we came to Berlin to extract.'

Engi listened to this exchange, understanding almost nothing. He didn't know where Rostock was, or Lübeck; he didn't know what *bearings* were, or how you found them (why had Rolf misplaced them in the first place, and why were they at, or near, the address he'd been given?). But the fact that he – they – were being aided by this curious creature pushed back his fears. There *was* a plan, even if he couldn't grasp it.

Rolf took a small roll of money and pocketed it. 'What will you do?'

The wounded man sighed and checked both ends of the street. 'Try to make myself either worthless or irritating. It's hard to know what line they'd consider not worth crossing.'

'Do you have anything?'

'Enough to embarrass, perhaps. Names they'd sooner no one else knew.'

'But once you've given them up …'

'I know. The good is that Gerd and I have no value to them other than for what we know. The bad is that there are no known rules yet. We could find ourselves on the sharp end of indifference or a burst of peevishness.'

'Can you not go to the Americans directly?'

'Who would I speak to? How could we be sure that we wouldn't be handed straight over to Oberursel, having already thrown away our only pair of nines?'

'The British?'

'I thought about that. But they'd sooner keep the Americans sweet than hurt Gehlen.'

'You're in the shit, brother.'

'And to think that a few weeks ago I was fretting about the job market.'

It was lighter now, the sky overcast. Early commuters were crossing Jonas-Strasse's southern extremity, too preoccupied to notice the conference being held at its mid-point. A street or two distant a mechanical digger fired consumptively to life, ready to raze a little more of the city's vast lunar landscape. Rolf shook the other man's hand once more and looked around as if wondering what came next. He opened his mouth and gave himself a little time to think about what to say.

'Would you have seen any of this coming?'

The wounded man shook his head. 'I don't see things coming. They arrive and I react, or hide. It's what life is.'

'A mystery, is what it is. I thought the war would kill me, or this wrong sort of peace. Never saw myself going beyond the uniform, the wire fence. Look at me now, shackled to a brat.'

These were harsh words, but Engi knew the tone meant something else. He might have called it affectionate, had his vocabulary not lacked the word. His anxiety had faded by now, gone to where only dark nights or loneliness might rouse it. He tugged at Rolf's coat.

'Can we go now?'

'Yes. But you'd better not mind plenty of walking.'

'I don't care, if it's out of Berlin.'

The two men looked at each other and laughed. The wounded man's face twisted badly as he did so, but to Engi it was no longer that of a *kobold*, and he smiled back (though he didn't know what he'd said that could have amused them).

'Here', said Rolf. 'I won't need this now.' He turned to the boy. 'We can risk a bus as far as Pankow. After that, we buy some food and work on our shoe leather.'

Fischer watched them until they reached the end of the street and turned into Bugenhagenstrasse. His mood had eased slightly, and he couldn't say why. He didn't dare return to the *Hotel Bad Gastein* to collect his meagre possessions, couldn't throw himself upon the hospitality of friends in the western sector of the city (he had none), had no idea where else he might find a bed to lie down and think about what came next without alerting someone who reported to Oberursel. All of that should have pressed heavily yet he felt detached, quarantined, permitted the same absurd sense of removal as if he were on the first day of his annual holidays and the world's shit had been put off for a fortnight. Was it sentimentality, he wondered, the happy prospect of at least one man and a child escaping the city?

He glanced back at the tiny part of it that had been Jonas-Strasse 17 and said his goodbyes to poor Frau Traugott and her waspish sister. The memories stirred something, and it occurred to him that there had been several boarding houses nearby, a little to the south of Putlitzstrasse s-bahn station, which over the years had degenerated gently into doss-houses for *fremdarbeiter* rail-gangers. If any survived, it wasn't likely that their charms had put them on Gehlen's list of suitable accommodation for agents.

Keeping distance between himself and possible surveillance of the *Bad Gastein* he went west as far as Oldenburgerstrasse before turning north. It was a good, pleasant walk, and the lingering effects of an evening spent hiding in Frau Beitner's battery-acid emporium and a subsequent night upon a cold, damp bench in the Tiergarten faded into the familiar dull ache of his wounds. He thought about the information in his pocket, delivered to him the previous day via Freddie Holleman (and carefully wrapped in a warning to get out of Berlin 'fucking quickly, you silly bastard'). The list was shorter than he'd hoped, longer than he'd expected, and it was difficult to gauge whether Zarubin had decided to keep him on the leash or provide everything he had. He recognized three names, knew why they *were* names and not just forgotten men; but the others he would have to deploy as a bluff in the hope that Gehlen knew what made them poisonous. He wished very much that Gerd Branssler was walking beside him, telling him how likely it was that the General would bow to the threat - be amenable to just forgetting two of his more troublesome ex-employees. He hoped, even more strongly, that Branssler was in condition still to offer an opinion on that or any other matter.

He came to broad Quitzowstrasse. To his left-hand side were the yards of the Moabit freight-station, where thousands of Jewish Berliner families had embarked to a bright new future in the east. Its single east-bound line had sneaked furtively around nearby Putlitzstrasse station, so that decent Aryan commuters hadn't needed to bother themselves with the consequences of their voting preferences. He considered that now, how he himself must have fretted about little things in his schedule, glanced indifferently at the trains as they passed by and not wondered at all why freight should be so carefully screened and guarded. It was an ugly thought, and he endured it only as long as it didn't strip his conscience with the force of a thrown tank-track.

At the corner of Putlitzstrasse (well to the north now of his hotel and its unsuspected collection of Fischer memorabilia) he bought a newspaper, intending to lose himself in the latest bad tidings and defer a decision upon *when*, and *how*. Once he'd paid for it the sum of his remaining cash stretched to a breakfast and a train ticket, which, if he could make the decision, might be sufficient. He added this very practical consideration to the weight of the argument for prompt action, and the scales, which had been tilting heavily the other way on the prospect of Maria-Therese's early widowhood, levelled very slightly - but not enough to make him courageous.

He realised that he was wandering. A few metres beyond the newspaper-seller he reached the first of the boarding houses he was seeking and continued past it (or rather, the rubble it had become). Ahead of him, the canal and the sprawl of the Rudolph-Virchow-Krankenhaus invited his idle curiosity and he accepted gratefully, hoping that enough of the embankment wall survived to allow him to sit and read his paper, to sift his options once more.

A man in his situation should have been more watchful. Before meeting Rolf and the boy he had been as twitchy as a cat in a police kennels, but since then his mood and the strengthening light had blunted too many of his nerve-endings. The streets, filling with Berliners, felt safe; he didn't notice that the company thinned out considerably once he was to the north of Putlitzstrasse station. When he came to the canal's south embankment he saw that it had been closed off in both directions for roadworks, creating a zone, perhaps a hundred metres to either side of him, in which he was the only pedestrian.

Or so he thought, until a slight shuffle behind him said otherwise. As he turned he took a quick step back, putting about two metres between himself and the knife. Its owner held it closely, into the body, and the way he was balanced on his toes suggested that it was about to be used.

'Thank you', said Fischer.

The man – his Tiergarten assailant of three days past, a bleak-faced, extremely fit-looking specimen – glanced quickly to each side and nodded. 'It's alright. I'm paid well.'

From his coat pocket Fischer removed the Steyr M1912 that Rolf had relinquished a few minutes earlier and shot the man in the head. The report was loud, but hardly an unexpected noise in contemporary Berlin. A British patrol, passing close by, would have investigated; but no German was going to move in the direction of more trouble than he'd signed for already. Fischer tossed the gun into the canal, looked around and then down at the corpse. It was laid on its side, considerately imitating a drunk sleeping off the previous night's damage.

'I meant, for making up my mind.'

61

There was an art to a stare. Hold a man's eyes until he looked away and you seized a high ground; add a slight curl to the lip and you told him exactly how little he was worth. A frown, though tempting, was almost always a mistake. It looked too much like over-acting – or worse, that one cared about the other's actions, or opinions, or appearance.

It was this last that Major Zarubin was attempting to comment silently upon. The man he had invited into his office, to whom he had offered a chair, occupied so perfect a state of shabbiness that one had to suspect a real effort had been made. In modern Berlin it could perhaps be argued that he had merely perfected a means of disappearing among the herd; but there was something wilfully, comprehensively dishevelled about this fellow that more or less spat in the Red Army's face and dared it to object.

Zarubin settled upon raised eyebrows, and waved vaguely to a small table to his left. 'Would you like a cup of tea?'

The man shook his head. 'Thank you, no, Comrade.' As he settled into the chair his already-pitiable physique collapsed like a beached jellyfish. He removed a pipe and tobacco from his pocket but paused as Zarubin pointedly, most definitely, frowned. As he opened his mouth to invite what was almost certainly going to be a curt refusal a lieutenant entered the room without knocking and placed a sheaf of papers on the desk. The stare *he* deployed at Zarubin's guest was a model of contempt, but it was as brief as his visit, and hardly offended.

'Rolf Hoelscher.'

'Sorry, comrade?'

'The man you briefed as an agent, and then brought to my attention?'

'Ah.' Wolfgang stirred slightly in his seat, as if to dislodge something about to sting him in the arse.

'His information was good. And bad. That is, most of it was nonsense, but I expected that. He's been useful, if not entirely honest about his relationship with the man he mentioned. Never mind. We can't expect truthfulness in our business, can we?'

Zarubin smiled as he said it, and Wolfgang's face paled slightly. 'I just reported what he'd sad to me.'

'Of course you did. You couldn't have known that he and his friend intended to take advantage of my trusting nature.'

'Absolutely not, Comrade Major.'

'Don't worry about it. I've spoken to Fischer and concluded our business. Well, almost. As for Hoelscher, well ...'

Wolfgang was till brooding upon *don't worry*, and hardly noticed the pause. 'Yes?'

'He strikes me as less than ... *enthusiastic* about the work he's been offered.'

'Oh, he's committed to the cause, comrade; no doubt about it.'

Zarubin pulled a face. 'Is he, though? We pulled him out of Bautzen, and one has to assume that a man would say just about anything to see the back of that place. His tutor at Moscow rated him quite highly, particularly for intelligence. But his very first assignment in Berlin went badly. He killed a man.'

'Yes, comrade.'

'Herr Peter Beckmann, a city councillor had was supposed to be bribing.'

'As you say.'

'I assume this to have been the result of an argument, or a taste for violence, or blind panic. Whichever the case, it hardly advanced the *cause*, did it?'

'No, comrade. But you said Beckmann may have tried to alert others to what he was doing.'

'Still, cutting the fellow's throat strikes me as a little excessive. And it was done with such skill ...'

'Yes, comrade?'

'It made me wonder whether the other side had managed to put a man in our midst.

Wolfgang blanched. 'Side?'

'I'm told it's a sporting metaphor. I meant Oberursel – Gehlen's gang.'

'Surely such a man would have instructions not to make himself conspicuous?'

'Given Herr Beckmann's relative unimportance, I would have to agree with you. They might sacrifice their man to achieve a great coup, but not less. And as a faithful servant of the Americans, Beckmann was someone they'd have preferred alive and well and irritating us in the Council Chamber.'

'So Rolf isn't a spy. I mean, one of theirs?'

Zarubin sighed. 'I doubt it. But he's obviously not a good return on Moscow's investment, and as venal as it seems they do like to get their money's worth. We shall have to retire him.'

'Retire, comrade? Do you mean ...?'

'What I meant by that was you.'

'But I've never done that! Even in the First War.'

'You're his handler. You took responsibility for him and it went very badly. Think of this as a sort of penance, or amends. Or the means of adding to our excellent opinion of you. Don't worry that it might be too easy; he appears to have gone into hiding, or fled. I'm sure you'll discover which. You can go now.'

After his guest had staggered out of the office Major Zarubin signed a few reports, altered others to repair his subordinates' exuberantly flawed grammar and made a telephone call to the General commanding the Border Guard in Mecklenburg-Vorpommern. This last chore took a little while, as both men had been cadets together in the Signal Corps before the War and the General was keen to reminisce about events that he found more amusing in retrospect than they had seemed at the time.

When he had managed to end the conversation and replace the receiver, Zarubin lifted it again and demanded his adjutant's presence. The man was admirably prompt, took his orders without comment and

disappeared. The remainder of the morning was given over to reading –
several of the interminable diktats from Moscow regarding the
administration of the SBZ, a pleasing report from an MGB agent in the
British Zone regarding food riots earlier that year and a translation of a
SSU briefing paper on Soviet intentions for Berlin which happened to be
remarkably inaccurate in every major detail. These baubles carried him
almost to lunch but he waited, using the time to tidy his desk and start on a
letter to his dead uncle's housekeeper, the only woman – indeed, human
being – he regarded as family. He had only begun the usual anodyne form
of words to express his hope for her good health when his adjutant
knocked on the door and waved in *Commandeur der VolksPolizei* Kurt
Beckendorp, whose red face spoke eloquently of his feelings regarding the
summons. Zarubin gave him a beaming smile.

'Commander, good morning. I need to ask a favour. I'm sure you
won't mind.'

62

For ten hours each day (excepting Sundays) the barrier-booth at the end of the Berlin platform of Frankfurt Hauptbahnhof was occupied by Eva, a middle-aged woman who hated her work with the vehemence that a university education brings to mindless toil. Her duties were simple, repetitive and exercised her intellect only to the extent that she had begun to question the very nature of time itself, and how it managed to slow so profoundly between a shift's start and end. When not clock-watching she sometimes tried to ease the tedium by guessing at the lives of travellers who handed their tickets to her, imagining secret *affaires de coeur*, desperate flights from vengeance, fugitive criminals and other variations upon circumstances more colourful than her own. When these dramas paled she would narrow her imagination and attempt merely to identify those on their first visit to Frankfurt. This was not a difficult exercise. Other than in those who were so crushed by their preoccupations that nothing intruded, a passage through one of the world's largest and most elegant interior spaces (one to which she herself had long been indifferent) could usually be read in a slightly awed gaze, a hesitation at the barrier and glance back, a hint of a mood lightened by the relatively sparse war damage. She was not so dulled by the job that her own mood was unaffected by these signs.

As even Eva had to admit, rush-hours were returning - slowly - to Frankfurt Hauptbahnhof. They couldn't yet be compared to the twice-daily invasions of the pre-war years, but train fares were cheap and most of the available, regular work in that part of Hesse was to be found within the city limits. The post-war depression lay heavily upon them still, but the tar bubbled and popped in places, and this was one of them. New staff were being hired, engineers were busy most days restoring and expanding the outdated signalling technology, and in the main concourse there had reopened a permanent newspaper and tobacco kiosk, heralding a further step upon the path to what once had been regarded as normality.

The busiest times of the day were the best, naturally, because time put on its running shoes. Eva could lose an hour or two as impatient queues backed up to have their tickets checked or taken, and was obliged sometimes to be slightly abrupt when a traveller decided that she was the best person to ask for local directions, thereby turning a queue into a blockage. Perversely, such people never seemed to need information at quiet times, when she would have been delighted to consume a few more of the day's minutes helping them.

But on this particular, peculiar day no-one was uncertain of his or her destination during the early morning press. She took tickets, answered brief questions about train times and even found herself on the end of several *good mornings* from passing commuters who could hardly manage a nod, usually. At 9.30am she was told by her supervisor that her application for re-training as a 'signalman' had been approved, and that the Controller himself had expressed his great satisfaction that a woman should apply for one of many vacancies in a notoriously masculine occupation. All of this put Eva in an uncharacteristically fine mood, one that required a monster to shake.

He came to the barrier after the rest of the passengers from the 10.05 Berlin train had passed through. She held out her hand and for a moment noticed nothing other than his hand, a reddened, quite mutilated thing (though it seemed dextrous enough), entirely covered in scar tissue. Of course, she glanced up at that and found a face which, offered a choice, she would have preferred to be much further from her own.

Her first thought was of Kraper's famous poster of Grock, each side of the half-and-half face shockingly different from the other. Employees of Deutsche Reichsbahn were of course expected to be professional and courteous at all times, and she almost managed to keep the shock from her face; but whatever he saw there didn't seem to offend him. He smiled (at least she believed it to be that), and raised his hat politely, revealing a similarly disarranged scalp.

'I wonder if you could direct me to this address?'

Eva took the piece of paper from his other hand (which was unmarked, quite normal) and read it. She knew the place immediately; it was a 1920s residential block near the river, one of the few in Sachsenhausen that had survived the bombing and street-fighting. It wasn't far, perhaps a kilometre from the station. She gave him simple directions which he didn't bother to take down.

He thanked her, raised his hat once more and passed on through the barrier. It was ridiculous - Germany was full of men wounded terribly in the war, walking corpses to remind folk who had lost it (should the fact escape their minds), yet she couldn't dislodge his face for more than an hour thereafter. Perhaps it had been the way in which its good part had functioned distinctly from the other, as if the two occupied different heads - or the same at different times, like shift-workers at a factory bench. The thought almost amused her, but that would have been shameful, given what had breached it. Eventually, the good news she had received earlier that morning crowded out the incident, though occasionally Grock, King of Clowns, popped back into her head and raised a smile.

Just south of the River Main, the apartment block at Schulstrasse 24 was maintained efficiently by its *portiersfrau*, Frau Ullman, as it had been since 1932. No one entered or departed the building without her knowing of it, save during brief periods when she was obliged to forage for the necessities that kept her building to a standard of cleanliness a surgeon would have envied. Her tenants were wholly satisfied with her work, regarding her in the same way they did the roof – not very often, but with absolute assurance of her integrity.

On this morning she was sat in her usual place beside the door, which was open wide enough for her to keep the hallway monitored as she sewed. A few familiar faces had passed by in the previous hour and a delivery of books awaited collection by the retired Professor in apartment 12. She couldn't inform him of this fact because the building's internal telephone system hadn't worked since February 1945; but he was a very regular gentleman, and always passed through the hall to take his daily walk after listening to the BBC news in German at 11am.

It was a few minutes before this expected encounter that the front doorbell rang. Frau Ullman placed her sewing box on the table and went to offer the caller the usual eight centimetres of gap through which he or she might make their supplications. As the door creaked open she looked instinctively towards the caller's midriff, as this was the height at which packages, letters or delivery slips were held for her perusal. Nothing being visible in this region, she raised her gaze to the caller's face.

Immediately, she thought of her friend Else's poor boy Gregor, badly wounded in the *Gneisenau* when the British bombed her Kiel dry-dock. He, too, had come home with a face like this, and about as much damage inside. It always broke her heart to see such visible evidence of what war did to men, and unthinkingly she allowed the door to open more than was prudent.

But he was very courteous, tipping his hat in the old way to greet her. He asked about the tenant of apartment 9, Frau Branssler, and whether he might have a word with her. Frau Ullman had to disappoint him, explaining that the lady's husband – who lived elsewhere, she couldn't say where, exactly – had called to collect her two days past, since when neither had returned. Curiously, this information was received with what she took to be satisfaction, if not euphoria. The wounded gentleman thanked her profusely for it and insisted upon kissing her hand (something that only her long-departed husband had ever done, and that when in drink), but when she asked if she might take a name in case Frau Branssler returned he merely winked and bid her good day.

Afterwards, she caught herself thinking of Else's boy once more - how she wished that he might have made so little of his own wounds. One needn't have all of a face to offer it to the world.

———

Private First Class Walter Gehringer was on stockade duty. It was his least favourite way to pass time, because this wasn't really a stockade, and a guy couldn't entertain himself by taunting the inmates, and at his post he had nothing better to look at than the weird, candy-box architecture south of his position and the occasional crock who staggered past the camp gates, dragging potatoes or whatever else he'd managed to find at the market. The only thing worth looking at - the town's girls - were all down the road in Frankfurt, or over at Bad Homburg, sucking officer cock. Hell, you couldn't even see the river properly from here.

The 'stockade' was a camp just outside Camp King, a wired area behind which, in Alaska House and a few outbuildings, a bunch of Krauts did things that USFET had decided they needed to do, and that was about all Gehringer or anyone else in his platoon knew. As an interrogation centre, Camp King had seen all sorts of Krauts – Nazi politicians, Nazi soldiers, Nazi scientists, just Nazis, Nazis swearing they weren't Nazis and even American Nazis (well, Axis Sally, anyway); but the ones in Alaska House did something that someone had decided other ranks needn't know about. The rest of the camp – the American rest – was run by Military Intelligence, so it wasn't too hard to guess at if a guy cared to guess, which Gehringer didn't. *These* Krauts could come and go without permission, mainly, so perhaps they weren't Nazis at all – at least, not the wrong sort of Nazis. It made him wonder why they had to have a gate here, and a guard; why it had to be him and not some other mug; why he couldn't be State-side already, discharged and starting his engineering course.

It was the sort of thing he thought a lot these days, most of all while getting busy getting older on sentry duty. The war was well over, the Krauts weren't ever, ever going to be a problem again and every letter from back home rubbed it in about how things were buzzing over there. He didn't begrudge the fact that fighting units had been at the front of the discharge queue, but it hadn't been his fault that he'd landed in Europe just in time to pat the back of the Third Reich as he showed it into its cell. That was two years ago, and he was now well beyond sick and tired of the Old Country, however much his grandmother had cried for just one last sight of it. In fact, if it were possible he would have flushed the damned language itself out of his head, but something you learned in the cradle isn't that easily dumped.

Today it was fine, light cloud with sunshine, which made him feel worse about what he was missing. He'd been at his post for two hours and it felt like three, and he wasn't due to be relieved until 6pm, which would give him about an hour to get back to barracks, have a shower and hope the other guys waited for him. Though not a single one of them had ever managed to attract the attention of a girl who wasn't uglier than a dog's ring-piece, their bright optimism continued to illuminate the truck's interior every time it drove them into Frankfurt for their *jungenausgehen*.

He was thinking about pretty girls still when he was front-and-centred by a local. The view was so surprising that he forgot not to talk in God's American.

'The circus left last week, pal.'

'I'm sorry, sir, I don't understand.'

His English wasn't bad - a little hesitant, and formal. But the voice was softer than the usual it-is-compulsory-or-forbidden noise the locals liked to make. Gehringer decided to make an effort.

'What is it you want?'

The guy pulled a stockade pass from his pocket and handed it over. 'I'd like to see the General.'

'Which General?'

'Wessel. General Wessel.'

Gehringer knew of Wessel, but it was news to him that he'd been a general. Nonplussed, he handed back the pass. 'But you've got the right authority. Just walk on in.'

'Ah, no, sir. I'd sooner you were here when he saw me. A witness, as it were. Would you mind giving my name?'

Gehringer enjoyed being a valet even less than a sentry, and was going to put the Kraut straight on that; but the *face* tugged a little on a string he hadn't known he possessed. Besides, it would allow him to move a few feet to the rear and ease the nagging pain in his lower back. He sighed. 'Wait.'

He entered the sentry booth, picked up the 'phone receiver and spoke briefly to order one of the post-room goons to the gates. He was there almost before Gehringer emerged from the booth (that was the great thing about Krauts; they respected authority no matter what the uniform), staring curiously through the gate at his messed-up compatriot.

Gehringer spoke German this time. 'He wants to see the General.'

'Which one?'

'Wessel.'

Freak Show cleared his throat. 'Tell him it's Fischer. Otto Fischer.'

If this guy was summoning a general and not sweating he must be something else – a Field Marshal, perhaps. But it occurred to Gehringer that the worst thing war does to Field Marshals is shaving nicks. Shaky hands hadn't given *this* guy what he'd got.

The post-room goon looked at the guard for guidance and received none. Finally, his eyebrows came down, the mouth closed and he went off to give the message. The Freak Show watched him disappear into Alaska House and then glanced around at the scenery, seemingly with all the anxiety of a man waiting at a bus stop. Ridiculously, Gehringer began to feel uncomfortable, and when the other man checked his wrist watch he almost told him that someone would be along in a minute, as if he were a fucking clerk calming an irate customer. At this the tugged string parted, and he settled on practising his scowl instead.

But it *was* a minute, more or less. Four men came to the gate, and one of them was Wessel. *He looks pissed* thought Gehringer, contentedly. The other three were the usual, suited or sweatered sorts that worked behind the wire but larger than average, and he assumed that a point was being made for the Freak Show's benefit.

'Please open the gate.'

Much as Gehringer didn't like taking orders from a Kraut he obeyed promptly, keen to see what happened next. But Wessel had the sense to keep whatever was biting him to himself. He gestured to his visitor; the Freak Show turned to the GI, said 'good morning' in English and obeyed the hand. As he had just returned to attention, Gehringer couldn't turn to see if the hired help laid hands upon him as they returned to Alaska House, but he was pretty sure they wanted to.

It was the last interesting thing that happened on his shift until the big guy came along. *That* was even more diverting, and afterwards Gehringer took some trouble to shape the anecdote for when he and the guys hit Frankfurt that evening.

63

At Rostock the Red Army had designated a stretch of Herweghstrasse as the refugee concentration point. The city's main railway station was less than two hundred metres' distant, so for once the business had been considered logically, perhaps even considerately. Looking around, Rolf could see that a lot of their fellow travellers needed as little further exercise as possible. He'd heard that typhus had been a big problem a year ago, that the Ivans had deliberately loaded infected Germans on to trains and ships and dispatched them as a thoughtful gift to the British. He couldn't see any signs of it now, but there was plenty of evidence of hunger and the further exhaustion that hopelessness brings on.

Engi had been silent since they'd arrived, which was a half-blessing. On their great trek (almost twenty kilometres before a kindly Soviet Transport Corps driver picked them up outside Birkenwerder and carried them all the way to Kessin), the boy had hardly drawn breathe other than to cram bread into his mouth between one question about their future and the next. Rolf wasn't yet familiar with the protocols of fatherhood but suspected that *shut up* was a bad start, so instead he had tried noncommittal noises, preoccupied silence and pointing out interesting features in the passing landscape, none of which had stemmed the torrent. He felt he understood now why his own parents had been so keen to get him into the *Wandervogel*.

But the first sight of refugees - lines of listless scarecrows, their meagre possessions bundled in filthy sheets and strapped to their backs - had entirely dammed the flow. It took no great insight to realise that Engi was seeing a dead mother and his first, fled future; he stood close to Rolf, taking care not to allow the slightest possibility that they might be separated, like a dog missing the comfort of a leash. Just before the sun went down they made a place for themselves between two Breslauer families and squatted on their coat tails. The presence of women seemed to calm the boy, and when Soviet soldiers distributed bread and water he watched them sharing it out among their children with almost forensic attention. Rolf had to make him eat his own ration, nagging it down with warnings of how unreliable the Ivans' mood could be.

They slept like foetuses, using each other's legs as pillows. It was a cool night but the press of bodies eased the worst of it, and even Rolf, his nerves fully charged for the coming test, recalled little of what made his entire body ache by dawn. When his bowels demanded that he visit the field latrine in the marshalling yards he made Engi sit closer to one of the Breslauer families, and when he returned sent the boy on the same errand in the company of three of their children. It was protection of sorts, but also camouflage.

Breakfast was a distribution of water only, which made him hope that their turn was coming soon. Rolf could speak enough Russian to ask the question, but it would pull him out of the crowd, draw attention they didn't need. He had just determined to remain invisible when the plan was spoiled by an old man, older than the Second Empire, shuffling along the line of refugees, trying to beg a smoke. His coat was tied with a trouser belt and the legs that protruded from beneath it were naked, their bone-thin ankles disappearing comically into a far larger man's boots. Rolf put a hand into his pocket and carefully worked a single cigarette from its pack. When it was loose he broke it between two fingers and removed a half. The old man took it, nodded and thanked him in a Moravian accent so thick he might have been speaking Czech. Rolf smiled and waved away his gratitude – a mistake, inviting the opening verses of a personal Jeremiad that was dampened neither by the audible sighs and rolling eyes of the Breslauer adults nor the growing attention of a nearby Soviet soldier, who slid his rifle from his shoulder and grasped it so as to deliver the butt playfully into a face.

The old fellow griped doggedly, and Rolf, not caring to join the injured list, didn't attempt to interrupt him. He waited for the blow to land, but some fragment of decency prefaced it with a warning shout. This was perfectly understood by everyone except the object of it, who ignored the interruption. Yet as the rifle came up a train whistle, carrying over Herweghstrasse from the North, caught the attention of every party (even those with strong and justified grievances regarding their present circumstances). The Soviet soldier settled upon a rough shove, which propelled the old man into the queue just where he wasn't wanted.

More whistles sounded, though these were powered by human mouths. The refugees climbed to their feet to collect up their belongings. Rolf and Engi gathered their own estate (comprised two small bags containing emergency rations of American spam and Russian tea) and took up the shuffle when it reached them. The boy seemed calm, steady, and Rolf forced a smile when he glanced up.

The line moved gradually, and divided near its head. Refugees with papers went to the left, while those who had been dispossessed of identity as well as homes and livelihoods were obliged to spell out their names to a Soviet officer sitting at a table in the middle of Herweghstrasse – a final, senseless humiliation that slowed their line considerably. Rolf had papers but Engi didn't of course; he put his hand on the boy's shoulder and pulled to the left.

'You're my son, right?'

They reached the divide, obeyed the shouted instructions and approached the rail barrier at which papers were being checked. Rolf held out his to a corporal.

'My boy, he's lost his papers.'

The corporal stared down at Engi for a moment and then back to Rolf's documents. He paid closer attention to the detail than a man at a bottleneck of beaten souls should have, and when he'd almost faded the papers with his glare he transferred his attention to a list on a clip-board. Several times it passed between them, painfully checking one unfamiliar script against another. Rolf knew far better than to ask whether there was a problem, but he felt the shakes coming on when the corporal turned to another soldier, pointed at the list and asked for a second opinion. When it came, the look of satisfaction on both their faces didn't need translation.

They were taken to an office in the station and told to wait. Rolf made the boy sit down, told him it was a mistake, that he shouldn't worry. He kept an eye on the door, wracked his memory for what it was that had set them on him, tried to isolate it within the broad expanse of his indifference to their aims, their doctrine, the times. It didn't reveal itself in the space of more than three hours, during which he listened to the train depart with their hopes for a new world. In all that time Engi didn't say a word, and Rolf couldn't imagine what was going through a young mind that already had logged enough misery for three lifetimes.

If he didn't know what he'd done he couldn't conceived excuses for it. Not that it mattered; if an alibi counted for anything in the Soviet system an entire generation of senior officers wouldn't have gone to the wall with puzzled expressions on their faces. Still, he'd make a point of asking when they asked him to stand at the edge of the trench. Before that, he'd do exactly what they wanted, admit to anything they needed. If he made them feel good the boy might not matter to them.

Eventually, he began to wonder why they were making him wait. It seemed a pointless gesture if a confession was unnecessary. And if they wanted him to squirm, surely they would have been present to witness it?

*Be calm.*

If it wasn't been for his little obligation Rolf could have been quite reconciled to the situation. He'd expected to be dead by now, erased at some Front or far away in rural Siberia – in either case a gift for the local soil-life. Ask any man in that condition if he'd settle for another six months and you'd have his hearty thanks. He couldn't complain, except for …

'I need to go to the toilet.'

Strange, how a boy who hadn't ever seen a toilet could put it that way.

'It won't be too long now. Hold it in, if you can. Or use the corner.'

Engi promptly stood up, went to the corner and pissed copiously. It wasn't going to please their hosts. The room was bare other than for the chair, a small cheap desk and a bulletin board with a Cyrillic timetable pinned to it, so the puddle had nowhere to hide. Rolf almost smiled. He might have to tell them that he'd become very frightened – after all, wasn't that the point of this dragging pause?

'I'm thirsty.'

'Make up your mind. Do you want water or to get rid of it?'

'Both.'

Rolf was dismissing the idea of marching to the door, flinging it open and demanding something to drink when he realised that in more than three hours here he hadn't thought to check whether it was even locked. This time he couldn't quash the smile. He was the ideal prey, perfectly resigned to his place at the kill.

'When can we go, Rolf?'

'I don't know. Soon, probably.'

Engi was considering *probably* still when the unlocked door opened. The Soviet corporal pushed in his head, gave the room a quick, sour glance and then waved in the man who stood behind him.

'Hello, mate.'

In his travelling outfit, Wolfgang was marginally more presentable than in his city ensemble, principally because the one – an old Wehrmacht field-coat, relieved of its epaulettes – covered the other. A grey handkerchief came out of one of its pockets and he dabbed away a memory of lunch that was adorning part of his heavy, Stalinesque moustache. He looked weary, very much like he wanted to be somewhere other than here.

Rolf nodded and forced himself not to ask the question.

Wolfgang gave the room a slightly longer examination that had the corporal. It seemed to bring him down further.

'Well, this is a mess, isn't it?'

Rolf followed the gaze. He saw nothing that wasn't Spartan-neat. 'Why is it?'

'I mean you, fucking off to the capitalists.'

'Who would care?'

'We would, mate. Family's important.'

As he said it Wolfgang looked at Engi for the first time.

'This is him, is it?'

'Is who?'

'The little bugger you didn't think to mention.'

'Why would I?'

'Don't be cheeky. The rules aren't written down, but you know it's against them.'

'He just attached himself. He isn't important.'

'No. Well ...'

Wolfgang patted his other pocket and withdrew a pistol, another Steyr. It seemed that the Red Army had a pile of those, too.

Rolf tried to feel, to think, nothing at all; but his heart pushed blood with the force of a breached storm-drain. 'Not the boy.'

The older man looked genuinely regretful. 'I'm sorry, mate. The Russian made a point of it.'

64

From the doorway, Fischer felt the refrigeration switch on as all eyes turned to take him in. He tried not to let it hurt his feelings

He was shoved from behind by one of men who had accompanied General Wessel to the gate. He didn't turn, but would have put dollars on it being the dark-haired Muscle, the one who fancied himself to be righteously outraged. The others had practised impassive as keenly as if they had stood in a witness parade.

Wessel came up from the rear of the queue, dismissed the escort and waved his unwelcome guest into the room. At a conference desk sat three men, only one of whom – Gehlen – Fischer recognized. Another had laid out a pen and paper neatly in front of him, the one who was going to make this semi-official. The third – a young, almost Semitic looking fellow with a very practised scowl – sat at Gehlen's other side, tapping the table with a coin. It was all very contrived, by men new to the subtler forms of intimidation.

'Sit, if you wish.'

'Thank you, Herr General.'

'Don't call me that. Sir will do.'

Wessel took his place at the table. For a few moments more the four men deployed their stares (distasteful, mildly disbelieving), and then Wessel recalled that he was the designated mouth.

'Why have you come?'

'To explain myself. Ourselves.'

'What is there to explain? You and Branssler were lying to us from the day you arrived.'

'Yes, we were.'

The young one snorted but said nothing. The clerk scribbled busily. Gehlen pondered the room's timbered ceiling. Wessel consulted his wristwatch, stretching the pause as one does when a plot swerves slightly from true.

'How much have you given to Karlshorst?'

'Nothing.'

'You were taken into the Soviet Zone and interviewed by MGB. We know that.'

'Yes, three days ago.'

'And you gave them ... nothing. It's very hard to believe.'

'Yet true, in fact. I wasn't required to offer anything. Our business was personal, in a sense.'

'They knew you to be employed by us, yet asked nothing about our operations?'

Fischer shifted slightly in his chair. 'They – he – didn't seem to be interested. At least, not in what I might say about them.'

Gehlen coughed gently. 'What was *personal* about your conversation?'

'The man who interviewed me – I know him, from Stettin. He was curious as to why I was back in Berlin.'

'Which must, therefore, have required that you speak of us, of Oberursel.'

'*Of*, yes. Not *about*. Our conversation settled upon Kurt Beckendorp - that is, the man known as Kurt Beckendorp.'

'Your confederate.'

Fischer couldn't help smiling. 'In a way.'

Wessel leaned forward. 'You, Branssler and Beckendorp conceived a plan to betray intelligence to MGB – probably via K5. We've been checking the data you've provided. It's bad.'

'Yes, it is.'

'Are you saying you were misled?'

'Not at all. We were almost entirely responsible for it. It didn't come from MGB, other than the organizational material about K5. Which is entirely accurate, apparently.'

'The names that you gave to us, of alleged spies …'

'We found dead men and dressed them up. If you're interested, we provided exactly the same to Karlshorst.'

Dumbfounded, Wessel glanced at Gehlen. 'Why would you do that?'

'To make time where there was none.'

'Time for what?'

'To find a door. To get out.'

'And MGB know this too?'

'They do.'

'Yet they don't seem to have put a bullet in the back of your head.'

'They have something you don't.'

Gehlen and the rest sat up.

'What's that?'

'A sense of humour.'

The dark one went darker still and muttered something. Wessel put a hand on his arm.

'Soviet Intelligence isn't renowned for it.'

'No. But I was lucky. The man who interviewed me, who knows me, is ... unusual. He's interested in what he finds ridiculous.'

'Give me his name.'

Fischer did so. He saw no recognition in their faces.

Gehlen tapped the table. 'But these are admissions, not explanations.'

'No. You referred to Kurt Beckendorp as our confederate. In fact, he's a friend.'

'Ah. And our discovery of his secret was what brought you to us.'

'It was what brought *me*. Gerd Branssler took the job in good faith, before Beckendorp became an issue.'

'Then you know his real name. May we have that also?'

'Not yet.'

'Why not?'

'You may not need it. But be assured that MGB know it, and don't care. So what you regard as a weapon isn't anything of the sort.'

'A man with another man's identity is, by definition, hiding something.'

Fischer glanced around the table. 'I'm glad you said that. It's something I'll be coming back to. You should know that Beckendorp is my fault, entirely. Four years ago it was most necessary that my friend disappear, for both our sakes. He took information with him that has never been used and is now quite useless. At the time, it may have kept us alive.'

'Can we know this information?'

'Certainly. It concerned a murder investigation conducted at Peenemünde. I was employed by General Walter Dornberger to find a culprit. Obviously, given the nature of the work conduced there, the business was considered most confidential.'

'Were you successful?'

'No, and yes. There was no murder, only a rather dextrous hand being played by the General against his competition.'

Gehlen's mouth twisted. 'Dornberger is a traitor to the German people.'

Fischer allowed himself to seem surprised. 'He works for the Americans. As do you.'

'We work *with* them, to a common end. He was attempting to sell himself to them even before the war's end.'

'A timing error, then. I understand they think quite highly of his team these days.'

'Never mind. So, the man now called Beckendorp assisted you with this investigation?'

'He did. He's a man of the street, but very shrewd. This is what has raised him so quickly in Berlin's *VolksPolizei*, and why MGB – or at least, a tiny part of it - don't care too much about his past.'

'If he were only a policeman, neither should we. But he's a communist, and probably a future light in K-5. Why shouldn't we regard him as an enemy?'

'For the same reason you shouldn't regard me as such. He and I – and Branssler, for that matter - have no ideals, no ideology, no faith in anything other than family and friendship. Beckendorp shaped himself to navigate the calmest waters, as sensible men do - believe me, he wouldn't wipe his arse on *Das Kapital*, Magna Carta or the US Constitution. Or perhaps he would. Either way, he has no intention of joining either side in your little war.'

'But as a German ...'

'Ach.' 'To even his own, intense surprise, Fischer waved down Gehlen. 'What's a German, anymore? To the Americans we're lapdogs, the Soviets pretend fraternal solidarity now they're done raping our wives and the British would like to us to agree to return to the Eighteenth Century. Germans don't have a say, and if they did it would be to beg some of that calm water and time to mend what's broken. We're too tired for *belief*.' He looked around the table once more. 'Those of us who think the war's over, that is.'

There was a faint commotion outside the building, but only Fischer seemed to notice it. Gehlen and Wessel were looking at each other - the one impassive, the other irritated still. The clerk (a grey little man, like so many of the bland bureaucratic monsters their world had raised) was waiting patiently for more to commit to paper while the swarthy young one stared straight at their visitor with what he doubtless hoped to be taken as utter revulsion. To Fischer it looked like air-sickness.

Wessel pursed his lips, shrugged. 'So, Beckendorp is a friend, a disinterested party. If he serves the enemy, nevertheless he wishes us no ill. No, it isn't enough, Herr Fischer. We have a duty to resist this threat to German civilization, a threat that's already proved all but fatal. We can't simply accept that men such as you and Branssler and your secretive friend can decide to detach themselves from the struggle, and without consequence. You say that MGB know everything about Beckendorp. Perhaps that's true, and that this curious Russian really does enjoy a joke. I doubt that K-5 will, however. Have you noticed how much more *humourless* the German communist is than his Russian comrade? Perhaps it's the grudge he's had to carry secretly all these years.'

Fischer rubbed his temple. 'You intend to betray him? To what possible purpose?'

'At the least, it should create considerable anxiety about Western penetration of the SED, which will be useful. With luck, a few blameless communists will go to the wall also, protesting their love of Chairman Stalin and all his works. You see, Fischer, this *is* a war, whether you wish it to be so or not, and any tactical advantage is to be seized upon. As ex-Fallschirmjäger, you must see this.' Wessel half rose from his seat and stared at the window. 'What *is* that noise?'

The door opened. Dark Haired Muscle entered - as outraged, seemingly, as when he'd escorted Fischer from the front gate. This time he had more cause, however. He held a handkerchief to his nose, which appeared to be broken (at least, it presented itself in a different direction than formerly). One of his eyes was beginning to close, and his shirt hung half off his back.

'It's …..' The voice was flat, nasal, almost unintelligible, but Fischer fancied that he'd caught the name.

Gehlen also looked outraged, though more at the interruption than its general condition. '*What?*'

'Branssler. We've got Branssler.'

65

'Why are you in that state?'

As distressed as he was, the Muscle had to restrain himself visibly. 'He resisted, sir.'

'But the American sentry? Surely … '

'We asked for assistance, but he said that the man had the proper pass, and passes were all that he dealt with. He just stood at his post, watching us trying to subdue Branssler. He was laughing!'

There was a commotion in the corridor, and the injured man stepped back hastily. Pushed from behind, Gerd Branssler half-fell into the room. He was filthy, bloodied, with a wild look in his bruised eyes that Fischer had seen only once previously, on a January evening, 1945, when his big fists had beaten a killer until a confession was no longer required or possible.

'Hello, Gerd', said Fischer, mildly. 'What are you doing?'

'Being an idiot. I went back to Greta's apartment to pick up things. The *portiersfrau* described you, said you'd been there this morning, looking for information. *Here* was obviously where you were going next.' For a few moments he glared at the two generals behind the desk and then stabbed a finger at them. 'They tried to have me killed.'

'Me also. What happened?'

'I discouraged the hired help. What happened with you?'

'I more than discouraged him.'

Wessel's face was by now a shade of deep ochre. 'You killed him?'

'He persisted.'

Gehlen coughed. 'We authorized it only after much thought. Clearly, men who pry into highly classified matters run a risk.'

Branssler tried out the finger once more, on Wessel's swarthy neighbour. 'It was this little bastard who told on me.'

'This is Brunner?'

'Yeah.'

Fischer smiled at the man. 'Sir, I have you on a list.'

'What's that supposed to mean?' A heavy accent, obviously Austrian.

Ignoring him, Fischer turned to Gehlen. 'Herr General, there was no threat, so your escalation wasn't necessary. All we wanted was to keep Beckendorp safe. We have – had – no interest in anything else, as I can prove to your satisfaction. You wanted to know his real name. It's Holleman, initial F.'

For a few moments no one said anything. Wessel pinched the bridge of his nose between thumb and forefinger. 'Christ. You were looking for …'

'We needed to be sure that if we disappeared him you couldn't follow. It's just a remarkable coincidence that the name should have been so similar.'

Gehlen and Wessel looked at each other once more, doing the silent conversation. 'What is it that you think you have?'

'Something the Americans may be interested to hear, should we not come to an arrangement.'

'What would *an arrangement* entail?'

'Amnesia. You forget that Branssler and I ever applied for a position here. You forget also about Kurt Beckendorp. We forget names in red files. And red files, of course. That's it. We don't even want severance terms.'

'*I* fucking well do.' Branssler took a half a step forward. 'They tried to make a widow of Greta.'

Hastily, Fischer grabbed an arm. 'Well, perhaps a personal reference, something about Herr Branssler's industry and application?'

Gehlen smiled coldly. 'I don't think so. You can of course inform the Americans of what we know. They may be irritated by it, but I hardly think it's going to make a difference. In the past two years, whole battalions of wanted men have been de-briefed by them and promptly hired.' He nodded towards the window. 'Many of them just down the road here, at Camp King. The traitor Dornberger was one of them. You may cause a small embarrassment, but I can accept that. Really, Fischer, you have very little in your hand.'

Fischer removed the piece of paper from his pocket. 'I have this. More names that you *know*, including this gentleman's.' He waved it at Brunner.

'That also is nothing, and for the same reason. If obliged, I can explain myself in terms of necessity, of making priorities in a difficult situation. I told you, this is war, and war is all about regrettable choices.'

Fischer looked down at his list. It was short, only five names. Gehlen was right, the Americans probably wouldn't care about them. They might insist that their pet General keep fewer secrets in future, but they weren't going to press him more than that. If circumstances changed they would be happy to pick out a couple of the names at random and have a show trial to reassure their public that the Reich's crimes were being punished, but Gehlen would be equally exonerated in the process. If this *was* a hand, it was somewhere short of a flush. Still, he wished now that he'd thought to make a few copies.

'As you say, Herr General. But it isn't the names here that will put you in a hole.' Fischer pushed the paper across the table. 'Please have it. I've made copies, obviously.'

Gehlen picked it up, read it with mild interest, said nothing.

'It's more a matter of provenance. You've spent … what, almost two years, moving Heaven, Hell and USFET to allow your organization to exist? You've been desperate for some sort of coup to prove your competence, which is why you took on the Beckendorp business in the first place when you should have been keeping your eyes to the front, on the real enemy. And it's why, I assume, you still wish to betray him, even though the advantage you'll gain isn't worth a hearty piss in a pot. But for the sake of that small satisfaction you're going to destroy everything.'

'How is that remotely possible?'

'As I say, provenance. What's on that list is nothing. Where it came from is everything.'

Wessel leaned across the table and tapped the clerk's hand. He stopped scribbling.

'I mentioned that there were copies. Actually, *this* is a copy. The original is franked *Ministerstvo Gosudarstvennoy Bezopasnosti SSSR*. As I say, the man has a sense of humour.'

'Why would he give this away?'

'Two reasons, I think. First, he's not really interested in fled war criminals, nor even what happens here at Oberursel. I believe that K-5 have been established as MGB's surrogates, to be your principal adversary on German territory. The Russians are focussed almost exclusively on the American threat, for obvious reasons. Second ...' Fischer paused and smiled, 'I think he hoped that I'd use it.'

Either the joke wasn't understood by the men at the other side of the table, or they didn't consider it amusing.

'Imagine what the Americans will say when they discover that this organization, a hopeful infant, has already been penetrated by Soviet Intelligence, and roughly by what the British call a fair mile. Do you think they'll pass it off as beginner's ill-luck, or cut their losses and your throats?'

Fischer stood up. He felt quite strangely tranquil, as if he'd been at the bottle since dawn. 'As I say, gentlemen, all we want is forgetfulness. You'll appreciate that we have no interest in revealing this information, even if to do so wouldn't amount to a death sentence.' He turned to Branssler. 'Shall we go, Gerd?'

At the door he paused and turned to Alois Brunner, a very small cog in a very young, still very hopeful organization.

'The Americans could well be interested in at least one name on that list. Someone they took the trouble to execute – even if they got the wrong man, poor bastard – isn't likely to be patted on the shoulder and told he's all square with them.'

66

*Maria-Therese Fischer: Proprietor, The Wall Laundry*

She should have been proud of it, but the thing was too surreal still, and if it hadn't been for Earl Kuhn it wouldn't have happened. She was an uneducated farm girl who had fled poverty into sexual slavery and then prostitution, and then fled further into a parlous, unforgiving new world. And now she was a businesswoman, an employer, a pillar of what one day might be a community once more.

The *wall* was long gone, of course, demolished to allow the old town to expand; but the road system commemorated it and local people would know what the name signified – continuity, something familiar in terribly changed times. Earl had thought that a tremendously good idea, the sort he should have had himself.

She had realised, finally, why he was doing this, being far more than a good friend. If she was happy here in Bremen then Otto would be happy also, and they would be content to stay - possibly forever. The revelation had made her quite angry for almost ten minutes. She didn't care to be manipulated, even if it was into warmth and security.

And what would she say to her husband, who scourged himself with illusions of inadequacy, of not being a provider to his family? It had been bad enough when she was merely washing nappies in her kitchen sink; if she started putting real food on the table he might expire from shame.

The thought came to her too often, and she forced it away. For some minutes now she had been bouncing Alisz's daughter Frida on her knee, and she feared that the excitement had brought on more laundry business.

She lifted the baby and pushed her nose against the offending area, something that, even three months earlier, she couldn't have imagined ever having the stomach for. Expertly, she stripped off the wet nappy, washed and dried the admirably passive Frida and wrapped her in a new item. All the while her head turned upon a hundred things that urgently needed to be arranged. She had never done anything like *this* before either, and she was terrified it might go wrong in some detail for which she'd taken responsibility. It was a big thing, and you only had a single chance to get it all just right.

She marvelled at how much filled her mind these days. As a tart she'd had to worry about beatings, infections and the local police. Then, it had been simple, a matter of keeping alive and fed in a city where Germans had been dispossessed, threatened, despised. Now she was safe, could eat as much as she wanted and wore a ring that said she was as good as anyone else, and there was hardly an hour in any day when she wasn't planning the next hour, *and* worrying about how to explain everything to Otto. And now this …

She glanced once more at the telegram on the table. At least she'd been given the small comfort of knowing that she wasn't yet a widow (though she'd always had a good figure for black). He deserved to be scolded for the risks he'd taken, but memories of how her father's shoulders were bent by his wife's unforgiving tongue had excised her own nagging gene. In any case, a homecoming should never be spoiled.

It would have been nice if he had managed to …

'Maria-Therese, do you have an iron?'

Alisz held out her blouse, which was very mildly creased. She had been trying to remain calm for most of the morning, but this profound crisis threatened to remove the grenade's pin. Had they been at the laundry there would have been a press to hand, but Maria-Therese didn't like bring her work home - in any case, the electricity supply to the apartment was still rationed to three evening hours per day.

'Alisz, your jacket will cover everything but the collar. Really, it doesn't matter, darling.'

Frida belched, and Maria-Therese grabbed a cloth to catch whatever came of it. Distracted, the baby's mother muttered something and moved on to her list's next drama. There was about a centimetre of brandy remaining in the bottle on the mantelpiece, and Maria-Therese was thinking about applying it medicinally to the girl when the apartment's front door opened and Odysseus stepped in, back from the wars.

'Otto!'

Somehow, Frida wasn't crushed in the tight hug that took up most of the next two minutes. When they parted (and Alisz had rescued her daughter), they examined each other carefully. She thought that he looked tired, older, the way a man does when looking after himself is a lost priority. He thought she looked as Penelope must have done, surrounded by her suitors. The second hug was tighter, a danger to any infant.

'Why didn't you send word?'

'I found a through-train, as quick as any telegram.' He look dazed, uncertain. 'But I can't stay, sweetheart. I stopped at the record shop on the way here, and Earl says he needs me for something important today, at 1pm. Do you mind?'

'Of course not. He's right, he does need you.'

Fischer glanced around his home and for the first time noticed the presence of guests. The girl was … Alisz, he recalled, one of Maria-Therese's two friends with American babies. She, too, looked better than he could recall – cleaner, neater, almost glamorous in fact. It made him wonder if he'd been without the company of women for too long.

'Hello, Alisz', he said.

'Hello, Herr Fischer.'

Maria-Therese laughed. 'That's all very well for now, Otto. But after one o'clock you must show her proper respect. You must call her Frau Kuhn.'

67

*Commandeur der VolksPolizei* Kurt Beckendorp scowled at the two men in front of him. Müller was used to the treatment and let it wash over him, but the new fellow wilted slightly.

'I have no fucking idea why I should be doing this. But someone I very much can't say *no* to wants it done. So that's that.'

Beckendorp addressed the new fellow directly. 'Do you know what we are?'

'Berlin *VolksPolizei*, Comrade Commander.'

'I said what, not who. *What* we are is a rat's nest of back-stabbing, arse-kissing rent-boys, all of us pretending to be the same thing but each answering to whichever of our esteemed Occupiers rings the bell and asks for his cock to be sucked. When they finally stop pretending to be allies and go their own ways we'll be pulled apart like the fellow who assassinated Henri IV, and then it'll be fucking chaos. *But*, we're also the only thing that Germans can come to when something goes bad for them. And how often is that?'

'Most days, comrade?'

'Most *hours*, lad. At Keibelstrasse we get an average of four to five hundred alleged crimes reported daily. This is not all strong stuff, of course. In a city where everyone argues about what belongs to whom we're the first call for every border dispute. But if you throw out the neighbours' spats and rattings we still log about four times what the pre-war Force had to deal with, and that's with four times fewer and less qualified men on the books. So you're very welcome, even if I don't look pleased to see you.'

The other man nodded but kept his mouth shut.

'I'm told you've just arrived in Berlin. You have family?'

'A son, comrade. His mother's dead.'

'Somewhere to live?'

'I'm looking at the m ...'

Muller coughed. 'There's a spare apartment in my building, the tenant died two weeks ago. Our landlord hasn't informed the Housing Committee yet.'

'Good. Reserve it for *VolksPolizei*, then. Use my name.'

The new man seemed genuinely pleased, and Beckendorp's iron heart softened slightly. At least the fellow wasn't the sort of little shit who believed that his powerful connections brought things to him as of semi-divine right.

'Alright. You've been assigned the rank of *unterkommissar*. Attach yourself like the clap to Müller here and listen to everything he tells you. I expect you to turn up for work every day, even if you've died the night before. I expect as much loyalty from you as anyone gets in this place. I also expect honesty, diligence, perseverance, and, above all, integrity.'

Keenly aware of his own egregious shortcomings in the first and last regard, the man who wasn't really Kurt Beckendorp cleared his throat, scratched his nose and turned to the too-high pile of files on his desk.

'Right, then. I'm told you're good. What do you know about murder?'

The man who wasn't really Rolf Hoelscher thought about that for a moment.

'Far too much, comrade.'

# Author's Note

The circumstances of the police visit to a farm near Rosenheim, and their examination of the papers of one Fritz Hollman, took place precisely as related by Fischer. Hollman was Josef Mengele, who used this and several other pseudonyms before he fled Germany in 1949. Gehlen's organization knew of Mengele's circumstances but did not betray him to the Allies. There is no evidence they aided him at any point.

Alois Brunner, in contrast, was sheltered for a time by the organization. During the war, Adolph Eichmann had regarded him as his most gifted associate, and he is said to have been responsible for sending over 100,000 French and Slovakian Jews to the gas chambers. Brunner never adopted a false identity while in Germany, as another former SS officer, Anton Brunner, had been executed by the Allies - for his own crimes and, in a case of mistaken identity, those of his near-namesake. In 1954, fearing discovery, Brunner fled to Syria via Egypt and adopted the pseudonym Georg Fischer. Among other activities, he later advised the Syrian Government on torture and interrogation techniques, and died – of natural causes – as late as 2012.

The Gehlen organization remained at Oberursel until early 1948, when the Americans transferred it to new headquarters at Pullach, near Munich. In the previous year, overall direction of the organization was relinquished by USFET to the CIA. On 1 April 1956 it was renamed the *Bundesnachrichtendienst* (Federal Intelligence Agency) and formally placed under the authority of the German Federal Republic. The organization enjoyed several intelligence coups during its years under

American patronage, but was remarkable for having been thoroughly infiltrated both by former Nazis and communist moles.

20295427R00242

Printed in Great Britain
by Amazon